2011 不求人文化

2009 懶鬼子英日語

www.17buy.com.tw

2005 意識文化

2005 易富文化

2003 我識地球村

2001 我識出版社

2011 不求人文化

2009 懶鬼子英日語

www.17buy.com.tw

2005 意識文化

2005 易富文化

2003 我識地球村

2001 我識出版社

全新制
TOEIC
Listening

50次多益滿分的怪物講師

多益聽力
答案＋解析本

自我檢測考試

001 (A)	002 (C)	003 (C)	004 (B)	005 (B)	006 (B)	007 (B)	008 (B)	009 (B)	010 (A)
011 (B)	012 (B)	013 (C)	014 (D)	015 (D)	016 (A)	017 (C)	018 (D)	019 (D)	020 (C)
021 (A)	022 (C)	023 (A)	024 (C)	025 (C)	026 (A)	027 (A)	028 (A)	029 (C)	030 (B)
031 (A)	032 (B)	033 (A)	034 (D)	035 (A)	036 (A)				

1.

(A) He's pouring water into a glass.
(B) He's setting a plate on a table.
(C) He's putting away some cups.
(D) He's drinking from a bowl.

（A）他正把水倒入玻璃杯。
（B）他正把盤子放在桌上。
（C）他正把一些杯子收好。
（D）他正從碗裡喝東西。

2.

(A) The men are making a copy.
(B) The men are stocking books on a shelf.
(C) The men are looking at a computer screen.
(D) The men are filing some papers.

（A）男士們正在影印。
（B）男士們正在把書存放在書架上。
（C）男士們正看著電腦螢幕。
（D）男士們正在整理一些文件。

3.

(A) The men are assembling a rack.
(B) Paint is being applied to a wall.
(C) Containers have been set on shelves.
(D) Flower pots are being piled in a corner.

（A）男士們正在組裝架子。
（B）油漆被塗在牆上。
（C）容器已經放在貨架上。
（D）花瓶被堆在角落。

4.

(A) They've placed their shoes on the sand.
(B) They're strolling along the shore.
(C) Seaweed has been left along the water's edge.
(D) The rock is casting a shadow.

（A）他們已經把鞋子放在沙灘上。
（B）他們沿著海邊散步。
（C）海藻被留在水的邊緣。
（D）石頭正投射出影子。

Part 2

5.

Who has the test results?
(A) That's what I thought.
(B) The secretary should have them.
(C) No, he hasn't.

誰有測驗的結果？
（A）那就是我所想的。
（B）祕書應該有。
（C）不，他沒有。

6.

Why weren't you at the party this afternoon?
(A) Yes, I wrote part of it.
(B) I thought it was tomorrow.
(C) I'll bring it later tonight.

為什麼你今天下午不在宴會中？
（A）是，我寫了其中一部分。
（B）我以為是明天。
（C）我今夜晚點會帶去。

7.

How do you like the new director?
(A) He's out of the office today.
(B) He's very demanding.
(C) No, that's not the right direction.

你的新主管怎麼樣呢？
（A）他今天不在辦公室。
（B）他要求很高。
（C）不，那不是對的方向。

8.

Could you come by my office before you leave?
(A) I don't know if the bill came this month.
(B) Sure. I'm on my way out now.
(C) No, she lives far away.

在你離開前，能到我辦公室來嗎？
（A）我不知道這個月帳單來了沒。
（B）當然，我正在下班的路上。
（C）不，她住得很遠。

9.

Have you contacted the travel agency, or do you want me to call them?
(A) Is that your phone number?
(B) I don't have time. Do you?
(C) No, I haven't had much yet.

你和旅行社聯繫了沒？還是由我來打電話給他們？
（A）那是你的電話號碼嗎？
（B）我沒有時間。你有嗎？
（C）不，我目前沒有很多。

10.

Did you make it to the new exhibit at the science museum?
(A) No, but I plan to next week.
(B) That's good news.
(C) Yes, to build a new museum.

你去過在科學博物館的新展覽會嗎？
（A）不，但我打算下週去。
（B）這真是個好消息。
（C）是的，為了蓋新的博物館。

11.

The marketing associate wasn't very helpful, was he?
(A) No, in the accounting department.
(B) I didn't think he was either.
(C) Thanks for your help.

行銷合夥人不太能幫忙，是吧？
（A）不，在會計部門。
（B）我也不認為他會幫忙。
（C）謝謝你的幫忙。

12.

The microphones in the auditorium aren't working.
(A) Sometime this morning.
(B) I'll get the technician.
(C) The desk is next to the computer.

禮堂的麥克風壞掉了。
（A）今天上午某個時候。
（B）我會去找技師。
（C）那張桌子在電腦旁。

Part 3

問題13~15請參考以下對話。

W : Excuse me. Can you tell me where a dry cleaner is here in the hotel? I spilt coffee on my shirt this morning, and need to have it cleaned within today.

M : Yes, there is one place located on the second floor. However, I don't think they offer express service. You'd better go to the one across from the hotel. I'm sure they can do the service.

W : What a relief! I'll go there right away. I need the shirt for a job interview tomorrow afternoon.

女：抱歉。可以告訴我這間飯店的乾洗店在哪嗎？今天早上我打翻咖啡在我的襯衫上，今日之內要清洗乾淨。
男：是，在二樓有。但我想他們不提供快速服務。您最好去飯店對面那家。我相信他們有提供快速服務。
女：真幸運！我馬上去。我明天下午的求職面試需要這件襯衫。

13.

Where are the speakers?
(A) In a bank
(B) In a shopping center
(C) In a hotel
(D) In a restaurant

說話者在哪裡？
（A）在銀行
（B）在購物中心
（C）在旅館
（D）在餐廳

14.

What does the woman want to do?
(A) Place an order
(B) Make a deposit
(C) Change her room
(D) Clean some clothes

這位女士想做什麼？
（A）下訂單
（B）存款
（C）換房間
（D）清洗衣物

15.

When is the interview?
(A) This morning
(B) This afternoon
(C) Tomorrow morning
(D) Tomorrow afternoon

什麼時候面試？
（A）今天上午
（B）今天下午
（C）明天早上
（D）明天下午

問題16~18請參考以下對話。

M：Hello, I'd like two tickets for Thursday night's theater performance.

W：I'm afraid all of the tickets are sold out for that performance.

M：Oh then, what about next week? Do you have tickets for next Saturday's performance?

W：Yes, we have. There are tickets for 7 p.m. and 9 p.m. Which would you like?

男：哈囉，我想要兩張週四晚上表演的門票。

女：那場表演所有的門票恐怕都賣完了。

男：哦，那麼下週的呢？有下週六表演的門票嗎？

女：是，有的。有晚上7點和晚上9點的。您想要哪一場的？

16.

Who most likely is the woman?
(A) A salesperson
(B) An athlete
(C) A security manager
(D) A museum curator

這位女士最有可能是什麼身分？
（A）一位售貨員
（B）一位運動員
（C）一位保全經理
（D）一位博物館館長

17.

What does the man want to do?
(A) Purchase a musical instrument
(B) Visit a museum
(C) Attend a performance
(D) Make a travel itinerary

這位男士想做什麼？
（A）購買樂器
（B）參觀博物館
（C）看表演
（D）安排旅遊行程

18.

What will the man probably do next?
(A) Complete a form
(B) Talk to the manager
(C) Listen to the music
(D) Purchase tickets

這個男士接著可能會做什麼？
（A）填寫表格
（B）與經理交談
（C）聽音樂
（D）購買門票

問題19~21請參考以下對話。

W：Becker, how's the marketing manager search going? Did you find anyone who is a good fit?

M：No. Personnel Department narrowed down the applications to two, but neither seems to be qualified. We're targeting young consumers in the clothing market. We need someone who has much experience in the related field.

W：I have a friend who is really qualified for the job. He's been with a clothing company for decades. Why don't you contact him to see if he's interested?

女：貝克，徵求行銷經理的事情進行得如何？你有找到任何合適的人嗎？

男：沒有。人事部門縮小應徵者範圍到兩位，但似乎沒有人符合資格。我們的目標是服裝市場的年輕消費者，我們需要一位在相關領域有豐富經驗的人。

女：我有一個朋友相當有資格來做這個工作。他在一家服裝公司幾十年了。你何不聯絡他，看看他有沒有興趣？

19.

Which department needs a new manager?
(A) Personnel
(B) Customer service
(C) Accounting
(D) Marketing

哪個部門需要新的經理？
（A）人事部門
（B）客戶服務部門
（C）會計部門
（D）行銷部門

20.

What qualification does the man mention?
(A) Willingness to travel
(B) Strong references
(C) Relevant experience
(D) A university degree

這位男士論及什麼資格？
（A）願意出差
（B）有力的推薦
（C）相關經驗
（D）大學學位

21.

What does the woman recommend?
(A) Contacting a possible candidate
(B) Transferring to another branch
(C) Placing an advertisement on the Internet
(D) Rescheduling some interviews

這位女士建議了什麼？
（A）聯繫一位可能的候選人
（B）轉換到另一家分公司
（C）在網路上登廣告
（D）重新安排一些面試

問題22～24請參考以下對話。

Bus schedule

Leaving Curvent Ave.	Arriving in Johnson St.
7:05	7:25
7:40	8:00
8:10	8:30
8:40	9:00

M : Can you come this Saturday to help out with the decoration for the exhibition?
W : Oh, what time should I arrive?
M : Can you come first thing in the morning at about 7:30? We need to get everything ready before the guests arrive at 9:30.
W : 7:30? Wow, it's quite early. That means I'll have to catch the first bus leaving Curvent Avenue.
M : The good thing is, if you work on the weekend, you get double hourly pay. The event tomorrow will last whole day till 5:30.
W : That's nice to know.

公車時刻表

當代街出發	抵達強森街
7:05	7:25
7:40	8:00
8:10	8:30
8:40	9:00

男：你這個星期六能來幫忙布置展覽會場嗎？
女：喔！我應該幾點抵達呢？
男：你能一早大概七點半就來嗎？我們需要在九點半客人抵達以前將所有東西準備就緒。
女：七點半？哇！真早！這表示我必須搭上第一班從當代街出發的巴士。
男：好消息是，如果你周末工作，你會拿雙倍的鐘點費。明天的展覽將持續一整天到五點半。
女：很棒！

22.

What is the woman asked to help?
(A) Reviewing a record
(B) Filing a report
(C) Decorating a stall
(D) Finding a bus schedule

女士被要求做什麼？
（A）審核紀錄
（B）報告歸檔
（C）布置攤位
（D）尋找公車時刻表

23.

Look at the graphic, what time will the woman get on the bus?
(A) 7:05
(B) 7:25
(C) 8:10
(D) 9:00

請看此圖，女士何時會搭上公車？
（A）7:05
（B）7:25
（C）8:10
（D）9:00

24.

What advantage does the man mention?
(A) Free meal
(B) Promotion
(C) Double pay
(D) Short work hours

男士提到什麼好處？
（A）免費餐點
（B）工作升遷
（C）雙倍薪水
（D）短的工時

Part 4

問題25~27請參考以下電話留言。

Hi, Erica. This is Madison Morton calling from Westwood Furniture store, and I'm a sales manager. I'm calling about the dress hanger you ordered from us last week. Unfortunately, the second type model you selected is not in stock. We can place a special order for it but I don't think we can get it in less than two months. However, we have the third type model available now. So I'd like to know whether you want to order the third type model or would rather wait for the second type model. I will leave for the day around six, so please call me back as soon as you get this message. Thank you.

嗨，艾瑞卡。這裡是西木傢俱店的麥迪森‧摩頓，我是銷售經理。我打來是有關上週您和我們訂購的衣架。很不巧的，您選的第二款沒有庫存。我們可以以下特別訂單，但我不認為我們能在兩個月之內拿到。然而，我們目前有第三款可提供。所以我想知道您是否要訂購第三款，或願意等第二款。我今天六點左右會離開，所以當您聽到這個留言，請盡快回電給我。謝謝！

25.

Who is the caller?
(A) An accountant
(B) A clothing maker
(C) A sales manager
(D) A fashion designer

來電者是誰？
（A）一位會計師
（B）一位服裝製造商
（C）一位銷售經理
（D）一位時裝設計師

26.

What might be the problem?
(A) An item is not available.
(B) Some documents are missing.
(C) Some products were damaged.
(D) The delivery is late.

有可能是什麼問題？
（A）有個項目不能提供。
（B）有些文件遺失了。
（C）有些產品被損壞了。
（D）延遲交貨。

27.

What does the caller need to know from Erica?
(A) The type of model she wants
(B) The time she will return to the office
(C) The cost of a specially ordered item
(D) The expected arrival time of delivery

留言者需要從艾瑞卡得知什麼？
（A）她想要的款式
（B）她會回到辦公室的時間
（C）特別訂購的金額
（D）預計配送抵達的時間

問題28~30請參考以下內容。

As you all know, our network equipment sales on the capital area have gone up. We expect the sales will continue to increase, so we're planning to start a new branch in Busan in early August. I'm appointed to head the sales department in Busan, so I will be leaving my position as sales manager in July. Several new employees will be hired to deal with the increased business, but of course, the same chance will be given to the experienced sales representatives within our company. All of you are invited to consider the possibility of transferring to Busan. Please give us some feedback within the next few weeks if you're interested in making this move.

如同大家所知道的，我們在首都地區的網絡設備銷售量上升了。我們期待銷量將繼續增加，所以我們計劃在八月初開始在釜山開設新的分公司。我被安排帶領釜山銷售部門，所以我將在七月離開銷售經理的職位。將有幾位新員工被雇用來處理增加的業務，當然，同樣的機會也會給予公司內經驗豐富的銷售代表們。請大家考慮調職到釜山的可能性。若您對此一變動有興趣，請在未來幾週之內給我們回應。

28.

Who is the speaker?
(A) A sales manager
(B) A maintenance worker
(C) A software designer
(D) A repair technician

誰是說話者？
（A）一位銷售經理
（B）一位維修工人
（C）一位軟體設計師
（D）一位維修技師

29.

What will happen in July?
(A) A company will stop its operation.
(B) Renovations on a new building will begin.
(C) The speaker will transfer to a new city.
(D) A presentation will be made at a meeting.

在七月會發生什麼？
（A）一個公司將停止其運作。
（B）一個新建築的裝修將開始。
（C）說話者將到新的城市。
（D）會議上將有一場報告。

30.

What does the speaker ask the listeners to consider?
(A) Meeting a project deadline
(B) Moving to a different office
(C) Recruiting more employees
(D) Modifying a building design

30.
說話者要求聽眾考慮什麼？
（A）遵守一個案子的最後期限
（B）轉換到不同的辦公室
（C）招募更多的員工
（D）修改建築設計

問題31~33請參考以下內容。

Welcome everyone to today's lecture series. Our featured speaker today is Mr. John Park, once the chairman of Stock Analyst Association. He is also an award-winning author of "Secret of Millionaire". Mr. Park will read excerpts from his book and answer questions from audience. Following that, he will be available to sign copies of his book. You can purchase the book at the back of the auditorium for twenty-five dollars. To get more information on his other books, you may refer to the brochures available there to anyone. Now, let's give a warm welcome to Mr. John Park.

歡迎大家來到今天的系列講座。我們今天的特別演講者，是曾為股票分析協會主席的約翰·帕爾可先生。他也是《百萬富翁先生的祕密》的獲獎作者。帕爾可先生將讀出他書中的摘要和回答聽眾的問題。之後，他將會為他的書簽名。您可於觀眾席後方以二十五美元購買這本書。若想知道有關於他其他書籍的更多資訊，您可以參考這邊提供的小冊子。現在，請給予約翰·帕爾可先生熱烈的歡迎。

31.

Who is Mr. Park?
(A) An author
(B) A conference organizer
(C) A bookstore owner
(D) A hotel receptionist

誰是帕爾可先生？
（A）一位作家
（B）一位會議舉辦人
（C）一位書店老闆
（D）一位旅館接待員

32.

What will Mr. Park talk about?
(A) His experience
(B) His book
(C) His heath
(D) His role as an analyst

帕爾可先生將談些什麼？
（A）他的經驗
（B）他的書
（C）他的健康
（D）他作為一位分析師的角色

33.

What can the listeners do at the back of the auditorium?
(A) Buy a book
(B) Read some signs
(C) Take a coffee break
(D) Register for future lectures

聽者可以在觀眾席後面做什麼？
（A）買書
（B）看一些告示
（C）小歇一下
（D）登記之後的演講

問題34～36請參考以下留言。

Hi, David, I am going to Toronto for an academic exchange next week, and I need you to plan an itinerary for me. Basically, I prefer direct flights with vegetarian meals. And airport pickup services need to be included as well. As far as I know, the meetings and seminars will be held at the City Garden Conference Center near downtown area. For convenience of travel, please book me a room at a hotel as close to the center as possible, so I don't need to worry about taxis. Also, I need to be back for a campus developing project the following Monday, so do make sure I return no later than Sunday afternoon. Thanks.

嗨，大衛，我下週要到多倫多參加學術交流，我需要你幫我計畫一份行程表。基本上我比較想要附素食餐點的直航班機。而且也要包含機場接送服務。據我所知，會議和研討會將會在靠近市中心的城市花園會議中心舉行，為了交通方便，請盡可能幫我在靠近會場的飯店訂一間房間，所以我不用擔心叫計程車的事情。還有，隨後的星期一，我需要回來參與校園開發企劃案，所以要確認我最晚星期天下午一定要回來。謝謝！

34.

Who is David, most likely?
(A) A hotel manager
(B) The speaker's boss
(C) A ticket agent
(D) The speaker's assistant

大衛最有可能是誰？
（A）飯店經理
（B）說話者的老闆
（C）售票人員
（D）說話者的助理

35.

Look at the graphic. Which hotel would the speaker prefer?
(A) Holiday Inn
(B) Shangri La Hotel
(C) Hilton Hotel
(D) Millington Hostel

請看此圖，說話者會比較喜歡哪一個飯店？
（A）假日旅館
（B）香格里拉飯店
（C）希爾頓飯店
（D）密靈頓旅舍

36.

Why does the speaker need to return early?
(A) To participate in a project
(B) To attend an academic exchange
(C) To see an old friend
(D) To avoid traffic jam

為何說話者需要提早回來？
（A）要參與企劃案
（B）要出席學術交流
（C）要見一個老朋友
（D）要避免交通壅塞

答案&解析

Chapter 01 一人獨照相片

Quiz |

Q1. (A) reading some materials
(B) drinking a glass of wine
Q2. (A) working at a warehouse
(B) carrying a bucket
Q3. (A) examining some documents
(B) wearing a wristwatch
Q4. (A) resting on a bench
(B) tying his shoelace

Q1

(A) **She is reading some materials.**
她正在讀一些資料。

(B) She is drinking a glass of wine.
她正在喝一杯葡萄酒。

Q2

(A) He is working at a warehouse.
他正在一間倉庫工作。

(B) **He is carrying a bucket.**
他正在搬運一個水桶。

Q3

(A) **He is examining some documents.**
他正在審查一些文件。

(B) He is wearing a wristwatch.
他正戴著手錶。

Q4

(A) **A man is resting on a bench.**
一個男人正在長椅上休息。

(B) A man is tying his shoelace.
一個男人正在綁他的鞋帶。

STEP 01 若沒答對會後悔的考題

例子 (A)	1. (B)	2. (B)	3. (B)	4. (C)

例子 美W

1 主詞	He, The man, A worker
2 大動作	working, using
3 小動作	wearing a helmet
4 背景／場所／其他	brick wall, bricks, a construction site

(A) A worker's using a tool.
(B) A worker's wearing a tool belt.
(C) A worker's loading bricks onto a cart.

（A）工人正使用工具。
（B）工人正戴著工具腰帶。
（C）工人正把磚頭裝到手推車上。

解說 照片裡的男生正拿著工具作業當中，所以（A）為答案。（B）不是答案，因為他沒有戴工具腰帶，而是戴著安全帽的狀態。（C）也不是答案，因為該男生雖然是正在拿磚頭做事情，但不是裝載當中，且照片裡也看不到手推車。　　　　　答案 (A)

詞彙 tool 工具　tool belt 工具腰帶　load 裝載　cart 手推車

1. 英M

1 主詞	He, The(A) man, A shopper
2 大動作	shopping
3 小動作	reaching for
4 背景／場所／其他	foods, groceries, a store

(A) The man is eating a meal.
(B) The man is shopping for groceries.
(C) The man is trying on a jacket.

（A）這個男人正在吃飯。
（B）這個男人正在購買食品雜貨。
（C）這個男人正試穿夾克。

解說 根據該男生在超市向陳列的食品伸手的動作可以知道他可能在購物當中，所以（B）為答案。（A）是故意誤導與用餐混淆的選項。（C）描述正在穿夾克的動作，而照片是穿著夾克的狀態，所以不是答案。

答案 (B)

詞彙 meal 餐飯　shop for 購買⋯　grocery 食品雜貨
try on 試穿

2. 澳 W

1 主詞	She, The(A) woman
2 大動作	wearing glasses
3 小動作	sitting
4 背景／場所／其他	a sofa, a table, plants, a room

(A) She's watching television.
(B) She's sitting on a sofa.
(C) She's reading a newspaper.

（A）她正在看電視。
（B）她正坐在沙發上。
（C）她正在閱讀報紙。

解說 該女生在沙發上坐著休息，所以（B）為答案。（A）論及照片裡沒有的名詞television，所以不是答案。（C）是故意誤導與照片裡出現的書混淆的選項，而且照片裡沒有出現報紙，也沒有正在閱讀的狀況。　　　　　　　　　　　　　　答案 (B)

詞彙 watch 看　sit 坐　sofa 沙發　newspaper 報紙

3. 美 M

1 主詞	He, The(A) man
2 小動作	looking at
3 背景	wearing a suit and a tie
4 背景／場所／其他	a watch, a wristwatch, a road

(A) The man is watching a game.
(B) The man is wearing a wristwatch.
(C) The man is adjusting his tie.

（A）這個男人正在觀看比賽。
（B）這個男人戴著手錶。
（C）這個男人正在調整他的領帶。

解說 該男生正在看著自己手腕上戴著的手錶，所以（B）為答案。（A）不是答案，因為該男生看著手錶，而不是看著比賽。（C）不是答案，因為沒有描述戴著領帶的狀態，而是描述了調整領帶的動作。　　　　　　　　　　　　　　答案 (B)

詞彙 wear 穿戴　wristwatch 腕錶　adjust 調整　tie 領帶

4. 美 W

1 主詞	She, The(A) woman, A girl
2 大動作	talking
3 小動作	sitting, holding
4 背景／場所／其他	a phone, a desk, a laptop, an office

(A) She's looking at a computer screen.
(B) She's sitting on a bench.
(C) She's talking over the phone.

（A）她正注視著電腦螢幕。
（B）她正坐在長椅上。
（C）她正在打電話。

解說 該女生正在打電話當中，所以（C）為答案。（A）不是答案，因為照片裡女生的視線沒有對著電腦，而是往別的方向。（B）不是答案，因為她不是在長椅上坐著。　　　　　　　　　　答案 (C)

詞彙 look at 注視　bench 長椅　over the phone 在電話上

STEP 02 考題實戰練習

1. (C)	2. (D)	3. (B)	4. (A)
5. (A)	6. (D)	7. (A)	8. (C)

1. 美 W
(A) A man is climbing up a ladder.
(B) A man is piloting a plane.
(C) A man is boarding an airplane.
(D) A man is entering a house.

（A）一個男人正在爬梯子。
（B）一個男人正駕駛飛機。
（C）一個男人正登上飛機。
（D）一個男人正進入一棟房子。

解說 該男生正在登上飛機當中，所以（C）為答案。（A）不是答案，因為他不是在踏上梯子，而是走上飛機的階梯。（B）不是答案，因為照片裡的男生正在登上飛機當中，而不是操作飛機。（D）不是答案，因為不是進屋，而是進飛機當中。　　答案 (C)

詞彙 climb up 向上爬　ladder 梯子　pilot 操作
board 搭乘

2. 美 M
(A) He is opening a car door.
(B) He is unlocking a metal gate.

(C) He is carrying a suitcase.
(D) He is wearing a suit and a tie.

（A）他正在開車門。
（B）他正將一道鐵門解鎖。
（C）他正提著一個手提旅行箱。
（D）他正穿著西裝和領帶。

解說 該男生穿著西裝，且戴著領帶，所以（D）為答案。（A）不是答案，因為他不是在開車門，而是在開房子的門。選項（B）我們無法知道是否為鐵門。（C）不是答案，因為他拿著的不是旅行包而是公事包。　　　　　　　　　　　　　　　答案 (D)

詞彙 **unlock** 解鎖　**metal gate** 鐵門　**carry** 提　**suitcase** 手提旅行箱　**a suit and a tie** 西裝和領帶

3. 英 M
(A) She's writing a letter.
(B) She's placing a file folder on the desk.
(C) She's putting some luggage on the floor.
(D) She's opening up a file cabinet.

（A）她正在寫一封信。
（B）她正把文件夾放在辦公桌上。
（C）她正把一些行李放在地板上。
（D）她正在開一個文件櫃。

解說 該女生正在將文件夾放在桌子上，所以（B）為答案。（A）不是答案，因為該女生不是在寫信。（C）不是答案，因為這不是放置包包的動作，而是將檔案夾放在桌子上的動作。（D）不是答案，因為論及了照片裡沒有的名詞file cabinet。　　　答案 (B)

詞彙 **write** 寫　**place** 放置　**file folder** 文件夾　**put** 放下　**luggage** 行李箱　**cabinet** 櫃子

4. 澳 W
(A) She's using the sink.
(B) She's washing her hands.
(C) She's eating dessert.
(D) She's opening a drawer.

（A）她正在使用水槽。
（B）她正在洗手。
（C）她正在吃甜點。
（D）她正打開抽屜。

解說 該女生正在水槽洗碗當中，所以（A）為答案。（B）不是答案，因為不是洗手，而是洗碗當中。（C）不是答案，因為不是吃東西，而是洗碗。（D）不是答案，因為論及了照片裡沒有的名詞drawer。　　　　　　　　　　　　　答案 (A)

詞彙 **sink** 水槽　**wash** 洗　**dessert** 點心　**drawer** 抽屜

5. 美 W
(A) A man is dragging some luggage.
(B) A man is filling a bag with some tools.
(C) A man is walking up the stairs.
(D) A man is paving the road.

（A）一個男人正拖著一些行李。
（B）一個男人正把一些工具裝進袋子裡。
（C）一個男人正在走上樓梯。
（D）一個男人正在鋪馬路。

解說 該男生雙手拉著旅行包，所以（A）為答案。（B）不是答案，因為論及了照片裡沒有的名詞tools，而且照片裡沒有出現裝載東西的動作。（C）不是答案，因為不是走階梯，而是在馬路上走路。（D）不是答案，因為不是鋪馬路，只是在馬路上走路的畫面。　　　　　　　　　　　　　答案 (A)

詞彙 **drag** 拖曳　**luggage** 行李　**fill** 裝滿　**walk up** 向上走　**stairs** 樓梯　**pave** 鋪平　**road** 道路

6. 美 M
(A) The man is storing some tools.
(B) The man is sweeping the floor.
(C) The man is removing his hat.
(D) The man is working outdoors.

（A）一個男人正存放一些工具。
（B）一個男人正在掃地。
（C）一個男人正拿掉他的帽子。
（D）一個男人正在戶外工作。

解說 該男生正在戶外工作中，所以（D）為答案。（A）不是答案，因為不是收拾工具的動作，而是拿著工具做事的畫面。（B）不是答案，因為不是掃地的畫面。（C）不是答案，因為該男生是戴著帽子，而不是在脫帽。　　　　　　　答案 (D)

詞彙 **store** 存放　**sweep** 掃　**remove** 移除　**outdoors** 戶外

7. 英 M
(A) A man is standing on the ladder.
(B) A man is installing a shelf.
(C) A man is writing a letter.
(D) A man is hammering a nail.

（A）一個男人正站在梯子上。
（B）一個男人正在安裝架子。
（C）一個男人正在寫信。
（D）一個男人正在槌釘子。

解說 該男生正站在梯子上做事，所以（A）為答案。（B）論及了照片裡沒有的名詞shelf，所以不是答案。（C）是故意用與ladder相近的發音letter來誤導的選項。（D）不是答案，因為看不出他是否在用槌頭。　　　　　　　　　　　　　答案 (A)

詞彙 **stand** 站立 **ladder** 梯子 **install** 安裝 **shelf** 架子 **write** 寫 **hammer** 用榔頭槌 **nail** 釘子

8. 澳 W

(A) She's looking at some plants.
(B) She's picking flowers in the garden.
(C) She's examining some documents.
(D) She's making a cup of coffee.

（A）她正在看一些植物。
（B）她正在花園裡摘花。
（C）她正在查閱一些文件。
（D）她正在沖一杯咖啡。

解說 該女生正在看著一些文件，所以（C）為答案。（A）不是答案，因為她不是在看花草，而在看文件。（B）不是答案，因為花是已經插在花瓶裡的。（D）不是答案，因為她拿著咖啡杯。　　答案 (C)

詞彙 **plant** 花草、植物 **pick** 摘採

Quiz |

Q1. (A) playing musical instruments
(B) clapping their hands
Q2. (A) wearing ties
(B) holding bags
Q3. (A) trying on shoes
(B) paying for goods
Q4. (A) holding a glass
(B) wearing a hat

Q1

(A) **They are playing musical instruments.**
他們正在演奏樂器。

(B) They are clapping their hands.
他們正在拍手。

Q2

(A) **The men are wearing ties.**
男人們打著領帶。

(B) The men are holding bags.
男人們正拿著袋子。

Q3

(A) Some shoppers are trying on shoes.
一些購物者正在試鞋子。

(B) **A man is paying for goods.**
一個男人正在付錢。

Q4

(A) **A woman is holding a glass.**
一個女人正拿著杯子。

(B) A man is wearing a hat.
一個男人戴著帽子。

STEP 01 若沒答對會後悔的考題

例子 (C)　　1. (C)　　2. (A)　　3. (C)　　4. (C)

例子 美W

1 主詞	They
2 概括性／群體性描述1	having a meal
3 概括性／群體性描述2	looking at each other
4 背景／場所／其他	food, dishes, table

(A) They're cooking some food.
(B) They're picking up some dishes.
(C) They're having a meal.

（A）他們正在烹調一些食物。
（B）他們正收拾一些碗盤。
（C）他們正在用餐。

解說 該男生和女生正在用餐當中，所以（C）為答案。（A）不是答案，因為不是在做菜，而是在吃著東西。（B）不是答案，因為雖然出現盤子，但不是在收拾的。 答案 (C)

詞彙 cook 烹調 pick up 拿起來 have a meal 吃飯

1. 英M

1 主詞	Some people, A woman
2 概括性／群體性描述	reading
3 個別描述	carrying a bag
4 背景／場所／其他	reading materials, train, suits and ties

(A) Some people are boarding a train.
(B) A woman is pointing at a distance.
(C) Some people are reading.

（A）有些人正在登上火車。
（B）一個女人正指著遠處。
（C）有些人正在閱讀。

解說 這些人正在閱讀某個東西，所以（C）為答案。（A）不是答案，因為他們不是在登上火車，而是已經在火車上。（B）不是答案，因為該女生是在看著東西，而不是指著。 答案 (C)

詞彙 board 搭乘 point at 指向 distance 距離 read 閱讀

2. 澳W

1 主詞	They
2 概括性／群體性描述1	facing each other
3 概括性／群體性描述2	sitting at the table
4 背景／場所／其他	cup, table

(A) They are looking at each other.
(B) They are holding cups.
(C) They are ordering a meal.

（A）他們正互相注視著。
（B）他們都拿著杯子。
（C）他們正在點餐。

解說 該男生和女生正在坐著互相注視，所以（A）為答案。（B）不是答案，因為杯子是在桌上擺著，而不是這些人拿著的。（C）是為了故意誤導而將照片裡坐在餐桌的人描述為點餐的選項。 答案 (A)

詞彙 look at each other 互相注視 hold 握 order 訂購 meal 餐點

3. 英M

1 主詞	The people, Some people
2 概括性／群體性描述	waiting in line
3 個別描述	standing apart from others
4 背景／場所／其他	stairs, vehicles, equipment

(A) They are driving up a hill.
(B) They are climbing over a wall.
(C) They are waiting in a line.

（A）他們正開車爬越一座小山。
（B）他們正爬過一堵牆。
（C）他們正在排隊等待。

解說 這些人正在排隊等著要坐纜車，所以（C）為答案。選項（A）會聽見照片裡沒有的名詞hill，所以不是答案。（B）也是聽見照片裡沒有的名詞wall，所以不是答案。 答案 (C)

詞彙 drive up 開車爬越 climb over a wall 攀爬越牆 wait 等待 in a line 排隊

4. 美W

1 主詞	Some people, A woman
2 概括性／群體性描述	walking, strolling
3 個別描述	riding, talking, wearing
4 背景／場所／其他	bicycle, phone, bag, street

(A) A bus is stopping for passengers.
(B) A woman is picking up her bag.
(C) A woman is talking on the phone.

（A）公車正在停車載客。
（B）一個女人正拿起她的背包。

（C）一個女人正在講電話。

解說 該女生正在打電話，所以（C）為答案。（A）裡聽見照片裡沒有的名詞bus，所以不是答案。（B）不是答案，因為她是將包包背著，而不是拿起來。
答案 (C)

詞彙 stop 停車　passenger 乘客　pick up 拿起
on the phone 在電話上

STEP 02　考題實戰練習

| 1. (B) | 2. (A) | 3. (D) | 4. (A) |
| 5. (D) | 6. (B) | 7. (A) | 8. (B) |

1. 美W

(A) They're writing on a chalkboard.
(B) They're working at a table.
(C) They're putting files in the cabinet.
(D) They're giving a presentation.

（A）他們正在寫黑板。
（B）他們正在桌邊工作。
（C）他們正在把文件放在櫃子裡。
（D）他們正在報告。

解說 （B）較接近描述這些人在桌上看文件，所以為答案。（A）不是答案，因為聽到照片裡沒有的名詞chalkboard。（C）不是答案，因為出現了照片裡沒有的名詞cabinet。（D）不是答案，因為這些人正在看著文件工作，而不是在發表當中。
答案 (B)

詞彙 write on 寫在…上　chalkboard 黑板　put 放
give a presentation 發表；報告

2. 美M

(A) A man is kicking a ball up in the air.
(B) Gardeners are trimming trees in a field.
(C) They're mowing a lawn in front of the house.
(D) Some plants in the park are being watered.

（A）一個男人正將球踢到空中。
（B）園丁正在田地修剪樹木。
（C）他們正在屋前的草坪除草。
（D）公園裡一些植物正在被澆水。

解說 該男生正在踢球，所以（A）為答案。（B）是故意用照片裡出現的trees來誤導的選項。（C）也是故意用照片裡看到的lawn來誤導的選項。（D）也是照片裡的plants來誤導的選項。
答案 (A)

詞彙 kick 踢　in the air 在空中　trim a tree 修剪樹木
field 田地　mow a lawn 除草　plant 植物

3. 英M

(A) Some people are resting in a park.
(B) Some people are eating in a restaurant.
(C) Some people are sweeping the floor.
(D) Some people are wearing coats and hats.

（A）有些人正在公園休息。
（B）有些人正在餐廳吃飯。
（C）有些人正在掃地。
（D）有些人穿著大衣和帽子。

解說 男生和女生正穿著大衣且戴著帽子，所以（D）為答案。（A）是聽到照片裡沒有的名詞park，所以不是答案。（B）不是答案，因為無法判定照片裡的地點是否為餐廳。（C）不是答案，因為這些人只是站著，而不是掃地當中。
答案 (D)

詞彙 rest 休息　sweep 掃　wear 穿戴

4. 澳W

(A) They are examining some papers.
(B) They are adjusting their glasses.
(C) They are taking some measurements.
(D) They are looking out the window.

（A）他們正在審閱一些文件。
（B）他們正在調整他們的眼鏡。
（C）他們正在進行一些測量。
（D）他們正看著窗外。

解說 這些人正在看著文件，所以（A）為答案。（B）不是答案，因為他們戴著眼鏡，而不是在調整當中。（C）不是答案，因為他們不是在測量，而是在看著文件。（D）是故意用照片裡出現的window來誤導的選項。
答案 (A)

詞彙 examine 審閱　paper 資料；報告　adjust 調整
take a measurement 測量　look out the window
看著窗外

5. 美W

(A) The people are greeting each other.
(B) The woman is driving a car.
(C) The woman is opening a car door.
(D) The man is handing a key to the woman.

（A）人們正在互相打招呼。
（B）這個女人正在開車。
（C）這個女人正在打開車門。
（D）這個男人正在將鑰匙交給這個女人。

解說 該男生將鑰匙給該女生，所以（D）為答案。（A）不是答案，因為他們只是互相面對，並不是在打招呼。（B）是故意用照片裡出現的car來誤導的選項。（C）也是故意用照片裡的car door來誤導的選項。
答案 (D)

詞彙 greet each other 互相問候　hand A to B 將A交給B

6. 美M

(A) The men are boarding a train.

(B) The men are walking on the railroad.

(C) The men are fixing a machine.

(D) The men are waiting at the railroad crossing.

（A）男人們正在登上列車。

（B）男人們正走在鐵道上。

（C）男人們正在修理機器。

（D）男人們正在等著穿過鐵路。

解說 該兩個男生正在鐵路上走著，所以（B）為答案。（A）是故意用train來誤導的選項。（C）是用照片裡沒有的名詞machine，所以不是答案。（D）不是答案，因為這些人是在鐵路上走著，而不是在平交道口上等待。　　　　　　　　　　　答案 (B)

詞彙 board 登乘　railroad 鐵路　fix 修理　machine 機器　wait 等候　railroad crossing 鐵路平交道

7. 英M

(A) Some people are shaking hands.

(B) A man is presenting his business card.

(C) A door is being checked by a repairman.

(D) One woman is closing the door behind her.

（A）有些人正在握手。

（B）有個男人正拿出他的名片。

（C）一扇門正由修理工人檢查中。

（D）一個女人正關上她身後的門。

解說 有兩個男生正在握手，所以（A）為答案。（B）裡聽到照片裡沒有的名詞business card，所以不是答案。（C）不是答案，因為無法知道該女生是否為修理工人。（D）不是答案，因為這扇門是已經關著的狀態。　　　　　　　　　　　答案 (A)

詞彙 shake hands 握手　present 展示　business card 名片　repairman 修理工人　close 關

8. 澳W

(A) Some people are screening some products.

(B) Some people are looking at a computer screen.

(C) Some people are helping each other move a computer.

(D) Some people are putting away some equipment.

（A）有些人正在檢查一些產品。

（B）有些人正在注視著電腦螢幕。

（C）有些人正在互相幫助搬動電腦。

（D）有些人正在收拾一些設備。

解說 有兩個女生正在看著電腦螢幕，所以（B）為答案。（A）是故意將當作名詞的screen改成動詞用以誤導的選項。（C）是用照片裡出現的單字computer來誤

導的選項。（D）不是答案，因為這些人是看著電腦螢幕，而不是收拾設備。　　　　　答案 (B)

詞彙 screen 檢查　look at 注視　each other 互相　move 移動　put away 收拾　equipment 設備

03 對照片裡的物件與背景的描述

Quiz |

Q1. (A) casting shadows　(B) being planted
Q2. (A) A table　　　　　(B) Diners
Q3. (A) being examined　(B) being assembled
Q4. (A) fountain, spraying
　　　 (B) trees, being trimmed

Q1

(A) **Trees are casting shadows.**
　　 樹木正投射出影子。

(B) Trees are being planted.
　　 樹木正在被種植。

Q2

(A) **A table has been set for a meal.**
　　 為了用餐，餐桌被擺設了。

(B) Diners are having their meals.
　　 用餐者正在吃飯。

Q3

(A) **A map is being examined.**
　　 地圖正在被查看中。

(B) A telescope is being assembled.
　　 望遠鏡正被組裝中。

Q4

(A) **The fountain is spraying into the air.**
　　 噴泉噴灑到空中。

(B) Some trees are being trimmed in the garden.
　　 花園裡的一些樹木正被修剪。

STEP 01　若沒答對會後悔的考題

例子 (B)　　1. (C)　　2. (A)　　3. (A)　　4. (B)

例子 美W

1 主要物件	lights
2 靜態性狀況1	(be/have been) turned on
3 靜態性狀況2	(be/have been) lined up
4 背景／場所／其他	wall, corridor, pedestrians

(A) A worker is fixing a lamp.
(B) Some lights have been turned on.
(C) A painting is hanging on the wall.

（A）一名工人正在修理一盞燈。
（B）有些燈被打開了。
（C）一幅畫正被掛在牆上。

解說 有一些燈正亮著，所以（B）為答案。（A）是故意用lamp來造成混淆的選項。（C）不是答案，因為並非有一幅畫掛在牆壁上，而是全部的牆壁上都有塗鴉。
答案 (B)

詞彙 worker 工人　fix 修理　lights 燈具　turn on 開　painting 畫作　hang 掛　wall 牆壁

1. 英M

1 人物的動作	A woman is watering some plants.
2 物件的立場	Plants are being watered.
3 背景／場所／其他	garden, plants, flowers

(A) Flowers are being planted.
(B) Bushes are being trimmed by the woman.
(C) Some plants are being watered.

（A）花草正在被種植。
（B）灌木叢正在被一個女人修剪。
（C）一些植物正在被澆水。

解說 該女生正在為花草澆水，所以（C）為答案。（A）是故意誤導而讓你聯想到種花的選項。（B）裡聽到照片裡沒有的名詞bushes，所以不是答案。
答案 (C)

詞彙 plant 種植　bush 灌木叢　trim 修剪　water 澆水

2. 澳W

1 主要物件	bed, lamps
2 靜態性狀況1	(be/have been) between the lamps
3 靜態性狀況2	(be/have been) turned on
4 背景／場所／其他	room, floor

(A) A bed is between the lamps.
(B) A maid is making the bed.
(C) Lamps are being turned on.

（A）一張床介於在檯燈之間。
（B）女傭正在整理床鋪。

（C）燈正被打開。

解說 這張床在檯燈之間，所以（A）為答案。照片裡沒有人，所以出現與人相關說法的（B）或聽到being的（C）不是答案。　　　　　　　　　　答案 (A)

詞彙 maid 女侍；女傭　make the bed 整理床鋪　turn on 開

3. 美M

1 人物的動作	A worker is measuring a piece of wood.
2 物件的立場	A piece of wood is being measured.
3 背景／場所／其他	ruler

(A) A piece of wood is being measured.
(B) There are machines at a construction site.
(C) A man is cutting down some trees.

（A）一塊木頭正被測量。
（B）在工地有一些機器。
（C）一個男人正在砍一些樹木。

解說 有個人正測量一塊木頭，所以（A）為答案。（B）裡聽到照片裡沒有的名詞machines，所以不是答案。（C）不是答案，因為不是將樹木砍下來，而是在測量木頭。　　　　　　　　　　答案 (A)

詞彙 a piece of 一塊的…　measure 測量　machine 機器　construction site 工地　cut down 砍伐

4. 美W

1 主要物件	painting, bed, dressers
2 靜態性狀況1	(be/have been) above the bed
3 靜態性狀況2	(be/have been) between the dressers
4 背景／場所／其他	room, window, curtain

(A) The curtain is covering the window.
(B) A painting is hanging above the bed.
(C) The floor is being cleaned.

（A）窗簾遮蓋著窗戶。
（B）一幅畫正掛在床的上方。
（C）地板正在被清掃。

解說 床舖的上方掛著一幅畫，所以（B）為答案。（A）不是答案，因為窗簾並非遮住窗戶，而是拉開

的。（C）不是答案，因為照片裡沒有人卻聽到being。　　　　　　　　　　答案 (B)

詞彙 cover 覆蓋　painting 畫作　above 上方　floor 地板　clean 清掃

STEP 02 考題實戰練習

| 1. (D) | 2. (B) | 3. (B) | 4. (A) |
| 5. (C) | 6. (D) | 7. (C) | 8. (C) |

1. 美W
(A) Storage tanks are being assembled.
(B) Industrial equipment is being inspected.
(C) Construction materials are burning.
(D) Smoke is rising into the air.

（A）儲存槽正在被組裝。
（B）工業設備正在被檢查。
（C）建築材料正在燃燒。
（D）煙霧正在上升到空中。

解說 煙霧正上升到空中，所以（D）為答案。（A）和（B）不是答案，因為照片裡沒有人卻聽到being。（C）不是答案，因為選項中出現了照片裡沒有的名詞construction materials。　　　　　　答案 (D)

詞彙 storage tank 儲存槽　assemble 組裝　industrial equipment 工業設備　inspect 檢查　construction materials 建築材料　burn 燃燒　smoke 煙　into the air 向空中

2. 美M
(A) Passengers are stepping onto a platform.
(B) The train is near the platform.
(C) People are purchasing tickets from machines.
(D) A train station is closed for repairs.

（A）乘客們正踏上月台。
（B）火車在月台處附近。
（C）人們正從機器購買票。
（D）火車站被關閉以維修。

解說 火車正在接近月台當中，所以（B）為答案。選項（A）和（C）因為照片裡看不到人，所以不是答案。（D）是故意用train station來誤導的選項。　　　　　　　　　　答案 (B)

詞彙 step onto 踏上…　near 近處　platform 月台　purchase 購買　train station 火車站　close 關閉　repair 修理

3. 英 M

(A) Groceries are being put in a bag.
(B) A purchase is being made.
(C) An assortment of items sits on a counter.
(D) A customer is removing an item from a shelf.

（A）雜貨正被放進一個袋子。
（B）一件採購正被進行中。
（C）在櫃檯上有各式各樣的物品。
（D）客人正從貨架上把一個品項移開。

解說 照片裡看得到付錢的畫面，所以（B）為答案。（A）裡聽到照片裡沒有的名詞bag，所以不是答案。（C）不是答案，因為商品不是擺在收銀台上面，而是陳列在收銀台後面。（D）不是答案，因為這個客人正在付錢當中，而不是移開商品。　　　答案 (B)

詞彙 grocery 雜貨　put 放　make a purchase 採購　an assortment of 各式各樣的　item 項目　sit 位於　customer 顧客　remove 移除　shelf 架子

4. 澳 W

(A) Boxes are stacked in a warehouse.
(B) Some boxes are laid down on the floor.
(C) The floor is being swept.
(D) Supplies are being unloaded in the warehouse.

（A）箱子被堆放在倉庫。
（B）一些箱子被放在地板上。
（C）地板正被打掃。
（D）備用品正在倉庫被卸貨中。

解說 這些箱子都堆放在倉庫裡，所以（A）為答案。（B）不是答案，因為這些箱子不在地板上，而在架子上。（C）和（D）不是答案，因為沒有人卻聽到being。　　　答案 (A)

詞彙 stack 堆置　lay down 放下　sweep 掃　supplies 備品；供應品　unload 卸貨　warehouse 倉庫

5. 美 W

(A) Some sailors are standing on a deck.
(B) Some ducks are swimming near a boat.
(C) Some boats are floating by the dock.
(D) Some boats are being tied up at the pier.

（A）一些船員正站立在甲板上。
（B）一些鴨子正游在一艘小船附近。
（C）一些船隻正在船塢旁浮著。
（D）一些船隻正停靠在碼頭。

解說 這些船隻都被綁在碼頭，所以（C）為答案。（A）不是答案，因為聽到照片裡沒有的名詞sailors。（B）不是答案，因為出現照片裡沒有的名詞ducks。（D）不是答案，因為照片裡沒有人卻聽到being。　　　答案 (C)

詞彙 sailor 船員　deck 甲板　float 浮在（水面上）

dock 船塢　be tied up 被綁　pier 碼頭

6. 美 M

(A) A vehicle is being parked.
(B) A vehicle is being repaired.
(C) A vehicle is being driven.
(D) A vehicle is being washed.

（A）一輛車子正被停放中。
（B）一輛車子正在被修理。
（C）一輛車子正在被駕駛。
（D）一輛車子正在被清洗。

解說 這些人正在洗車，所以（D）為答案。（A）不是答案，因為這輛車子不是正被停車當中。（B）不是答案，因為這輛車子不是正在被修理。（C）不是答案，因為不是開車當中。　　　答案 (D)

詞彙 vehicle 車輛　park 停車　repair 修理　drive 駕駛　wash 洗

7. 英 M

(A) Diners are eating sandwiches at a table.
(B) A table is covered with a newspaper.
(C) Chairs are around the table.
(D) Some chairs are occupied.

（A）用餐者正在桌上吃三明治。
（B）餐桌被用報紙蓋著。
（C）椅子圍著桌子。
（D）有些椅子有人坐。

解說 餐桌的周圍擺著一些椅子，所以（C）為答案。（A）不是答案，因為照片裡沒有人，而且也聽到照片裡沒有的名詞sandwiches。（B）不是答案，因為照片裡沒有報紙。（D）不是答案，因為不只是一些椅子沒人坐，而是全部的椅子都沒人坐。　　　答案 (C)

詞彙 diner 用餐者　cover 覆蓋　newspaper 報紙　occupied 已佔用的

8. 澳 W

(A) The woman is next to the hotel.
(B) The woman is putting her shoes in the drawer.
(C) The suitcase is full of clothes.
(D) The suitcase is being assembled.

（A）這個女人正在旅館旁邊。
（B）這個女人正把她的鞋子放進抽屜。
（C）這個手提箱裝滿了衣服。
（D）這個手提箱正在被組裝。

解說 該手提箱裝滿著衣服，所以（C）為答案。（A）不是答案，因為無法知道該女生在哪裡，只有看到她在室內而已。（B）不是答案，因為該女生雖然正在收鞋子，但不是放在抽屜裡而是放在手提箱裡。（D）不是答案，因為該女生不是在組裝東西。　　　答案 (C)

詞彙 next to 在…旁邊　put 放　suitcase 旅行手提箱
full of 充滿…　clothes 衣服　assemble 組裝

Quiz |

Q1. (A) eating in a restaurant
(B) being served in a restaurant
Q2. (A) working outdoors
(B) climbing down the ladder
Q3. (A) leaving the stage
(B) playing musical instruments
Q4. (A) using a mouse
(B) typing on a keyboard

Q1
(A) **People are eating in a restaurant.**
人們正在餐廳吃飯。.

(B) The food is being served in a restaurant.
餐廳裡供應著食物。

Q2
(A) **Workers are working outdoors.**
工人正在戶外工作。

(B) The men are climbing down the ladder.
男人們正在爬下梯子。

Q3
(A) Some musicians are leaving the stage.
一些音樂家正在離開舞台。

(B) **People are playing musical instruments.**
人們正在演奏樂器。

Q4
(A) She's using a mouse.
她正在使用滑鼠。

(B) **She's typing on a keyboard.**
她正在使用鍵盤打字。

STEP 01 若沒答對會後悔的考題

例子 (B)	1. (C)	2. (B)	3. (B)	4. (A)

例子 美 W

1 狀況	餐廳
2 對人物的描述	X
3 對物件的描述	be unoccupied
4 背景／場所／其他	table, outdoors, shadows

(A) A waiter is taking an order.
(B) The tables are unoccupied in a restaurant.
(C) People are helping themselves to the food.

（A）一個服務生正在接受客人點餐。
（B）餐廳的桌子還未被佔用。
（C）人們自助取用食物。

解說 餐桌和椅子都空著，所以（B）為答案。（A）不是答案，因為出現照片裡沒有的名詞waiter。（C）不是答案，因為照片裡沒有人出現。　　　答案 (B)

詞彙 take an order 服務點餐　unoccupied 無人佔用
help oneself to 自助食用…

1. 英 M

1 狀況	交通
2 對人物的描述	getting in the car
3 對物件的描述	be open
4 背景／場所／其他	car, door, tire

(A) A girl is checking the tire.
(B) A girl is driving a car.
(C) A girl is entering the car.

（A）一個女孩正在檢查輪胎。
（B）一個女孩正在開車。
（C）一個女孩正進入汽車。

解說 該女孩正在進入車子裡，所以（C）為答案。（A）是故意用tire來誤導的選項。（B）是故意用car來誤導的選項。　　　答案 (C)

詞彙 check 檢查　tire 輪胎

2. 澳 W

1 狀況	工作場所
2 對人物的描述	carrying a box
3 對物件的描述	be stacked
4 背景／場所／其他	warehouse, corner

(A) A man is standing in a warehouse.
(B) A man is carrying a box.
(C) Some boxes are being loaded.

（A）一個男人正站在倉庫裡。
（B）一個男人正搬著一個箱子。
（C）一些箱子正被裝載。

解說 該男生正拿著箱子移動當中，所以（B）為答案。（A）不是答案，因為該男生不是站著，而是在移動當中。（C）不是答案，因為有一些箱子堆著，但不是在被堆放當中。　　　答案 (B)

詞彙 warehouse 倉庫　carry 搬運　load 承裝

3. 美 M

1 狀況	公司
2 對人物的描述	examining papers
3 對物件的描述	be seated
4 背景／場所／其他	office, table, chair

(A) The seats are unoccupied.
(B) Some people are examining papers.
(C) A man is placing a file in the cabinet.

（A）座位沒有人坐。
（B）有些人正在查閱文件。
（C）一個男人正把文件夾放在櫃子裡。

解說 這些人看著文件並且對話當中，所以（B）為答案。（A）不是答案，因為這些座位坐著人，而不是空著的。（C）是故意用cabinet來誤導的選項。　答案 (B)

詞彙 unoccupied（座位）無人佔用的　examine 查閱
papers 文件　place 置放

4. 美 W

1 狀況	戶外／其他
2 對人物的描述	X
3 對物件的描述	floating, in the water
4 背景／場所／其他	shadow, clouds, sky

(A) Some boats are floating in the water.
(B) Some boats are tied up at the dock.
(C) People are rowing a boat.

（A）一些船隻正浮在水上。
（B）一些小船被綁在碼頭。
（C）人們正在划船。

解說 這些船隻正浮在水上，所以（A）為答案。（B）不是答案，因為出現了照片裡沒有的名詞dock。（C）不是答案，因為照片裡沒有人。 答案 (A)

詞彙 float 浮在（水面上） tied up 被綁著 dock 碼頭 row（用槳）划

1. (C)	2. (B)	3. (B)	4. (B)
5. (C)	6. (A)	7. (D)	8. (B)

1. 美W

(A) Wine bottles have fallen on the ground.
(B) A shopper is paying for the purchase.
(C) Some bottles are lined up on the shelves.
(D) A woman is lifting up a crate.

（A）紅酒瓶掉到地上。
（B）一位購物者正在為採購付費。
（C）一些瓶子在貨架上排成一列。
（D）一個女人正舉起一個箱子。

解說 架子上陳列著瓶子，所以（C）為答案。（A）不是答案，因為照片裡看不到ground。（B）不是答案，因為照片裡看不到錢，卻聽到paying for。（D）不是答案，因為照片裡看不到crate。 答案 (C)

詞彙 fall 掉落 shopper 購物者 pay for 付費 shelf 架子 lift up 舉起

2. 美M

(A) A waitress is taking an order.
(B) There's some food on the serving dishes.
(C) People are eating a meal.
(D) There are some empty seats.

（A）一位女服務生正在接受客人點餐。
（B）上菜盤上有一些食物。
（C）人們正在吃飯。
（D）有一些空座位。

解說 盤子上有食物，所以（B）為答案。（A）不是答案，因為無法知道將食物拿過來的人是男的還是女的，而且也不是正在幫客人點菜。（C）不是答案，因為照片裡沒有用餐的人。（D）不是答案，因為出現了照片裡沒有的名詞seats。 答案 (B)

詞彙 take an order 服務點餐 serving dish 上菜盤 eat a meal 用餐 empty 空的

3. 英M

(A) He's setting the timer.
(B) He's checking the tire.

(C) He's pushing the cart.
(D) He's repairing the helmet.

（A）他正在設定計時器。
（B）他正在檢查輪胎。
（C）他正在推車。
（D）他正在修理安全帽。

解說 該男生正在檢查輪胎，所以（B）為答案。（A）是故意用tire的相似音timer來誤導的選項。（C）也是故意用car的相似音cart來誤導的選項。（D）不是答案，因為該男生在修理車子，而不是修理安全帽。 答案 (B)

詞彙 set 設定 push 推 repair 修理

4. 澳W

(A) He's filling a bag with dirt.
(B) He's digging a hole with a shovel.
(C) He's tying plants to a frame.
(D) He's planting flowers.

（A）他正在把土裝進袋子裡。
（B）他正在用鏟子挖一個洞。
（C）他把植物綑綁於框架。
（D）他正在種花。

解說 該男生正在用鏟子挖土當中，所以（B）為答案。（A）不是答案，因為出現了照片裡沒有的名詞bag。（C）是故意用plants來誤導的選項。（D）不是答案，因為出現了照片裡沒有的名詞flowers。 答案 (B)

詞彙 fill 裝 dirt 土 dig a hole 挖洞 shovel 鏟子 tie 綁 plant 種植；植物

5. 美W

(A) They are writing in their notebooks.
(B) A woman is pointing to a building.
(C) They are looking at a laptop.
(D) A woman is passing paper to her co-worker.

（A）他們正寫在筆記本上。
（B）一個女人正指著一棟樓。
（C）他們正在看著筆記型電腦。
（D）一個女人正將報告交給她的同事。

解說 這些人正在看著laptop而說話當中，所以（C）為答案。（A）是故意用notebook來誤導的選項。（B）不是答案，因為不是女生而是男生指著東西，而且其所指著的對象也不是大樓而是laptop。（D）不是答案，因為照片裡看不到拿東西給別人的動作。 答案 (C)

詞彙 notebook 筆記本 point to 指向… pass 傳遞 co-worker 同事

6. 美M

(A) The conference room is unoccupied.

(B) The office furniture is being moved.
(C) The desk is being cleaned.
(D) The table has been set for a meal.

（A）會議室沒人使用。
（B）辦公傢俱正被搬動中。
（C）桌子正被清理中。
（D）因為要用餐，餐桌已擺設好了。

解說 該會議室是空著的，所以（A）為答案。（B）和（C）不是答案，因為照片裡沒有人卻聽到being。（D）是故意用table來誤導的選項。　　　　答案 (A)

詞彙 conference room 會議室　unoccupied 無人佔用的
furniture 傢俱　move 搬動　clean 清掃　set the table
擺設餐桌　meal 餐

7. 英M
(A) A cake is being sliced.
(B) A lamp is being turned off.
(C) Customers are being served.
(D) Candles are being lit.

（A）一塊蛋糕正被切下。
（B）一盞燈正被關掉。
（C）客人正在被服務。
（D）蠟燭正被點亮。

解說 蛋糕上的蠟燭正被點亮，所以（D）為答案。（A）是故意用cake來誤導的選項。（B）不是答案，因為出現了照片裡沒有的名詞lamp。（C）不是答案，因為無法知道照片裡的人是否為客人，且也不知道是否在接受服務。　　　　答案 (D)

詞彙 slice 把…切成薄片　turn off 關　serve 服務
candle 蠟燭　light 光亮；點亮

8. 澳W
(A) Plants are being watered in the garden.
(B) The women are sitting on a bench.
(C) The women are watching a game.
(D) A woman is wandering about in a forest.

（A）花園裡的植物正在被澆水。
（B）這些女人正坐在長椅上。
（C）這些女人正在觀看比賽。
（D）一個女人正在森林中徘徊。

解說 這些女生正在長椅上坐著聊天當中，所以（B）為答案。（A）是故意用周遭背景的單字plants來誤導的選項。（C）不是答案，因為她們不是在看著比賽。（D）不是答案，因為她們不是在森林裡徘徊當中。　　　　答案 (B)

詞彙 wander about 徘徊；四處走　forest 森林

---

05 Who、Where 疑問句

Quiz |

Q1. (1) Who's going to　(2) Who handles
　　　(3) Who should I　(4) Who's in charge
Q2. (1) ⓐ　(2) ⓑ　(3) ⓐ
Q3. (1) Where should I　(2) Where do you
　　　(3) Where is　(4) Where does
Q4. (1) ⓐ　(2) ⓑ　(3) ⓐ

Q1

(1) <u>Who's going to</u> speak at the meeting after work?
誰將會在下班後的會議上演講？

(2) <u>Who handles</u> complaints regarding our products?
誰處理對我們產品的投訴？

(3) <u>Who should I</u> contact for the meeting?
有關這場會議我應該與誰聯繫？

(4) <u>Who's in charge</u> of safety inspections for your plant?
誰負責你們工廠的安全檢查？

Q2

(1) Who's going to be in charge of the project?
　ⓐ **John, our vice president.**
　ⓑ I meet him quite often.

誰將要負責這個專案？
ⓐ 我們的副總裁約翰。
ⓑ 我經常見到他。

(2) Who will be responsible for taking notes for the meeting?
　ⓐ They are Mr. Parks.
　ⓑ **I think Jackson will.**

誰將負責在會議中做記錄？
ⓐ 他們是帕克先生們。
ⓑ 我認為是傑克森。

(3) Who can help this customer?
　ⓐ **I have some time right now.**
　ⓑ It's our custom.

誰能幫忙這位客人？
ⓐ 我現在有一點時間。
ⓑ 這是我們的習慣。

Chapter 05_ Who、Where 疑問句　**025**

Q3

(1) Where should I sign my name on these forms?
我應該在這些表格的哪裡簽署我的名字？

(2) Where do you plan to visit this weekend?
你計劃本週末拜訪哪裡？

(3) Where is the nearest pharmacy?
哪裡是最近的藥店？

(4) Where does the company have its main office?
公司的總辦公室在哪裡呢？

Q4

(1) Where was his article published?
ⓐ **On page 12 in the newspaper.**
ⓑ Yes, last Thursday.

他的文章被刊登在哪裡？
ⓐ 在報紙的第十二頁上。
ⓑ 是的，上週四。

(2) Where is the copy machine?
ⓐ I like coffee.
ⓑ **We don't have one.**

影印機在哪裡？
ⓐ 我喜歡咖啡。
ⓑ 我們沒有。

(3) Where can I get directions to the city hall?
ⓐ **I can give them to you.**
ⓑ He's a new director.

我能在哪裡得知去市政府的方向？
ⓐ 我可以告訴你。
ⓑ 他是一位新的主任。

STEP 01 若沒答對會後悔的考題

1. (B)　　2. (A)　　3. (B)　　4. (A)　　5. (B)

1. 美 M　美 W

1 疑問詞	Where
2 動詞（動作）	is
3 對象／場所／其他狀況	the conference room

Where's the conference room?
(A) There's room in the cabinet.
(B) It's down the hall.

會議室在哪裡？
（A）在櫃子裡有空間。
（B）它在走廊盡頭。

解說 聽到了where，就知道答案要選包含場所說法（down the hall）的選項，因此（B）為答案。雖然（A）用了同音字room，但這裡的意思為「空間」。
答案 (B)

詞彙 conference room 會議室　room 房間；空間
cabinet 櫃子

2. 英 M　澳 W

1 疑問詞	Who
2 動詞（動作）	is going to be working on
3 對象／場所／其他狀況	the renovation project

Who's going to be working on the renovation project?
(A) The facilities department will.
(B) The projector isn't working.

誰將會去做修繕計畫？
（A）設施部門會。
（B）投影機無法正常運轉。

解說 聽到了who，就知道答案要選包含部門名稱（facilities department）的選項，因此（A）為答案。（B）不是答案，且只用了同音字working，而這裡的意思為「運轉」，所以與考題裡的意思「做；做事」有差異。
答案 (A)

詞彙 work on... 從事於…　renovation 修繕　working 運轉

3. 美 W　美 M

1 疑問詞	Where
2 主詞／動詞（動作）	is he going
3 對象／場所／其他狀況	this afternoon

Where's he going this afternoon?
(A) At the store.
(B) To the post office.

他今天下午將去哪裡？
（A）在商店。
（B）到郵局。

解說 聽到了where，就知道答案要選包含地點說法（to the post office）的選項，因此（B）為答案。雖然（A）也是地點說法，但該考題需要的答案，需要包含表達方向性或動作性的介系詞。（A）用了沒有動作性的at，

所以不能作為答案。　　　　　　答案 (B)

詞彙 this afternoon 今天下午　**post office** 郵局

4. 美M 英M

1 疑問詞	Who
2 動詞（動作）	wrote
3 對象／場所／其他狀況	today's meeting agenda

Who wrote the today's meeting agenda?
(A) I think Miyumi did.
(B) No, we're out of paper.

今天的會議程程是誰寫的？
（A）我想是米友美。
（B）不，我們的紙用完了。

解說 聽到了who，就知道答案要選包含人名（Miyumi）的選項，因此（A）為答案。（B）不是答案，因為對於疑問詞疑問句，不可以用Yes或No來回答。　答案 (A)

詞彙 write 寫　**meeting agenda** 會議議程
out of paper 把紙用完了

5. 美W 澳W

1 疑問詞	Where
2 主詞／助動詞（動作）	can I buy
3 對象／場所／其他狀況	tickets for tonight's play

Where can I buy tickets for tonight's play?
(A) I feel like playing tennis after work.
(B) At the theater.

我能在哪買到今晚舞台劇的門票？
（A）我想在下班後打網球。
（B）在劇院。

解說 聽到了where，就知道答案要選包含地點說法（at the theater）的選項，因此（B）為答案。（A）是故意用類似發音playing來誤導的選項。　答案 (B)

詞彙 buy 買　**play** 舞台劇；玩…（遊戲／運動）　**feel like -ing** 想要做…　**after work** 下班後　**theater** 劇院

STEP 02 考題實戰練習

1. (A)	2. (B)	3. (B)	4. (B)	5. (C)	6. (B)
7. (B)	8. (B)	9. (B)	10. (A)	11. (C)	12. (C)

1. 美M 美W
Where's the sales department?
(A) Next to the payroll office.
(B) No, I didn't sell all of them.
(C) Miss Jefferson from the marketing department.

銷售部門在哪裡？
（A）在發薪辦公室的旁邊。
（B）不，我沒有賣掉全部。
（C）行銷部門的傑弗森小姐。

解說 聽到了where，就知道答案要選包含地點說法（next to the payroll office）的選項，因此（A）為答案。（B）不是答案，因為對於疑問詞疑問句，是用No來回答的。（C）是對who疑問句的回答，而且故意用了department來誤導的，所以不是答案。　答案 (A)

詞彙 sales department 銷售部門　**payroll office** 薪資辦公室　**sell** 賣　**marketing department** 行銷部門

2. 美W 英M
Who's going to take the CEO to the hotel?
(A) Tomorrow morning.
(B) His secretary will.
(C) Thanks for the directions.

誰將帶CEO去飯店？
（A）明天早上。
（B）他的祕書會。
（C）謝謝您告訴我方向。

解說 聽到了who，就知道答案要選包含職稱（secretary）的選項，因此（B）為答案。（A）是對於when疑問句的回答。（C）是對「我幫你的忙」等說法回答的方式。在該考題裡若沒有聽到疑問詞，有可能會被「帶去飯店」誤導。　答案 (B)

詞彙 take 某人 **to** 某個場所 帶某人去某處　**secretary** 祕書　**directions** 方向；指示

3. 美M 澳W
Where are the vegetables stored after they've been picked?
(A) He'll go to the store tomorrow.
(B) In refrigerated storage containers.
(C) Because it might spoil.

蔬菜被摘完後儲存在哪裡？

（A）他明天將去商店。
（B）在冷藏保管容器裡。
（C）因為它可能會腐壞。

解說 聽到了where，就知道答案要選包含地點說法的選項，因此（B）為答案。（A）是故意用stored的類似發音store來誤導的選項。（C）是對於why疑問句的回答

方式。　　　　　　　　　　　答案 (B)

詞彙　vegetable 蔬菜　store 商店　pick 摘取
refrigerated storage container 冷藏保管容器　spoil
（食物）腐壞

4. 美M 美W
Where can I find the factory manager?

(A) At 10 p.m.
(B) Go to the second door on the left.
(C) They're on the top shelf.

我在哪裡可以找到廠長？

（A）晚上十點。
（B）往左邊第二道門去。
（C）它們在貨架最上層。

解說　聽到了where，就知道答案要選包含地點說法（to
the second floor）的選項，因此（B）為答案。（A）是
對於when疑問句的回答方式，所以不是答案。（C）是
包含地點說法的陷阱。該考題的工廠長是單數名詞，所
以不可以用they來說。　　　　　　　答案 (B)

詞彙　factory manager 廠長　shelf 架子

5. 英W 英M
Who will be interviewing the applicants?

(A) 5 applicants so far.
(B) Yes, I have a job interview today.
(C) I'll ask Ms. Shimamura to do it.

誰即將和申請者面談？

（A）到目前為止五位申請者。
（B）是，今天我有求職面試。
（C）我會請島村女士來做。

解說　聽到了who，就知道答案要選包含人名（Ms.
Shimamura）的選項，因此（C）為答案。（A）是故意
用同音字applicants來誤導的選項。（B）不是答案，因
為對疑問詞疑問句用Yes來回答的。　　答案 (C)

詞彙　applicant 申請者　so far 到目前　job interview 求職
面試　ask 某人 to 動詞原形 要求某人作某事

6. 美M 美W
Who should I ask if I need more paper for the copier?

(A) Yes, he asked me to.
(B) Speak to the department administrator.
(C) The newspaper's delivered every morning.

若我需要更多影印紙，我該向誰詢問？
（A）是的，是他要求我的。
（B）和該部門管理者說。
（C）報紙在每天早上遞送。

解說　聽到了who，就知道答案要選包含職稱（department

administrator）的選項，因此（B）為答案。（A）是對於
疑問詞疑問句用Yes來回答，所以不是答案。（C）是故
意用paper的類似發音newspaper來誤導的選項。　答案 (B)

詞彙　copier 影印機　department administrator
部門管理者　newspaper 報紙　deliver 配送

7. 英M 澳W
Where did you put the shipment of machine parts
that arrived yesterday?

(A) It's a fact.
(B) They're in the store room.
(C) They're made of metal.

你把昨天送達的機器零件貨運放在哪？
（A）這是事實。
（B）它們在儲藏室。
（C）它們以金屬製成。

解說　聽到了where，就知道答案要選包含地點說法（in
the store room）的選項，因此（B）為答案。（A）是
用了完全無關的回答方式，所以不是答案。選項（C）
要看machine parts來判斷，這應該是對於what疑問句的
回答方式。　　　　　　　　　　　　　答案 (B)

詞彙　put 放　shipment 貨運　machine parts 機械零件
arrive 抵達　fact 事實　store room 儲藏室　metal 金屬

8. 美M 美W
Who's available to give the closing speech?

(A) It closes at five.
(B) Dr. Sheppard can do it.
(C) I love peaches.

誰能為閉幕演講？
（A）它在五點關閉。
（B）雪帕德博士可以。
（C）我愛桃子。

解說　聽到了who，就知道答案要選包含人名（Dr.
Sheppard）的選項，因此（B）為答案。（A）是用
closing的類似發音closes來誤導的選項。（C）是用
speech的類似發音peaches來誤導的選項。　答案 (B)

詞彙　available 可用的；有空的
give the closing speech 做閉幕演講　peach 水蜜桃

9. 美W 英M
Who has the test results?

(A) That's what I thought.
(B) The secretary should have them.
(C) No, he hasn't.

誰有測驗結果？
（A）那就是我所想的。
（B）祕書應該有。

028

（C）不，他還沒。

解說 聽到了who，就知道答案要選包含職稱（secretary）的選項，因此（B）為答案。（A）是對於陳述句或否定、附加、一般疑問句的回答方式。（C）不是答案，因為對於疑問詞疑問句，是用No來回答的。　　答案 (B)

詞彙 result 結果　secretary 祕書

10. 澳W 美W

Where do you file the meeting records?

(A) In the cabinet over there.
(B) Every Friday afternoon.
(C) Our past records are no longer available.

你把會議記錄歸檔在哪？
（A）在那邊的櫃子。
（B）每個星期五下午。
（C）我們之前的記錄已不能用了。

解說 聽到了where，就知道答案要選包含地點說法的選項，因此（A）為答案。（B）是對於How often疑問句的回答方式。（C）是故意用同音字records來誤導的選項。　　答案 (A)

詞彙 file 歸整檔案　record 記錄　every 每個…
no longer available 不再能使用

11. 英M 澳W

To whom should I address this package?

(A) He should do it.
(B) A suit and a tie.
(C) Dr. Kun Tao.

包裹的收件地址該寫誰？
（A）他應該做的。
（B）西裝和領帶。
（C）康陶博士。

解說 To whom也是與who疑問句同類的考題，因此以人名來回答的（C）為答案。選項（A）無法知道he是指誰，所以不是答案。（B）是故意用address的類似發音dress來誤導的選項。　　答案 (C)

詞彙 address 寫收件人姓名地址　package 包裹
a suit and a tie 西裝和領帶

12. 美W 美M

Where should I go to buy some presents for our customers?

(A) They were impressed by the presentation.
(B) About twenty dollars.
(C) Try the department store near the ABC Bank.

我該去哪買給我們顧客的禮物？
（A）他們認為那個報告讓人印象深刻。

（B）約二十元。
（C）試試去ABC銀行附近的百貨公司。

解說 聽到了where，就知道答案要選包含地點說法（near the ABC Bank）的選項，因此（C）為答案。（A）是故意用presents的類似發音presentation來誤導的選項。（B）是對於How much的回答方式，但也是可以和presents（禮物）做聯想來回答，所以得小心。　　答案 (C)

詞彙 present 禮物　impressed 印象深刻的　department store 百貨公司　near 在…附近

Quiz

Q1. (1) When does　(2) When did
　　 (3) When will　(4) When were
Q2. (1) ⓑ　(2) ⓐ　(3) ⓑ
Q3. (1) Why are　(2) Why was
　　 (3) Why hasn't　(4) Why don't
Q4. (1) ⓑ　(2) ⓑ　(3) ⓐ

Q1

(1) When does your flight leave?
您的航班什麼時候離開？

(2) When did you sign up for the conference?
你什麼時候報名這個會議的？

(3) When will the new manager start?
新的經理將於什麼時候開始？

(4) When were those articles written?
那些文章是什麼時候寫的？

Q2

(1) When is the new product going to be released?
　ⓐ At least twice a week.
　ⓑ **In October, I believe.**

新產品將於什麼時候上市？
ⓐ 至少一週兩次。
ⓑ 我想是在十月。

(2) When will the factory begin production?
　ⓐ **In less than two months.**
　ⓑ At the new plant.

工廠什麼時候將開始生產？
ⓐ 兩個月內。
ⓑ 在新工廠。

(3) When did Mr. Tanaka call?
　ⓐ At her office.
　ⓑ **About three hours ago.**

田中先生什麼時候打電話的？
ⓐ 在她的辦公室。
ⓑ 約三小時前。

Q3

(1) Why are you walking so fast?
你為什麼走這麼快？

(2) Why was that company so profitable last year?
為什麼那間公司去年獲利這麼高？

(3) Why hasn't the meeting started yet?
會議為什麼還不開始呢？

(4) Why don't we meet after lunch to discuss the budget?
我們何不在午餐後見面討論預算呢？

Q4

(1) Why can't we take the highway?
　ⓐ By train.
　ⓑ **It's closed for road repairs.**

我們為什麼不走高速公路？
ⓐ 坐火車。
ⓑ 它因為道路維修而封閉。

(2) Why are so many people standing near the park?
　ⓐ Have a seat.
　ⓑ **That's a bus stop.**

為什麼很多人站在公園附近？
ⓐ 請坐。
ⓑ 那是一個巴士站。

(3) Why don't we take a quick break?
　ⓐ **I can't. I've got too much to do.**
　ⓑ Sorry, I didn't mean to break it.

我們何不小歇一下？
ⓐ 我不能。我有太多事要做。
ⓑ 對不起，我不是故意打破它的。

STEP 01　若沒答對會後悔的考題

1. (A)	2. (B)	3. (B)	4. (A)	5. (B)

1. 美M 美W

1 疑問詞＋時間點	When are
2 主詞／動詞（動作）	you going
3 對象／場所／其他狀況	to Shanghai

When are you going to Shanghai?
(A) Not until December.
(B) To see some potential clients.

你何時去上海？
（A）十二月。
（B）去拜訪潛在客戶。

解說 聽到了when are，就可以知道要選以未來時間說法（not until December）回答的（A）為答案。（B）是對於why疑問句的回答方式，所以不是答案。
答案 (A)

詞彙 potential client 潛在客戶

2. 英M 澳W

1 疑問詞＋助動詞	Why did
2 主詞	Mr. Lawyer
3 動詞（動作）	change his job

Why did Mr. Lawyer change his job?
(A) We need to hire several new people.
(B) He found a more challenging position.

為什麼羅約先生換了他的工作？
（A）我們需要聘請一些新人。
（B）他找到一個更具挑戰性的職位。

解說 聽到了why did，就可以知道是詢問理由的why。兩個選項都是以句子的形式，所以是全部得聽完才能回答的考題。「找到了具有挑戰性的職位，所以換了工作」是有邏輯的組合，所以（B）為答案。（A）是故意用hire來誤導的選項。
答案 (B)

詞彙 change 改變 job 職業 hire 雇用 challenging 具有挑戰性的

3. 美W 美M

1 疑問詞＋時間點	When's
2 主詞	the next step of the study
3 動詞（動作）	supposed to begin

When's the next step of the study supposed to begin?
(A) I'll study it every day.
(B) It'll start within the next month.

這個研究的下一步預計什麼時候開始？
（A）我將每天學習。
（B）它將會在下月之內開始。

解說 聽到了when's，就可以知道要選包含未來時間的說法（within the next month）的（B）為答案。（A）是表達頻率的說法，所以是對於how often的回答方式，

且也是故意用同音字study來誤導的選項。 答案 (B)

詞彙 step 步驟 be supposed to 預計… within 在…之中

4. 美M 英M

1 疑問詞＋助動詞	Why has
2 主詞	the board
3 動詞（動作）	reorganized our company

Why has the board reorganized our company?
(A) To make us more efficient.
(B) In three hours.

董事會為什麼將我們公司改組？
（A）為了使我們更加有效率。
（B）三小時之內。

解說 聽到Why has，就要知道是詢問理由的why，所以用「to＋動詞原形」回答的（A）為答案。（B）是未來時間點的說法，所以是對於when疑問句的回答方式。 答案 (A)

詞彙 reorganize 重新組織 efficient 有效率的

5. 美W 澳W

1 疑問詞＋助動詞	Why don't
2 主詞	we
3 動詞（動作）	meet in the lobby

Why don't we meet in the lobby?
(A) Because it's a good place.
(B) Sure, what time do you want to meet?

我們何不在大廳見面？
（A）因為它是一個好地方。
（B）當然，你想什麼時候見面呢？

解說 聽到why don't，就可以知道是建議的why，因此以表達肯定、許可回答方式的（B）為答案。（A）是對理由的why的回答方式。 答案 (B)

詞彙 meet 見面 lobby 大廳 place 場所

STEP 02 考題實戰練習

1. (B)	2. (C)	3. (C)	4. (C)	5. (B)	6. (B)
7. (B)	8. (C)	9. (A)	10. (C)	11. (C)	12. (B)

1. 美M 美W

When can I schedule an appointment with Dr. Yang?

(A) A ten-minute walk from here.
(B) Any time after 4:00 p.m.
(C) Could you, please?

我什麼時候能預約楊醫師？
（A）從這裡步行十分鐘。
（B）下午四點後的任何時間。
（C）可否麻煩您？

解說 聽到了when can，就可以知道以未來時間點說法（after 4:00 p.m.）回答的（B）為答案。（A）是對於where疑問句的回答方式。（C）是對於Could I的回答方式，也是故意誤導為和Could you混淆的選項。
答案（B）

詞彙 schedule an appointment 安排預約 any time 任何時候

2. 美W 英M

Why are you leaving so early?

(A) Do you know where he lives?
(B) Yes, I wake up early.
(C) I'm running late for the meeting.

你為何這麼早離開？
（A）你知道他住哪裡嗎？
（B）是的，我很早起床。
（C）我開會遲到了。

解說 Why後面沒有don't，所以是詢問理由的疑問句，因此當作理由的（C）為答案。（A）的lives為leaving的類似發音，所以不是答案。（B）是對疑問詞疑問句用Yes來回答的，所以不是答案。
答案（C）

詞彙 leave 離開 so early 很早 wake up 起床 late 遲的；晚

3. 美M 英W

Why didn't you come to the seminar?

(A) It's just down the hall.
(B) It went very well, thanks.
(C) I was too busy.

你為什麼沒來研討會？
（A）它就在走廊的盡頭。
（B）它進行得非常好，謝謝你。
（C）我太忙了。

解說 Why後面聽到的不是don't而是didn't，所以是詢問理由的疑問句，因此作為沒有到研討會的理由的（C）為答案。（A）是對於where疑問句的回答方式。（B）是對於how的回答方式，且故意和come產生聯想而誤導

的選項。
答案（C）

詞彙 go very well 進行得很好 busy 忙碌的

4. 美M 美W

When did you finish the project?

(A) He finished it last week.
(B) You can't use the projector until three p.m.
(C) I'm still working on it.

你什麼時候完成這個計畫的？
（A）他上週完成了。
（B）你下午3點前不能使用投影機。
（C）我仍在處理當中。

解說 若是聽到了when did就立刻選包含過去時間點說法的（A）那就錯了。一樣包含時間點說法的（B）也不是答案。這兩個選項的主詞都不對。表達為「仍然處理當中」的（C）才是答案。
答案（C）

詞彙 finish 完成 use 使用 work on 處理

5. 澳W 英M

When does the department store open?

(A) Open the door, please.
(B) At 10 a.m., I think.
(C) Next to the payroll office.

百貨公司何時營業？
（A）請開門。
（B）我想是上午十點。
（C）在發薪辦公室旁邊。

解說 聽到了when does，就可以知道用未來時間點說法（at 10 a.m.）回答的（B）為答案。（A）是故意用同音字open來誤導的選項。（C）是對於where疑問句的回答方式，所以不是答案。
答案（B）

詞彙 department store 百貨公司 payroll office 發薪辦公室

6. 美M 美W

When's your business trip to Tokyo?

(A) Yes, it went pretty well.
(B) Next Friday.
(C) No, it's within walking distance.

你何時到東京出差？
（A）是的，它進行得相當好。
（B）下週五。
（C）不，它在步行距離之內。

解說 若聽到了when's，就可以知道以未來時間點說法（next Friday）回答的（B）為答案。因為是對於疑問詞疑問句用Yes來回答，所以（A）不是答案。（C）是對於疑問詞疑問句用No來回答，所以也不是答案。
答案（B）

詞彙 business trip 商務出差 go pretty well
進行得相當好 within walking distance 在步行距離

7. 英M 澳W

Why hasn't the new carpet arrived yet?

(A) By train, I think.
(B) I'll call the delivery company.
(C) I'll have it dry-cleaned.

為什麼新的地毯還沒到？
（A）我認為是搭火車。
（B）我會打電話給快遞公司。
（C）我會把它乾洗。

解說 Why後面沒有聽到don't，所以是詢問理由的疑問句。（B）裡聽到間接迴避性的回答，所以是答案。（A）是對於詢問交通方式的how的回答方式，所以不是答案。（C）是故意用dry-cleaned來與carpet產生聯想而誤導的選項。　　　　　　答案 (B)

詞彙 arrive 抵達 delivery company 快遞公司
dry-cleaned 乾洗

8. 美M 美W

Why do you think everyone is so busy lately?

(A) Yes, all of them.
(B) Sorry, I can't be there on time.
(C) We got a lot of new orders.

你認為為什麼最近每個人都這麼忙？
（A）對，他們全部。
（B）抱歉，我無法準時到那裡。
（C）我們接到很多新訂單。

解說 Why後面沒有聽到don't，所以是詢問忙碌的原因的疑問句。因此（C）為答案。（A）是對於疑問詞疑問句用Yes來回答的，所以不是答案。（B）是對於建議的why的回答方式，所以不是答案。　答案 (C)

詞彙 so busy 很忙 lately 最近；近期 on time 準時
a lot of 很多 order 訂單

9. 美W 英M

When is the next play going to start?

(A) Tonight, at 7:30.
(B) Yes, that's a good one.
(C) There are five players.

下一場舞台劇何時開始？
（A）今晚七點三十分。
（B）是的，這個不錯。
（C）有五名選手。

解說 聽到了when is，就可以知道用時間點說法（at 7:30）回答的（A）為答案。（B）是對於疑問詞疑問句用Yes來回答的，所以不是答案。（C）是故意用play

的近似發音players來誤導的選項。　　　答案 (A)

詞彙 play 演出；演劇 player 選手

10. 澳W 美W

Why was the itinerary changed?

(A) Sorry, I'm too busy.
(B) I'll make an appointment.
(C) Because Mr. Tanaka couldn't be here then.

行程為什麼改變了？
（A）很抱歉，我太忙了。
（B）我將會預約。
（C）因為田中先生那時不能在這裡。

解說 Why後面沒有聽到don't，所以是詢問旅遊行程改變的理由的疑問句。因此（C）為答案。（A）是對於建議的why的回答方式，所以不是答案。（B）是故意用appointment（約定）來與itinerary（旅遊行程）產生聯想而誤導的選項。　　　　答案 (C)

詞彙 itinerary 旅程計畫 change 改變 too busy
太忙碌 make an appointment 預約 then 那時候

11. 英M 澳W

When will you return to your hometown?

(A) He'll be out of the town today.
(B) In the city.
(C) Within a week.

你什麼時候回到你的家鄉？
（A）他今天將出差。
（B）在城市。
（C）在一個星期內。

解說 若聽到了when will，就可以知道以時間點說法（within a week）回答的（C）為答案。（A）用了不對的主詞，所以不是答案。（B）是對於where疑問句的回答方式，所以不是答案。　　　　答案 (C)

詞彙 return 返回 hometown 故鄉 be out of the town
出差

12. 美W 美M

Why weren't you at the party this afternoon?

(A) Yes, I wrote part of it.
(B) I thought it was tomorrow.
(C) I'll bring it later tonight.

為什麼你今天下午不在派對中？
（A）是的，我寫了一部分。
（B）我以為是明天。
（C）我今夜稍晚會帶去。

解說 Why後面沒有聽到don't，所以是詢問「今天下午不在派對裡的理由」的疑問句。因此（B）為答案。

（A）是對於疑問詞疑問句用Yes來回答的，所以不是答案。（C）是故意用tonight來與afternoon產生聯想而誤導的選項。　　　　　　　　　答案（B）

詞彙　write 寫　part 部分　bring 帶來　later tonight 今夜稍晚

Quiz |

Q1. (1) What kind, buy　(2) What time
　　 (3) What, doing　(4) What, think
Q2. (1) ⓑ　(2) ⓐ　(3) ⓐ
Q3. (1) How long　(2) How much
　　 (3) How do you like　(4) How about
Q4. (1) ⓐ　(2) ⓑ　(3) ⓑ

Q1

(1) What kind of ticket did you buy?
你買了哪一種票？

(2) What time did Mr. Rose leave the office?
羅斯先生什麼時候離開辦公室的？

(3) What are you doing after work?
下班後你將會做些什麼？

(4) What do you think of our advertising strategy?
你認為我們的廣告策略如何？

Q2

(1) What are you ordering?
　ⓐ No, thanks. I have one.
　ⓑ **The chicken sandwich.**

　你正在訂購什麼？
　ⓐ 不，謝謝。我有一個。
　ⓑ 雞肉三明治。

(2) What's the due date for this report?
　ⓐ **Next Friday.**
　ⓑ Only three.

　這份報告的截止日期是什麼時候？
　ⓐ 下星期五。
　ⓑ 只有三個。

(3) What are you doing after work?
　ⓐ **I'm going fishing.**
　ⓑ She's not at home.

　下班後你將會做些什麼？
　ⓐ 我將會去釣魚。
　ⓑ 她不在家。

Q3

(1) How long did your interview last?
你的面試花了多久時間？

(2) How much did the lunch cost?
午餐花了多少錢？

(3) How do you like your coffee?
你要如何調配你的咖啡？

(4) How about shipping the orders this afternoon?
要不要今天下午將訂單出貨？

Q4

(1) How many rooms do you need to book?
ⓐ **Just one.**
ⓑ Around 3 o'clock.

您需要預訂多少房間呢？
ⓐ 只要一間。
ⓑ 大約是三點。

(2) How do you commute to work?
ⓐ No, not every day.
ⓑ **By train.**

你如何去上班？
ⓐ 不，不是每天。
ⓑ 坐火車。

(3) How would you like to play a game of tennis this afternoon?
ⓐ Unfortunately, I didn't.
ⓑ **That's a good idea.**

今天下午打網球賽如何？
ⓐ 真不幸，我沒有做。
ⓑ 那是個好主意。

STEP 01　若沒答對會後悔的考題

1.(A)	2.(A)	3.(B)	4.(A)	5.(B)

1. 美M 美W

1 疑問詞	What
2 決定類別的單字	drink

What would you like to drink?
(A) A glass of water, please.
(B) I'd be delighted.

你想喝點什麼？
（A）請給我一杯水。
（B）我會很喜歡的。

解說 What後面聽到及物動詞drink，所以這裡的what是詢問接受動作的對象。（A）用接受drink的對象來回答，即為答案。（B）是故意用與would you like發音相近的delighted來誤導的選項。　　答案 (A)

詞彙 a glass of water 一杯水　delight 高興；喜歡

2. 英M 澳W

1 疑問詞	How
2 決定類別的單字	long

How long will this light bulb last?
(A) At least five years.
(B) To make the room bright.

這個燈泡能一直用多久？
（A）至少五年。
（B）為了讓房間變明亮。

解說 聽到了how long，就可以知道用期間來回答的（A）為答案。（B）是故意用light的相似發音bright來誤導的選項。　　答案 (A)

詞彙 light bulb 燈泡　last 持續　bright 明亮

3. 美W 美M

1 疑問詞	What
2 決定類別的單字	time

What time is the meeting scheduled to start?
(A) He's just started working here.
(B) Not for an hour.

這個會議被訂在幾點開始？
（A）他才剛到這裡開始工作。
（B）在一小時後。

解說 聽到了what time，就可以知道是詢問時間的what，所以用時間說法（not for an hour）來回答的（B）為答案。（A）的主詞不相合，所以不是答案。　　答案 (B)

詞彙 be scheduled to 預定…　start 開始

4. 美M 英M

1 疑問詞	How
2 決定類別的單字	about

How about meeting in the lobby?
(A) That would be nice.
(B) You should meet him.

在大廳見面如何？
（A）那樣很好。

(B) 你應該和他見面。

解說 這是建議的how。所以對於建議以肯定或允許說法來回答的（A）為答案。（B）是meeting的相似發音meet來故意誤導的選項，而且這裡的him也無法得知是誰。　　　　　　　　　　　　　　　答案 (A)

詞彙 meet 見面　lobby 大廳

5. 美W 澳W

1 疑問詞	What
2 決定類別的單字	think

What do you think of our design proposal?
(A) I believe it's a good sign.
(B) I was very impressed.

你認為我們的設計方案如何？
（A）我相信它是個好徵兆。
（B）我深深被感動了。

解說 這是詢問意見的what。包含形容詞（impressed）的句子常常表達意見。（A）是故意用design的相似發音sign來誤導的選項。　　　　答案 (B)

詞彙 proposal 設計方案　sign 徵兆　impressed 有深刻印象的

STEP 02　考題實戰練習

1. (B)	2. (A)	3. (B)	4. (B)	5. (A)	6. (B)
7. (C)	8. (B)	9. (B)	10. (B)	11. (B)	12. (A)

1. 美M 美W

What flavor of soup would you like?
(A) Some soup and salad.
(B) What do you recommend?
(C) That's my favorite.

你想喝什麼口味的湯呢？
（A）一些湯和沙拉。
（B）你推薦什麼？
（C）這就是我最喜歡的。

解說 What後面聽到及物動詞like，所以這裡的what是詢問接受動作的對象。（B）是詢問「給我的建議」的「間接、迴避性回答方式」，即為答案。（A）是故意用一樣的單字（soup）來誤導的選項。（C）裡面無法知道that指的是什麼，所以不是答案。　　答案 (B)

詞彙 flavor 味道　soup 湯　recommend 建議　favorite 喜歡的（東西）

2. 美W 英M

What files do I need to bring on Tuesday?
(A) The ones on my desk.
(B) Yes, let's speak then.
(C) Because I haven't seen them.

我週二需要攜帶哪些檔案（夾）？
（A）我辦公桌上的那份。
（B）是的，我們到時說吧。
（C）因為我還沒有看見他們。

解說 What後面聽到及物動詞bring，所以這裡的what是詢問接受動作的對象。因此，以bring的受詞來回答的（A）為答案。（B）是對於疑問詞疑問句用Yes來回答，所以不是答案。（C）是對why疑問句的回答方式，而且無法知道這裡的them是指什麼。　答案 (A)

詞彙 file 文件（夾）　bring 攜帶

3. 美M 澳W

How long have you worked at your company?
(A) About 4 kilometers from here.
(B) It will be three years next month.
(C) It doesn't work properly.

你在貴公司工作多久了？
（A）從這裡起約四公里。
（B）到下個月就三年了。
（C）它不能正常運作。

解說 聽到了how long，就可以知道以期間說法回答的（B）為答案。（A）是對於where的回答方式，且故意和long產生聯想而誤導的選項。（C）的work是worked的相似發音，但這裡的意思不是「工作」，而是「運作」。　　　　　　答案 (B)

詞彙 work 運作　properly 正常地

4. 美M 美W

How many people are attending the product demonstration?
(A) It tends to be.
(B) Everyone from the research division.
(C) For the next 10 to 12 months.

有多少人會出席產品展示會？
（A）它傾向那樣。
（B）研究部門的每一個人。
（C）在未來十至十二個月當中。

解說 聽到了how many，所以用「全部」或「一部分」來回答的（B）為答案。（A）是故意用attend的相似發音tend來誤導的選項。（C）是對how long的回答方式，所以不是答案。　　　　答案 (B)

詞彙 attend 出席 demonstration 展示會 research division 研究部門

5. 澳 W 英 M

What color are you painting the wall?

(A) Light brown, I think.
(B) Three weeks from now.
(C) The cooler's over there.

你用什麼顏色來塗牆壁？
（A）我打算用淺棕色。
（B）從現在起三個星期。
（C）冷卻器在那裡。

解說 What color後面聽到及物動詞painting，所以這裡的what是詢問接受動作的對象。（A）用painting的受詞補語來回答，即為答案。（B）是對於when的回答方式。（C）是故意用color的類似發音cooler來誤導的選項。　　　　　　答案 (A)

詞彙 paint 塗 wall 牆壁 light brown 淺棕色 cooler 冷卻器；冷藏庫 over there 位在那裡

6. 美 M 美 W

How much is the admission to this museum?

(A) About an hour.
(B) Only 5 dollars.
(C) Bikes aren't allowed in this area.

這個博物館的入場費多少錢？
（A）大約一小時。
（B）只要五元。
（C）在這個地區不准騎腳踏車。

解說 聽到了how much和admission，就可以知道是詢問費用的how。因此以費用回答的（B）為答案。（A）是對於how long的回答方式。（C）是故意讓admission和allowed產生聯想的選項。　　答案 (B)

詞彙 admission 入場費 museum 博物館 allow 准許

7. 英 M 澳 W

What's the best way to reach your employer?

(A) I can't reach it.
(B) About ten kilograms.
(C) Try calling her mobile phone.

聯繫你老闆最好的方式是什麼？
（A）我無法到達。
（B）約十公斤。
（C）試試打她的手機。

解說 這是詢問方法（the best way）的what。（C）就是在論及方法，即為答案。（A）是故意用同音字（reach）來誤導的選項。（B）是故意讓way和ten kilograms產生聯想而誤導的選項。　　答案 (C)

詞彙 way 方法 reach 與…聯繫 employer 雇主 about 大約 try 嘗試 mobile phone 行動電話

8. 美 M 美 W

How did you learn about this job?

(A) I'm still learning how.
(B) I read about it in the newspaper.
(C) About a month ago.

你怎麼知道這個工作的？
（A）我現在仍然在學。
（B）我在報紙上讀到它的。
（C）大約一個月前。

解說 這是詢問方法的how。所以（B）為答案。（A）是故意用learn的相似發音learning來誤導的選項。（C）是對於when的回答方式，所以不是答案。　　答案 (B)

詞彙 job 職業 newspaper 報紙

9. 美 W 英 M

What time is the meeting scheduled to start?

(A) He's just started working here.
(B) Not for an hour.
(C) In the auditorium.

會議訂於什麼時候開始？
（A）他才剛到此開始工作。
（B）一個小時之後。
（C）在演講廳。

解說 聽到了what time，就可以知道是詢問時間的what。因此，以時間說法（not for an hour）來回答的（B）為答案。（A）是故意用start的相似發音started來誤導的選項，而且也無法知道He是指誰。（C）是對於where疑問句的回答方式，所以不是答案。　　答案 (B)

詞彙 be scheduled to 預訂 start 開始 just 剛才 auditorium 演講廳

10. 澳 W 美 W

What's Mr. Thomas doing during his leave of absence?

(A) No, I think he's in today.
(B) He's taking courses at the community center.
(C) He lives far away.

湯瑪士先生在他的休假期間要做什麼？
（A）不，我想他今天有上班。
（B）他在社區活動中心參加課程。
（C）他住得很遠。

解說 What後面聽到doing，所以是詢問行為的what。因此包含行為說法（將要參加課程）的（B）為答案。（A）是對於疑問詞疑問句用Yes來回答的，所以不是答案。（C）是故意用leave的類似發音lives來誤導的選

項。 答案 (B)

詞彙 during 在…期間 leave of absence 休假 be in 有上班 course 課程 community center 社區活動中心 far away 相當遙遠

11. 英M 澳W

How do you like the new director?
(A) He's out of the office today.
(B) He's very demanding.
(C) No, that's not the right direction.

你的新主管怎麼樣呢？
（A）他今天不在辦公室。
（B）他的要求很高。
（C）不，這不是正確的方向。

解說 聽到了詢問意見的How do you like，所以表達意見的（B）為答案。若在考題裡只有聽到new director，就很容易選擇（A），但這是一種陷阱，而且（A）也不是表達意見的。（C）是故意用director的相似發音direction來誤導的選項。 答案 (B)

詞彙 director 主管 office 辦公室 demanding 要求很高的 direction 方向

12. 美W 美M

How's the ice cream?
(A) It's quite good.
(B) I'm feeling better, thanks.
(C) Thanks for the favor.

這個冰淇淋如何？
（A）相當好。
（B）我感到好些了，謝謝。
（C）謝謝你的幫忙。

解說 對於詢問狀態的how is以包含形容詞的句子回答的（A）為答案。選項（B）的內容和冰淇淋無關，而是表達情緒的說法。（C）是故意用冰淇淋flavor的相似發音favor來誤導的選項。 答案 (A)

詞彙 quite good 相當好 feel better 感到較好一點 favor 善意；好意

---

08 提出建議的句子與選擇疑問句

Quiz

Q1. (1) Would you
(2) Could you
(3) Don't you want
(4) Let's

Q2. (1) ⓑ (2) ⓑ (3) ⓐ

Q3. (1) seven, eight
(2) talk now, you busy
(3) initial this, sign by full name
(4) Which

Q4. (1) ⓐ (2) ⓐ (3) ⓑ

Q1

(1) **Would you** like to join us for the party?
你願意跟我們去參加派對嗎？

(2) **Could you** lend me your newspaper?
你能借我你的報紙嗎？

(3) **Don't you want** to see the baseball game tonight?
你今晚不想看棒球賽嗎？

(4) **Let's** try the new cafeteria.
我們試試看新的自助餐廳吧。

Q2

(1) Could you give me a call at the office later?
ⓐ I've already put it on your desk.
ⓑ **Sure, I'll call you around five.**

你稍後能打電話到辦公室找我嗎？
ⓐ 我已經放在你的桌上了。
ⓑ 當然，我大約在五點打電話給你。

(2) Do you need any help moving these boxes?
ⓐ He's moving to the city.
ⓑ **I'd appreciate that.**

你需要任何幫助來搬這些箱子嗎？
ⓐ 他正搬家到這個城市。
ⓑ 那樣我會很感激的。

(3) Let's go to the Italian restaurant on Main Street.
ⓐ **That sounds good.**
ⓑ The food wasn't ready.

我們去大街上的義大利餐廳吧。
ⓐ 那聽起來不錯。
ⓑ 食物還沒準備好。

Q3

(1) Should we order <u>seven</u> dishes or <u>eight</u>?
我們應該點七道菜還是八道菜呢？

(2) Can we <u>talk now</u> or are <u>you busy</u>?
我們可以現在談嗎？還是你正在忙？

(3) Should I just <u>initial this</u> or <u>sign by full name</u>?
我應該只簽姓氏還是簽全名？

(4) Which <u>parking area</u> is for <u>employees</u>?
哪個停車場是給員工的？

Q4

(1) Do you prefer a window or an aisle seat?
  ⓐ **Either one is fine with me.**
  ⓑ Sure, you can sit here.

你比較想要靠窗還是靠走道的座位？
  ⓐ 對我來說哪個都好。
  ⓑ 當然，你可以坐這裡。

(2) Would you rather fly or take a train to the meeting?
  ⓐ **I'd prefer to take an airplane.**
  ⓑ The training should be very useful.

你想要搭飛機還是搭火車去開會？
  ⓐ 我想要搭飛機。
  ⓑ 訓練應該相當有用。

(3) Which restaurant should we eat dinner at?
  ⓐ We can meet today.
  ⓑ **Either one is fine.**

我們應該在哪家餐廳吃晚餐呢？
  ⓐ 我們今天可以見面。
  ⓑ 哪一家都很好。

STEP 01　若沒答對會後悔的考題

| 1. (A) | 2. (A) | 3. (B) | 4. (A) | 5. (B) |

1. 美M 美W

| 1 決定類別的線索 | Would you like me to |
| 2 動詞與其他 | make you some tea |

Would you like me to make you some tea?
(A) That's okay. I'll make some myself.
(B) She likes to see the dessert menu.

你要我幫您泡點茶嗎？
（A）沒關係。我會自己弄的。
（B）她喜歡看甜點菜單。

解說 聽到了Would you like me to，就可以知道是建議。因此，否定或拒絕說法之後再附加說明的（A）為答案。（B）是故意用dessert menu來與tea產生聯想而誤導的選項，且也無法知道其主詞she指的是誰，所以不是答案。　　　　　　　　　　答案 (A)

詞彙 make 人 some tea 泡茶給某人　dessert 甜點

2. 英M 澳W

| 1 決定類別的線索 | in the cafeteria or my office |
| 2 動詞與其他 | prefer to meet |

Would you prefer to meet in the cafeteria or my office?
(A) Anywhere is fine.
(B) Yes, I agree with you.

你想在自助餐廳還是在我辦公室見面？
（A）任何地點都好。
（B）是的，我同意你。

解說 聽到了or就可以知道是選擇疑問句。因此包含表達「任何」的any的（A）為答案。（B）是對於選擇疑問句用Yes來回答，所以不是答案。　　　答案 (A)

詞彙 prefer 較願意；較喜歡　cafeteria 自助餐廳　agree with 同意…

3. 美W 美M

| 1 決定類別的線索 | Please |
| 2 動詞與其他 | take a copy of the sales contract |

Please take a copy of the sales contract.
(A) Yes, I'm sure he did.
(B) I already have one, thanks.

請拿一份銷售合約。
（A）是的，我確定他做了。
（B）我已經有一份了，謝謝。

解說 聽到了Please就可以知道是建議。因此，省略了否定或拒絕說法而直接用附加說明來回答的（B）為答案。（A）裡無法知道he指的是誰、did指的是什麼行為，所以不是答案。　　　　　　答案 (B)

詞彙 take a copy 拿走一份　sales contract 銷售合約　already 已經

4. 美M 英M

1 決定類別的線索	Monday or Tuesday
2 動詞與其他	reschedule the meeting

Can you reschedule the meeting for Monday or Tuesday?
(A) How about Monday?
(B) No, they are behind schedule.

你能重新安排會議於星期一或是星期二嗎？
（A）星期一如何？
（B）不，他們的進度落後了。

解說 聽到了or就可以知道是選擇疑問句。（A）是拿選擇事項以反問句的方式回答，即是答案。（B）是對於選擇疑問句以No來回答，所以不是答案。　答案 (A)

詞彙 reschedule 重新安排行程　meeting 會議
be behind schedule 落後於計畫的進度

5. 美W 澳W

1 決定類別的線索	Do you mind
2 動詞與其他	waiting in the lobby

Do you mind waiting in the lobby?
(A) To my mind, she's right.
(B) Absolutely not.

你介不介意在大廳等？
（A）照我的想法，她是對的。
（B）絕對不會。

解說 聽到了Do you mind就可以知道是建議。mind有「介意」的意思，所以（B）的「完全不」，也就是「允許」的意思，即為答案。（A）是故意用同義字mind來誤導的選項，且也無法知道she指的是誰。
答案 (B)

詞彙 mind 介意　lobby 大廳　to my mind 照我的想法
right 正確的；對的　absolutely not 絕對不

STEP 02　考題實戰練習

1. (B)	2. (A)	3. (B)	4. (C)	5. (B)	6. (A)
7. (B)	8. (B)	9. (B)	10. (B)	11. (C)	12. (A)

1. 美M 美W

Would you like to read the magazine when I finish?
(A) No, can you repair it?
(B) No, thanks. I already bought a copy.
(C) Yes, I'd love to lead.

當我看完後，你想閱讀這本雜誌嗎？
（A）不，你可以修它嗎？
（B）不，謝謝。我已經買了一份。
（C）是的，我很想要領導大家。

解說 聽到了建議的Would you，所以表達否定或拒絕的（B）為答案。（A）是無厘頭的回答。（C）是故意用read的類似發音lead來誤導的選項。　答案 (B)

詞彙 magazine 雜誌　finish 完成　repair 修理
a copy 一份　lead 領導

2. 美W 英M

Do you want some fruit or ice cream?
(A) Either one is okay.
(B) Sure. Help yourself.
(C) Yes, it was nice.

你想要一些水果或冰淇淋嗎？
（A）其中任一個都可以。
（B）當然，請隨意。
（C）是的，它是很好的。

解說 聽到了句子中間的or就可以知道是選擇疑問句。因此，表達「任何一個（either）」的（A）為答案。（B）是對於建議的回答方式，而不是答案。（C）是對於「單字 or 單字」的選擇疑問句用Yes來回答，所以不是答案。　答案 (A)

詞彙 help oneself 隨意食用

3. 美M 澳W

Would you like to try this shirt on instead?
(A) It isn't that short.
(B) What size is it?
(C) Yes, we have.

你想換成這件襯衫試試看嗎？
（A）它不是那麼短。
（B）它的尺寸是多少？
（C）是的，我們有。

解說 聽到了Would you就可以知道是建議。（B）是反問形式的回答方式，總是能夠成為答案。（A）故意用了shirt的類似發音short來誤導的選項。（C）是不符合考題內容的回答。　答案 (B)

詞彙 try on 試穿　instead 取代　short 短的　size 尺寸

4. 美M 美W

We need to check your passport or your driver's license for identification.

(A) Yes, I am.
(B) Leave your car here.
(C) Oh, I don't have either.

我們需要檢查您的護照或駕駛執照來確認身份。
（A）是，我是。
（B）把你的車留在這裡。
（C）噢，我任何一個都沒有。

解說 聽到了句子中間的or就可以知道是選擇疑問句。（C）用either來表達「任何一個」，即為答案。（A）是對於「單字 or 單字」的選擇疑問句用Yes來回答，所以不是答案。（B）是故意用car來與driver's license產生聯想而誤導的選項。 答案 (C)

詞彙 **check** 檢查 **passport** 護照 **driver's license** 駕照 **identification** 身份檢查 **leave** 遺留；留下

5. 澳W 英M

Which is the fastest way to get to the bank, Islington Road or the highway?

(A) You can park your car in the garage.
(B) They're both about the same.
(C) To cash a check.

哪個是到銀行最快的方法呢？伊斯林頓路還是高速公路？
（A）你可以把車停在車庫。
（B）它們兩個都差不多。
（C）為了兌現一張支票。

解說 聽到了Which與or就可以知道是選擇疑問句。（B）用both來表達「兩個都是」，即為答案。（A）是故意用car來與road和highway產生聯想來誤導的選項。（C）是故意用cash a check來與bank產生聯想來誤導的選項。 答案 (B)

詞彙 **way to get to** 去某處的路 **park** 停車 **garage** 車庫 **cash a check** 兌現支票

6. 美M 美W

Do you need a lift to the convention?

(A) I'd appreciate that.
(B) I'm not sure I can lift this box alone.
(C) I enjoy their conversation, too.

要不要載你到會議去？
（A）謝謝你。
（B）我不確定我能否獨自舉起這個箱子。
（C）我也喜歡他們的談話。

解說 聽到了建議的Do you need，所以表達肯定或允許的（A）為答案。（B）是故意用同音字lift來誤導的，

則這裡的意思不是「載人」而是「舉起」，所以不是答案。（C）是故意用convention的相似發音conversation來誤導的選項。 答案 (A)

詞彙 **lift** 搭載 **convention** 會議 **appreciate** 感謝 **alone** 獨自 **conversation** 對話 **too** 也

7. 英M 澳W

Could you come by my office before you leave?

(A) I don't know if the bill came this month.
(B) Sure. I'm on my way out now.
(C) No, she lives far away.

在你離開前，能順便到我辦公室來嗎？
（A）我不知道這個月帳單來了沒。
（B）當然，我正在下班路上。
（C）不，她住得很遠。

解說 聽到了建議的Could you，所以表達肯定或允許之後附加說明的（B）為答案。（A）是故意用come的類似發音came來誤導的選項。（C）也是故意用leave的類似發音lives來誤導的選項。 答案 (B)

詞彙 **come by** 順路訪問 **leave** 離開 **bill** 帳單 **far away** 遠

8. 美M 美W

Which restaurant would you like to recommend?

(A) Dinner is at 7 p.m.
(B) How about the Korean one?
(C) Yes, it's quite good.

你會推薦哪家餐廳？
（A）晚餐在晚上7點。
（B）韓式餐廳如何？
（C）是的，它相當不錯。

解說 Which是表達選擇疑問句的單字，而此類型答案傾向於包含one。因此（B）為答案。（A）是故意用dinner來與restaurant產生聯想而誤導的選項。（C）是對於選擇疑問句用Yes來回答，所以不是答案。 答案 (B)

詞彙 **recommend** 推薦 **dinner** 晚餐 **How about?** 如何？ **quite** 相當；很

9. 美W 英M

Have you contacted the travel agency or do you want me to call them?

(A) Is that your phone number?
(B) I don't have time. Do you?
(C) No, I haven't had much yet.

你和旅行社聯繫了沒？還是由我來打電話給他們？
（A）那是你的電話號碼嗎？
（B）我沒有時間。你有嗎？

（C）不，我目前沒有很多。

解說 聽到了句子中間有or就可以知道是選擇疑問句。在此，將B變形的（B）為答案。（A）是故意用phone number來與contacted產生聯想而誤導的選項。若只聽到Have you而立刻選（C）No, I haven't.的話就錯了。

答案 (B)

詞彙 contact 聯絡 travel agency 旅行社 phone number 電話號碼

10. 澳W 美W

Don't you want to take a taxi?

(A) Thanks, I'll take some, please.
(B) No, I'd like to walk.
(C) No, I talked to him this morning.

你不想搭計程車嗎？
（A）謝謝，我取用一些吧。
（B）不，我想走路。
（C）不，我今天上午和他說過了。

解說 聽到了Don't you want，就可以知道是間接的建議。因此，表達否定或拒絕之後附加說明的（B）為答案。（A）是故意用同音字take來誤導的選項，在這裡的意思為「取用」。（C）是故意用相似發音talked來誤導的選項。

答案 (B)

詞彙 take a taxi 搭計程車 would like to 想要…

11. 英M 英W

Can you stay a little longer or do you need to leave now?

(A) No, I don't need them.
(B) The sleeves are too long.
(C) I'll let you know in a second.

你能多待一下還是你現在就要離開呢？
（A）沒有，我不需要他們。
（B）袖子太長了。
（C）我很快會讓你知道。

解說 聽到了句子中間的or就可以知道是選擇疑問句。（C）是間接迴避性回答方式，即為答案。（A）是故意用同音字need來誤導的選項。（B）是故意用longer的相似發音long來誤導的選項。

答案 (C)

詞彙 stay 停留；待著 a little longer 再久一點點 sleeves 袖子

12. 美W 美M

Let's stop by the construction site next week.

(A) I'll be out of town next week.
(B) That's the resident's apartment.
(C) To build a new convention hall.

我們下週去一下工地吧。
（A）我下週將要出城。
（B）那是居民的公寓。
（C）為了建立一個新的會議廳。

解說 聽到了Let's就可以知道是建議。因此，表達否定或拒絕之後附加說明的（A）為答案。（B）是故意用apartment來與construction產生聯想來誤導的選項。（C）也是故意用build來與construction site產生聯想來誤導的選項。

答案 (A)

詞彙 stop by 順路訪問 construction site 工地 resident 居民 apartment 公寓 convention hall 會議廳

Quiz

Q1. (1) Are, happy   (2) Did, arrive
     (3) Do, have   (4) Will, speak
Q2. (1) ⓐ   (2) ⓑ   (3) ⓐ
Q3. (1) like   (2) been trained
     (3) lived here   (4) ordered
Q4. (1) ⓑ   (2) ⓐ   (3) ⓐ

Q1

(1) Are you happy with your computer software?
你對你的電腦軟體滿意嗎？

(2) Did the shipment arrive yesterday?
貨運昨天到了嗎？

(3) Do you have these shirts in other colors?
這些襯衫你有其他顏色嗎？

(4) Will you speak at the sales meeting?
你將在銷售會議上演講嗎？

Q2

(1) Did we renew that contract last month?
ⓐ **Yes, on 20ᵗʰ.**
ⓑ That's a great idea.

我們上個月更新過合約嗎？
ⓐ 是的，在二十號時。
ⓑ 那是個很棒的主意。

(2) Have you already had breakfast?
ⓐ This train does go fast.
ⓑ **No, I'm really hungry.**

你已經吃過早餐了嗎？
ⓐ 這台火車的確開得很快。
ⓑ 沒有，我真的很餓。

(3) Are there any extra tea cups?
ⓐ **In the cupboard, over the sink.**
ⓑ I made it this morning.

有任何多餘的茶杯嗎？
ⓐ 在水槽上方的櫥櫃裡。
ⓑ 我今天早上做好了。

Q3

(1) Don't you like the book?
你不喜歡這本書嗎？

(2) Haven't you been trained to use that software?
你不是受過訓練使用那個軟體嗎？

(3) You've lived here for a while, haven't you?
你已經住在這裡一段時間了，不是嗎？

(4) You ordered more stationary, didn't you?
你訂購了更多的文具，不是嗎？

Q4

(1) It's hot in the building, isn't it?
ⓐ Yes, it's a pleasant weather.
ⓑ **I'll turn on the air conditioner.**

這棟大樓裡面很熱，不是嗎？
ⓐ 是的，這是個舒服的天氣。
ⓑ 我來打開冷氣。

(2) There's no restaurant around here, is there?
ⓐ **There used to be one.**
ⓑ I just bought some groceries.

這附近沒有餐廳，是嗎？
ⓐ 以前有一家。
ⓑ 我剛買了一些雜貨。

(3) Didn't Ms.Johnson buy printer papers last week?
ⓐ **She's getting them today.**
ⓑ Put them in his office.

上週強森小姐沒有買印表機的紙嗎？
ⓐ 她今天會買的。
ⓑ 把那些放在他的辦公室。

STEP 01 若沒答對會後悔的考題

1. (B)	2. (A)	3. (B)	4. (A)	5. (A)

1. 美 M 美 W

1 助動詞 + 主詞 + 動詞	Are you going
2 受詞與其他	to the workshop next weekend

Are you going to the workshop next weekend?
(A) About weekly training schedules.
(B) Yes, I'm looking forward to it.

你下週會去工作坊嗎？
（A）有關於週訓練計畫。
（B）是的，我很期待。

解說 沒有出現疑問詞、否定詞、以及附加問句尾巴，所以是一般疑問句。若要回答「將要去」，用Yes，不

是的話用No。（B）說Yes之後以「很期待」來附加說明，即為答案。（A）是對於「這場工作坊是有關什麼的？」的回答。　　　　　答案(B)

詞彙　workshop 工作坊　training schedule 訓練計畫　look forward to 對…期待

2. 英M 澳W

| 1 助動詞＋主詞＋動詞 | Didn't you organize |
| 2 受詞與其他 | the company banquet last year |

Didn't you organize the company banquet last year?
(A) Yes, you attended, right?
(B) Which bank is closer?

你不是籌辦了公司去年的宴會嗎？
（A）是的，你參加了，對嗎？
（B）哪家銀行比較近？

解說　有否定詞在最前面出現了，所以是否定疑問句。將此否定詞拿掉了之後，如果要表達「籌辦了」，就是Yes，不是的話就是用No來回答。因此說Yes之後再附加說明的（A）為答案。（B）是故意用banquet的相似發音bank來誤導的選項。　答案(A)

詞彙　organize 籌畫舉辦　banquet 宴會　attend 參加

3. 美W 美M

| 1 助動詞＋主詞＋動詞 | Did you deliver |
| 2 受詞與其他 | the document in person |

Did you deliver the document in person?
(A) The personnel department.
(B) No, I sent it by fax.

你親自遞送了文件嗎？
（A）是人事部門。
（B）不，我用傳送過去的。

解說　沒有出現疑問詞、否定詞、以及附加問句尾巴，所以是一般疑問句。若要說「親自遞送的」就用Yes，不是的話用No來回答。（B）是說了No之後再說「用傳真送過去的」的，即為答案。（A）是用person的相似發音personnel來誤導的選項。　答案(B)

詞彙　deliver 投遞；配送　document 文件資料　in person 親自　personnel department 人事部　by fax 用傳真方式

4. 美M 英M

| 1 動詞＋形容詞 | are delicious |
| 2 主詞與其他 | These sandwiches / aren't they? |

These sandwiches are delicious, aren't they?
(A) Yes, I like this kind.
(B) No, I can't wait to have some.

這些三明治很美味，不是嗎？
（A）是的，我喜歡這一種。
（B）不，我等不及要吃一些。

解說　這是在最後部分有尾巴的附加問句。將此尾巴拿掉了之後，若要表達「好吃」，就用Yes，不是的話就用No來回答。因此，Yes後面附加說明的（A）為答案。（B）是說了No之後卻加上Yes的附加說明，所以不是答案。　答案(A)

詞彙　delicious 美味的　kind 種類　can't wait to 等不及

5. 美W 澳W

| 1 主詞＋助動詞＋動詞 | We haven't missed |
| 2 受詞與其他 | the train, have we? |

We haven't missed the train, have we?
(A) No, it's just arrived.
(B) She's been gone since yesterday.

我們還沒錯過這班火車，是嗎？
（A）不，它剛剛才到。
（B）她從昨天開始不在的。

解說　這是在最後部分有尾巴的附加問句。將此尾巴和否定詞拿掉了之後，若要表達「錯過火車」就用Yes，若不是的話就用No來回答。因此，No後面附加說明的（A）為答案。（B）不是答案，因為無法知道she是在指誰。　答案(A)

詞彙　miss 錯過　arrive 抵達　since 自從…

STEP 02　考題實戰練習

1. (B)　2. (C)　3. (B)　4. (B)　5. (B)　6. (A)
7. (A)　8. (B)　9. (B)　10. (A)　11. (A)　12. (A)

1. 美M 美W

Are you taking the clients out for lunch today?

(A) The chicken sandwich, please.
(B) Yes, would you like to join us?
(C) The food there is always delicious.

你今天要帶客戶出去吃午餐嗎？
（A）請給我雞肉三明治。
（B）是的，你想加入我們嗎？
（C）那兒的菜永遠很美味。

解說 沒有出現疑問詞、否定詞、以及附加問句尾巴，所以是一般疑問句。若要表達「帶出去」，就用Yes，不是的話就用No來回答。（B）是說了Yes之後將附加說明以反問形式來表達。（A）是故意用sandwich來與lunch產生聯想而誤導的選項。（C）不是答案，因為there指的是某地點。　　　　　　　答案 (B)

詞彙 take out 帶出去　always 總是

2. 美W 英M
Aren't you going to call the doctor this afternoon?

(A) At our last meeting.
(B) I go about twice a month.
(C) I gave him a call this morning.

你今天下午不打電話給醫生嗎？
（A）在我們最後一次的會議。
（B）我大約每月去兩次。
（C）我今天上午打過電話給他了。

解說 有否定詞出現於最前面，所以是否定疑問句。將此否定詞拿掉了之後，若要表達「將要打電話」就用Yes，若要表達「不會打電話」就用No回答。因此，將No省略了之後，以「今天上午打過電話給他了」來附加說明的（C）為答案。（A）是對於未來時態用過去時態來回答，所以不是答案。（B）是故意用going的相似發音go來誤導的選項。　　　答案 (C)

詞彙 last 上次的　about 大約　twice a month 一個月兩次

3. 美M 澳W
The concert starts at 9 o'clock, doesn't it?

(A) That's the music store.
(B) I think the time should be on the ticket.
(C) I found the ending better.

演唱會在9點鐘開始，不是嗎？
（A）那是間唱片行。
（B）我想入場票上應該有時間。
（C）我認為結局的部分好一些。

解說 這是在句子最後出現尾巴的，所以是附加問句。將此尾巴拿掉了之後，若要表達「在九點開始」就用Yes，若不是就用No來回答。因此將No省略了之後附加說明的（B）為答案。（A）是故意用music來與concert產生聯想來誤導的選項。（C）是故意用ending來與starts產生聯想來誤導的選項。　答案 (B)

詞彙 concert 演唱會　start 開始　music store 唱片店　ending 結局；結束

4. 美M 美W
Our clothing sales have gone up this year, haven't they?

(A) No, he hasn't been there.
(B) Yes, I believe so.
(C) See you next month.

今年我們的服裝銷售增加了，不是嗎？
（A）沒有，他沒去過那裡。
（B）是的，我相信是這樣。
（C）下個月見。

解說 這是在句子最後出現尾巴的，所以是附加問句。將此尾巴拿掉了之後，若要表達「增加了」就用Yes，若不是就用No來回答。因此Yes後面附加說明的（B）為答案。（A）不是答案，因為無法知道主詞he指的是誰。（C）是故意用next month來與this year產生聯想而誤導的選項。　　答案 (B)

詞彙 clothing 衣服　sales 銷售量　go up 上升　I believe so 我相信如此

5. 澳M 英M
Are there any tickets available for today's play?

(A) It's probably the most valuable skill.
(B) I'm afraid they're all sold out.
(C) You must present your ticket.

有今天舞台劇的門票嗎？
（A）它可能是最具價值的技術。
（B）恐怕已經都賣完了。
（C）你必須出示你的票。

解說 沒有出現疑問詞、否定詞、以及附加問句尾巴，所以是一般疑問句。若要表達「有門票」就用Yes，不是的話就用No來回答。（B）是將No省略之後以「都賣完了」來附加說明的答案。（A）是故意用valuable來與available產生混淆的選項。（C）是故意用相似發音ticket來產生混淆的選項。　答案 (B)

詞彙 available 可用的　play 舞台劇　probably 可能　valuable 具有價值的　skill 技術　sold out 賣完了　present 出示

6. 美M 美W
Did you make it to the new exhibit at the science museum?

(A) No, but I plan to next week.
(B) That's good news.
(C) Yes, to build a new museum.

你去過在科學博物館的新展覽會嗎？
（A）不，但我打算下週去。

（B）這真是個好消息。
（C）是的，為了蓋新的博物館。

解說 沒有出現疑問詞、否定詞、以及附加問句尾巴，所以是一般疑問句。若要表達「能參加」就用Yes，不是的話就用No來回答。因此No之後附加說明的（A）為答案。（B）是故意用news來與new產生混淆的選項。（C）是故意用同音字new和museum來產生混淆的選項。 答案(A)

詞彙 **make it to** 到某處 **exhibit** 展示會 **museum** 博物館 **build** 建造

7. 英M 澳W
Didn't Ms. Johnson file the insurance paperwork last week?

(A) I'll ask her.
(B) The tiles arrived yesterday.
(C) The plastic ones look better.

強生女士上週沒有將保險文件歸檔嗎？
（A）我再問她。
（B）昨天瓷磚到了。
（C）塑膠的那個更好看。

解說 有否定詞出現於最前面，所以是否定疑問句。將此否定詞拿掉了之後，若要表達「將保險文件歸檔了」就用Yes，若不是就用No來回答。（A）是用成為答案機率很高的「間接迴避性回答」，即為答案。（B）是故意用file的相似發音tiles來產生混淆的選項。（C）是故意用plastic來與paper產生聯想來誤導的選項。 答案(A)

詞彙 **file** 整理歸檔 **insurance paperwork** 保險文件 **tile** 瓷磚 **arrive** 抵達 **plastic** 塑膠的

8. 美M 美W
Jacob will be able to reschedule the appointment, won't he?

(A) Yes, he's just been appointed.
(B) Yes, he will do it right away.
(C) Too many times.

雅各將能重新安排這個約會，不是嗎？
（A）是的，他剛被任命。
（B）是的，他會馬上做的。
（C）太多次了。

解說 這是在句子最後出現尾巴的，所以是附加問句。將此尾巴拿掉了之後，若要表達「能重新安排約會」就用Yes，若不是就用No來回答。因此說Yes之後附加說明的（B）為答案。（A）是故意用appointment的相似發音appointed來產生混淆的選項。（C）是故意用times來與reschedule和appointment產生聯想來誤導的選項。 答案(B)

詞彙 **be able to** 動詞原形 能夠做某事 **reschedule an appointment** 重新安排約定 **appoint** 任命 **right away** 立刻

9. 美W 英M
The marketing associate wasn't very helpful, was he?

(A) No, in the accounting department.
(B) I didn't think he was either.
(C) Thanks for your help.

行銷合夥人不太能幫忙，是吧？
（A）不，在會計部門。
（B）我也不認為他很會幫忙。
（C）謝謝你的幫忙。

解說 這是在句子最後出現尾巴的，所以是附加問句。將此尾巴拿掉了之後，若要表達「很有幫助」就用Yes，若不是就用No來回答。因此將No省略了之後附加說明的（B）為答案。選項（A）No之後的附加說明不妥當，而且故意用accounting department與marketing產生聯想來誤導。（C）是故意用help來與helpful產生混淆的選項。 答案(B)

詞彙 **associate** 同僚 **helpful** 有幫助的 **accounting department** 會計部門

10. 澳W 美W
Do you have any plans for this weekend?

(A) We're going hiking on Saturday.
(B) No, it was a guided tour.
(C) I put the plants by the window.

這個週末你有任何計畫嗎？
（A）我們週六將要去健行。
（B）不，這是有導遊的導覽。
（C）我把植物放在窗邊。

解說 沒有出現疑問詞、否定詞及附加問句，所以是一般疑問句。若要表達有計畫就用yes，沒有就用no回答，因此省略掉yes後再附加說明的（A）為答案。選項（B）在no後面的附加說明不妥當，而（C）是故意用plans的相似發音plants來產生混淆。 答案(A)

詞彙 **plan** 計畫 **this weekend** 這個週末 **hiking** 登山 **guided** 導遊陪伴的 **put** 置放 **plant** 植物

11. 英M 澳W
Isn't that training session scheduled to last 2 hours?

(A) Yes, it will end on time.
(B) No, the train departs at 5:03.
(C) I believe it's yours.

培訓課程不是預定持續兩個小時嗎？
（A）是的，它會準時結束。
（B）不，火車在五點零三分出發。
（C）我相信它是你的。

解說 有否定詞出現於最前面，所以是否定疑問句。將此否定詞拿掉了之後，若要表達「預訂持續」就用Yes，若不是就用No來回答。因此說Yes之後附加說明的（A）為答案。選項（B）No後面的附加說明不妥當，而且故意用training的相似發音train來產生混淆。（C）是故意用yours來與hours產生混淆的選項。

答案 (A)

詞彙 training session 訓練課程 be scheduled to 動詞原形 預訂… last 持續 end 結束 on time 準時 depart 出發

12. 美W 美M

This plant was constructed about two years ago, wasn't it?

(A) Yes, I think that's right.
(B) Was the result satisfactory?
(C) It looks like a good plan.

這家工廠是大約兩年前建造的，不是嗎？
（A）是的，我認為那是對的。
（B）結果令人滿意嗎？
（C）它看起來像是個好計畫。

解說 這是在句子最後出現尾巴的，所以是附加問句。將此尾巴拿掉了之後，若要表達「建造的」就用Yes，若不是就用No來回答。因此說Yes之後附加說明的（A）為答案。（B）是故意用satisfactory來與factory、plant產生聯想來誤導的選項。（C）是故意用plant的相似發音plan來產生混淆的選項。 答案 (A)

詞彙 plant 工廠 construct 建造 about 大約 result 結果 satisfactory 令人滿意的 plan 計畫

Chapter
10 陳述句、間接疑問句

Chapter **10** 陳述句、間接疑問句

Quiz |

Q1. (1) I'd like to
(2) I thought
(3) There's
(4) I think, forgot

Q2. (1) ⓑ (2) ⓐ (3) ⓑ

Q3. (1) Can you tell me when
(2) Do you know why
(3) Have you decided which
(4) I don't remember who

Q4. (1) ⓐ (2) ⓐ (3) ⓐ

Q1

(1) I'd like to make a reservation.
我想要預約。

(2) I thought you already left for Seoul.
我以為你已經往首爾去了。

(3) There's a phone call for you.
有一通找你的電話。

(4) I think I forgot my wallet.
我覺得我忘了我的皮夾。

Q2

(1) I'd like to confirm my appointment time.
ⓐ Thanks, I'm glad you like it.
ⓑ **What is your name?**

我想確認我預約的時間。
ⓐ 謝謝，我很高興你喜歡它。
ⓑ 您的名字是什麼？

(2) I think Henry's a great designer.
ⓐ **I believe so.**
ⓑ I read the sign.

我認為亨利是個偉大的設計師。
ⓐ 我相信是這樣。
ⓑ 我看到告示了。

(3) I can't find my notebook anywhere.
ⓐ I found it boring.
ⓑ **Have you checked the conference room?**

我到處都找不到我的筆記本。
ⓐ 我覺得很無聊。
ⓑ 你有檢查過會議室嗎？

Q3

(1) Can you tell me when you bought your car?
你能告訴我你什麼時候買了你的車呢？

(2) Do you know why the budget meeting was canceled?
你知道為什麼預算會議被取消嗎？

(3) Have you decided which computer to buy?
你決定要買哪台電腦了嗎？

(4) I don't remember who is supposed to water the plant.
我不記得是誰該給花草澆水。

Q4

(1) Can you tell me when the report is due?
ⓐ **Next week, perhaps.**
ⓑ I can do it.

你能告訴我報告的截止日期嗎？
ⓐ 也許是下星期。
ⓑ 我可以做。

(2) Do you know where I can buy a plane ticket?
ⓐ **You can purchase it on the Internet.**
ⓑ It does look plain.

你知道我在哪兒能買到機票嗎？
ⓐ 你可以上網訂購。
ⓑ 它的確看起來很平凡。

(3) I don't know how to use the copy machine.
ⓐ **Let me show you.**
ⓑ With sugar, please.

我不知道如何使用這台影印機。
ⓐ 讓我做給你看。
ⓑ 請加糖，謝謝。

STEP 01 若沒答對會後悔的考題

1. (A)　　2. (A)　　3. (B)　　4. (B)　　5. (B)

1. 美M 美W

| 1 決定類別的單字 | I really like |
| 2 其他 | the magazine I'm reading |

I really like the magazine I'm reading.
(A) Which issue is it?
(B) No, you should follow me.

我真的很喜歡我正在讀的這本雜誌。
（A）是哪一期？
（B）不，你應該跟著我。

解說 有I really like而且也沒有尾巴，所以是表達意見的陳述句。因此以反問句來回答的（A）為答案。如果將考題裡面的reading聽成leading，就很容易選（B）當作答案，因為可能聯想到follow，但該選項就是陷阱。
答案 (A)

詞彙 magazine 雜誌　issue 期數　follow 跟隨

2. 英M 澳W

| 1 決定類別的單字 | I've forgotten how |
| 2 其他 | to use this software |

I've forgotten how to use this software.
(A) Morris can help you figure it out.
(B) You may try a different size.

我忘了如何使用這個軟體。
（A）莫里斯可以幫助你了解。
（B）你可以試試看不同的尺寸。

解說 以I've forgotten開始，所以是陳述句，而句子裡面包含了how，所以也具有間接疑問句的色彩。選項（A）是對於how的回答方式，說別人會幫忙，此即為答案。如果將考題裡面software的ware聽成wear（穿衣服）的話，有可能選（B）為答案，因為可以聯想到「試穿別的大小」。
答案 (A)

詞彙 forget 忘記　figure out 理解；了解　try 嘗試

3. 美W 美M

| 1 決定類別的單字 | I heard |
| 2 其他 | the show's been postponed |

I heard the show's been postponed.
(A) Thanks, I'll answer the phone.
(B) Really? When's the new date?

我聽說這個表演被延期了。
（A）謝謝，我將會接電話。
（B）真的？新的日期是什麼時候？

解說 以主詞開頭，是陳述句。因此以反問句來回答的（B）為答案。（A）是故意用postponed的相似發音phone來誤導的選項。
答案 (B)

詞彙 postpone 延期　answer the phone 接電話

4. 美M 英M

1 決定類別的單字	Can you tell me how
2 其他	to fix the printer

Can you tell me how to fix the printer?
(A) There are some papers in the staff room.
(B) I'm afraid I don't know.

你能告訴我如何修理這台印表機嗎？
（A）在職員室有一些紙（報告）。
（B）恐怕我不知道。

解說 得注意聽Can you tell me後面出現的how，然後找出對於how的回答。選項（B）是用「不知道」類型的間接迴避性回答，即為答案。（A）是故意用papers來與printer產生聯想來誤導的選項。 答案 (B)

詞彙 fix 修理 staff room 職員室

5. 美W 澳W

1 決定類別的單字	I'll need
2 其他	some help moving these desks

I'll need some help moving these desks.
(A) Yes, these days.
(B) I can give you a hand.

我需要一些幫忙來搬這些桌子。
（A）是的，這幾天。
（B）我可以幫你。

解說 以主詞開頭而且也沒有尾巴，所以是陳述句。對於「需要幫忙」以答應幫忙的說法回答的（B）為答案。（A）是故意用和考題裡一樣的單字these來產生混淆的選項。 答案 (B)

詞彙 move 搬移 these days 最近 give someone a hand 幫助某人

STEP 02 考題實戰練習

1. (B)	2. (B)	3. (A)	4. (A)	5. (A)	6. (A)
7. (B)	8. (B)	9. (A)	10. (B)	11. (A)	12. (A)

1. 美M 美W

I think the picture in the booklet is too light.
(A) I thought we needed two lights.

(B) Could it be darkened?
(C) Several color photos.

我認為這本小冊子的圖片太淡了。
（A）我以為我們需要兩個燈。
（B）它有可能被加深嗎？
（C）幾張彩色照片。

解說 出現I think而且沒有結尾，所以是表達意見的陳述句。以反問句回答的（B）為答案。（A）是故意用同音字light來誤導的選項。（C）是故意用photos來與picture產生聯想的選項。 答案 (B)

詞彙 booklet 小冊子 light 淡的；燈具 darken 加深顏色

2. 美W 英M

I thought Ms. Wagner was going to lead the workshop.
(A) I haven't read it yet.
(B) No, she's on vacation.
(C) It comes in today.

我以為華格納女士將會領導這個工作坊。
（A）我還沒有讀過。
（B）不，她在休假中。
（C）它在今天進來。

解說 出現I thought而且沒有尾巴，所以是表達意見的陳述句。先說No之後附加說明的（B）為答案。（A）是故意用lead的相似發音read來誤導的選項。（C）是故意用comes來與going產生聯想來誤導的選項。 答案 (B)

詞彙 lead 領導 on vacation 休假中 come in 進入

3. 美M 澳W

Have you heard when the construction of the new office will be finished?
(A) Yeah, by the end of December.
(B) We'll work on the instructions.
(C) About 5 years old.

你有聽說什麼時候新辦公室將會完工嗎？
（A）有啊，十二月底。
（B）我們將弄說明書。
（C）大約五歲左右。

解說 在Have you heard之後出現了when，所以是要對於when回答的間接疑問句。因此以時間說法回答的（A）為答案。（B）是故意用construction的相似發音instructions來誤導的選項。（C）是對於How old的回答方式。 答案 (A)

詞彙 construction 建設 finish 完成 work 工作 instruction 說明書 about 大約

4. 美M 美W

I'd like to make reservations for dinner tonight.

(A) Can I have your name?

(B) Two nights only.

(C) Let's have a rest for a while.

我想預訂今晚晚餐的座位。
（A）請告訴我您的大名。
（B）只有兩晚。
（C）我們休息一會兒吧。

解說 以I'd like to開始而且沒有尾巴，所以是陳述句。因此以反問句回答的（A）為答案。（B）是故意用tonight的相似發音two nights來產生混淆的選項。（C）是故意用reservations的相似發音rest來產生混淆的選項。 答案 (A)

詞彙 make a reservation 預訂 have a rest 休息 for a while 一會兒

5. 澳W 英M

That construction work outside surely is noisy.

(A) Why don't you close the windows?

(B) The instructions are on the back.

(C) Inside the restaurant.

外面在施工真的很嘈雜。
（A）你為什麼不把窗關上？
（B）說明在背面。
（C）在餐廳內。

解說 以主詞開始而且沒有尾巴，所以是陳述句。聽到noisy，因此可以知道是提出問題狀況的句子。因此提供解決方法的（A）為答案。（B）是故意用construction的相似發音instructions來產生混淆的選項。（C）是故意用inside來與outside產生聯想來誤導的選項。 答案 (A)

詞彙 construction work 施工 outside 戶外 noisy 吵雜 close 關 inside 在…內

6. 美M 美W

Can you please tell me where to find Dr. Tang's office?

(A) He works in the next door building.

(B) We haven't been booked yet.

(C) She found it this morning.

你可以告訴我湯博士的辦公室在哪兒嗎？
（A）他在隔壁大樓工作。
（B）我們還沒有被預約。
（C）她今天上午發現的。

解說 出現Can you please tell me，所以接著得要聽到where的部分。這是要對於where做回答的間接疑問句。因此以場所說法回答的（A）為答案。（B）的主詞為

we，但無法知道是在指誰。（C）也是無法知道she指的是誰，且故意用find的相似發音found來產生混淆的選項。 答案 (A)

詞彙 next-door 隔壁的 book 預約

7. 英M 澳W

I've hired two software engineers.

(A) It's hard to use.

(B) Are they going to start within this week?

(C) We projected higher sales.

我聘請了兩名軟體工程師。
（A）它很難用。
（B）他們將在這週內開始嗎？
（C）我們預估了更高的銷量。

解說 以主詞開始而且沒有尾巴，所以是陳述句。以反問句回答的（B）為答案。（A）是故意用hired的相似發音hard來產生混淆的選項。（C）也是故意用hired的相似發音higher來產生混淆的選項。 答案 (B)

詞彙 hire 雇用 hard 困難 use 使用 within 在…之內 project 預估

8. 美M 美W

I can't get the computer to start.

(A) I went out this morning.

(B) Do you want me to try?

(C) He starts tomorrow.

我無法啟動電腦。
（A）我今天早上外出過。
（B）你要讓我試試看嗎？
（C）他從明天開始。

解說 聽到否定詞，所以是提出問題狀況的句子。以主詞開頭而且沒有尾巴，所以是陳述句。「can't get 名詞 to do」是一種提出問題狀況的說法。因此以包含解決方法的反問句回答的（B）就是答案。（A）是無厘頭的回答。（C）是故意用一樣的start來產生混淆的選項。 答案 (B)

詞彙 go out 外出 try 嘗試

9. 美W 英M

Do you know who's responsible for this project?

(A) Yes, the marketing manager is.

(B) Yes, it's next Monday.

(C) About new products.

你知道誰負責這個計畫嗎？
（A）是的，是行銷經理。
（B）是的，在下週一。
（C）有關於新產品。

解說 聽到Do you know之後，還得要聽到who，然後對於who做回答的間接疑問句。說Yes之後以職稱來回答的（A）為答案。（B）是對於when的回答方式，所以不是答案。（C）是對於what的回答方式，而且故意用project的相似發音products來產生混淆的選項。 答案 (A)

詞彙 be responsible for 負責… marketing manager 行銷經理 product 產品

10. 澳W 美W

The microphones in the auditorium aren't working.

(A) Sometime this morning.
(B) I'll get the technician.
(C) The desk is next to the computer.

禮堂的麥克風壞掉了。
（A）今天上午某個時候。
（B）我會去找技師。
（C）那張桌子在電腦旁。

解說 以主詞開頭而且沒有尾巴，所以是陳述句。在句中有聽到否定詞，所以這是提出問題狀況的。因此以解決方法回答的（B）為答案。（A）是對於when的回答方式，所以不是答案。（C）是故意用desk和computer來與microphones產生聯想來誤導的選項。 答案 (B)

詞彙 microphone 麥克風 auditorium 禮堂 work 運作 sometime 某個時候

11. 英M 澳W

Our sales fell by ten percent last quarter.

(A) Decrease in demand is the main reason.
(B) Our new sales goals.
(C) I'm getting used to this weather.

我們上一季的銷售額下降了百分之十。
（A）需求下降是主要的原因。
（B）我們的新的銷售目標。
（C）我習慣於這種天氣。

解說 以主詞開頭而且沒有尾巴，所以是陳述句。因此做附加說明的（A）為答案。（B）是故意用同個字sales來產生混淆的選項。若將考題誤解為「溫度下降了」，有可能會錯選（C）的選項。 答案 (A)

詞彙 fall 下降 last quarter 前一季 decrease 減少 demand 需要 main 主要的 goal 目標 get used to 名詞 習慣於…

12. 美W 美M

Do you know why the company outing was cancelled?

(A) Probably because of the bad weather.
(B) Can we meet in two hours?
(C) I haven't heard of that company.

你知不知道為什麼公司郊遊被取消了？
（A）可能是因為天氣不好。
（B）我們能在兩小時內見面嗎？
（C）我沒聽說過那家公司。

解說 聽到Do you know之後，要注意聽why的部分，然後要對於why回答的間接疑問句。以「because of 名詞」回答的（A）為答案。若在考題裡只聽到了cancelled，那麼選項（B）的「見面吧」可能會產生聯想而選錯。（C）是故意用同個字company來產生混淆的選項。 答案 (A)

詞彙 outing 郊遊 cancel 取消 probably 可能 because of 因為 bad weather 氣候不佳

Quiz I

1. (A)	2. (B)	3. (A)	4. (A)
5. (A)	6. (A)	7. (A)	8. (A)

Q1 美M 美W

M : **Did you see** the new documentary with Larry Martin on television last night? It was so informative!

W : I wanted to see it, but I wasn't able to leave for the day until 9. I think Larry Martin is a great host.

男：昨晚你在電視上有看賴瑞・馬汀主持的新記錄片嗎？它相當有教育性！

女：我想看，但是在九點前我不能下班。我認為賴瑞・馬汀是很棒的主持人。

這段談話主要是有關於什麼？
（A）一個電視節目
（B）一部新上映的電影

解說 聽到mainly about，就可以知道是「詢問主題的考題」。透過與Have you seen類似的Did you see，藉由其後面出現的「昨晚在電視上／新的紀錄片」，可以知道（A）為答案。　　　　　　　　　　答案 (A)

詞彙 documentary 記錄片　informative 有益的；有教育性的　leave for the day 下班　host 主持人

Q2 英M 澳W

M : Hi, Christina. We talked about going to a movie tonight. Do you still remember?

W : Oh no, **I forgot!** I'm sorry I can't make it to the movies tonight. My cousin is visiting me from New York, and I'm taking her out for dinner at a new restaurant near my house.

男：嗨，克莉絲汀娜。我們討論過今晚要去看電影。你還記得嗎？

女：噢不，我忘了！我很抱歉今晚我不能去看電影。我的表親從紐約來拜訪我，我要帶她出去到我家附近的一間新餐廳吃晚餐。

這個女人的問題狀況是什麼？
（A）她找不到可以坐的位子。
（B）她不能和這個男人去看電影。

解說 「有什麼問題／狀況？」類的考題就是在詢問主題。將I forgot後面聽到的「不能去看電影」做變化來表達的（B）為答案。　　　　　　答案 (B)

詞彙 go to a movie 去看電影　can't make it to 不能做⋯ take人out 和某人出去

Q3 美W 英M

W : Hi. **I'm calling to** know what the number is for the City Bank located in Middletown.

M : Do you have a particular address in mind? I see two branches in the computer listings.

女：您好。我打電話來是要知道在中區的城市銀行的電話是幾號。

男：您記得特定的地址嗎？我在電腦的列表裡看到有兩家分行。

這通電話的目的是什麼？
（A）為了得到一個電話號碼
（B）為了寄送一個包裹

解說 詢問通話目的的考題就是在詢問主題。將核心說法I'm calling to後面出現的「為了知道號碼」做變化來表達的（A）為答案。　　　　答案 (A)

詞彙 located 位於⋯　particular 特定的　have（名詞）in mind 記得某事物　computer listing 電腦列表清單

Q4 澳W 英M

W : Dr. Min's office. How may I help you?

M : Hi, my name is Mike, one of Dr. Min's patients. **I'd like to** know the result of my physical examination. Can I speak to him for a minute?

女：閔醫師辦公室。我可以給您什麼幫助嗎？

男：您好，我的名字是麥可，我是閔醫師的病患之一。我想知道我的健康檢查結果。我能和他通一下電話嗎？

為什麼這個男人和這個女人聯繫？
（A）為了詢問有關檢查結果
（B）為了做預約

解說 「為什麼聯繫」類的考題也是在詢問主題的類型。將核心說法I'd like to後面出現的「為了知道健康檢查結果」做變化來表達的（A）為答案。　　答案 (A)

詞彙 physical examination 檢康檢查　for a minute 暫時；一下子　exam result 檢查結果　make an appointment 做預約

Q5 英M 英W

M : Good morning. Can you tell me where to go to open a savings account?

W : I can do that for you here. Do you have either a driver's license or a passport with you?

男：早安，你能告訴我要到哪裡可以開儲蓄帳戶嗎？

女：我可以在這裡幫你開。你有駕照或是護照嗎？

說話者很有可能在哪裡？
（A）在銀行
（B）在會計師事務所

解說 「開帳戶」類的說法是在「銀行」聽的到的。

答案 (A)

詞彙 open a savings account 開儲蓄帳戶
driver's license 駕照　passport 護照

Q6 美W 美M

W：Here is my laptop. How long do you think it will take to fix the problem?

M：Please pick it up by five thirty. I think I'll need about an hour to cleanse the hard drive, check for viruses and upgrade the memory.

女：這是我的筆記型電腦。你認為修復這個問題會需要多久？
男：請在五點三十分來拿。我想我需要大約一小時來清理硬碟、檢查有沒有病毒和升級記憶體。

說話者很有可能在哪兒？
（A）在電腦維修中心裡
（B）在汽車展覽會中

解說 聽到電腦有問題且詢問何時領取電腦，所以可以猜測是在「電腦維修中心」進行的對話。　答案 (A)

詞彙 laptop 筆記型電腦　take 花時間　pick up 領取
exhibition 展覽會

Q7 美W 英M

W：David, I heard there's going to be a product demonstration this afternoon for our computer models for next year.

M：Certainly. I'm going to attend it. Where is the meeting supposed to be held?

女：大衛，我聽說今天下午將有一場我們明年電腦模型的產品展示會。
男：確實。我將會去參加。會議應該會在哪裡舉辦呢？

說話者可能是為誰工作？
（A）一家電腦製造商
（B）一家廣告公司

解說 work for（公司名稱）是指「某家公司的職員」。這個考題詢問說話者的公司是什麼，換句話說就是詢問說話者是誰的考題。以上的對話需將該女性的話全部都聽完才能了解內容。說出「參加我們電腦模型的產品展示會」的人，可以認為是在「電腦製造商」上班的。

答案 (A)

詞彙 product demonstration 產品展示會　attend 參加
be supposed to 應該　hold 舉行

Q8 漢W 美M

W：Shawn, welcome to National Heavy Equipment. We're very happy you joined our sales team. Today, you'll start your training with Ms. Chen, who will be your manager in the sales

department.

M：Well, could you please let me know in detail what type of clients I'll be working with?

女：尚恩，歡迎來到國家重型設備。我們非常高興你加入我們的銷售團隊。今天，你會跟著你未來銷售部門的經理陳女士開始訓練。
男：那麼，你能讓我詳細知道我和哪一類型的客戶一起工作嗎？

這個男人很有可能是什麼人？
（A）一位銷售專員
（B）一個重要的客戶

解說 會聽到「很高興你加入了我們的銷售團隊」這句話的人，應該就是「銷售專員」吧。A representative不是指代表者，而是「職員／專員」的意思。　答案 (A)

詞彙 sales department 銷售部門　in detail 詳細的　work with... 共事；一起工作

STEP 01　若沒答對會後悔的考題

1 (A)	2 (A)	3 (B)	4 (B)
5 (A)	6 (B)	7 (B)	8 (A)
9 (A)	10 (C)	11 (C)	12 (A)
13 (B)	14 (C)		

1. 英M 美W

1 找出核心詞彙	topic
2 了解類型	詢問主題
3 看選項	停車規定或城市公園

M：Alicia, **have you heard** the parking rules on city streets are strictly enforced? I think you have to move your car off the street.

W：Really? I didn't know about that. I guess I'd better move my car before the meeting starts.

男：亞麗莎，你聽說過在市街的停車規定要嚴格執行嗎？我覺得你應該把你的車從街道移開。
女：真的嗎？我不知道那些消息。我想我最好在會議開始前把車移開。

這段談話主要是有關於什麼？
（A）新的停車規定
（B）一個城市公園

解說 透過核心詞彙topic就可以知道是「詢問主題」的考題。藉由Have you heard後面出現的「停車規定要嚴格執行」，可以知道（A）為答案。　答案 (A)

詞彙 parking rules 停車規定 enforce 實施 move the car off 把車移開 had better 最好是～

2. 澳W 英M

1 找出核心詞彙	problem
2 了解類型	詢問主題
3 看選項	不能運作或寄錯東西

W：Hello, GW Telecom Technical Support. McDori speaking. What can I do for you?

M：Hi, **I have a problem** with this mobile phone that I bought yesterday. It shuts itself off whenever I try to make a call.

女：您好，GW電信科技支援中心。我是麥多莉。有什麼我能為您做的嗎？

男：您好，我昨天買的行動電話有點問題。每當我試著要打電話時，它會自動關機。

這個問題狀況可能是什麼？
（A）電話不能正常運作。
（B）送出了錯誤的樣本。

解說 「有什麼問題／狀況」也是在詢問主題的考題，在一段對話裡不會出現數個問題狀況。將「我有個問題」後面出現的「每當我試著要打電話時，它會自動關機」以概括性的敘述做變化來表達的（A）為答案。
答案（A）

詞彙 mobile phone 行動電話 shut off（指電器）關閉 try to... 嘗試做某事 make a call 打電話

3. 美W 美M

1 找出核心詞彙	discussing
2 了解類型	詢問主題
3 看選項	銷售報告或午餐計劃

W：Hi, James. Several sales representatives are having lunch with our clients. Would you like to join us? We're going to the new Italian restaurant down the street.

M：I wish I could. But I have a budget meeting at 1 p.m.

女：您好，詹姆士。有好幾位銷售代表要和我們的客戶吃午餐。你想要加入我們嗎？我們將會去在街底新開的義大利餐廳。

男：我希望我可以。但是我在下午一點鐘有預算會議。

說話者在討論什麼？
（A）一個銷售報告
（B）午餐計畫

解說 透過核心詞彙discussing，就可以知道為「詢問主題的考題」。前面出現的疑問句就是詢問主題類型考題的答案線索。將「我們要吃飯，一起來吧」以概括性的敘述做變化來表達的（B）為答案。
答案（B）

詞彙 sales representative 銷售代表 down the street 在街底 budget meeting 預算會議

4. 澳W 英M

1 找出核心詞彙	call
2 了解類型	詢問主題
3 看選項	寄送包裹或要求修理

W：Good afternoon, Campbell Property Management.

M：Hello, this is Andrew Peterson from TTS corporation. **I'm calling to** request that someone come over to do some repairs. We're having trouble with the lights in the front office. For some reason, they aren't working. Could you send someone over to fix them?

女：午安，坎貝爾物產管理。

男：您好，我是TTS公司的安德魯·彼德森。我打電話是請求一個人來做點維修。我們辦公室前面的燈光有問題。因為某種原因，它們不能運作。你能派個人過來修理它們嗎？

為什麼這個男人打電話給這個女人？
（A）他需要寄送一個包裹。
（B）他的辦公室需要修理。

解說 「為什麼打電話」類型也是詢問主題的考題。將核心說法I'm calling to後面出現的「請求派一個人做點維修」做變化來表達的（B）為答案。
答案（B）

詞彙 light 燈具 for some reason 某個原因 work 運作 send over... 派送

5. 美W 美M

1 找出核心詞彙	where
2 了解類型	詢問地點
3 看選項	郵局或禮品店

W：I want to send this gift to my friend in New York. Can you tell me how much it costs to send it there?

M：Well, for standard delivery, it costs 11 dollars per kilogram, but it will take about ten days to get there.

女：我想寄這個包裹給我在紐約的朋友。你能告訴我寄到那裡需要多少費用嗎？

男：嗯，一般郵寄每公斤費用是十一元，但是大約需要十天才能夠到達那邊。

這個女人很有可能是在哪裡工作呢？
（A）在一間職業介紹所
（B）在一家機械公司

說話者很有可能在哪裡？
（A）在郵局
（B）在一家禮品店

解說 透過「郵資多少錢」和「一般郵件」等說法，可以猜測是在「郵局」。　　　　　　　　　答案（A）

詞彙 cost 費用　standard delivery 一般配送
per... 每…　about 大約　get 到達

6. 澳W 英M

1 找出核心詞彙	man
2 了解類型	詢問說話者
3 看選項	電腦技師或營業員

W : Hi, I'm looking for a portable computer to use during my business trip. Can you help me?
M : Sure. Would you like a simple laptop or a laptop with more advanced features?

女：您好，我正在尋找一台在出差期間使用的攜帶型電腦。你能幫忙我嗎？
男：當然。你想要簡單的筆記型電腦還是有較多進階功能的筆記型電腦？

這個男人很有可能是什麼人？
（A）一個電腦技術員
（B）銷售員

解說 會聽到「尋找攜帶性電腦」這類話的人，可能就是「銷售員」。　　　　　　　　　　答案（B）

詞彙 look for... 尋找　portable computer 攜帶用電腦
business trip 出差　feature 機能

7. 美W 美M

1 找出核心詞彙	woman, work
2 了解類型	詢問說話者
3 看選項	職業介紹所或機械公司

W : Welcome to Korea Heavy Machinery. After the morning orientation session, Ms. Yang, who will be your manager, will explain why our customers are proud to use our machinery.
M : Thank you.

女：歡迎來到韓國重機。在上午的訓練指導講習後，將成為你們經理的楊女士會說明為什麼我們的顧客會很自豪使用我們的機械。

男：謝謝你。

這個女人很有可能是在哪裡工作呢？
（A）在一間職業介紹所
（B）在一家機械公司

解說 「說話者在哪裡工作」類的考題是詢問說話者的職業，所以有時候不一定與「對話的地點」有關。透過該女性話語當中的公司名稱與「使用我們的機械」，可以知道（B）為答案。　　　　　　　答案（B）

詞彙 orientation session（新生）訓練指導講習　be proud to... 自豪於…

8. 美M 澳W

1 找出核心詞彙	man
2 了解類型	詢問說話者
3 看選項	辦公用品店或配送公司

M : GW's Office Mart, good afternoon. This is Martin. How may I help you?
W : Hi, this is Maria Hernandez with the Dublin office. I'm calling about the office supplies I ordered from your company last week.

男：這是GW辦公用品賣場，午安。我是馬汀。我可以幫助您嗎？
女：您好，我是都柏林辦公室的瑪莉亞·荷南茲。我打電話來是關於我上週從你們公司訂購的辦公室用品。

這個男人很有可能是在哪裡工作呢？
（A）在辦公用品店
（B）在配送公司

解說 透過該男性說的公司名稱與該女性說的「上週從你們公司訂購的辦公室用品」，可以知道該男性是在「辦公用品店」工作的。　　　答案（A）

詞彙 office supply 辦公用品

問題9～10請參考以下對話。 美W 英M

1 找出核心詞彙	calling, woman
2 了解類型	詢問主題、說話者
3 看選項的詞彙	瑕疵品，丟失的東西，發票
	店主，銷售人員，客服職
4 預測對話內容	詢問問題，解決方式

W : Hello, [10]M&D Pictures. Customer Service Department. This is Jane Fuller. How may I help you?

M : Hi, [9]I'm calling about a camera I bought

from your store two weeks ago but for some reason I haven't been able to get it to work properly.

W : Well, all our products have a one-year warranty, so your camera is still covered. The easiest thing would be for someone to take a look at it. I recommend you bring it to the service center.

女：您好，M&D相片公司顧客服務部。我是珍·富勒。我可以如何幫助您？

男：您好，我打電話來是有關於兩週前從你們店裡買的相機，因為某些原因我無法使它正確運作。

女：好的，我們所有的產品都有一年的保固，因此您的相機仍在保固期。最簡單的方式是有人幫你看看。我建議您將它帶來服務中心。

詞彙 for some reason 某原因 be able to 能做 properly 正確地 warranty 保固 covered 在保固有效期 take a look at 看一看

9.

這個男人為什麼打電話？
（A）討論一件有瑕疵的商品
（B）報告丟失的東西
（C）要求收據

解說 透過核心詞彙calling，可以知道是詢問主題的考題。藉由在核心說法I'm calling about後面出現的「在你們商店買的相機、無法正常運作」，可以知道（A）為答案。 答案（A）

詞彙 defective merchandise 有缺點的商品 lost 弄丟；遺失 ask for 要求 receipt 收據

10.

這個女人很有可能是什麼人？
（A）店老闆
（B）手機銷售人員
（C）客戶服務職員

解說 接電話的女性話語裡有答案的線索。另外，聽到該男性說的「無法正常運作」這類的話的人應該是（C）。 答案（C）

詞彙 mobile phone 行動電話 salesperson 銷售員 representative 代表人

問題11～12請參考以下對話。 漢W 英M

1 找出核心詞彙	discussing, where
2 了解類型	詢問主題、地點
3 看選項的詞彙	籌備活動，價格，地點
	音樂廳，樂器行，道路上
4 預測對話內容	在演奏廳準備表演。

W : Could you tell me [11] where the stage manager is? I want to ask him where to position some of these instruments on stage.

M : Well, I guess [12] he should be here 3 hours before the concert starts, but it seems like he's going to be a little late.

W : You have his mobile phone number, right? I'd better confirm the position over the phone.

女：你能告訴我舞台總監在哪裡嗎？我想問他這些樂器要放在舞台哪裡。

男：嗯，我想在音樂會開始前三小時他應該會在這裡，但是看來他似乎將會有一點晚到。

女：你有他的行動電話號碼，對吧？我最好打電話來確認位置。

詞彙 stage manager 舞台督導 instrument 樂器 seem like 似乎是… over the phone 透過電話

11.

說話者正在討論什麼？
（A）某些樂器的價格
（B）劇院的位置
（C）活動的準備工作

解說 透過核心詞彙discussing，可以知道是詢問主題的考題。若Could you tell me等說法在對話前面部分出現，也能當作詢問主題的考題的答案線索。將後面出現的「問樂器要放在哪裡」以概括性的敘述做變化來表達的（C）為答案。 答案（C）

詞彙 price 價格 location 位置 theater 劇場 preparation 準備

12.

說話者很有可能在哪裡？
（A）在音樂廳
（B）在唱片店
（C）在路上

解說 透過「樂器要放哪裡」、「音樂會開始前在這兒」等線索，可以知道是在「音樂廳」。 答案（A）

詞彙 music shop 唱片店

問題13～14請參考以下對話。 [美M] [美W]

1 找出核心詞彙	where, man
2 了解類型	詢問地點、說話者
3 看選項的詞彙	會議，詢問處，面試
	快遞人員，接待員，面試者
4 預測對話內容	求職者在服務台詢問面試地點。

M：Excuse me. [14]I'm here to interview with Mr. Dotson in the accounting department.

W：[13]Please sign in, and here is your ID badge for visitors. The interview is going to be held on the 9th floor.

M：Certainly. [13]Can you tell me where the elevator is?

男：打擾一下。我來這兒是和會計部門的道森先生面試的。
女：請簽名，這是您的訪客證。面試將在九樓舉行。
男：沒問題。你能告訴我電梯在哪裡嗎？

詞彙 accounting department 會計部門 sign in 簽名 ID badge 名牌

13.
這段談話很有可能是在哪裡發生的？
（A）在會議中
（B）在服務台
（C）在面試中

解說 「給訪客證的地方」、「有人告訴你電梯在哪裡的地方」應該是服務台。　　　　　答案 (B)

詞彙 reception desk 服務台

14
這個男人很有可能是什麼人？
（A）快遞人員
（B）櫃檯人員
（C）求職面試者

解說 說出「我是來面試的」人，應該是「求職者」。　　　　　答案 (C)

詞彙 delivery man 快遞人員 receptionist 櫃檯人員 job interviewee 求職面試者 cf. interviewer（面試官）

STEP 02 考題實戰練習

1. (B)	2. (D)	3. (B)	4. (B)	5. (D)	6. (B)
7. (C)	8. (D)	9. (D)	10. (C)	11. (B)	12. (C)

問題1～3請參考以下對話。 [美W] [澳W]

W1: Hi, Maria. It's Joanna. [1]Can you give me a ride to work this morning? My car broke down late last night, and it's being fixed in the repair shop.

W2: I'd be delighted to, but I have to go into work early to prepare for an important meeting. [2]Do you mind leaving 30 minutes earlier than usual?

W1: [2]Not at all! I will be ready to be picked up in 10 minutes.

W2: [3]You can make that 20. I need some time to get dressed before going out.

女1：您好，瑪麗亞，我是喬安娜。今天早上你能否載我一程去上班？昨天深夜我的車壞了，它在修車廠維修。
女2：我很樂意，但我得很早去上班去準備一個重要會議。你介不介意比平常提早三十分鐘出門？
女1：不介意！我會加速在十分鐘內準備好。
女2：你可以有二十分鐘。出門前，我需要一些時間換衣服。

詞彙 give someone a ride 載某人一程 repair shop 修理廠 30 minutes earlier than usual 比平常早三十分鐘 be ready to 準備好做 pick up 整理 make it（時間）在某時間做… get dressed 換衣服 go out 外出

1.
說話者主要在討論什麼？
（A）提早的會議
（B）去上班的方式
（C）修理工人的問題
（D）一個新的工作時間表

解說 這是詢問主題的考題。在對話前段部分出現的疑問句可以當作答案線索。「載我一程去上班」已經決定其主題，所以將此變化後來表達的（B）即是答案。　　　　　答案 (B)

詞彙 way to get to 去…的方向 mechanic 修理工人 schedule 日程表

2.
說話者同意做什麼事？
（A）順道去修理店。
（B）與客戶聯絡。
（C）共乘一台計程車。
（D）早一點去上班。

解說 在此對話裡，由「介不介意…？」與「不介意」的問答過程當中，可以看出「同意」了什麼事情。將「比平常提早三十分鐘」以簡化的敘述來表達的（D）為答案。　　　　　答案 (D)

詞彙 stop by 順道去… contact 聯絡 share 分享

3.

說話者在什麼時候可能見面？
（A）在十分鐘後
（B）在二十分鐘後
（C）在三十分鐘後
（D）在四十分鐘後

解說 這是詢問具體事項／具體時間點的考題。「十分鐘後」是陷阱，而「二十分鐘後」的（B）才是答案。
答案（B）

詞彙 meet 見面 in（時間名詞）在多久之後

問題4～6請參考以下對話 英M 美W

M: [4]Town Post Office, how may I help you?

W: Hi, [5]I'd like to know how much you charge for sending a package to Korea. And how long does it take for the package to get there?

M: Well, standard delivery for packages is 11 dollars per kilogram, and it could take up to 10 days to arrive. If you tell me how much it weighs, I can give you a price.

W: I'm not sure how heavy it is. [6]I'll weigh it then call you back. Thanks.

男：這是鄉鎮郵局，需要什麼協助嗎？
女：您好，我想知道寄包裹到韓國要多少費用？還有要花多少時間可以寄達？
男：嗯，一般郵寄的包裹是每公斤十一元，而且可能需要十天會到。若你能告訴我它有多重，我可以告訴你費用。
女：我不太確定它的重量。我會秤一下然後回電給你。謝謝。

詞彙 charge for 收費 package 包裹 standard delivery 一般郵寄 take up to 10 days 要花十天 weigh 有…重 call back 回撥

4.

這個男人的工作很有可能是什麼？
（A）倉庫工人
（B）郵局職員
（C）旅行社職員
（D）電話公司接線員

解說 接電話時說「這是…郵局」，所以可以猜測為「郵局職員」。
答案（B）

詞彙 warehouse 倉庫 worker 工人 clerk 職員 travel agent 旅行社 operator 接線生

5.

這個女人為什麼打電話？
（A）詢問郵遞區號
（B）請教問路
（C）找一些有關旅遊的信息
（D）詢問價格

解說 聽到核心說法I'd like to。透過在後面出現的「多少費用」，可以知道是「詢問價格的狀況」。 答案（D）

詞彙 ask for 要求 postal code 郵遞區號 driving direction 道路指南 tour 旅遊 inquire about 詢問有關… price 價格

6.

這個女人接下來可能會做什麼？
（A）完成文書業務
（B）秤重一件包裹
（C）郵寄一些信件
（D）購買機票

解說 只要聽到在I'll後面的部分就可以回答。代名詞it是指包裹，所以（B）為答案。 答案（B）

詞彙 complete 完成 paperwork 文書業務 mail 郵寄 purchase 購買 flight ticket 飛機票

問題7～9請參考以下對話 美W 美M

W: Excuse me. Can you tell me where the dry cleaner is [7]here in the hotel? I spilt coffee on my shirt this morning, and [8]need to have it cleaned today.

M: Yes, there is one located on the second floor. However, I don't think they offer express service. You'd better go to the one across from the hotel. I'm sure they can do it within a few hours.

W: What a relief! I'll go there right away. [9]I need the shirt for a job interview tomorrow afternoon.

女：抱歉。你能告訴我這家飯店的乾洗店在哪嗎？今天早上我打翻咖啡在我的襯衫上，今日之內要清洗乾淨。
男：是，在二樓有。但我想他們不提供快速服務。您最好去飯店對面那家。我相信他們在幾個小時之內做得到。
女：真幸運！我要馬上去。我明天下午的求職面試需要這件襯衫。

詞彙 dry cleaner 乾洗 spill 溢出 express service 快速服務 across from 在…對面 right away 立刻 job interview 求職面試

7.

說話者在哪裡？
（A）在銀行
（B）在購物中心
（C）在飯店
（D）在餐廳

解說 聽到線索「這家飯店」！若知道了對話的地點能聯想到相關核心詞彙，就更容易回答考題。例如，銀行

的核心詞彙（open a bank account）、購物中心的核心詞彙（looking for）、餐廳的核心詞彙（order、menu）等。 答案 (C)

詞彙 shopping center 購物中心　restaurant 餐廳

8.

這個女人想要做什麼？
（A）下訂單
（B）存款
（C）更換她的房間
（D）清潔一些衣服

解說 這是詢問要求事項的考題。該女性話裡的核心詞彙為need to，將其後面的「清洗」做變化來表達的（D）為答案。 答案 (D)

詞彙 place an order 下訂單　make a deposit 存款
clean 清洗　clothe 衣服

9.

面試是什麼時候？
（A）今天上午
（B）今天下午
（C）明天早上
（D）明天下午

解說 interview和appointment的附近很常有答案的線索。在其後聽到的（D）為答案。 答案 (D)

詞彙 interview 面試

問題10～12請參考以下對話和圖表。 美W 美M

Flight number	Departure	Destination
CK 106	Taipei	Singapore
[11]CK 381	Taipei	Sydney
CK 997	Taipei	Tokyo
CK 639	Taipei	Bangkok

W : Kingsman [10]Travel Agency, may I help you?

M : Hello, [10]I would like to book a ticket to Sydney.

W: Certainly. When is your date of departure, please?

M : Friday, [12]January 3. I'll return to Taipei on January 10.

W : So it's a round-trip ticket for next week.

班機號碼	出發地	目的地
CK 106	台北	新加坡
CK 381	台北	雪梨
CK 997	台北	東京
CK 639	台北	曼谷

女：金士曼旅行社，有什麼能為您服務的嗎？
男：哈囉！我想要訂一到雪梨的機票。
女：當然。請問您的出發日是何時？
男：星期五，一月三日。我一月十日回台北。
女：所以是一張下周的來回機票。

詞彙 travel 旅遊　help 協助；幫忙　would like 想要（較want有禮貌）　book a ticket 訂票　Sydney 雪梨　certainly 當然　date of departure 出發日　please 請問　Friday 星期五　January 一月　round-trip ticket 來回機票　next week 下星期　flight number 班機號碼　departure 出發　destination 目的地　Singapore 新加坡　Tokyo 東京　Bangkok 曼谷

10.

這段對話主要是關於什麼？
（A）訂電影票
（B）訂飯店房間
（C）訂飛機票
（D）訂晚餐席位

解說 這是詢問「對話主題是什麼」的「簡單選項類考題」。由對話中「旅行社」及「我想要訂一張到雪梨的機票」可推斷選項（C）訂飛機票為正確答案。 答案 (C)

詞彙 movie 電影　hotel 飯店　flight 航班

11.

請看此圖，男士會搭哪一個航班？
（A）CK 106
（B）CK 381
（C）CK 997
（D）CK 639

解說 圖表中台北飛雪梨的班機為CK381，所以選項（B）為正確答案。 答案 (B)

詞彙 take a flight 搭航班

12.

男子將離開多久？
（A）3天
（B）5天
（C）7天
（D）10天

解說 這是詢問「時間長度」的「簡易時間計算」問題。男子說「一月三日（出發）。我一月十日回台北」，10－3＝7，所以他將離開7天。 答案 (C)

詞彙 how long 多久　be away 離開，不在

Quiz |

1. (A)	2. (B)	3. (B)	4. (A)
5. (A)	6. (B)		

Q1 英M 美W

M : You'll have to complete the application form and bring it to me. Would you like me to mail or fax the form to you?

W : Well, my fax machine is being fixed. **Could you** send it to me in the mail?

男：你必須完成這份申請表並且帶來給我。你希望我用郵寄還是傳真這份表格給你呢？

女：好的，我的傳真機正在修理中。你能用郵寄的給我嗎？

這個女人要求這個男人做什麼？
（A）郵寄一份資料
（B）派一位維修人員

解說 透過核心詞彙ask，可以知道是詢問「要求事項」的考題。將核心說法Could you後面出現的「用郵寄的給我」以概括性的敘述做變化來表達的（A）為答案。
答案（A）

詞彙 complete 完成 application form 申請表 bring 帶來 fix 修理 in the mail 以郵件 document 文件 repairperson 修理工人

Q2 英M 澳W

M : Hello, my name is Henry Han from City Times. I'd like to talk to your sales manager, Sandra Oh.

W : I'm afraid she is no longer in our sales department. The new sales manager is John Celina. **Would you like me to** connect you with him?

男：您好，我是城市時報的亨利‧韓。我想和你們的銷售經理珊卓拉‧歐通話。

女：恐怕她已經不在我們的銷售部門了。新的銷售經理是約翰‧塞里納。你要我幫你轉接給他嗎？

這個女人提議做什麼？
（A）下材料訂單
（B）轉接這通電話

解說 出現核心詞彙offer，可以知道是詢問「建議事項」的考題。透過與核心說法Could you類似的Would

you like me，藉由其後面出現的「幫你轉接給他」，可以知道（B）為答案。
答案（B）

詞彙 sales manager 銷售經理 be no longer 不再是… connect 連接 place an order for 下訂某物 transfer （電話）轉接

Q3 英M 澳W

M : This copy machine broke down again! I'm worried because I need to make copies for my presentation tomorrow morning.

W : Don't worry. Why don't you keep preparing for your presentation? **I'll** call the technician about fixing this machine.

男：這台影印機又壞了！我很擔心，因為我明天早上的報告需要複本。

女：別擔心，你何不繼續準備你的報告？有關這台機器的修理，我會打電話給技師。

這個女人接下來很有可能會做什麼？
（A）修理這台機器
（B）打電話

解說 出現核心詞彙do next，可以知道是詢問「下一個行程」的考題。透過在核心說法I'll後面出現的「打電話給技師」，可以知道（B）為答案。
答案（B）

詞彙 copy machine 影印機 break down 故障 make a copy 複印 presentation 發表 prepare for 準備… technician 技術員 fix 修理 repair 修理 make a phone call 打電話

Q4 英M 美W

M : I think we need to hire several part-time workers to help us move the office.

W : You're right. We can't do all of the preparation work ourselves. **Let me** search for a hiring agency to find us some people as soon as possible.

男：我想我們需要雇用幾位計時工作人員來幫忙我們搬遷辦公室。

女：你是對的。我們無法自己做全部的準備工作。讓我找招聘公司以儘可能快點幫我們找到人。

這個女人說她將會做什麼？
（A）尋找一間招聘公司
（B）申請一個臨時工作

解說 出現核心詞彙she will do，可以知道是詢問「下一個行程」的考題。透過在核心說法Let me後面出現的「找招聘公司」，可以知道（A）為答案。
答案（A）

詞彙 part-time worker 計時工作人員 move the office 搬遷辦公室 preparation work 準備工作 hiring agency 招聘公司 temporary 臨時的

Q5 澳W 英M

W : Frank. How's it going with editing the <u>new book</u>? Will it be released to the bookstores as scheduled?

M : I don't think so. The author of the book wanted to make last-minute changes, so I **won't** be able <u>to get the book out</u> **until this March.**

女：法蘭克，新書的編輯進行得如何呢？它將會按照計畫在書店上市嗎？

男：我不這麼認為。這本書的作者到最後突然要做修正，因此到三月前我將無法出版這本書。

根據這個男人的談話，在三月可能會發生什麼事？
（A）將會出一本新書。
（B）一位新的編輯將被雇用。

解說 透過未來時間點in March，可以知道是在詢問「下一個行程」的考題類型。「在三月之前無法出版」意思就是要三月以後才能出版。因此（A）為答案。

答案 (A)

詞彙 edit 編輯 release 出刊 as scheduled 依時間計畫表 author 作者 make last-minute changes 最終的修正 not A until B 在B時間前不會發生A

Q6 美W 美M

W : I'll be out of the town this week. Why don't I e-mail you a draft of the report first? You can take a look before I come back.

M : Definitely, **I'll** <u>read it</u> **this week**. Then we can set up a time to talk about it later.

女：我這週要出城。我何不將報告的草稿用電子郵件先寄你？你可以在我回來前先看看。

男：肯定的，我將會在這週看它。然後我們晚一點可以約個時間來討論它。

這個男人說他這星期將會做什麼？
（A）去出差
（B）閱讀文件

解說 this week是核心詞彙，在對話內容與考題裡出現了相同的this week說法，因此在this week的前後會有答案的線索。因此把「將會看它」以概括性的敘述做變化來表達的（B）為答案。

答案 (B)

詞彙 out of the town 出城 a draft of the report 報告的草稿 take a look 看 definitely 肯定地 set up a time 約時間 talk about it later 晚一點來討論它 go on a business trip 出差

---

1 (B)	**2** (B)	**3** (A)	**4** (A)
5 (B)	**6** (A)	**7** (B)	**8** (B)
9 (C)	**10** (A)	**11** (C)	**12** (C)
13 (A)	**14** (C)		

1. 英M 美W

1 找出核心詞彙	woman ask
2 了解類型	詢問要求事項
3 看選項	給地址或訂單編號

M : Hi. My name is Bill Brown. I'm calling about a printer that I ordered from you two weeks ago. It hasn't arrived yet.

W : Sure. I'd be happy to help you. **Can you** tell me your order number, please?

男：我的名字是比爾·布朗。我打電話來是有關於兩週前我和你們訂購的印表機。它到現在還沒有來。

女：當然。我很樂於幫助您。可否告訴你的訂單編號嗎？

這個女人要求這個男人做什麼？
（A）給她正確的地址
（B）告訴她訂單編號

解說 出現核心詞彙woman ask，可以知道是詢問「要求事項」的考題。透過在核心說法Can you後面出現的「告訴我你的訂單編號」，可以知道（B）為答案。

答案 (B)

詞彙 I'd be happy to 我很樂於… order number 訂單編號

2. 美W 美M

1 找出核心詞彙	request
2 了解類型	詢問要求事項
3 看選項	別的預約時間，或去辦公室的方向

W : **Could you** tell me where Mr. Wilson's office is? I forgot to ask when I made the interview appointment.

M : He's on the 8th floor. Turn left after you get off the elevator and go all the way down the hallway. It's right next to the sales department. Good luck with the interview.

女：你能告訴我威爾森先生的辦公室在什麼地方嗎？我預約面試時忘記問了。

男：他在八樓。出電梯後左轉，然後走廊直走到底。它在銷售部門的右邊。祝您面試幸運。

這個女人請求什麼事？
（A）別的預約時間
（B）去辦公室的方向

解說 透過核心詞彙request，可以知道是詢問「要求事項」的考題。透過在核心說法Could you後面出現的「告訴我威爾森先生的辦公室在什麼地方」，可以知道將此以概括性的敘述做變化來表達的（B）為答案。
答案（B）

詞彙 interview appointment 面試預約 get off 下車 all the way down the hallway 走廊直走到底 next to 在…旁 sales department 銷售部門 Good luck. 祝幸運。 directions to 去…的方向

3. 英M 美W

1 找出核心詞彙	woman suggest
2 了解類型	詢問建議事項
3 看選項	使用別的影印機，或打電話給技師

M : I want to make some copies before the budget meeting starts, but all of the machines are being used. The only copier not being used is in the accounting department, but it's out of order.

W : In that case, **why don't you** try the photocopiers downstairs in the lobby? It should be available, but you'll need to pay for the copies.

男：在預算會議前我想要影印一些東西，但是所有的機器都正被使用中。唯一沒有被使用的在會計部門，但是它壞了。

女：若是那樣，你何不試試在樓下大廳的影印機？它應該可以用，但是您將需要付費影印。

這個女人建議這個男人做什麼？
（A）使用另一台影印機
（B）打電話給技師

解說 透過核心詞彙woman suggest，可以知道是詢問「建議事項」的考題。藉由在核心說法why don't you後面出現的「使用在樓下大廳的影印機」，可以知道將此以概括性的敘述做變化來表達的（A）為答案。
答案（A）

詞彙 make a copy 做複印 accounting department 會計部門 out of order 故障 in that case 那樣的話 available 可以使用 pay for… 為…付費 technician 技術員

4. 美M 澳W

1 找出核心詞彙	woman offer
2 了解類型	詢問建議事項
3 看選項	拿名片或搬移書架

M : I need to confirm the position of the bookshelf first so that we can have the books placed correctly. But the library director hasn't come in yet. Do you know his mobile phone number?

W : Actually I have his business card in my car. I'll go and get it.

男：我需要先確認書架的位置，這樣我們才能把書置放正確。但是圖書館的管理人還沒有來。你知道他的行動電話號碼嗎？

女：事實上我車上有他的名片。我去拿。

這個女人提議做什麼？
（A）拿名片
（B）搬移書架

解說 透過核心詞彙offer，可以知道是詢問「建議事項」的考題。透過在核心說法I'll後面出現的「去拿（名片）」，可以知道（A）為答案。
答案（A）

詞彙 bookshelf 書架 library director 圖書館管理人 come in 到達 mobile phone number 行動電話號碼 business card 名片

5. 英M 美W

1 找出核心詞彙	do next
2 了解類型	詢問下一個行程
3 看選項	退費或帶來照片

M : Hi. I'm here to pick up some photos. My name is Jack Mayers. I had my photos taken on Monday. The person who helped me said they should be ready to be picked up today.

W : I have your information right here. You had passport photos taken. I'll go get them for you.

男：您好。我來拿一些照片。我的名字是傑克‧梅約。我在星期一拍了照片。幫忙我的人說它們應該在今天會準備好可以領。

女：我這邊有您的資料。您照了護照相片。我去拿來給您。

這個女人接下來可能會做什麼？
（A）發出退款
（B）帶來一些照片

解說 透過核心詞彙do next，可以知道是詢問「下一個行程」的考題。透過在核心說法I'll後面出現的「去拿（相片）來給您」，可以知道（B）為答案。 答案 (B)

詞彙 pick up 領取 be ready to 準備好 passport photo 護照相片 get（某物）for you 拿某物給你 bring 帶來

6. 美W 美M

1 找出核心詞彙	do next
2 了解類型	詢問下一個行程
3 看選項	完成表格或配送貨品

W：According to the company policy, all requests for office supplies must be made in writing. <u>Probably the easiest thing to do would be to fill out a supplies request form placed at the human resources department's entrance.</u>

M：Oh, I see. That certainly would be very easy. **I'll** do it right away. Thank you for your help.

女：依據公司的政策，所有的辦公用品申請書都必須用寫的。最簡單的方法可能是填寫放在人力資源部門入口處的辦公用品申請表格。
男：噢，我知道了。那當然非常容易。我將會馬上去做。謝謝你的幫忙。

這個男人接下來可能會做什麼？
（A）完成表格
（B）配送貨品

解說 透過核心詞彙do next，可以知道是詢問「下一個行程」的考題。透過在核心說法I'll後面出現的「馬上去做（填寫申請表格）」，可以知道（A）為答案。
答案 (A)

詞彙 according to 根據… request 申請書 office supply 辦公用品 in writing 用寫的 fill out 填寫 human resources department 人力資源部門 entrance 入口 right away 立刻 complete 完成 deliver 配送

7. 澳W 美M

1 找出核心詞彙	this afternoon
2 了解類型	詢問下一個行程
3 看選項	報告或為會議準備

W：I heard you visited our office in New York to get some ideas about how we can expand our customers here in United States. <u>Are you going to share your ideas at our marketing</u>

<u>meeting tomorrow morning</u>?

M：I will. **I'm going to** take some time **this afternoon** to get all my information organized.

女：我聽說你為了取得一些我們如何在美國擴大顧客群想法，所以拜訪了我們的紐約辦公室。你會在明天上午的行銷會議上分享你的想法嗎？
男：我會的。今天下午我將會花一些時間整理我的資訊。

這個男人今天下午將會做什麼？
（A）發表報告
（B）為會議做準備

解說 這是詢問「下一個行程」的考題。在對話內容與考題裡出現了相同的this afternoon說法，因此在this afternoon的前後就有答案的線索。該女性同意「分享你的想法」這項建議，然後說「下午將會整理資訊」，這就是「準備會議」的意思。 答案 (B)

詞彙 get some ideas 得到一些想法 share 分享 take some time 花一些時間 organized 整理 give a presentation 發表 prepare for 為…準備

8. 英M 美W

1 找出核心詞彙	Monday
2 了解類型	詢問下一個行程
3 看選項	辦公室會關閉或介紹員工

M：I heard we're going to work with the <u>new programmer</u> soon. I guess she's in the middle of her training courses. Do you know when she starts in our office?

W：Yes, <u>her first day will be **Monday**. She will be introduced to everyone at our team meeting on that day.</u>

男：我聽說我們很快將要和新的程式設計師一起工作。我猜她還在她的訓練課程中。你知道什麼時候來上班嗎？
女：是的，星期一將是她的第一天。她在那天的會議裡會被介紹給我們團隊的每一個人。

星期一將會發生什麼事？
（A）一間辦公室將關閉。
（B）會介紹一位員工。

解說 Monday是核心詞彙，在對話內容與考題裡出現了相同的Monday說法，因此在Monday前後就有答案的線索。將「她（新的程式設計師）將被介紹」以概括性的敘述做變化來表達的（B）為答案。 答案 (B)

詞彙 in the middle of 在…當中 training course 訓練課程 first day 第一天 introduce 介紹 on that day 在那一天 be closed 被關閉

問題9～10請參考以下對話。 美W 英M

1 找出核心詞彙	woman ask, do next
2 了解類型	詢問要求事項、接下來的內容
3 看選項	確認配送，下訂單，修理
	電話，退還，尋找地址
4 預測對話內容	要求修理服務之後，
	撥打電話確認細節。

W : Max, the sales department called and said something about a broken air conditioner. ⁹Can you go and see if you can fix it? An important meeting with potential customers starts right after lunch, and they want to make sure it works properly before the meeting.

M : Oh, I have a couple of urgent repairs first thing this morning. Can you check if someone can stay around until 12:00 p.m. or so? I should be able to look at it right before lunch time.

W : ¹⁰I'll call and find out. I'll let you know in a while.

女：馬克斯，銷售部門打來說些關於空調壞掉的事。你能去看看能否修理它嗎？有一場和潛在客戶的重要會議在午餐後馬上要開始，所以他們希望務必在會議前它能正常運作。

男：噢，今天早上我有幾個緊急的維修。你可以確認一下大約到中午十二點左右有人可以在附近嗎？我應該可以在午餐前去看看。

女：我會打電話找一下。我一會兒後會讓你知道的。

詞彙 sales department 銷售部門 broken 故障 fix 修理 potential customer 潛在客戶 properly 正常地 urgent 修理 repair 修理 stay around 在附近 or so 大約 be able to 可以 look at 看 find out 查找 in a while 一會兒後

9.
這個女人要求這個男人做什麼？
（A）檢查配送
（B）訂一些設備
（C）做維修

解說 透過核心詞彙woman ask，可以知道是詢問「要求事項」的考題。藉由在核心說法Can you後面出現的「去看看你能否修理它」，可以知道（C）為答案。

答案 (C)

詞彙 check on 確認 delivery 配送 order 下訂單 equipment 設備

10.
這個女人接下來可能會做什麼？
（A）打電話
（B）退還一些商品
（C）找一個地址

解說 透過核心詞彙do next，可以知道是詢問「下一個行程」的考題。透過在核心說法I'll後面出現的「打電話找一下」，可以知道（A）為答案。 答案 (A)

詞彙 make a phone call 打電話 return 返回 merchandise 商品 address 地址

問題11～12請參考以下對話。 美W 美M

1 找出核心詞彙	woman ask, do next
2 了解類型	詢問要求事項、接下來的內容
3 看選項	退款，餐點，換座位
	完成表格，取消預約，談話
4 預測對話內容	要求變更座位之後與家人確認

W : Hi, my sister and I just checked in. I found our seats are near the back of the plane in row 40. ¹¹Would it be possible to change them to exit row seats?

M : Let me see. You're flying to Detroit, right? Yes, I do have 2 seats available, but you'll have to pay extra 30 dollars for each seat.

W : Sounds reasonable, but ¹²I should check with my sister before paying for them.

女：您好，我姊姊和我剛報到。我發現我們的座位靠近飛機後面的第四十排。有可能換到出口附近一排的座位嗎？

男：讓我看看。你們要飛行到底特律，對嗎？好的，我有兩個可用的位子，但是每個座位您必須付額外三十元。

女：聽起來蠻合理的，但是付費前我必須和我姊姊確認。

詞彙 check in （航空）報到 Would it be possible...? （某事）有可能嗎？ exit row seat 出口附近一排的座位 reasonable 合理 pay for 為…付費

11.
這個女人要求什麼？
（A）退款
（B）一份餐點
（C）換座位

解說 出現核心詞彙ask，可以知道是詢問「要求事項」的考題。透過與核心說法Can you類似的Would it be possible，藉由其後面出現的「換到出口附近一排的座位」，可以知道將此以簡單型式變化來表達的（C）為

答案。 答案 (C)

詞彙 refund 返還 meal 餐食 seat change 換座位

12.

這個女人接下來會做什麼？
（A）完成一份表格
（B）取消預約
（C）和她的姊姊談話

解說 出現核心詞彙do next，可以知道是詢問「下一個行程」的考題。透過與核心說法I'll類似的I should，藉由其後面出現的「和我姊姊確認」，可以知道將此換句話說來表達的（C）為答案。 答案 (C)

詞彙 complete 完成 form 表格 cancel 取消 reservation 預約 talk to 和某人說話

問題13～14請參考以下對話。 英M 澳W

1 找出核心詞彙	woman ask, do next
2 了解類型	詢問要求事項、接下來的內容
3 看選項	保留，給收據，郵寄東西
	離開，閱讀，寫
4 預測對話內容	要求保管商品後，填寫名字。

M : Thank you for shopping at Shoes Heaven. What can I do for you?

W : I'd like to buy these shoes at a reduced price, but I found the sale starts tomorrow. ¹³Could you hold them for me? I'll be out of town all day tomorrow.

M : Sure, no problem. The sale goes through the weekend. So you can come anytime this weekend. ¹⁴Just write your name here, and ¹⁴I'll put the boots aside for you.

男：感謝您來到鞋子天堂購物。有什麼我能為您做的嗎？
女：我想要以特價的價格買這些鞋子，但是我發現明天才開始打折。你可以為我保留它們嗎？明天我將要出城一整天。
男：當然，沒有問題。打折活動會持續到週末。因此您可以在這個週末任何時間過來。將您的名字寫在這兒，我會為您把靴子放在一旁。

詞彙 at a reduced price 以降低的價格… hold 保留 be out of town 出城 all day 整天 go 持續 put…aside 放在一旁

13.

這個女人要求這個男人做什麼？
（A）把一些商品放在一旁

（B）給這個女人一份收據
（C）郵寄這個女人購買的東西給她

解說 出現核心詞彙woman ask，可以知道是詢問「要求事項」的考題。透過在核心說法Could you後面出現的「為我保留它們」，與該男生說的「為您把鞋子放在一旁」，可以知道（A）為答案。 答案 (A)

詞彙 merchandise 商品 receipt 收據 mail 郵寄 purchase 購買

14.

這個女人接下來可能會做什麼？
（A）離開這家店
（B）看報紙
（C）寫一些東西

解說 透過核心詞彙do next，可以知道是詢問「下一個行程」的考題。該男性說的最後一句會決定該女性的下一個動作。若該男生說「請寫下您的名字」，該女性接下來可能會進行（C）。 答案 (C)

詞彙 leave 離開 newspaper 報紙 write something down 寫一些東西

STEP 02 考題實戰練習

1. (C)	2. (B)	3. (D)	4. (D)	5. (B)	6. (B)
7. (D)	8. (D)	9. (C)	10. (C)	11. (B)	12. (A)

問題1～3請參考以下對話。 美M 美W

M : Good evening, Marie. ¹How's everything going with your bread factory? I was in the area and thought I'd come by to see how the new baking system is working.

W : Oh, ²I find that the system you sold us is fantastic. It's a lot more convenient to have the bread dough shaped and baked automatically.

M : I am sure it is worth the money. It saves time and cuts back on flour use, and it should increase your production. Does it seem that you produced more bread this month?

W : Hopefully. ³We are expecting large orders next week, and I'm sure we can meet the deadline this time.

男：晚安，瑪麗。你的麵包工廠營運得如何？我在這附近，我想說來了解一下新烘烤系統運作得如何。
女：哦，我認為你賣給我們的系統太棒了。它非常便於使生麵成型和

自動烘烤。

男：我確信它值得花那筆錢，這樣可以節省時間和減少麵粉的使用，並增加您的產量。你覺得這個月生產了更多麵包嗎？

女：希望是。下週我們期待有大訂單，現在我敢確定我們能在截止日期前完成。

詞彙 bread factory 麵包工廠　come by 來到　bread dough 生麵糰　shape 塑型　bake 烘培　automatically 自動地　worth 值得　cut back on 減少　meet the deadline 在截止日期時　this time 目前

1.

說話者很有可能在哪裡？
（A）在施工現場
（B）在一家花店
（C）在一間工廠
（D）在一家雜貨店

解說 將「你的麵包工廠營運得如何」與「我想是否能了解一下新烘烤系統運作得如何」連接起來推論的話，就可以知道是在「工廠」。　　　　答案 (C)

詞彙 construction 施工　grocery store 雜貨店

2.

說話者正在談什麼？
（A）降低包裹費用的方法
（B）一些新設備的好處
（C）一棟大樓的建設
（D）訂購物品的過程

解說 透過核心詞彙discussing，可以知道是詢問「主題」的考題。將「新的系統非常方便」與「節省時間和減少麵粉的使用，並增加產量」以概括性的敘述做變化來表達的（B）為答案。　　　　答案 (B)

詞彙 packaging 包裹　benefit 益處　equipment 設備　process 程序　order goods 訂貨物

3.

根據這段對話，下週將會發生什麼？
（A）老舊的系統將會被檢查。
（B）陳列箱將被換掉。
（C）工人們將超時工作。
（D）會有訂單下來。

解說 next week是核心詞彙，在對話內容與考題裡出現了相同的next week說法，因此在next week的前後會有答案的線索。將「我們期待有大訂單」以概括性的敘述做變化來表達的（D）為答案。若是主動句，常常會改成被動句來出現。　　　　答案 (D)

詞彙 inspect 檢查　display case 陳列箱　replace 替換　work overtime 超時工作　place an order 處理訂單

問題4～6請參考以下對話和圖表。 美 W　美 M

Types of tickets	Per person	Remarks
Children	$ 750	Age 13 to 17
[5]Adult regular	$ 1,000	Adult over 18
[5]Adult special	$ 500	Handicap caregiver
Group ticket	$ 800	Starting group of 10

[5]* 6 free wheelchair seats for each performance

W : [4]Martha Gram Theater, may I help you?

M : I'd like to inquire about the dance program this Sunday, please.

W : Yes, it'll be a performance given by a group from Taiwan called the Cloud Gate. How many tickets would you need?

M : [5]We need three. But one of us will be coming in a wheelchair. Do you have any seats accommodating it?

W : We do. [5]There are 6 free wheelchair seats for every performance. The main caregiver also gets to pay half price for entry. And there are ramps on every floor of the building.

M : That's very nice. What time does the show begin?

W : At 7:00 sharp. [6]I suggest you arrive at least 15 minutes early to avoid rushing.

M : Fine. Please arrange seats for the three of us, thank you.

門票類別	每人售價	備註
孩童票	$ 750	13歲到17歲
一般成人票	$ 1,000	18歲以上
特別成人票	$ 500	殘障照護人員
團體票	$ 800	最少10人以上

* 每場表演提供 6張免費輪椅座

女：瑪莎葛蘭姆劇院。哪裡能為您效勞嗎？
男：我想詢問關於這個星期天的舞蹈節目。
女：它是一個由台灣叫做雲門的團體所表演，您需要幾張門票呢？
男：我們需要三張。不過我們其中一位將坐輪椅來。你們有輪椅專用的座位嗎？
女：我們有！每一場表演有6張免費的輪椅座。主要的照護者入場半價。而且建築物的每一個樓層都有輪椅專用道。
男：太好了。表演何時開始呢？
女：7點整。我建議您至少以15分鐘以到場，以避免人潮過多。
男：好。請幫我們3人安排座位。謝謝。

詞彙 theater 劇院 inquire about 詢問 dance program 舞蹈節目 performance 演出 group 團體 wheelchair 輪椅 accommodate 為……提供便利；關照 main caregiver 主要照顧者 half price 半價 ramp 坡道 floor 樓層 sharp 準時地 suggest 建議 at least 至少 avoid 避免 rushing 倉促 arrange 安排

4.

女士在哪裡工作？
（A）在博物館
（B）在購物中心
（C）在書店
（D）在劇院

解說 這是詢問「地點」的「簡短選項類考題」。一開始女士便報出工作單位「瑪莎葛蘭姆劇院」，所以正確答案是（D）在劇院。　　　　　　答案 (D)

詞彙 museum 博物館 mall 購物中心 bookstore 書店 theater 劇院

5.

請看此圖，男士需要付多少錢？
（A）$ 1,000
（B）$ 1,500
（C）$ 2,000
（D）$ 2,500

解說 這是詢問「應付價格」的「簡易計算題」。對話中可知將有3位觀眾，其中1位乘坐輪椅。而女士提到輪椅座位免費，照護者票價半價，而最後一位是一般全票，對應到表格價位為$1,000 + $500 + $0 = $1,500，所以答案是（B）。　　　　　　答案 (B)

詞彙 money 錢；款項 pay 支付

6.

女士建議男士做什麼？
（A）用信用卡支付
（B）允許時間就座
（C）事前取票
（D）做照護者

解說 這是詢問「建議事項」的「簡短選項類考題」，核心語是「建議做什麼」。在此女士說：「我建議您至少15分鐘以前到場，以避免人潮過多」做變化表達的（B）為答案。　　　　　　答案 (B)

詞彙 credit card 信用卡 allow 允許 be seated 就座 pick up 提貨、接人 ahead of time 事前 caretaker = caregiver 照護者

問題7～9請參考以下對話。 美M 澳W

M : Ms. Waldron? [7]Did you hear the decorations you ordered for the company awards banquet just arrived?

W : Yes, I did. [8]Could you pick up the supplies and deliver them to the main hall this Friday by 2:00? One truck should be enough. And [9]please don't forget to hand the receipt over to the accounting department when you're finished.

M : Certainly. [9]Don't you need a copy of it for your records?

W : Yes, I do. Please copy and give it to my assistant to file.

男：沃爾倫女士嗎？你有聽說你幫公司頒獎典禮訂的裝飾品剛剛到達了嗎？
女：有的。你能在這週五兩點前取貨並送到大廳？一台卡車應該就夠。當你完成時，請別忘了將收據給會計部門。
男：當然。你不需要一份影本做記錄嗎？
女：是的，我要。請複印並把它給我的助理歸檔。

詞彙 decoration 裝飾品 award banquet 頒獎典禮 pick up 領取 deliver A to B 將A配送到B hand... over to 將…交給… receipt 收據 accounting department 會計部門 be finished 完成後 file 存檔；歸檔

7.

說話者正在討論什麼？
（A）退貨的規定
（B）預約時間表上的衝突
（C）會計軟體的問題
（D）即將來臨的活動的用品

解說 出現核心詞彙discussing，可以知道是詢問「主題」的考題。透過在核心說法Did you hear後面出現的「你幫公司頒獎典禮訂的裝飾品」，可以知道將此以概括性的敘述做變化來表達的（D）為答案。　答案 (D)

詞彙 policy 政策 return 返還 goods 貨物 conflict 衝突 appointment schedule 預約時間表 upcoming 即將到來的

8.

這個女人要求這個男人做什麼？
（A）參加典禮儀式
（B）準備工作坊
（C）領退款
（D）做配送

解說 透過核心詞彙woman ask，可以知道是詢問「要求事項」的考題。透過在核心說法Could you後面出現的「取貨並送到大廳」，可以知道將此以概括性的敘述做變化來表達的（D）為答案。　　答案 (D)

詞彙 ceremony 儀式 organize 準備 get a refund 領退款 make a delivery 做配送

9.

這個男人詢問什麼？
（A）一個檔案夾
（B）一個旅遊行程
（C）一份收據
（D）一台影印機

解說 「詢問什麼」類型也是在詢問「要求事項」。「不需要一份（收據的）影本嗎？」就是在詢問「收據」的說法。　　　　　　　　　　　　　　答案 (C)

詞彙 file folder 檔案夾 itinerary 日誌 photocopier 影印機

問題10～12請參考以下對話。 英M 美W

M：**10**Have you heard the company just launched a new website? I had a look at it, and found it wonderful.

W：Yes, I saw it this morning. At a glance, it looks a lot better than the old one. I think it should be very helpful for our business.

M：Of course, it will be much easier for customers to order our products online. And **11**a new web-based e-mail system could keep employees updated even away from the office.

W：I didn't realize that. Well, that solves my problems. **12**I'm leaving for a conference on Monday, and I was concerned about missing important e-mail.

男：你有聽說公司剛剛推出一個新的網站嗎？我看了一下，覺得它太棒了。

女：是的，我今天早上看到了。略看一下，看起來比舊的好多了，我想它應該會對我們的業務非常有幫助。

男：當然，它將讓客戶更容易上網訂購我們的產品。而新的網路版電子郵件系統能讓員工們隨時知道最新消息，即使員工離開辦公室。

女：我沒發現這個。不過，那解決了我的問題。我週一有個會議要去，而我正在擔心會錯過重要的電子郵件。

詞彙 launch 開始 at a glance 看一眼 online 線上 keep 人 updated 讓某人隨時知道最新消息 away from 離開某處 realize 實現 solve 解決 leave 離開某處 conference 會議 be concerned about 擔心有關於…

10.

這段談話的主題是什麼？
（A）一場即將來臨的會議
（B）修訂過的安全規定
（C）一個新網站

（D）網路購物

解說 透過核心詞彙main topic，可以知道是詢問「主題」的考題。透過在核心說法Have you heard後面出現的「公司剛剛推出一個新的網站」，可以知道（C）為答案。　　　　　　　　　　　　　　答案 (C)

詞彙 upcoming meeting 即將來臨的會議 revise 修訂 safety regulation 安全規定

11.

根據這個男人的談話，這家公司的員工現在能做什麼？
（A）得到免費的配送
（B）離開辦公室可以確認電子郵件
（C）申請旅遊小冊子
（D）線上登錄活動

解說 這是詢問「具體事項的考題」。「員工能做」為核心詞彙，而在對話中與此有關的，就是在中間出現的「能讓員工更新資料，即使員工離開辦公室」，即是指在辦公室以外的地方也能看電子郵件。　　答案 (B)

詞彙 free delivery 免費配送 apply for 申請… sign up for 登錄…

12.

這個女人說她星期一將會做什麼？
（A）離開去開會
（B）線上訂備品
（C）為預算得到許可
（D）升級網站

解說 這裡的Monday，在對話裡沒有經過paraphrasing，所以是核心詞彙。因此Monday前後就有答案的線索。將「我週一有個會議要去」變化而表達的（A）為答案。　　　　　　　　　　　　　　答案 (A)

詞彙 depart 出發 order 下訂單 supply 備品；材料 approval 同意 budget 預算

Quiz

| 1. (B) | 2. (B) | 3. (B) | 4. (A) |

Q1 美M 美W

M : Hi, Christina. I just heard the assembly line was down at the Kings Bread factory. Will the shipment of the cakes for the Komparin Corporation be affected?

W : No, fortunately it won't. **I've got** an e-mail **this morning** saying that the order was sent yesterday.

男：克莉絲汀娜，您好。我剛聽說金氏麵包工廠的裝配線停了。要給康沛瑞公司的蛋糕配送會受影響嗎？

女：不，很幸運不會。我今天上午收到一封電子郵件說那張訂單是昨天就被送出了。

這個女人今天早上收到了什麼？
（A）一份訂單
（B）一封電子郵件

解說 此為詢問及物動詞（receive）的受詞為何的簡短選項類的考題。在對話內容與考題裡常以相同的this morning說法出現，在此前後會出現答案；但receive常被換句話說變成get。因此，在I've got之後、this morning之前聽到的an e-mail為答案的線索。（B）為答案。　　　　　　答案 (B)

詞彙 **assembly line** 裝配線　**factory** 工廠　**affect** 影響
fortunately 幸運地　**get** 收到

Q2 英M 澳W

M : Griffin, It's 4:10 p.m. now, and I think I heard you have to leave at 4 p.m. for an appointment today.

W : You're right. **I'm having my eyes examined at 4:30 p.m.**, but I have to finalize this report.

男：格里芬。現在是下午四點十分，我想我有聽說你在今天下午四點鐘有約會要離開。

女：你說得對。我在下午三十分要檢查我的眼睛，但我必須要做完這份報告。

這個女人的預約是什麼時候？
（A）在下午四點鐘
（B）在下午四點三十分

解說 透過核心詞彙appointment，可以知道是詢問「時間點」的簡短選項類的考題。在與appointment有相關

的I'm having my eyes examined前後聽到的到時間點at 4:30 p.m.，所以（B）為答案。　　　　　答案 (B)

詞彙 **leave** 離開　**appointment** 約會　**examine** 做檢查
finalize 使…完成

Q3 澳W 英M

W : Excuse me. Is there a grocery store around here? I'd like to buy some fresh fruit for dinner this evening.

M : There's one on Madison Street, just across the Central Bank. But **you'll have to hurry because** everything will be sold out quickly in the evening.

女：打擾一下。這附近有雜貨店嗎？為了今天晚餐，我想買點新鮮的水果。

男：在麥迪遜街上有一家，就在中央銀行的對面。但你必須快點，因為到了晚上所有東西都將很快被搶購一空。

為什麼這個女人應該要快點？
（A）有某個人正在等她。
（B）水果將要缺貨了。

解說 這是詢問「理由」的「句子選項類的考題」，其核心詞彙為hurry。將hurry後面表達理由的「所有東西都將很快被搶購一空」做變化來表達的（B）為答案。
　　　　　　　　　　　　　　　　　　答案 (B)

詞彙 **grocery store** 雜貨店　**around here** 附近
sold out 賣完　**business** 公司　**out of stock** 缺貨

Q4 美M 美W

M : Silvia, will the company pay the travel expenses this time?

W : They'll pay for the **registration fee**, but as for the airfare, I should cover it myself this time although the company paid for the plane tickets for the conference in January.

男：蘇維亞，這次公司將會支付出差費嗎？

女：他們將會支付報名費，但是就機票費而言，這次我應該自己付的，雖然公司為一月份的會議支付過機票費。

有關於報名費用的事這個女人說了什麼？
（A）它將由公司支付。
（B）到一月截止。

解說 出現say about，所以是詢問「意見」的「句子選項類的考題」。將registration fee前面的意見「他們（公司）將會支付」以被動語態句子作變化的（A）為答案。
　　　　　　　　　　　　　　　　　　答案 (A)

詞彙 **travel expense** 出差費　**pay for** 為…付費
registration fee 報名費　**airfare** 機票費
cover （費用上）負擔

1 (A)	2 (B)	3 (B)	4 (A)
5 (B)	6 (B)	7 (A)	8 (B)
9 (C)	10 (A)	11 (C)	12 (A)
13 (C)	14 (C)		

1. 美W 英M

1 找出核心詞彙	presentation
2 了解類型	詢問意見的考題
3 看選項	完成得很好，或送去給公司總裁

W：Tom! You gave an excellent **presentation** this morning! I wonder if you could give your input to Morris for his report.

M：Well, I wish. But I'm afraid I have to finish this feasibility analysis for the upcoming project by tomorrow.

女：湯姆！今天上午你的報告太棒了！我想問你能否對莫里斯的報告給些你的意見。

男：嗯，我希望可以。但是我恐怕得為了即將到來的企劃案，在明天之前完成這份可行性分析。

有關於報告的事，這個女人說了什麼？
（A）它相當好。
（B）它被送去給公司總裁。

解說 有say about，所以是詢問「意見」的「簡短選項類的考題」。透過在presentation附近的意見「報告太棒了」，可以知道（A）為答案。 答案 (A)

詞彙 give a presentation 做報告 input 意見；協助 feasibility analysis 可行性分析 upcoming 即將到來的

2. 澳W 英M

1 找出核心詞彙	How, get, destination
2 了解類型	詢問方法（交通方式）的考題
3 看選項	搭計程車或走路

W：I have a job interview at the GW Corporation in half an hour. I'm not sure if I have time to walk there or maybe I should take a taxi.

M：It's just a 5-minute walk. Go along this street and turn right then you **get to** the building. The company's really not that far.

女：我半小時之後在GW公司有現場面試。我不確定我有沒有時間走到那兒，還是我也許應該搭計程車。

男：它只要走五分鐘。沿著這條街走然後右轉，那樣你就到那棟樓了。那家公司真的不太遠。

這個女人很有可能將如何到她的目的地？
（A）搭計程車
（B）走路

解說 how後面聽到get與destination，就可以知道為詢問「交通方式」的「簡短選項類考題」。對於該女性的疑問「有沒有時間走到那兒，還是應該搭計程車」，該男性回答「只要走五分鐘」，所以（B）為答案。 答案 (B)

詞彙 job interview 求職面試 half an hour 三十分鐘 take a taxi 搭計程車 get to 到達某處

3. 美M 美W

1 找出核心詞彙	leave work
2 了解類型	詢問時間點的考題
3 看選項	晚上六點或晚上七點

M：Jessica, has the shipment of projectors arrived yet? We have to place them in the meeting room before we leave work.

W：Well, the shipping company said it should be here by 6 p.m. so I think we can finish all the preparation work by 7 p.m. Then we can **call it a day**.

男：傑西卡，投影機的貨運到了嗎？我們得在下班前把它們置放在會議室呢。

女：嗯，貨運公司說它應該在下午六點半之前會到這裡，所以我想我們可以在晚上七點之前完成所有準備工作。然後我們就能下班。

說話者很有可能將在什麼時候下班？
（A）在晚上六點鐘
（B）在晚上七點鐘

解說 這是詢問「時間點」的「簡短選項類考題」。在 leave（或是意思相同call it a day）附近聽的到「我想我們可以在晚上七點之前完成所有準備工作」，所以可以知道（B）為答案。六點鐘是貨運來的時間，這是陷阱。 答案 (B)

詞彙 place 置放 leave work 下班 shipping company 貨運公司 preparation work 準備工作 call it a day 下班

4. 英M 美W

1 找出核心詞彙	Mario Ortiz
2 了解類型	詢問具體人物的考題
3 看選項	設計師或製造商

M : The sales figures on our mobile phone have been rising since last quarter. I think It's because <u>the new GW phone incorporated **Mario Ortiz's** new design.</u>

W : It's been a long time since we manufactured a phone that has had such a tremendous impact.

男：我們行動電話的銷售數據從上一季起一直上升。我認為這是由於新的GW電話結合了馬力歐‧奧蒂斯的新設計。

女：我們很久以來沒有生產過有這麼巨大影響力的行動電話了。

馬力歐‧奧蒂斯是什麼人？
（A）一位設計師
（B）一位製造商

解說 這是詢問「具體人物」的「簡短選項類考題」。Mario Ortiz為核心詞彙。在Mario Ortiz附近聽到「結合了馬力歐‧奧蒂斯的新設計」，所以可以知道Mario Ortiz為設計師。　　　　　　　　　答案 (A)

詞彙 sales figure 銷售數據　mobile phone 行動電話　rise 上升　incorporate 和…結合　manufacture 製造　tremendous 巨大的　impact 影響

5. 美M 澳W

1 找出核心詞彙	Saturday
2 了解類型	詢問具體地點的考題
3 看選項	歌劇院或美術館

M : Mary, <u>where are you planning on taking the overseas clients</u> on **Saturday**? <u>The art museum or the opera hall is convenient.</u>

W : I'd like to take them to the art museum. They have an exhibit right now featuring work from several well-known contemporary artists.

男：瑪麗，你打算週六帶海外客戶去哪裡？美術館或歌劇院都很方便。

女：我想帶他們去美術館。他們正有一場展出一些知名當代藝術家的作品的展覽。

這個女人計畫星期六將要去什麼地方？
（A）去歌劇院
（B）去美術館

解說 這是詢問「具體地點」的「簡短選項類考題」。像Saturday這樣具體時間點為很好的線索，且其附近的句子也有答案的線索。對於「週六將帶海外客戶去哪裡？」，以「想帶他們去美術館」回答，所以（B）為答案。　　　　　　　　　答案 (B)

詞彙 take 帶…去某處　overseas client 海外客戶　art museum 美術館　right now 正在　A feature B 以B為特色的A　well-known 有名的　contemporary artist 當代藝術家

6. 美W 英M

1 找出核心詞彙	late
2 了解類型	詢問理由的考題
3 看選項	弄錯時間表或航班耽誤

W : Excuse me. Do you know when the afternoon session for Newton Corporation begins? **I came late because** <u>my flight was delayed.</u>

M : No, I don't, but you can find a schedule of all the sessions at the information desk in the conference room.

女：抱歉，你知道牛頓公司下午的會議什麼時候開始嗎？因為我的班機被延誤，所以我遲到了。

男：不，我不知道，但你可以在會議室的諮詢台找到所有的會議日程。

為什麼這個女人遲到？
（A）她弄錯時間表了。
（B）她的航班耽誤了。

解說 這是詢問「理由」的「句子選項類考題」。在late（或與late意思相同的句子）附近有線索。聽到「我的班機被延誤」，所以（B）為答案。　　　　答案 (B)

詞彙 session 會議　be delayed 被延誤　information desk 諮詢台　conference room 會議室

7. 美M 美W

1 找出核心詞彙	must be completed
2 了解類型	詢問行為對象的考題
3 看選項	培訓課程或辦公室整修

M : I heard the company has hired several new programmers to work on our new project. When will they start?

W : They're not actually working at our office yet. **They have to finish** <u>their training session first.</u> Their first day will be Monday.

男：我聽說我們公司為了處理新的企劃雇用了一些新程式設計人員。他們什麼時候會開始？

女：他們還沒有實際在我們辦公室工作。他們要先完成他們的培訓課程。他們第一天上班將是在星期一。

根據這個女人的談話，什麼必須先完成？

（A）培訓課程

（B）辦公室整修

解說 這是詢問「行為的對象」的「簡短選項類考題」。核心詞彙「必須被完成」變成「他們要先完成」，所以要被完成的就是培訓課程。（A）為答案。

答案 (A)

詞彙 programmer 程式設計師 work on 在⋯工作 finish 完成 training session 培訓課程 first day 第一天

8. 美W 英M

1 找出核心詞彙	last week
2 了解類型	詢問行為的考題
3 看選項	寄很大的包裹或訂購軟體

W : Hi, I ordered the computer software package from your company **last Monday**. And it hasn't arrived yet. Could you look up my order, please?

M : Sure. What's the name on the order, and when did you place it?

女：你好。上星期一我從你們公司訂了一套電腦軟體。它還沒有送到。你能查一下我的訂單嗎？

男：當然，訂單上的姓名是什麼，還有你什麼時候下的訂單？

這個女人說她上個星期做了什麼？

（A）寄了一大包包裹

（B）訂購了軟體

解說 這是詢問「行為」的「句子選項類考題」。核心詞彙last week在對話裡通常會改變成其他說法，如對話中出現的last Monday。將在last Monday附近的「訂了一套電腦軟體」簡化後來表達的（B）為答案。 答案 (B)

詞彙 order 下訂單 look up 查閱 place an order 下訂單

問題9～10請參考以下對話。 美W 美M

1 找出核心詞彙	woman surprised, wish to purchase
2 了解類型	詢問理由、數量的考題
3 看選項	行程變化，沒有座位，沒有直航服務 一，二，六
4 預測對話內容	訝異沒有直航班機，因此購買需轉機的機票

W : Excuse me, when's the next flight to Osaka?

M : Unfortunately, there is no direct flight to Osaka. You need to stop over in Tokyo. Then there is a connecting flight to Osaka. The next flight to Tokyo departs at 6 p.m.

W : ⁹No direct flight to Osaka? I'm surprised! I thought it would be a direct trip. Well, okay then, ¹⁰please give me a single ticket to Tokyo.

女：打擾一下，下一個前往大阪的航班是什麼時候呢？

男：很不巧的，沒有直飛到大阪的航班。你需要在東京停留。會有轉機航班到大阪。下一班到東京的班機在下午六點出發。

女：沒有直飛到大阪的班機？我真是驚訝！我以為這會是直飛的行程。嗯，好的，那麼請給我一張到東京的機票。

詞彙 direct flight 直飛航班 stop over 在中途停留 connecting flight 轉機航班

9.

為什麼這個女人感到驚訝？

（A）行程改變了。

（B）沒有座位了。

（C）沒有直航服務。

解說 這是詢問「理由」的「句子選項類考題」。將「我真是驚訝」附近的理由「以為這會是直飛的行程」做變化來表達的（C）為答案。 答案 (C)

詞彙 schedule change 行程變更 left 留下 direct service 直航服務

10.

這個女人希望買多少張票？

（A）一張

（B）兩張

（C）六張

解說 這是詢問「數量」的「簡短選項類考題」。核心詞彙「希望買」（或與此相同意思的句子）附近出現「給我一張單程票」，所以（A）為答案。 答案 (A)

詞彙 purchase 購買

問題11～12請參考以下對話。英M 澳W

1 找出核心詞彙	currently working on, man thank
2 了解類型	詢問行為的對象、理由的考題
3 看選項	併購，發表，建設企劃 推薦，延長期限，建議
4 預測對話內容	老闆正在進行建築個案當中，因為將他推薦給老闆而表達感謝。

M : Christina, the assignment you gave me is nearly complete. I'm in the process of taking a final look at it.

W : Oh, the top priority has changed. [11]The president just called. He is working on a construction project for a new client. [12]He needs someone with extensive knowledge about construction regulations, so I recommended you.

M : [12]Thanks. That sounds like a great opportunity for me.

男：克莉絲汀娜，你給我的任務已快完成了。我正在做最後瀏覽。
女：噢，首要事項有變化了。總裁剛剛打過電話。他為一位新客戶正在進行一項建設企劃。他需要在建設法規上有廣泛知識的人，所以我推薦了你。
男：謝了。對我來說，這聽起來像是個相當好的機會。

詞彙 assignment 任務 nearly complete 接近完成 be in the process of 在…的過程 take a look at 瀏覽 top priority 首要事項 work on 在…做事 construction project 建設企劃 extensive knowledge 廣泛的知識 regulation 法規 recommend 推薦 opportunity 機會

11.
這個總裁正在進行什麼事？
（A）一項商業併購
（B）一場會議的發表
（C）一項建設企劃

解說 這是詢問「行為的對象」的「簡短選項類考題」。核心詞彙「正在進行當中」附近出現「總裁剛剛打過電話、他正在進行一項建設企劃」，所以將此做變化來表達的（C）為答案。 答案（C）

詞彙 currently 現在 merger 併購 presentation 發表

12.
為什麼這個男人感謝這個女人？
（A）因為向總裁推薦他

（B）因為為他的報告延長期限
（C）因為提供給他一些建議

解說 這是詢問「理由」的「句子選項類考題」。在核心詞彙「感謝」附近出現「所以我推薦了你」，所以將此做變化來表達的（A）為答案。 答案（A）

詞彙 extend 延長 deadline 最後期限 offer 提供 advice 建議

問題13～14請參考以下對話。美M 美W

1 找出核心詞彙	waiting for, waiting
2 了解類型	詢問具體人物、時間長短的考題
3 看選項	客戶，經理，修理工 一小時，二小時，三小時
4 預測對話內容	等修理工等了三小時

M : Isn't the fax machine still working yet?

W : No, it isn't. [13, 14]We've been waiting for it to be fixed for three hours. But I called the maintenance department again, and they can take a look at it sometime this afternoon.

M : This afternoon? I am expecting very important document to be faxed this morning. Is there another machine I can use?

男：傳真機仍然還不能用嗎？
女：不，它不能。我們一直在等它修好等了三個小時。但是我有再打電話給維修部，他們可以在今天下午某個時間來看看。
男：今天下午？我正預期一份非常重要的文件今天早上要傳真過來。有另一台機器可以讓我使用嗎？

詞彙 fax machine 傳真機 wait for 等待… maintenance department 維修部門 take a look at 看一下 important 重要 document 文件；資料

13.
這些工作者在等什麼人？
（A）一位商業客戶
（B）一位辦公室經裡
（C）一位修理工

解說 這是詢問「具體人物」的「簡短選項類考題」。Waiting for為核心詞彙，透過在該核心詞彙附近出現的「等它被修好、打電話給維修部」等話語，可以猜測正在等「修理工」。 答案（C）

詞彙 business client 商業客戶 manager 經理 repairperson 修理工

14.

他們等了多長的時間？
（A）一小時
（B）兩小時
（C）三小時

解說 這是詢問「時間長短」的「簡短選項類考題」。其核心詞彙也是waiting，透過其後面出現的three hours，就可以知道答案。　　　答案（C）

詞彙 wait 等待

STEP 02　考題實戰練習

1. (C)　2. (A)　3. (D)　4. (D)　5. (C)　6. (A)
7. (D)　8. (D)　9. (D)　10. (A)　11. (D)　12. (B)

問題1～3請參考以下對話 [美W] [英M]

W：Good morning. Have you talked with Marsha about arranging for the sales meeting on Tuesday?

M：She just called. [1,2]The quarterly sales report expected to arrive yesterday came in this morning. She needs to analyze all the data, so she asked if we could reschedule the meeting for Wednesday.

W：Well, [2]I'm leaving for a business trip on that day, but I can make myself available for an early morning meeting. Would you call her and reschedule the meeting?

M：Sure. [3]I'll reach her as soon as possible.

女：早安，你有和瑪莎談到關於在星期二安排銷售會議嗎？
男：她剛剛打電話來。原本預計昨天要到的季度銷售報告，在今天早上才來。她需要分析所有的數據，所以她要求我們是否能重新安排會議在星期三。
女：嗯，那天我要出差，但我能儘量參加晨間會議。你可以打電話聯繫她，並重新安排會議嗎？
男：當然，我會盡快聯繫她。

詞彙 talk with 和…談話　arrange for 安排…
quarterly sales report 季度銷售報告　come in 到達
analyze 分析　leave 離開　business trip 出差　reach 聯絡
as soon as possible 儘快

1.

為什麼瑪莎要求將會議延後？
（A）她正在等一位客戶。
（B）她出差了。
（C）某個訊息被延誤了。
（D）沒有會議室可以提供。

解說 這是詢問「理由」的「句子選項類考題」。核心詞彙「將會議延後」在對話中是以「是否能重新安排會議在星期三」來表達，且其前面出現「她需要分析所有的數據，所以她要求」，所以將此做變化來表達的（C）為答案。　　　答案（C）

詞彙 wait for 等待…　client 客戶　be delayed 被延誤
available 能夠使用

2.

這個會議很有可能將在什麼時候被舉辦？
（A）在星期三上午
（B）在星期三下午
（C）在星期四上午
（D）在星期四下午

解說 這是詢問「時間點」的「簡短選項類考題」。該男性說「是否能重新安排會議在星期三」，接著該女性說「我能儘量參加晨間會議」，所以可以猜測「星期三上午」將開會。　　　答案（A）

詞彙 be held 被舉辦

3.

這個男人接下來很有可能會做什麼？
（A）安排旅行時間表
（B）準備銷售報告
（C）尋找研究資料
（D）想要和瑪莎聯絡

解說 這是「下一個行程」的考題。do next為核心詞彙，將核心說法I'll後面聽到的「聯繫到她」做變化來表達的（D）為答案。　　　答案（D）

詞彙 travel schedule 旅行時間表　prepare 準備　look for 尋找　research data 數據研究資料　try to 嘗試做…　contact 聯絡

問題4～6請參考以下對話 [澳W] [美M]

W：Becker, [4]how's the marketing manager search going? Did you find anyone who is a good fit?

M：No. The personnel department narrowed down the applications to two, but neither seems to be qualified. We're targeting young consumers in the clothing market. [5]We need someone who has extensive experience in the related field.

W：I have a friend who is really qualified for the job. He's been with a clothing company for decades. [6]Why don't you contact him to see if he's interested?

女：貝克，尋求行銷經理的事情進行得如何？你有找到任何不錯適合的人嗎？

男：沒有。人事部門縮小應徵者範圍到兩位，但似乎沒有一個具有資格。我們的目標是服裝市場的年輕消費者，我們需要一位在相關領域有豐富經驗的人。

女：我有一個朋友相當有資格來做這個工作。他在一家服裝公司幾十年了。你何不聯絡他，看看他有沒有興趣？

詞彙 marketing manager 行銷經理　search 尋找 personnel department 人事部門　narrow down 縮小　application 申請　qualified 合格　target 目標 young consumer 年輕消費者　experience 經驗 related field 相關領域　decade 十年　contact 聯絡

4.

哪一個部門需要一位新的經理？
（A）人事
（B）客戶服務
（C）會計
（D）行銷

解說 這是詢問對象為什麼的「簡短選項類考題」。「需要一位新的經理」為核心詞彙。透過「尋求行銷經理的事情進行得如何」，可以猜測新的經理就是行銷部門的經理。　　　　　　　　　　　答案 (D)

詞彙 personnel 人事　customer service 客戶服務 accounting 會計　marketing 行銷

5.

這個男人提到什麼資格條件？
（A）願意出差
（B）強力的推薦
（C）相關的經驗
（D）大學學位

解說 這是詢問對象為什麼的「簡短選項類考題」。「資格條件」為核心詞彙，在後面出現的「我們需要…的人」與核心詞彙意思相同，因此將「一位在相關領域有豐富經驗」做變化來表達的（C）為答案。　答案 (C)

詞彙 qualification 資格條件　mention 提及… willingness 願意　reference 推薦　relevant 有關的 university degree 大學學位

6.

這個女人建議了什麼？
（A）聯絡可能的候選人
（B）調到另一個分公司
（C）在網路上登廣告
（D）重新安排一些面試的時間

解說 透過woman recommend，可以知道是「詢問建議事項的考題」。由核心說法why don't you後面出現的「聯絡他看看他有沒有興趣」，可以知道將此做變化來表達的（A）為答案。　　　　　　　　　　答案 (A)

詞彙 possible 可能性　candidate 候選人 transfer to 轉換到…　place an advertisement 登廣告

reschedule 重新安排日程

問題7～9請參考以下對話。 美 W 英 M

W：Hi, Mr. Writer. **7**I'm leaving my job here to move to New York. That's why I asked to meet with you.

M：Oh, we are sorry to lose you. **8**Your idea on our clothing design was very creative and garnered good feedback. Our market share has increased thanks to your effort.

W：Thank you. I've loved working with you. **8, 9**It's been a great honor to be a part of such a highly recognized clothing firm, but the design school I dreamed of is in the New York area, and I'd like to take this opportunity to expand my knowledge.

女：瑞特先生您好。我即將離開這裡的工作前往紐約。這是我要求和您見面的原因。

男：噢，我們很遺憾失去你。你的想法對我們的服裝設計來說很有創意，引起很好的回饋。我們的市場占有率已經增加，歸功於你的努力。

女：謝謝你，我很喜歡和您一起工作。能成為高名聲的服裝公司的一員，這是很大的榮耀，但我夢想進入的設計學校在紐約，我想把握這個機會擴展我的學識。

詞彙 leave a job 離職　move 移動　meet with 與…見面　lose 失去　creative 創意　garner 回饋　market share 市場佔有率　effort 努力　work with 與…一起工作　honor 光榮　highly recognized 高名聲　design school 設計學校　dream of 夢想…　take an opportunity 把握機會 knowledge 知識

7.

為什麼這個女人想和這個男人談話？
（A）討論客戶滿意度
（B）要求調任
（C）要求一些建議
（D）提出她的辭呈

解說 這是詢問「理由」的「句子選項類考題」。「為什麼和這個男人談話」，在對話裡變成「要求和您見面的原因」，在其前後出現了「離開這裡的工作前往紐約」，所以將此做變化來表達的（D）為答案。
答案 (D)

詞彙 talk to 和…談話　discuss 討論　customer satisfaction 顧客滿意度　transfer 轉換　ask for 要求 recommendation 建議　resignation 辭呈

8.

說話者很有可能在哪裡工作？
（A）在旅行社
（B）在廣告公司

(C) 在設計學校
(D) 在服裝公司

解說 透過「你的想法對我們的服裝設計來說很有創意，引起很好的回饋」、「能成為高名聲的服裝公司的一員」，可以知道在「服裝公司」工作。 答案 (D)

詞彙 travel agency 旅行社 advertising firm 廣告公司

9.

有關於紐約這個女人說了什麼？
(A) 她的家族住在那裡。
(B) 有很多觀光名勝。
(C) 有很多服裝店。
(D) 有她想去的學校。

解說 出現 say about，所以是詢問「意見」的「簡短選項類考題」。透過在 New York 前後的線索「我夢想進入的學校在紐約」、「我想把握這個機會擴展我的學識」，可以知道答案為（D）。 答案 (D)

詞彙 tourist attraction 觀光名勝

問題10～12請參考以下對話和圖表。美 M 英 W

Yokoi Restaurant
Lunch Specials

1. Chicken Teriyaki w / Rice $17
2. Vegetable Yakisoba $15
3. Tempura w / Rice $16
4. [11]California Roll $18

M : [10]Miss, sorry to have you wait for so long. We are a little short-handed today.

W : That's OK. I don't mind. [12]Everyone knows that the dishes at Yokoi Restaurant are well worth waiting for. So, what do you recommend for today?

M : Well, here's a list of the chef's lunch special. The Chicken Teriyaki is very nice and tender. And it is quite popular, too.

W : Mmm…, sounds good, but I feel like eating something cold… [11]I think I'll try number 4. And give me a glass of cola with that.

橫井餐廳
中午特餐

1. 照燒雞肉附白飯 $17
2. 蔬菜炒麵 $15
3. 天婦羅附白飯 $16
4. 加州卷 $18

男：小姐，不好意思讓您久等。我們今天有點人手不夠。

女：沒關係。我不介意。大家都知道橫井餐廳的菜餚很值得等待。那麼，你今天推薦什麼呢？

男：嗯，這裡是主廚的中午特餐可供選擇的項目。照燒雞肉很不錯也很嫩。而且也很受歡迎喔！

女：嗯……聽起來蠻好的，不過我想吃點涼菜，我看我試試4號餐好了。也給我來杯可樂。

詞彙 wait 等待 short-handed 人手不足 mind 介意 dish 菜餚 restaurant 餐廳 worth 值得的 recommend 推薦 a list of 一列 chef 主廚 special 特別 chicken 雞肉 teriyaki 蘸糖色烤、照燒（一道日式料理）tender 嫩 popular 受歡迎的 feel like 想要 cold 冰涼的；寒冷的 glass 玻璃杯

10.

是什麼事情造成了拖延？
(A) 餐廳人手不足。
(B) 主廚上班遲到。
(C) 侍者在聊天。
(D) 服務生罷工。

解說 這是詢問「原因、理由」的「簡短選項類考題」。核心語是「造成拖延」，男士第一句話說的「我們今天有點人手不夠」與選項（A）是同義表達。 答案 (A)

詞彙 cause 造成 delay 延遲 understaffed 人員不足 late for work 上班遲到 server 侍者 chat 聊天 waiter 服務生 on strike 罷工

11.

請看此圖，女士點了哪一道菜？
(A) 照燒雞肉附白飯
(B) 蔬菜炒麵
(C) 天婦羅附白飯
(D) 加州卷

解說 這是詢問「選項為何」的「簡短選項類考題」。女士說想要試試4號餐，看表格中4號餐是「加州卷」，所以答案是（D）。 答案 (D)

詞彙 rice 米飯 vegetable 蔬菜 yakisoba 日式炒麵 tempura 天婦羅 California roll 加州卷

12.

女士對於餐廳有何暗示？
(A) 服務生總是很慢。
(B) 餐廳風評不錯。
(C) 空調很冷。
(D) 食物不太好吃。

解說 這是詢問「暗示、引申含意」的「簡短選項類考題」。核心語是 imply about。女士說「大家都知道橫井餐廳的菜餚很值得等待」做變化來表達的（B）為答案。 答案 (B)

詞彙 imply 暗示 slow 慢的 reputation 名聲；風評 air conditioning 冷氣冷調 food 食物

3

Quiz |

1. (B)　　　2. (B)　　　3. (A)　　　4. (A)

Q1 美W 英M

W : Hi, Peter. Have you booked your flight for the conference in **New York** yet? Do you prefer to take the 9 o'clock flight on Wednesday evening or the 11 o'clock flight on Thursday morning?

M : Wednesday's flight would be better. That way, we can take a short break before the conference begins on Friday morning.

女：您好，彼得。您已經訂好到紐約開會的班機了嗎？您想要星期三晚上九點的航班還是星期四早上十一點的航班？

男：週三的航班比較好。這樣我們可以在週五上午會議開始前短暫休息一下。

說話者為什麼要去紐約？
（A）參觀名勝
（B）參加會議

解說 看到考題裡的「去紐約」，可以預測以「業餘活動」或「通勤／交通／搜尋」為主體。透過該女性說的「到紐約開會」，可以知道答案為「參加會議」。
答案 (B)

詞彙 book 預約　prefer 較願意…　take a break 暫歇一下　attraction 觀光名勝　attend 參加

Q2 澳W 美M

W : Hi, Richard. Are you ready for the presentation this afternoon?

M : Not quite. There is a **problem**. I've finished and saved the presentation files in my laptop. I tried to connect it with the projector, but the projector is not working.

女：嗨，理查。今天下午的報告你準備好了嗎？

男：還沒有。有點狀況。我完成了之後把報告文件儲存在我的筆記型電腦裡面了。我試著把它連接到投影機，但是投影機無法運作。

這個男人提到什麼問題？
（A）有些工作者很早離開了。
（B）投影機故障了。

解說 看到考題裡的problem，可以預測以「故障／修理／維修」為主體。透過在problem後面出現的「投影機無法運作」，可以知道將此做變化來表達的（B）為答案。
答案 (B)

詞彙 not quite 尚未完成　laptop 筆記型電腦　connect 連接　work 運作　out of order 故障

Q3 英M 美M

M1 : Thanks for meeting with me, Mr. Lee. As you can see in last year's expense report, we overspent last year. **I want to talk about** some ways to cut back on costs next year.

M2 : Well, to stay within the budget, I think we need to limit our expenses on office supplies.

男1：李先生，謝謝您和我見面。如您在去年的費用報告上所見，去年我們超支了。我想談談一些來削減明年的成本的方法。

男2：嗯，為了保持在預算範圍內，我認為我們需要限制辦公用品上的支出。

這場會議的目的是什麼？
（A）如何減少花費
（B）如何擬訂預算

解說 藉由考題裡面的「會議的目的」與選項，可以預測其主題為「會議內容」。由「我想談談一些來削減明年的成本的方法」能判斷（A）為答案。
答案 (A)

詞彙 expense 費用　cut back on 削減…
stay 保持　budget 預算　limit 限制　office supply 辦公用品　reduce 減少　draw up 降低

Q4 美M 澳W

M : Have you heard that **Ms. Sato** has been promoted to vice president of sales?

W : Yes, and I heard she is hiring more salespeople to expand into the overseas market.

男：妳有聽說佐藤女士晉升為銷售副總了嗎？

女：是的，而且我聽說她正雇用更多銷售人員以拓展海外市場。

關於佐藤女士說到了什麼？
（A）她晉升了。
（B）她最近被雇用。

解說 藉由選項可以預測以「雇用／升遷／人事變動」為主體。Ms. Sato或she附近會出現答案，而在此就出現了「晉升」。
答案 (A)

詞彙 promote 晉升；升遷　vice president 副總
雇用　expand into 拓展；擴張　overseas market 海外市場

1 (A)	2 (B)	3 (A)	4 (B)
5 (A)	6 (A)	7 (B)	8 (A)
9 (B)	10 (B)	11 (C)	12 (B)
13 (C)	14 (B)		

1. 美W 美M

1 找出核心詞彙	man want
2 了解類型	訂票／開票或訂貨／配送
3 看選項	訂購來回票或旅行書

W : Thank you for calling Fantasia Travel Service. How may I help you?

M : Hello, this is Danny Kim from CS Corporation. I'm planning to go on a business trip this weekend. **I'd like to** take a flight leaving for New York tomorrow night and return on Sunday morning.

女：感謝您致電想曲遊服務中心。我能給您什麼幫助嗎？
男：你好，我是CS公司的丹尼‧金。我計畫這週末要出差。我想搭明天晚上去紐約的航班，並在週日上午回來。

這個男人想要做什麼？
（A）訂購來回票
（B）訂購一本旅行書

解說 透過選項可以預測以「訂票／開票」或「訂貨／配送」為主體。與旅行社職員通話的男性說「我想搭明天晚上去紐約的航班」，所以可以猜到他想訂購飛機票。　　　　　　　　　　　　答案 (A)

詞彙 business trip 出差　leave for 離開並去某地　return 返回　round trip ticket 來回票　order 下訂單

2. 英M 澳W

1 找出核心詞彙	man late to work
2 了解類型	通勤／交通／搜尋
3 看選項	車禍或道路封閉

M : I can't believe that I spent 3 hours on the way to work today. I was caught in traffic on Highway 238.

W : Wow, what a long time! I heard that there was a car accident and the highway was temporarily blocked. You should have taken an alternate road to be here on time.

男：我不敢相信，我今天在路上花了三個小時才到公司。我在238號高速公路上塞車。
女：哇，這麼久！我聽說有車禍，道路暫時封鎖。你應該開替代道路就能準時了。

為什麼這個男人上班遲到？
（A）他遇到車禍。
（B）道路被封閉了。

解說 藉由選項可以猜測以「通勤／交通／搜尋」為主體。有事故所以道路封閉為原因。但在此並沒有暗示該男性發生車禍。　　　　　　　　　　答案 (B)

詞彙 spend 花費　work 上班　accident 事故 temporarily 暫時地　blocked 封鎖的 take an alternate road 駕駛替代道路　closed 封閉的

3. 美M 澳W

1 找出核心詞彙	their products
2 了解類型	訂貨／配送
3 看選項	可在線上訂購或價錢合理

M : We're going to be so busy today. We got a batch of **orders** last night from our website.

W : It's not that surprising. Since the holiday is coming, I expect many people will be ordering cakes and chocolates before or during the holiday.

男：我們今天將會很忙。我們的網站昨晚收到了一批訂單。
女：這並不令人驚訝。因為假期即將來臨，我預計很多人會在節日前或這期間訂蛋糕和巧克力。

說話者對他們的產品做了什麼建議？
（A）可以在線上被訂購。
（B）價錢很合理。

解說 透過選項可以猜測以「訂貨／配送」為主體。「從我們的網站收到了一批訂單」即是指「可以在線上被訂購」。　　　　　　　　　答案 (A)

詞彙 batch 一批；一次份量　holiday 節日　product 產品 reasonably 合理地　priced 價錢

4. 英M 美W

1 找出核心詞彙	problem
2 了解類型	故障／修理／維修／改善
3 看選項	印得太深或雙面影印

M : Hi, **I'm having trouble** with my X2 photocopier. I can't make double-sided copies by using the special printing features. Can you help me with this?

W : Okay. Have you read the user manual? If not, please consult page 77 of the manual.

男：嗨，我的X2影印機有點問題。我不能使用特殊影印功能來做雙面複印。你能幫助我嗎？

女：好的。你讀過使用手冊了嗎？如果沒有，請參考手冊第七十七頁。

影印機有什麼問題？
（A）印得太深了。
（B）不能雙面影印。

解說 透過考題與選項可以猜測以「故障／修理／維修／改善」為主體。在此，problem變成trouble提供了線索，因此將其後面出現的「我不能做雙面複印」做簡單變化來表達的（B）為答案。　　　答案(B)

詞彙 photocopier 影印機　make a copy 影印　double-sided 雙面的　by -ing 在…的情形下　feature 功能　user manual 使用手冊　consult 參考　copier 影印機　two sides 雙面

5. 美M 美W

1 找出核心詞彙	meeting with the customers
2 了解類型	準備會議／安排時間
3 看選項	今天或明天

M : Ms. Leskey called me yesterday and said her flight back to Boston has been canceled due to the bad weather, and she couldn't get another flight.

W : But **the meeting with our customers** is at 5 p.m. today. We'd better push back the meeting until tomorrow if she doesn't get here on time.

男：雷思琪小姐昨天打電話給我，說由於天候不佳，她回波士頓的航班被取消了，而她無法接上其他航班。

女：但和我們客戶的會議在今天下午五點。如果她不能準時到這兒，我們最好延後會議到明天。

和顧客的會議是在什麼時候？
（A）今天
（B）明天

解說 透過考題可以猜測以「準備會議／安排時間」為主體。與顧客的會議是今天五點鐘，所以today為答案。必須注意不要被「延後會議到明天」誤導了。
　　　答案(A)

詞彙 cancel 取消　bad weather 天候不佳　push back 延後　on time 準時

6. 英M 澳W

1 找出核心詞彙	topic of the seminar
2 了解類型	會議內容
3 看選項	網路銀行或廣告趨勢

M : Hi, Christina. How was the **seminar** yesterday? It was about current trends in online banking, wasn't it?

W : Yes, and it was very good. Guwon, the instructor, was well-organized and covered a lot in two hours.

男：嗨，克里斯汀娜。昨天研討會如何？它是有關於網路銀行目前的趨勢，是嗎？

女：是的，它非常好。講師高文很有條理，並在兩小時內論及很多內容。

這場研討會的主題是什麼？
（A）網路銀行
（B）廣告趨勢

解說 透過考題可以猜測以「會議內容」為主體。這是該男性提及研討會的內容並向該女性確認的狀況。將seminar附近聽到的online banking做變化來表達的（A）為答案。　　　答案(A)

詞彙 current 現今的　trend 趨勢　instructor 講師　well-organized 很有系統　cover 涵蓋

7. 美M 美W

1 找出核心詞彙	going to Hong Kong office
2 了解類型	僱用／升遷／人事變動
3 看選項	拜訪競爭對手的公司或管理

M : Did you hear that Ms. Adler is **moving to the Hong Kong office**? It was so unexpected because she has only been here for two months.

W : Yes, I heard. **She is going to** manage the sales team there.

男：你有聽說阿德勒女士將調到香港辦事處嗎？真是出乎意料，因為她在這裡只待了兩個月。

女：是的，我聽說她要去管理那邊的銷售團隊。

為什麼阿德勒女士將要去香港辦公室？
（A）拜訪競爭對手的公司
（B）管理銷售團隊

解說 透過考題與選項可以猜測以「僱用／升遷／人事變動」為主體。對話裡「她將要去管理那邊的銷售團

隊」，句中的there就是考題所指的Hong Kong office，句中的she就是考題所指的Ms. Adler。因此（B）就是答案。 答案 (B)

詞彙 manage 管理 visit 拜訪 rival company 競爭對手的公司

8. 英M 美W

1 找出核心詞彙	man want to talk to Ms. Sato
2 了解類型	薪水／費用
3 看選項	員工福利或加薪

M : Good morning, my name is James Keenan. I'm here to **meet with Ms. Sato to talk about my employee benefits.**

W : Ms. Sato is in the meeting right now. But, here is some information on health and other benefits to read while you are waiting.

男：早安，我的名字是詹姆斯·基南。我來這兒和佐藤女士見面，討論我的員工福利。

女：佐藤女士現在正在開會。不過這裡有一些關於健康和其他福利的資訊，在等待的時候可以看看。

為什麼這個男人想要和佐藤女士說話？
（A）討論他的員工福利
（B）討論加薪

解說 透過考題與選項可以猜測以「薪水／費用」為主體。透過出現於開頭部分自我介紹後面的話語，可以知道是要來談「員工福利」的。 答案 (A)

詞彙 benefit 福利 right now 現在 discuss 討論 pay raise 加薪

問題9～10請參考以下對話 美M 澳W

1 找出核心詞彙	woman, man want
2 了解類型	詢問說話者、行為的簡短選項類考題
3 看選項	旅行社職員，售票員，保全人員
	看電影，看表演，規劃旅行
4 預測對話內容	男人想買表演入場券，和賣票的人對話

M : Hello, <u>9, 10 I'd like two tickets for Thursday night's theater performance.</u>

W : <u>9 I'm afraid all of the tickets are sold out for that performance.</u> Would you like me to check if there are some tickets for next week?

W : Yes, I'd appreciate that. Do you have tickets for next Saturday performance?

男：你好，我想要兩張週四晚上戲場表演的門票。

女：我恐怕那場表演所有的門票都已經賣完了。妳希望我幫妳看看下星期是否有票呢？

男：是的，謝謝你。有下週六表演的票嗎？

詞彙 theater 劇場 performance 表演 sold out 賣完了 appreciate 感謝

9.

這個女人很有可能是什麼？
（A）旅行社職員
（B）售票員
（C）保全人員

解說 該男性說「想買門票」，而該女性說「都賣完了」，所以可以知道該女性為售票員。 答案 (B)

詞彙 travel agent 旅行社 salesperson 銷售員 security guard 保全人員

10.

這個男人想要做什麼？
（A）看電影
（B）看表演
（C）做旅行規劃

解說 這是該男性想買表演門票的狀況，所以可以說是他想看表演。 答案 (B)

詞彙 attend 參加 make arrangement 做規劃

問題11～12請參考以下對話。 英M 澳W

1 找出核心詞彙	discussing, immediately
2 了解類型	詢問主題、行為的簡短選項類考題
3 看選項	貨運費，損壞的部分，訂購物的配送，
	傳達訊息，配送商品，尋找遺失的商品
4 預測對話內容	配送上有問題，要求再次寄送

M : Hello, this is Nicholas Reed from AK Machine Parts. I'm returning your message regarding your concern about <u>11 getting your order within this week.</u>

W : <u>Yes, in fact most of our order came in yesterday, but one part is missing. Have you shipped all the parts we ordered?</u>

M : Well, <u>12 the feed pump was temporarily out of stock yesterday. I'll send it immediately, so</u>

you can get it no later than this weekend.

男：你好，我是AK機械零件公司的尼古拉斯·瑞德。我是來回覆您的留言，您在意這週之內能否收到您的貨物。

女：是的，實際上我們貨物大多是在昨天收到的，但有一部份還沒看到。你有運送出我們訂購的所有的零件嗎？

男：嗯，供水幫浦昨天暫時缺貨。我會立即寄送它，所以您最晚可以在週末前收到。

詞彙 return 回覆　in fact 事實上　part 部份　missing 遺失　ship 配送　feed pump 供水幫浦　temporarily 暫時地　out of stock 缺貨　immediately 立即　no later than 不晚於

11.

說話者在討論什麼？
（A）貨運費
（B）損壞的部分
（C）訂購物的配送

解說 透過考題與選項可以猜測以「訂貨／配送」為主體。但是這是只聽前段部分無法找到主題的難題，必須要聽到中間部分才行。由於是零件漏掉所以要求再配送的狀況，因此「訂購物的配送」為其主題。　答案 (C)

詞彙 shipping charge 貨運費　damaged 損壞的　delivery 配送　order 訂購

12.

這個男人說他將立刻要做什麼？
（A）傳達訊息
（B）運送一些商品
（C）找遺失的東西

解說 immediately是常做為線索的副詞。send it裡的send可以改成ship，it是指漏掉的零件，也就是merchandise，所以（B）為答案。　答案 (B)

詞彙 deliver 配送　merchandise 產品　locate 找出某物　missing 遺失

問題13～14請參考以下對話。美W 美M

1 找出核心詞彙	applying for, interviewed
2 了解類型	詢問動作的對象、數量的
	簡短選項類考題
3 看選項	人事經理，研究分析師，編輯助理
	一位，兩位，三
4 預測對話內容	申請編輯助理職位的人總共有兩位

W : Hi, Jeff. **13**I'm here to see if you're having any luck finding me an assistant editor.

M : Well, we've got a lot of applications. **14**I've narrowed it down to two candidates, so I'd

like to set up interviews with them. Do you have time to meet with them next Tuesday?

W : I'm afraid I'm not available at that time. But I'm free Thursday morning.

女：你好，傑夫，我來這裡看看你有沒有運氣幫我找到一個編輯助理。

男：嗯，我們收到了很多申請書。我已經將範圍縮小到兩個候選人了，所以我想和他們安排面試。你下星期二有時間與他們會面嗎？

女：恐怕那個時候我不行。但我星期四上午有空。

詞彙 assistant editor 編輯助理　application 申請者　narrow down 縮窄　candidate 候選人　set up 決定；選定　available 能夠用的

13.

應徵者申請的是什麼職位？
（A）人事經理
（B）研究分析師
（C）編輯助理

解說 透過考題與選項可以猜測以「雇用／升遷／人事變動」為主體。透過「幫我找到一個編輯助理」與「我們收到了很多申請書、想和他們安排面試」，可以知道應徵者是來申請編輯助理職位的。　答案 (C)

詞彙 position 職位　apply for 申請…　personnel 人事部　research analyst 研究分析師

14.

有多少申請者將被面試？
（A）一位
（B）兩位
（C）三位

解說 該男性說「已經將範圍縮小到兩個候選人了，所以我想和他們安排面試」，所以申請者為兩位。
　　　　　　　　　　　　　　　　　答案 (B)

詞彙 applicant 申請者　interview 面試

STEP 02　考題實戰練習

1. (D)　2. (C)　3. (B)　4. (D)　5. (D)　6. (C)
7. (C)　8. (A)　9. (A)　10. (B)　11. (B)　12. (D)

問題1～3請參考以下對話和圖表。美M 美W

	Items	Sets needed
1	Cartridges and toners	5
2	**3**Folders and labels	15
3	Staplers and staples	8
4	Paper and envelopes	10

M : Tracy, can you help to **¹make copies of this document**, please?

W : Oh, I'm afraid I can't have it done right away. **²Our copy machine is out of ink.** I have called to order from the supplier, and they won't make a delivery until this afternoon.

M : If that's the case, did you make a survey of what other office supplies we may need? It would be more efficient to buy them all at once instead of making partial orders separately.

W : I did, but you didn't reply… I thought you are not in need. Well, what do you need to order then?

M : **³Maybe some folders and labels will come in handy. They'll make it easier for me to organize the data on my desk.**

W : All right. No problem. I'll call the supplier and add to the original order.

	品名	需要套數
1	墨水匣及碳粉	5
2	檔案夾及標籤	15
3	釘書機及釘書針	8
4	紙張及信封	10

男：翠西，可以麻煩你可以幫忙影印這份文件嗎？
女：喔，我恐怕沒辦法馬上做喔。我們影印機的墨水匣沒有墨水了。我已經打電話向供應商訂購了，他們今天下午才會送貨。
男：若是這樣的話，你有調查一下我們還需要什麼其他文具嗎？全部一起買會比分批買要有效率。
女：我有，可是你沒回信……我以為你沒有需求呢！那麼，你要訂購些什麼嗎？
男：可能買些檔案夾和標籤會很好用。它們會讓我方便整理桌上的資料。
女：好的，沒問題。我會打電話給供應商追加訂購。

詞彙 **make copies** 影印 **document** 文件 **I'm afraid** 恐怕 **have it done** 完成它 **right away** 立即 **copy machine** 影印機 **supplier** 供應商 **make a delivery** 送貨 **make a survey** 調查 **office supply** 辦公室文具用品 **efficient** 有效率的 **instead of** 而不是 **partial** 部分的 **separately** 分開地 **in need** 有需求 **handy** 好用的 **organize** 整理；組織 **data** 資料 **add to** 增加；擴充 **original** 原始的；原先的

1.
他們最可能在哪裡工作？
（A）洗衣店
（B）超市
（C）麵包店
（D）律師事務所

解說 這是詢問「地點」的「簡短選項類考題」。核心語是「在哪裡工作」。由於對話內容是關於辦公室「影印文件」、「墨水匣」等物件，只有選項（D）最符合。 答案 (D)

詞彙 **laundry** 洗衣店 **supermarket** 超市 **bakery** 麵包店 **law firm** 律師事務所

2.
為何女士無法為男士影印？
（A）影印機故障
（B）她不會操作機械
（C）墨水匣沒有墨水
（D）男士沒禮貌

解說 這題是詢問「原因，理由」的「句子選項類考題」。女士提到「我們影印機的墨水匣沒有墨水了」，所以答案是（C）。 答案 (C)

詞彙 **broken** 故障 **operate** 操作 **polite** 有禮貌的 **manner** 方式；態度

3.
請看此圖，哪一項可能會有變動？
（A）墨水匣及碳粉
（B）檔案夾及標籤
（C）釘書機及釘書針
（D）紙張及信封

解說 這是詢問「可能變動的選項」的「簡短選項類考題」。男士說「可能買些檔案夾和標籤會很好用。」而這也是女士會增加訂購的項目，對應的答案是（B）。 答案 (B)

詞彙 **cartridge** 墨水匣 **toner** 碳粉匣 **folder** 檔案夾 **label** 標籤 **stapler** 釘書機 **staple** 釘書針 **paper** 紙張 **envelope** 信封

問題4～6請參考以下對話。 美 W 美 M

W : Hi, my name is Sara Wilson, and **⁴I ordered some books from your store yesterday.** However, I don't think I will be home next week to receive the delivery. **⁵Can you have the package delivered to my office, instead?**

M : I'm afraid we've already sent out your order, Ms. Wilson. If no one confirms the receipt of the delivery, **⁶the package will be returned to us. Then, we will call you to set up a new delivery date.**

W : Then should I pay for an extra fee to get it?

M : In fact, yes, you should. There will be an additional charge.

女：您好，我的名字是莎拉‧威爾遜，我昨天從您的商店訂購一些書籍。但是，我想我下週不會待在家收到投遞。你可以把包裹改送到我的辦公室嗎？

男：恐怕我們已經送您的訂單了，威爾遜女士。如果沒有人確認簽收，包裹將被退還給我們。之後，我們會打電話給您安排新的寄送日期。

女：那我該付額外的費用嗎？

男：實際上來說，是的，您應該是。這將有一筆額外的收費。

詞彙 order 下訂單 receive 收到 delivery 配送 package 包裹 confirm 確認 receipt 領取 pay for 付費 extra fee 額外費用 in fact 事實 additional charge 額外費用

4.

這個男人可能在哪裡工作？
（A）在郵局
（B）在快遞公司
（C）在修理廠
（D）在書店

解說 這是詢問該男性的職業的考題。透過該女性說的「從您的商店訂購一些書籍」，可以知道該男性在書店工作。　　　　　　　　　答案 (D)

詞彙 post office 郵局 delivery company 快遞公司 repair shop 在修理廠 bookstore 在書店

5.

為什麼這個女人聯絡這個男人？
（A）為了登廣告
（B）為了付運費
（C）為了討論遺失的貨物
（D）為了變更配送地址

解說 對於電話上的對話，問「為什麼聯絡」的考題是詢問主題的。仔細看該考題與選項之後，大概可以知道「訂貨／配送」類的主題。Can you後面出現「把包裹改送到我的辦公室」，所以（D）為答案。　答案 (D)

詞彙 place an advertisement 登廣告 shipping charge 運費 missing 遺失的 change 變更

6.

當這個男人收到這個女人的包裹時，他將會做什麼？
（A）保留它待領
（B）提供免費配送
（C）安排新配送時間
（D）給她退費

解說 「收到這個女人的包裹時」，這句話以該男性角度來說就變成「包裹將被退還給我們，之後…」。將後面出現的「安排新的寄送日期」做變化來表達的（C）為答案。　　　　　　　答案 (C)

詞彙 pickup 領取 refund 退費

問題7～9請參考以下對話。 英 M 澳 W

M : Rachel, **7, 8**can you help Jeff with the work on how to market our new line of ice cream? Jeff asked me to find someone to work with him.

W : Why not? We used to collaborate before, and the results were always successful.

M : Yes, that's why Jeff suggested working with you. He is well aware that you're experienced in marketing ice cream, so he needs your advice.

W : Okay, **8, 9**let me call him to see if he can begin the project today. I want to get it started as soon as possible.

男：瑞琪爾，有關於如何向市場推出我們新的冰淇淋，你能夠幫忙傑夫嗎？傑夫要我找人和他一起做。

女：有何不可？我們之前曾經合作，結果總是很成功。

男：對，這就是為什麼傑夫提議與你一起工作。他很清楚你在行銷冰淇淋上有經驗，所以他需要你的意見。

女：沒問題，讓我打電話給他看看他是否可以今天開始這個計畫。我想盡快開始。

詞彙 Why not? 為何不？ used to 曾經 collaborate 共事 successful 成功的 suggest 建議 be aware that 知道 be experienced in 有經驗於 advice 建議 as soon as possible 儘可能地快

7.

說話者很有可能在什麼部門工作？
（A）顧客服務
（B）技術支援
（C）行銷
（D）會計

解說 思考「如何向市場推出新的商品」的部門是哪裡？就是行銷部門嘛！　　　　　　答案 (C)

詞彙 customer service 顧客服務 technical support 技術支援 marketing 行銷 accounting 會計

8.

這個男人說傑夫要求了什麼？
（A）計畫上的協助
（B）對行銷預算的許可
（C）不同的工作時間安排
（D）轉換到其他分公司

解說 考題裡的Jeff requested，在對話裡變成Jeff asked 來出現。透過後面出現的「要我找人和他一起做」與「開始這個計畫」，可以知道是為了一項計劃來要求協助的。　　　　　　　　　　答案 (A)

詞彙 approval 同意 budget 預算 transfer 轉換 branch 分公司

9.

這個女人接下來將會做什麼？
（A）與同事聯絡
（B）與一些顧客見面
（C）參加研討會
（D）面試求職者

解說 let me是詢問「下一個行程」考題的核心說法，接在後面出現的是「打電話給他看看」，所以將這部份做變化來表達的（A）為答案。contact是比call還要更概括性的說法。　　　　　　　　　答案 (A)

詞彙 contact 聯絡　co-worker 同事　customer 顧客　attend 參加　job candidate 工作候選人

問題10～12請參考以下對話。 美M 美W

M：Hi, Susan. I was a little late for the meeting, and [10]I missed some parts of the meeting. Could you tell me what the sales manager said about the Hong Kong office?

W：He said the [11]Hong Kong group's doing great. They've boosted their sales this quarter by focusing on teenage consumers in their advertisement.

M：Great! So the manager suggests that we target younger people so our branch may raise our sales, too, right?

W：You're right. And [12]he said another meeting is scheduled for next week to discuss the details.

男：您好，蘇珊。我開會有點晚到，錯過了會議裡某些部分。你能告訴我，關於香港辦公室，銷售經理說了些什麼嗎？
女：他說，香港團隊做得非常好。他們在本季廣告中對準青少年消費者大力宣傳，快速提高了銷售量。
男：太棒了！所以經理建議我們將目標放在更年輕的人，而我們的分部也就更能提高我們的銷售，對嗎？
女：你說得對。他說下週要另開一次會議來討論細節。

詞彙 late 遲；晚　miss 錯過　part 部份　manager 經理　boost 強力推銷　focus on 聚焦於…　advertisement 廣告　target 目標　branch 分公司　raise 上升　detail 細節事項

10.

這個男人問這個女人做什麼？
（A）去另一間辦公室的方式
（B）會議內容的詳情
（C）廣告商清單
（D）支援銷售提案

解說 仔細觀察這三個考題，可以知道「會議內容」為主題，似乎是與「業績／策略」相關的內容呢！透過man ask，可以知道是詢問要求事項的考題，所以在對

話裡其答案線索為Could you tell me附近的內容。這個狀況是錯過了會議並要求對方告訴他相關內容，所以
（B）為答案。　　　　　　　　　答案 (B)

詞彙 how to 做…的方法　list 清單　advertiser 廣告商　assistance 支援；協助　proposal 提案

11.

香港辦公室的員工做了什麼？
（A）設計了新產品
（B）增加了銷售量
（C）分析了銷售報告
（D）完成了他們的訓練

解說 專有名詞通常會以相同的形式在考題與對話錄音裡出現，是簡單又重要的核心詞彙。因此，將Hong Kong office改說Hong Kong group的部分附近會出現答案。boost與increase是意思相近的單字。　答案 (B)

詞彙 increase 增加　analyze 分析　finish 完成

12.

根據這個女人所言，下週將會發生什麼？
（A）一位經理將退休。
（B）一位客戶將抵達。
（C）一間公司將被併購。
（D）一場會議將被舉辦。

解說 這是詢問「下一個行程」的考題，且next week為核心詞彙。該女性說「要開另一次會議來討論細節」，所以（D）為答案。　　　　　　　　　答案 (D)

詞彙 occur 發生　retire 退休　customer 顧客　acquire 獲取　hold 舉行

Quiz |

1. (A)　　　2. (A)　　　3. (B)　　　4. (A)

Q1 美W 美M

W : Have you heard about the GWF Restaurant on Main Street?

M : Yes. **I saw** a really positive review **in the newspaper**. It said that the newly hired chef apparently specializes in international dishes.

女：你聽說了關於在曼因街上的GWF餐廳的事嗎？
男：是的。我在報上看到了很正面的評論。它說新聘用的主廚顯然專長於國際化的料理。

根據這段對話，這個男人在報紙上看到了什麼？
（A）一則評論家的評語
（B）一個職缺

解說 若先知道在報紙上常常出現的，是針對電影／表演／餐廳的評論，就可以猜測到對話主題為「電影／表演／外食／興趣」。因此將核心詞彙saw與in the newspaper之間的positive review以概括性的敘述做變化來表達的（A）為答案。　　　答案(A)

詞彙 positive 正面的 review 評論 newspaper 報紙 apparently 顯然地 specialize in 專長於… international 國際化的 dish 料理 critic 評論家 job opening 職缺

Q2 澳W 英M

W : Hi, Jim, it's Mary. Do you **have any plans for the long weekend**?

M : Yes. I am excited to go to Dubai. I heard about some good restaurants near my hotel and also a wonderful museum in the city.

女：吉姆你好，我是瑪麗。這個長週末你有任何計畫嗎？
男：是的。我很興奮要去杜拜。我聽說在我住的旅館附近有一些不錯的餐廳，而且在市區也有很棒的博物館。

這個男人這週末將要做什麼？
（A）參觀一座城市
（B）舉辦派對

解說 透過考題裡的do this weekend，可以預測以「度假計劃」為主題。核心詞彙weekend後面出現的「很興奮要去杜拜」，可以知道他要去參觀一座城市。　答案(A)

詞彙 plan 計畫 weekend 週末 museum 博物館 visit 參觀 hold 舉辦

Q3 澳W 英M

W : **This photocopier** is one of the most popular models we have in the store. **It comes with** complimentary copy papers and ink cartridges.

M : That's a good offer, but isn't it too difficult to install it by myself?

女：這台影印機是在我們店裡最受歡迎的款式之一。它附有免費的影印紙和墨水匣。
男：這是個很好的銷售活動，但是由我自己來安裝它不會太困難嗎？

什麼東西被包含於這台影印機的購買？
（A）免費安裝
（B）免費備品

解說 看考題與選項可以預測到對話的地點為「商店」。「和影印機一起提供…」的說法是以it comes with來表達的，而後面出現的免費的影印紙和墨水匣可以換成「免費備品」來表達。　　　答案(B)

詞彙 photocopier 影印機 popular 受歡迎的 come with 與…一起的 complimentary 免費的 offer 提供 by oneself 藉由某人自己 include 包括 installation 安裝 supply（事務）用品

Q4 美W 美M

W : Dr. Min's office. How may I help you?

M : My name is John Clark. **I'd like to** make a dental appointment. I'd like to see a doctor as soon as possible. It seems I developed a cavity in one of my lower back teeth.

女：閔醫生辦公室。我能如何幫助您？
男：我的名字是約翰・克拉克。我想要做牙科預約。我想要儘可能快點就診。在我的後下方牙齒好像有了蛀牙。

為什麼這個男人打電話到閔醫生辦公室？
（A）為了安排預約
（B）為了推銷產品

解說 透過考題與選項可以知道接電話的人工作的地方是「醫院」。為什麼打電話到醫院呢？聽對話之前已經可以預測到答案了，在核心說法I'd like to後面出現的「牙科預約」簡化成「預約」。　　　答案(A)

詞彙 make an appointment 預約 see a doctor 就診 as soon as possible 儘快 develop a cavity 有了蛀牙 lower back teeth 後下方牙齒

1 (B)	2 (A)	3 (B)	4 (A)
5 (A)	6 (B)	7 (B)	8 (A)
9 (A)	10 (A)	11 (C)	12 (A)
13 (C)	14 (C)		

1. 美M 澳W

1 找出核心詞彙	going to Tokyo
2 了解類型	通勤／交通／搜尋或度假計劃
3 看選項	進行調查或拜訪同事

M : I heard you'll be taking off next week. Where are you **going**?

W : **To Tokyo**. I'm visiting a former colleague I got to be very close with when I worked there. I've been itching to meet her but, I'm worried because the bank has been so busy lately. We're understaffed.

男：我聽說你下週要休假。你要去哪裡？

女：去東京。我要去拜訪以前我在那裡工作時非常要好的同事。我很渴望與她見面，但是我也很擔心，因為銀行最近相當忙。我們的人員不足。

為什麼這個女人要去東京？
（A）為了進行調查
（B）為了拜訪以前的同事

解說 核心詞彙going to Tokyo附近有答案。在選項中，將「拜訪以前的同事」的colleague改成了co-worker來表達。　　　　　　　　　　　　　　答案 (B)

詞彙 take off 休息　former 以前的　colleague 同事　itching to 對…渴望　understaffed 人員不足　conduct a survey 進行調查　co-worker 同事

2. 英M 美W

1 找出核心詞彙	not yet gone to the event
2 了解類型	電影／表演／外食／興趣
3 看選項	沒空或不喜歡

M : **Have you been to the Magic Art exhibition yet**? It's amazing to see so many three-dimensional paintings and drawings.

W : **I wish. But** I've been too busy working since I got promoted to manager. How long will the exhibit be in town?

男：你去過神奇美術展了嗎？看到那麼多立體的繪畫和素描真令人感到驚奇。

女：我希望可以。但是自從我晉升成為經理工作一直很忙。這個展覽將會在市區多久呢？

為什麼這個女人還沒有去過這個活動？
（A）她沒有太多空閒時間。
（B）她不喜歡這項活動。

解說 event是具體活動的概括性單字。在此將「工作一直很忙」改成了「沒有太多空閒時間」來表達。　　　　　　　　　　　　　　答案 (A)

詞彙 exhibit 展覽　three-dimensional 三度空間；立體的　get promoted 晉升　event 活動　free time 空閒時間

3. 美W 美M

1 找出核心詞彙	shopping for
2 了解類型	商店
3 看選項	妹妹或兒子

W : Hi, I'm looking for a sweater. I hope to get it for my son's birthday next week. I think he'd like one of these sweaters, but are any of these available in blue?

M : Unfortunately we don't have any blue sweaters in stock, but we can order one from our warehouse. They usually deliver in less than three days.

女：你好，我正在找一件毛衣。為了我兒子下個禮拜的生日，我希望拿到它。我想他會喜歡這其中一件毛衣，但是這有任何藍色的嗎？

男：很不巧的我們庫存裡沒有任何藍色的毛衣，但是我們可以從我們的倉庫訂一件。他們通常會在三天之內配送。

這個女人買東西給誰？
（A）她的妹妹
（B）她的兒子

解說 透過核心詞彙shopping for，可以知道這是在「商店」裡，店員與客人之間發生的對話。looking for為商店相關的核心詞彙，藉由在其後面出現的「為了我兒子下個禮拜的生日，我希望拿到它」，可以知道（B）為答案。　　　　　　　　　　　　　　答案 (B)

詞彙 look for 尋找　sweater 毛衣　available 能夠　unfortunately 不幸地；不巧　warehouse 倉庫　deliver 配送

4. 美W 英M

1 找出核心詞彙	Where
2 了解類型	詢問對話地點的考題
3 看選項	錄影帶出租店或汽車出租店

W : Good morning. I want to return this videotape that I borrowed last week. Is it overdue?

M : Let me check. Oh, this was due last Friday. You have to pay a $1 late charge per day.

女：早安。我要還上週借的錄影帶。它逾期了嗎？

男：讓我確認一下。噢，上週五是到期日。你要付每日一元的逾期費。

這段談話很有可能是在哪裡發生的？

（A）錄影帶出租店

（B）汽車出租店

解說 這是詢問對話地點的考題。需要看著選項反向預測答案。若（A）為答案，可能會出現borrowed、return等的單字。若（B）為答案，可能會出現book或check out等的說法。對話裡出現的是歸還videotape的狀況，所以（A）為答案。　　　　　　　答案（A）

詞彙 return 歸還　borrow 借出　overdue 逾期　due 期限 pay 付費　late charge 逾期費　per 每…　take place 發生 video rental store 錄影帶出租店

5. 英M 澳W

1 找出核心詞彙	Where
2 了解類型	詢問對話地點的考題
3 看選項	藥局或餐廳

M : Hello, I'd like to get this prescription refilled, please. My name is Mark Johnson, and I have used this pharmacy before.

W : All right. As we're busy, it will take a little while. Why don't you come back in an hour to pick it up?

男：你好，我想要補充這個處方藥。我的名字是馬克‧強森，我之前在這間藥局開過藥。

女：好的。因為我們很忙，這將需要一段時間。你何不在一個小時後回來領取它呢？

說話者在哪裡？

（A）在藥局

（B）在餐廳

解說 這是詢問對話地點的考題。需要看著選項反向預測答案。若（A）為答案，可能會出現prescription等的

單字。若（B）為答案，可能會出現order或menu等的單字。在此對話裡除了出現prescription，也聽得到「之前在這間藥局開過藥」，所以（A）為答案。　　答案（A）

詞彙 get prescription refilled 以處方箋再次領藥 pharmacy 藥局　come back 回來　pick up 領取

6. 美M 美W

1 找出核心詞彙	call the bank
2 了解類型	銀行
3 看選項	詢問營業時間或開戶資訊

M : Hello, **I'm calling to** know how long it usually takes to open a new bank account.

W : Well, usually it takes about half an hour except in the morning when our bank gets crowded. If you want to save some time, download the application form from our website and fill it out before your visit.

男：你好，我打電話來是想知道開一個新帳戶需要多久時間？

女：嗯，除了早上我們銀行人很多的時候之外，平常大約要花半小時。如果你要省一點時間，在你來之前先從我們網站上下載申請表之後填寫它。

為什麼這個男人打電話給銀行？

（A）為了詢問營業時間

（B）為了得到開戶資訊

解說 透過考題可以知道接電話的人在銀行工作。將核心詞彙I'm calling to後面的「想知道開一個新帳戶需要多久時間」以概括性的敘述做變化來表達的（B）為答案。　　　　　　　　　　　　　　　答案（B）

詞彙 open a bank account 開銀行帳戶　about 大約 crowded 擁擠的　save 存款　download 下載　application form 申請表　fill out 填寫　inquire about 詢問有關… opening hour 營業時間

7. 澳W 英M

1 找出核心詞彙	mechanic not able to help the woman
2 了解類型	修理站
3 看選項	無法拿到零件或太忙

W : Hi. I'd like to drop off my car for repairs. I got into an accident last night.

M : Well, **our mechanic** is really busy today. But if you want to leave your car here tonight, we will call you to give you an estimate in the morning.

女：您好，我要把我的車留下來修理。我昨晚遇上了事故。
男：我們的修理師今天真的很忙，但如果你想今晚把你的車留在這裡，我們早上會打電話給你估價。

為什麼修理師今天無法幫忙這個女人？
（A）他無法拿到零件。
（B）他今天太忙。

解說 透過考題可以知道對話的地點為「汽車維修站」。因此將「修理師真的很忙、早上會給你打電話」做變化來表達的（B）為答案。　　　　答案 (B)

詞彙 drop off my car for repairs 把車留下來修理
accident 事故；意外　mechanic 修理師　leave 留下
give an estimate 估價　be able to 能夠…　part 零件

8. 美W 英M

1 找出核心詞彙	fee
2 了解類型	停車場或博物館
3 看選項	五元或二元

W : Excuse, me. I parked my car here in the parking area all this morning. But I found I am a little short of cash. Can I pay by credit card?

M : Yes, you can. Let me see how much you should pay. Well, you came here at 9:30 and now it's 11:30. **You owe** 5 dollars for 2 hours.

女：抱歉，我今天整個上午將車停在這個停車場。但是發現我現金有點不夠。我可以用信用卡支付嗎？
男：是的，可以。讓我看看你應該付多少。嗯，你在九點三十分到這兒，現在是十一點三十分。兩小時你要付五元。

費用是多少錢？
（A）五元
（B）兩元

解說 透過考題可以知道對話地點為「停車場」或「博物館」。在對話裡，將fee改成了「你要付」來表達，所以後面出現的五元為答案。　　　　答案 (A)

詞彙 park 停車　parking area 停車場　all morning 整個上午　pay 付費　by credit card 用信用卡…　owe 尚未付的款項　fee 費用

問題9~10請參考以下對話。 美W 英W

1 找出核心詞彙	discussing, see on the website
2 了解類型	詢問主題或行為對象的簡短選項類考題
3 看選項	購物中心，公寓，天氣
	廣告，評論，天氣
4 預測對話內容	透過廣告得知新購物中心的相關消息。

W1 : What a rainy day outside! [9]I was hoping that I'd go to the outdoor shops downtown today, but not in this weather.

W2 : [9]Do you want to go to the Mega Mall with me instead? It's just opened.

W1 : That sounds good to me. I've wanted to shop there since [10]I saw the ad on the website.

女：外面真是個大雨天了！我本來希望今天去市區的戶外用品店，但不是在這樣的天氣。
男：你想改成和我一起去巨霸商場嗎？它剛開幕。
女：這聽起來不錯。自從我在網站上看到了廣告，我一直想去那裡購物。

詞彙 a rainy day 下雨天　outdoor shop 戶外運動用品店
instead 替換　ad 廣告

9.
這些女人主要在討論什麼？
（A）購物中心
（B）一間公寓
（C）天氣

解說 在對話裡，對於建議的說法「去商場」表達了同意，所以可以知道（A）為答案。　　　　答案 (A)

詞彙 discuss 討論　shopping complex 購物中心
apartment 公寓　weather 天氣

10.
說話者在網站上看到了什麼？
（A）一則廣告
（B）一則評論家的評論
（C）天氣資訊

解說 see on the website為核心詞彙，此對話裡在saw（由see變化而來）與on the website之間會出現答案。ad是advertisement的縮寫。　　　　答案 (A)

詞彙 advertisement 廣告　critic 評論家　review 評論

問題11～12請參考以下對話。 英M 美W

1 找出核心詞彙	Where, concern
2 了解類型	詢問地點、主題的考題（問題狀況或令人擔心的事情也是一種主題）
3 看選項	服裝店，街角，乾洗店 需要快速服務，需要去電影院的方向，遺失票
4 預測對話內容	詢問有關快速服務的洗衣店。

M : Hi, **11, 12I'd like to have this business suit cleaned for a banquet I am attending tonight. Can you do it right away?**

W : **12I'm afraid that I can't do it today. We are too busy to process your order at this time.**

M : Okay. **11, 12Are there any other dry cleaners that might be able to take care of my order?**

男：您好，為了我今晚參加的宴會，我想要清洗這套西裝。你能馬上做嗎？

女：恐怕我今天沒辦法做。我們今天太忙，不能在這個時候處理您的要求。

男：好的。有任何其他的乾洗店可以處理我的要求嗎？

詞彙 business suit 西裝　cleaned 清洗　banquet 宴會 attend 參加；出席　right away 立刻　process 處理 dry cleaner 乾洗　take care of 做處理

11.
說話者在哪兒？
（A）在服裝店
（B）在街角
（C）在乾洗店

解說 這是詢問對話地點的考題。透過「我想要清洗這套西裝」，可以知道在乾洗店。　　答案（C）

詞彙 clothing store 服裝店　dry cleaner's 乾洗店

12.
這個男人關心什麼？
（A）他需要快速完成的服務。
（B）他需要去電影院的方向。
（C）他遺失了音樂會的票。

解說 此狀況為乾洗店職員說「今天太忙，而不能在這個時候處理」，所以該男性在找別的店，因此（A）為答案。　　答案（A）

詞彙 concern 擔心　finish 完成　quickly 快速地 directions 方向　theater 電影院　lose 遺失

問題13～14請參考以下對話。 美M 澳W

1 找出核心詞彙	Where, in Sydney
2 了解類型	詢問地點、理由的句子選項類考題
3 看選項	戲院，辦公室，博物館 參加會議，買房子，度假
4 預測對話內容	在博物館的男人說他正在雪梨度假。

M : Excuse, me. **13Can you tell me where the science exhibit is being held?**

W : It's on the second floor up to the main stairways to your left. **13Have you ever been to our museum?**

M : No. **14This is the first time visiting Sydney. I'm spending my vacation here at my uncle's house.** He moved here several months ago.

男：抱歉，你能告訴我科學展覽在哪裡舉辦嗎？

女：在你左邊的主樓梯間往上的二樓空間。你有來過我們的博物館嗎？

男：沒有。這是我第一次來雪梨。我在這兒我叔叔的家渡假。他在幾個月前搬到這裡的。

詞彙 exhibit 展覽　hold 舉辦　stairway 樓梯　museum 博物館　move 搬移　several 數個

13.
說話者很有可能在哪裡？
（A）在戲院
（B）在辦公室
（C）在博物館

解說 透過「科學展覽在哪裡舉辦」與「我們的博物館」，可以知道博物館為對話地點。　　答案（C）

詞彙 theater 電影院

14.
為什麼這個男人在雪梨？
（A）他正在參加會議。
（B）他正在買房子。
（C）他在渡假。

解說 地名或人名本身成為很好的核心詞彙。對話裡出現Sydney，所以其附近有答案。該男性說在度假，（C）即為答案。　　答案（C）

詞彙 attend 參加；出席　conference 會議　buy 買 vacation 渡假

| 1. (A) | 2. (B) | 3. (A) | 4. (A) | 5. (B) | 6. (D) |
| 7. (B) | 8. (C) | 9. (A) | 10. (D) | 11. (A) | 12. (D) |

問題1～3請參考以下對話。 英M 美W

M：I haven't been able to go out since ¹I moved into my new apartment. Finally, I'm done unpacking. So I can look around the city.

W：Well, ²I recommend you go to the outdoor music concert this weekend.

M：I heard about that concert from a radio ad. The city holds it every year, right?

W：Yeah, unless you hate large crowds, you will have fun. There will be several music stages installed, and ³the local restaurants will be giving out samples of their food. I'm sure you'll be excited.

男：自從搬到新公寓後我一直無法出門。終於我都拆箱完畢了。因此我可以好好看看這個城市。
女：那麼，我建議你這週末去戶外音樂會。
男：我從電台廣告裡知道這個音樂會。城裡每年都舉辦。對嗎？
女：對啊，除非你討厭一大堆人群，你會覺得很好玩的。那會安裝幾個演出舞台，還有當地的餐廳將會給免費試吃。我相信你會很興奮的。

詞彙 go out 外出 finally 終於 unpack 拆封 look around 四處看看 recommend 建議 outdoor 戶外 ad 廣告 hold 舉行 install 設置 give out 分發

1.
這個男人最近做了什麼？
（A）搬到一間新公寓
（B）管理一間餐廳
（C）申請一個職位
（D）休假

解說 透過在前面部分出現的「自從搬到新公寓後我一直無法出門、終於可以好好看看這個城市」。可以知道「最近搬來的」。 答案 (A)

詞彙 recently 最近 manage 管理 apply for 申請 open position 職缺 take time off work 休假

2.
這個女人建議了什麼？
（A）在戶外市場購物
（B）去一場音樂表演
（C）聽廣播
（D）與導遊商量

解說 核心詞彙suggest在對話中是以recommend表達，在對話裡recommend附近會出現答案。 答案 (B)

詞彙 performance 表演 consult 諮詢；商談 travel guide 旅行導覽

3.
當地的餐廳將會提供什麼？
（A）提供免費試吃
（B）持續營業到很晚
（C）舉辦烹飪課
（D）發行禮券

解說 對話裡的核心詞彙為the local restaurants，將核心詞彙附近的「給免費試吃」在選項裡改以「提供免費試吃」來表達。 答案 (A)

詞彙 provide 提供 offer 提供 complimentary 免費的 organize 舉辦 class 課程

問題4～6請參考以下對話。 澳W 美M

W：Thank you for calling Ellen Jay Bookstore. What can I do for you?

M：Hello, I'd like to buy a newly released book, *Back To Nature*, reviewed in today's newspaper. But ⁴I don't remember how to get to your store. Is it on 14th street or 16th street? I'm going to stop by your store on my way home.

W：Neither. We're located on 17th Street, and you need to walk three blocks down. However, ⁵we're closing in five minutes. ⁶You'll have to come tomorrow, instead. We're open at 9 a.m.

女：感謝您來電艾倫傑書店。我能為您做些什麼嗎？
男：您好，我想購買在今天的報上受評論的新上市的書《回歸自然》。但我不記得怎麼去你的店。是在第十四街還是十六街？我要在我回家的途中順便去你的商店。
女：都不是。我們位在第十七街附近，你需要往下走三個街區。但是我們在五分鐘內將打烊。您明天再來，我們在上午九點營業。

詞彙 bookstore 書店 newly released book 新上市的書 newspaper 報紙 stop by 順便去 on one's way 在…的途中 locate 位在 close 打烊 instead 做為替代

4.
為什麼這個男人要打電話？
（A）為了得到去書店的方向
（B）為了詢問營業時間
（C）為了要求配送
（D）為了取消一項訂購

解說 詢問來電的目的的考題是要詢問「主題」的。在核心說法I'd like to後面接著but，在but之後的內容即為答案。 答案 (A)

詞彙 direction 方向 inquire about 詢問有關於… store's hours 營業時間 ask for 要求 delivery 配送

5.

有關於這家店這個女人說了什麼？
（A）它遷移到新地區。
（B）它快打烊了。
（C）某些項目缺貨。
（D）有個職缺。

解說 這是詢問意見的句子選項類考題，答案在於對話的後面部分。將「在五分鐘內將打烊」做變化來表達成「快打烊了」的（B）為答案。 答案 (B)

詞彙 be about to 能夠… be short of …短缺 job vacancy 職缺

6.

這個女人要求這個男人做什麼？
（A）參考地圖
（B）稍晚再回撥電話
（C）完成某件工作
（D）明天到店裡來

解說 這是詢問要求事項的考題。將核心說法you'll have to後面出現的「明天再來」做變化來表達的（D）為答案。 答案 (D)

詞彙 consult 參考 map 地圖 call back 回撥電話 later 稍晚一點 complete 完成 visit 拜訪

問題7～9請參考以下對話。 美W 英M

W：Thank you for calling Dr. Johnson's office. How may I help you?

M：Hello, my name is David Wilson, one of Dr. Johnson's patients. ⁸I'm calling about the medicine he prescribed. I want to change it to another one.

W：I'm afraid ⁷Dr. Johnson is away from the office to attend a medical conference. Since it doesn't seem to be an emergency, ⁹let me put you through to Dr. Lee's office. She's been taking his job during his absence.

女：謝謝您來電強生醫生辦公室。我能給您什麼幫助嗎？
男：您好，我的名字是大衛‧威爾遜，是強生醫生的病人之一，我打電話來是有關他開給我的藥。我想改成另一種。
女：很可惜強生醫生離開辦公室，去參加一場醫學會議了。既然這事似乎不緊急，我幫你把電話接到李醫生的辦公室。他不在時她一直代理他的工作。

詞彙 patient 病人 medicine 藥 prescribe 處方 away from 離開…的 conference 會議 emergency 緊急狀況 take 承擔 absence 不在

7.

強生醫生在哪裡？
（A）和病人在一起
（B）在一場會議
（C）在別的辦公室
（D）在渡假

解說 這不是詢問對話的地點，而是詢問特定人物所在地點的考題。Dr. Johnson的附近出現「離開辦公室去參加一場醫學會議」，所以（B）為答案。 答案 (B)

詞彙 on vacation 休假中

8.

為什麼這個男人打電話到強生醫生的辦公室？
（A）為了說有關報告的事
（B）為了做預約
（C）為了討論處方
（D）為了有關帳單詢問

解說 透過該男性說的核心詞彙calling about後面出現的「關他開給我的藥」與「我想改換成另一種」等的線索，可以知道（C）為答案。 答案 (C)

詞彙 talk about 討論 presentation 演講 schedule an appointment 預約時間 ask about 詢問有關於… bill 帳單

9.

這個女人接下來很有可能會做什麼？
（A）轉接電話
（B）聯絡強生醫生
（C）預約
（D）取消訂單

解說 這是詢問下一個行程的考題。將核心詞彙let me後面出現的put you through改成類似說法的（A）為答案。 答案 (A)

詞彙 transfer 轉換 contact 聯絡 make an appointment 做預約 cancel 取消

問題10～12請參考以下對話和圖表。 美M 英W

Items	Price
¹²T-shirt	$100/ea
Baseball hat	$50/ea
Key chain	$10/ea
Postcard	$5/ea

M：Hello, ¹⁰I am looking for some souvenir to take home. Is there anything you'd recommend?

W : You've come to the right place. Our store carries the most comprehensive selection in town. No matter it's baseball hats, T-shirts,... or key chains, postcards... All items will let you carry the best memories of the trip back home.

M : [11]I think these T-shirts are very cute. I'd like to buy one for each of my family. What sizes do you have?

W : It comes in three sizes – large, medium, and small. For adults, I think large will do. Medium is more for teenagers, and size small fits even younger age groups.

M : Well, [12]I think I'll carry two large T-shirts and two small T-shirts. How much is it totally?

品項	價格
T恤	$100 / 每件
棒球帽	$50 / 每頂
鑰匙圈	$10 / 每單品
明信片	$5 / 每張

男：哈囉！我想找一些紀念品帶回家，不知你有沒有什麼推薦的呢？

女：你來對地方了！我們是城裡貨樣最齊全的店！不管是棒球帽、T恤、鑰匙圈、明信片…所有的品項都會讓您將這趟旅程最好的回憶帶回家。

男：我覺得這些T恤非常可愛，我想幫我家人一人買一件。你們有什麼尺寸？

女：有大、中、小三種尺寸。成人的話，可穿大號；中號比較是青少年穿；小號是為更年幼的族群設計。

男：好！我想我要帶兩件大號、兩件小號。總共多少錢？

詞彙 **look for** 尋找 **souvenir** 紀念品 **take home** 帶回家 **recommend** 推薦 **carry** 攜帶；販售 **comprehensive** 完整的、全面的 **selection** 挑選 **no matter** 不論 **baseball hat** 棒球帽 **T-shirt** T恤 **key chain** 鑰匙圈 **postcard** 明信片 **item** 項目 **memory** 回憶 **trip** 旅遊 **cute** 可愛的 **each** 每個的 **size** 尺寸 **large** 大號 **medium** 中號 **small** 小號 **teenager** 青少年 **fit** 適合 **even younger** 甚至更年輕的

10.

此對話在哪裡發生？

（A）在漢堡店
（B）在珠寶店
（C）在服飾店
（D）在紀念品店

解說 這是詢問「地點」的「簡短選項類考題」。男士詢問店員「我想找一些紀念品帶回家，不知你有沒有什麼推薦的呢？」可推斷答案是選項（D）。 答案 (D)

詞彙 **burger** 漢堡 **jewelry** 珠寶 **clothing** 服飾 **souvenir** 紀念品

11.

男士想買什麼回家？

（A）T恤
（B）帽子
（C）厚運動褲
（D）磁鐵

解說 這是詢問「購買項目為何」的「簡短選項類考題」。男士說「我覺得這些T恤非常可愛，我想幫我家人一人買一件。」所以選項（A）是正確答案。

答案 (A)

詞彙 **sweat pants** 厚運動褲 **magnet** 磁鐵

12.

請看此圖，男士需要支付多少錢？

（A）$250
（B）$300
（C）$350
（D）$400

解說 這是詢問「應支付價格為何」的「簡易計算題」。男士提到「我想我要帶兩件大號、兩件小號」所以總共4件T恤。對應到表格每件T恤$100元，所以 $4 \times \$100 = \$400$，正確答案是（D）。 答案 (D)

詞彙 **need** 需要 **pay** 支付

<table>
<tr><td></td></tr>
</table>

<table>
<thead>
<tr><th>Chapter 16</th><th>對話內容較長的考題</th></tr>
</thead>
</table>

16 對話內容較長的考題

STEP 01 若沒答對會後悔的考題

1 (C)	2 (A)	3 (C)	4 (C)
5 (B)	6 (C)	7 (B)	8 (D)

1. 美W 美M

1 找出核心詞彙	reject
2 了解類型	詢問原因
3 看選項	男子在做某事

W : Can you please fix my computer for me? It doesn't work.
M : **I am busy** with my speech for tomorrow. Can't you fix it by yourself?

女：你可不可以幫我修電腦？它壞掉了。
男：我在忙明天的演講。不能你自己修一下嗎？

為何男士回絕了女士的要求？
（A）因為他在睡覺
（B）因為他快要出門
（C）因為他在工作
（D）因為他在講電話

解說 看題目便可知道這是「女子提出請求，男子回絕」的對話內容，要特別注意男子回絕的理由，男子說「I am busy with my speech for tomorrow.」可知道他在忙，但忙什麼呢？在忙隔天的演講，也就是他正在工作。 答案 (C)

2. 美M 英W

1 找出核心詞彙	purpose
2 了解類型	詢問對話主題
3 看選項	預訂某物

M : Hi, **I need to make a reservation** for this Friday night, seven PM.
W : Sure, may I have your name and number of guests, please?
M : It's Brian. We need a table for four.

男：嗨！我需要預約這禮拜五晚上七點。
女：沒問題。麻煩可以給我您的大名及來賓人數嗎？
男：我叫布萊恩。我們需要四個人的座位。

男士來電的目的是什麼？
（A）訂餐桌
（B）訂車票
（C）訂房間
（D）訂班機

解說 題目在詢問對話的目的，這類訊息會出現在對話的開頭。果不其然，男子開頭就說「I need to make a reservation for this Friday night, seven PM.」之後又表示「We need a table for four.」。故可判斷這通電話（男子）的目的是餐廳訂位。 答案 (A)

3. 美W 美M

1 找出核心詞彙	where, work at
2 了解類型	詢問對話人物的資訊
3 看選項	工作地點

W : Hi, Mr. Hunter. **This is Star Travel Agency**. We are sorry to notify you that your flight to Tokyo tomorrow has suddenly been cancelled due to the typhoon.
M : That's terrible. I have been expecting that trip.

女：嗨，杭特先生。這裡是星辰旅行社。我們很抱歉要通知您，您明天飛往東京的航班因為颱風而突然取消。
男：太糟糕了！我一直在期待這個旅程。

女士在哪裡工作？
（A）一家航空公司
（B）一個歐洲政府
（C）一家旅行社
（D）一個旅遊景點

解說 從題目的選項可知，應該是與旅遊有關的訊息通知，而這類的對話內容，可能是「航空公司工作人員與顧客、旅行社工作人員與顧客」這兩種。貼下來可聽對話的開頭，女子一開始就表明是旅行社的來電，故答案選（C）。 答案 (C)

4. 美M 美W

1 找出核心詞彙	thinking about
2 了解類型	詢問對話人物的打算
3 看選項	想做的事

M : **I am thinking about** quitting my job and starting a business on my own. What do you think?
W : Mmm... if you want to succeed, you need a lot of money to get started.

男：我在想要辭去工作自己創業。你覺得呢？
女：嗯。如果你想要成功的話，你需要很多錢才能開始。

男士想要做什麼？
（A）結婚
（B）買車
（C）創業
（D）買房

解說 從題目的選項可知此題在詢問男子想做的事情，可能是在告知對方，或是想跟對方商量，因此對話中應該會出現I want...或是I am thinking...這類的句型。找到這樣的句型，就知男子的打算，便可知正確答案為（C）。 答案 (C)

5. 美W 英W

1 找出核心詞彙	where, take place
2 了解類型	詢問對話的地點
3 看選項	地點

W1：Wow, so many passengers **on the train**! Why are there so many people?
W2：Because today is a national holiday. Many people would like to go out for a tour just like us.

女：哇，火車上好多乘客！為什麼有這麼多人呢？
男：因為今天是國定假日，很多人想出去旅遊，就像我們一樣。

對話發生在哪裡？
（A）候車室
（B）火車上
（C）售票處
（D）月臺處

解說 從題目的選項可知此題在詢問對話發生的地點，觀看選項，可知應該是在車站，但是在車站的哪裡呢？答案就在女生講的第一句話「... so many passengers on the train!」。 答案 (B)

6. 美M 美W

1 找出核心詞彙	complaining
2 了解類型	詢問對話人物（女子）的意見
3 看選項	抱怨的事項

M：These accounts are <u>so confusing that we can't sort them out at all</u>.
W：Don't worry; we are looking for temporary accountants.

女：這些帳目太混亂了，我們兩個根本整理不了。
男：別擔心，公司在招聘臨時會計。

女子在抱怨什麼？
（A）公司離家太遠了。
（B）工資沒有發放。
（C）帳目太混亂了。
（D）帳目失蹤了。

解說 題目直指詢問「女子」的抱怨事項，所以要特別注意女子所說的話。女子在講帳目混亂的事宜，故答案應選（C）。 答案 (C)

7. 美M 英W

1 找出核心詞彙	business, work for
2 了解類型	詢問對話人物（女子）的身分
3 看選項	行業、公司

M：Good afternoon. I **subscribe to your periodical**. I signed up for twelve months, but since July, I haven't received any deliveries.
W：Yes, that seems to be a mistake.

男：午安。我訂閱你們的期刊。我訂了12個月，但從七月開始就沒有收到任何投遞。
女：是的，這似乎出錯了。

女子從事於哪一個行業？
（A）醫療機構
（B）雜誌出版社
（C）會計師事務所
（D）貨運公司

解說 題目在詢問女子的工作地點。若對話是由女子開頭的話，通常會先自我介紹，這時就可以得知女子從事的行業。但此段對話是由男子開頭，男子所述說的內容與女子的工作有關，男子提到「subscribe to your periodical」，要知道periodical是magazine的一種，故可推論女子的工作地點為（B）雜誌社。 答案 (B)

8. 美M 美W

1 找出核心詞彙	inquire
2 了解類型	詢問物品的所在位置
3 看選項	各種事項

M：Lisa, do you know where <u>they keep</u> the original blueprints for the Royal Hotel? I can't find them in our archives.
W：As far as I know, they were removed from our archives and sent to the architect's office.

男：麗莎，你知道他們將皇家旅館的原始藍圖存放在哪裡嗎？我在檔案櫃找不到。
女：據我所知，藍圖被移出檔案室，並送到建築師事務所。

女：據我所知，藍圖被移出檔案室，並送到建築師事務所。

男子詢問什麼？
（A）建築物的地址
（B）檔案室的密碼
（C）建築師的聯繫資訊
（D）某些文件的位置

解說 看題目可知詢問的內容是「男子詢問的問題」，因此掌握男子對話重點是答題的關鍵。題目使用很多與對話一樣的詞彙，意圖造成考生的混淆，但只要聽到男子說「where」，便可把選項（B）和（C）刪除。接下來聽到他要找的是藍圖的位置，並非建築物的地址，固可將（A）刪除，得到答案（D）。這裡的document指的是blueprint。　　　　　　　　　　　　　答案 (D)

STEP 02　考題實戰練習

1 (A)	2 (C)	3 (B)	4 (D)
5 (A)	6 (C)		

問題1～3請參考以下對話與圖表。 美W 英W 美M

W1 : With regard to how to increase sales of products, [1,2] I think we should lower prices and insist on small profits but quick turnover.

W2 : I don't agree. The cost of raw materials and advertising has raising a lot. [2]If we adopt the method you said, we will have no profit.

M　: Both of you are right, but we have to consider the actual situation. Our products are unsalable abroad, largely because we haven't opened the local market. [2]I suggest that we should contact more with local supermarkets and shopping malls and intensify publicity.

W1 : [3]I still stick to my idea.

女1：關於增加產品的銷量，我認為應該降低價格，堅持薄利多銷的方法。
女2：我不同意，原料和廣告費用都大幅度上漲了，如果採用你所說的方法，我們就沒有什麼利潤可賺了。
男：你們說的都沒錯，但是我們要考慮到實際情況。我們的產品在國外滯銷，很大一部原因是因為沒有打開當地的市場。我建議應該加強和當地超市、商場的聯繫，加大宣傳力度。
女1：我還是堅持我自己的想法。

詞彙 turnover 營業額 adopt 採用 actual 實際的，現實的 unsalable 滯銷的 intensify 加強；增加 stick 堅持

1.
第一個人的建議是什麼？
（A）降低價格
（B）提高價格
（C）加大宣傳力度
（D）提高品質

解說 這是詢問對話細節的考題，題目已經直指第一個人，只要聽到女子說「I think we should lower prices」，便可知到答案應選（A）。　　　　答案 (A)

詞彙 lower 降低 increase 增加 intensify 加強 publicity 宣傳

2.
關於這三個人的想法，哪一項是正確的？
（A）他們三個人的想法是一致的。
（B）只有兩個人的想法是一致的。
（C）每個人的想法都不同。
（D）只有兩個人提出了想法。

解說 對話中的三個人都提出了不同的想法，（C）是正確答案。　　　　　　　　　　　　答案 (C)

3.
第二位女子說「我堅持我的想法」是什麼意思？
（A）她太固執了。
（B）她認為自己的想法是最好的。
（C）她堅決不同意第三個人的想法。
（D）她會妥協的。

解說 這是詢問某句話背後含意的考題。說話者的個性無法因一句話而判斷，排除（A）；在對話中沒有提到堅決不同意第三個人，排除（C），同樣地，也沒有表示同意。「stick to sb.'s idea」是表示堅持意見的意思，所以此題選（B）。　　　　　　　　答案 (B)

詞彙 stubborn 固執的；倔強的

問題4～6請參考以下對話與圖表。 美W 美M 英W

W1 : Are you Mr. Smith? I'm Lynn. She's Lucy. We were [4]sent here to meet you.

M　: [6]I'm so glad you've come to meet me.

W2 : Mr. Smith, you have [4,6]stayed on the plane for twelve hours; you must be tired. We have booked a hotel not far from our company for you. You can take a rest first.

M　: It's very thoughtful of you, [5]but I'm going to meet your manager after a while.

W1 : How about we take you to the hotel to arrange your luggage first?

M　: [6]That's settled.

女1：您是史密斯先生吧，我是琳恩，她是露西，公司派我們來接您。

男：你們來接我，我真是太高興了。

女2：史密斯先生，您坐了十二個小時的飛機，肯定很累了。我們已經為您預定了離公司不遠的酒店，您可以先去休息。

男：你們考慮的真周到，但我等一下要和你們經理見面。

女1：我們先將您送到飯店安置行李吧！

男：就這麼辦吧。

詞彙　tired 疲倦的；累的 thoughtful 體貼的 luggage 行李

4.

這些女子在做什麼？

（A）預定機票
（B）買機票
（C）登機
（D）接機

解說　根據對話中的We were sent here to meet you和後文中出現的plane可知，他們是在接機。　　答案 (D)

詞彙　reserve 預定 boarding 登機 airport 機場

5.

史密斯先生說「但我等下要和你們經理見面」是什麼意思？

（A）他沒有時間去酒店休息。
（B）他不能入住酒店。
（C）他不想去酒店。
（D）他沒有必要去酒店。

解說　這是詢問某句話背後含意的考題。在對話中女子建議史密斯先生先去飯店休息，但史密斯先生回答說他要去和經理見面，也就是說他沒有時間去酒店，所以答案選（A）。其它選項和文意不符。　　答案 (A)

6.

根據對話，哪一項是不正確的？

（A）史密斯先生在飛機上待了十二個小時。
（B）史密斯先生接受了他們的建議。
（C）史密斯拒絕了他們來接機。
（D）史密斯很高興他們來接機。

解說　這是在詢問對話細節的考題。根據對話內容可知，史密斯先生在飛機上待了十二個小時，故（A）可刪除。對於先去放行李的提議，史密斯先生也同意，故（B）也可以刪除。他們已經來接機，且史密斯先生表示很高興，所以（C）的表述有誤，是正確答案。

答案 (C)

詞彙　suggestion 建議 refuse 拒絕 glad 開心的

Chapter 17　與圖表相關的考題

STEP 01　若沒答對會後悔的考題

1 (A)

1. 英W　美M

1 找出核心詞彙	floor
2 了解類型	詢問樓層
3 看圖表	大樓的樓層表
4 看選項	樓層
5 聽錄音來確認答案	

Floor	Tenants
5	P & R Accounting
4	Princess Orthopedics
3	Champion Software
2	Positive Advertisement
1	Castle Real Estate

W：Hi, I can't find the Hollywood Film. Which floor should I go to?

M：They are on the same floor as Positive Advertisement.

樓層	住戶
5	P & R會計
4	公主整形外科
3	冠軍軟體公司
2	正向廣告
1	城堡仲介公司

女：你好，我找不到「好萊塢影片」，我應該去哪層樓呢？
男：他們和「正向廣告」同一層樓。

看圖示。女子要去哪個樓層？

（A）2樓
（B）3樓
（C）4樓
（D）5樓

解說　看題目便可知道這是「與公司所在樓層有關」的對話內容，要特別注意講到公司位置、樓層的訊息，男子說「They are on the same floor as Positive Advertisement.」可知道女子想找的公司和「Positive

Advertisement」在同一層樓。再對照圖表，可知「Positive Advertisement」在二樓，故答案為（A）。

答案 (A)

1 (B)	2 (C)	3 (D)	4 (D)
5 (B)	6 (C)	7 (A)	8 (C)
9 (D)	10 (B)	11 (C)	12 (D)

問題1～3請參考以下對話與圖表。美W 美M

Order	NO. 86425
Items / quantity	**Unit price**
Highlighter / 200	0.5 dollar
Duplicating paper / 200 boxes	30 dollars / box
²Stapler / 20	15 dollars

W : Hello, what can I do for you?

M : ¹Have the office supplies we ordered last week arrived?

W : Yes, they arrived just yesterday, but ²the price of the stapler has been adjusted. The manufacturer raised the original price by 3%.

M : Do you mean we have to pay 3% more?

W : Yes.

M : In this case, ³I think our order will have to be adjusted, too. We only have so such money for them.

訂單	編號：86425
物品 / 數量	單價
螢光筆 / 200支	0.5美元
複印紙 / 200盒	每盒30美元
釘書機 / 20個	15美元一個

女：你好，需要幫忙嗎？
男：我們上周訂購的辦公用品到貨了嗎？
女：是的，昨天剛到，但是釘書機的價格有所調整。廠家把原先的價格提高了3%。
男：你的意思是我們要多付3%嗎？
女：的確。
男：既然這樣的話，我想我們的訂單也要調整一下，我們只用這麼多錢購買。

詞彙 office supply 辦公用具 stapler 釘書機
manufacturer 製造商 adjust 調整

1.
男士的目的是什麼？
（A）和女士談判
（B）來取辦公用品
（C）說明女士處理訂單
（D）和女士討價還價

解說 這是詢問對話主題的考題，根據對話中男士的第一句話Have the office supplies we ordered last week arrived可知，男士的目的是取貨，選（B）。　答案 (B)

詞彙 purpose 目的 negotiate 協商

2.
按照女士的話，男士應該為釘書機付多少錢？
（A）300美元
（B）255美元
（C）309美元
（D）200美元

解說 圖表中顯示了釘書機的單價是15美元，20個釘書機的價格是300美元，按照女士的話，釘書機的價格上漲了3%，不用真的去計算費用，只要找到比原本應付的300美元多的選項即可，所以選（C）。　答案 (C)

3.
男士最後的話是什麼意思？
（A）他要取消訂單。
（B）他要放棄購買釘書機。
（C）他要全部購買全部的複印紙。
（D）他要少買釘書機。

解說 這是詢問男子意圖的考題，男子最後的話是：我想我們的訂單也要調整一下，我們只用這麼多錢購買，言外之意就是，價格上漲了，但是貨款不變，那麼釘書機的數量就會少，選（D）。　答案 (D)

詞彙 cancel 取消 fewer 較少的

問題4～6請參考以下對話與圖表。英W 美W

Interview Notice

• All applicants are requested to come to our company for an interview at ten a.m. next Monday.

• The interview is divided into three rounds and will be completed within a week.

• Candidates should be formally dressed.

⁶6 June, 2017

W1 : Have you arranged the ⁴interview time, Devena?

W2 : Yes, the form is already on your desk.

W1 : I see. How many interviewees are there in all?

W2 : In addition to the **⁵two candidates** to be interviewed by the general manager, <u>there are 20 others</u>.

W1 : Remember to publish the interview notice online.

W2 : I'm just going to do it.

面試通知

- 請所有應聘者在下週一上午十點來公司參加面試。
- 面試分為三輪，將在一周內完成。
- 應聘者應穿著正式。

2017年6月6日

女1：德維娜，面試時間你安排好了嗎？

女2：已經好了，表格已經放在你的辦公桌上了。

女1：我知道了。一共有多少面試者？

女2：除了總經理要親自面試的兩位應聘者，還有20位。

女1：你要記得把面試通知發佈到網上。

女2：我正要去做呢。

詞彙 arrange 安排 interviewee 面試者 candidate 應徵者 publish 公告；發布 notice 通知；公告

4.

他們在談論什麼？

（A）關於雇用人數

（B）關於培訓時間

（C）關於面試結果

（D）關於面試時間

解說 在對話中的第一句就可聽到女子詢問是否把面試時間安排好了，雇用人數、培訓時間和面試結果在對話中均沒有提及。　　　　　　　　　答案 (D)

詞彙 employee 員工 training 訓練 result 結果

5.

一共有多少位面試者？

（A）20

（B）22

（C）18

（D）23

解說 在對話中女子問一共有多少面試者，第二名女子回答說：出了總經理要親自面試的兩位，還有20位，即總共有22位面試者，選（B）。　　答案 (B)

6.

面試在什麼時候進行？

（A）下個月

（B）這周五

（C）下周

（D）下下周

解說 表格中的第一條明確提到了所有的面試者應在下周一上午十點參加面試，也就是說面試是在下周進行的，選（C）。　　　　　　　　　　　答案 (C)

詞彙 hold 舉辦

問題7～9請參考以下對話與圖表。 美M 美W

The Names of The Film	Time	Price
Love and Other Drugs	7:30	35 dollars
Love Actually	8:00	40 dollars
Midnight in Paris	8:30	35 dollars
The Holiday	9:00	35 dollars
⁸*The Painted Veil*	9:30	40 dollars

M : Bonnie, I've heard that a lot of science fiction movies have been released recently. Would you like to go to see a movie with me?

W : **⁷**<u>Yes. I'd like to.</u> But I prefer movies about love.

M : **⁹**<u>If so, you can watch a science fiction movie with me first, and then I'll watch a romantic movie with you.</u> Ok?

W : **⁷**<u>Sure.</u> But I don't know what romantic movies have been showing recently.

M : That's OK. We can browse these kinds of movies on the computer, and then book tickets. By the way, **⁸**<u>we only have time after nine.</u>

電影名稱	時間	價錢
《愛情與靈藥》	7:30	35美元
《真愛至上》	8:00	40美元
《午夜巴黎》	8:30	35美元
《戀愛假期》	9:00	35美元
《面紗》	9:30	40美元

男：邦妮，我聽說最近上映了很多部的科幻電影，你有興趣和我一起去看嗎？

女：是的，我很願意去。但是我更喜歡講述愛情的電影。

男：如果是這樣的話，你先陪我看科幻電影，我再陪你看愛情電影。可以嗎？

女：當然可以了。但是我還不知道最近上映了什麼愛情電影。

男：沒關係，我們可以透過電腦瀏覽這類電影，然後再訂票。順便說一下，我們只有九點以後有時間。

詞彙 science fiction movie 科幻電影 release 上映 recently 最近

7.

女子是否會和男子一起去看科幻電影？
（A）是的，她會的。
（B）不，她不會。
（C）沒有提到。
（D）不，她很願意。

解說 這個問題需要將整段對話聽完才能夠作答，根據對話中的內容，女子說自己想看愛情電影，然後男子出主意，看完科幻再看愛情電影，邦妮同意了，因此（A）正確。 答案 (A)

詞彙 mention 提及

8.

他們會選擇哪部愛情電影？
（A）《愛情與靈藥》
（B）《午夜巴黎》
（C）《面紗》
（D）《戀愛假期》

解說 這個題目需要搭配電影時刻表，對話中男子說的最後一句話By the way, we only have time after nine，再對照時刻表，九點半之後的只有《面紗》這部電影，因此他們只能選擇這部，故答案為（C）。 答案 (C)

詞彙 drug 藥 midnight 午夜 veil 面紗

9.

我們從對話中了解到什麼？
（A）他們是情侶。
（B）男子非常喜歡看科幻電影。
（C）女子不喜歡看科幻電影。
（D）男子尊重女子的選擇。

解說 根據對話中的內容，女子想看愛情電影，男子就和她商量看完科幻就看愛情電影，故選（D）。
答案 (D)

詞彙 dialogue 對話 respect 尊重

問題10～12請參考以下對話與圖表。 英W 美M

Broadway musical *The Sound of Music*
Time: forty past six in the evening of
　　　May 6, 2018
Venue: Art Gallery
Seat: Row 25, No. 6
Fare: 890 dollars
Ticket No.: 22852582

W : What kind of music do you like?

M : ¹¹I like all kinds of music, but I like jazz and country music recently.

W : Well. Did you go to the country music concert held yesterday?

M : No, I didn't know where it was. But I went to see a musical yesterday.

W : WOW! I went to the musical, too. Give me your ticket and let me see ¹²if we were in the same place.

M : Ok. Here you are.

百老匯音樂劇《音樂之聲》
時間：2018年5月6日晚上6點40
場館：藝術館
座位：25排6號
票價：890美元
票號：22852582

女：你喜歡哪種音樂？
男：我喜歡所有的音樂，但是最近我喜歡爵士樂和鄉村音樂。
女：好吧，昨天舉辦的鄉村音樂演奏會你去了嗎？
男：沒有，我不知道在哪裡。但是我昨天去看了音樂劇。
女：哇哦！我也去看了音樂劇。把你的門票給我，讓我看看是否我們在同一個地方。
男：好的，給你。

詞彙 jazz 爵士 country music 鄉村音樂 concert 音樂會 musical 音樂的

10.

男子幾點去看音樂劇？
（A）6:20
（B）6:40
（C）7:20
（D）7:40

解說 這題需要對照圖表，根據圖表的時間可知是forty past six，與（B）項的twenty to seven表達的是同一個意思，都是指「六點四十」。 答案 (B)

詞彙 employee 員工 training 訓練 result 結果

11.

男子喜歡流行音樂嗎？
（A）不喜歡，他喜歡爵士樂和鄉村音樂。
（B）不，他喜歡除了流行音樂的所有音樂。
（C）是的，他喜歡所有的音樂。
（D）是的，他喜歡除了爵士樂和鄉村音樂以外的所有音樂。

解說 根據對話中的內容I like all kinds of music, but I like jazz and country music recently，因此可知是喜歡所有的音樂，故選（C）。 答案 (C)

詞彙 except 除此之外 beside 之外

12.

以下正確的是？
（A）他們都喜歡流行音樂。
（B）男子只喜歡爵士樂和鄉村音樂。
（C）女子看了鄉村音樂演奏會。
（D）他們現在在同一個城市。

解說 這題需要聽完所有的對話內容後，才能夠作答。根據對話中的男子說的最後一句話here you are，可知他們是在同一個城市，故選（D）。　　　答案（D）

Quiz |

1. (B)　　　**2.** (A)　　　**3.** (A)　　　**4.** (A)

Q1 美 W

This is Emily Wang from Dr. Edgar's office. **I would like to speak with you about** your appointment at 4 p.m. tomorrow. As this is your first visit, please arrive 10 minutes earlier to fill out some forms.

我是埃德加醫生辦公室的艾蜜莉・王。我想告訴您有關您明天下午四點的預約。由於這是您第一次來，請您提早十分鐘到填寫一些表格。

這通留言的目的是什麼？
（A）為了邀請一位演講者
（B）為了確認預約

解說 在考題裡看到message的同時，就可以知道該錄音為「電話錄音」類型。由考題的purpose也能知道這是詢問主題的，答案線索在錄音的前段／中間部分。錄音裡聽到詢問主題類考題的核心詞彙I'd like to speak with you，在此之後就有線索。將「我想告訴您有關您明天下午四點的預約」改成「為了確認預約」來表達的（B）為答案。　　　答案（B）

詞彙 **appointment** 預約　**fill out** 填寫　**form** 填寫　**confirm** 確認

Q2 美 M

Hi, this is Mark Peterson from Central Bank. I was very impressed with your resume, and I would like to meet you for an interview. **Please bring** a picture ID on the interview date.

你好。我是中央銀行的馬克・彼得森。我對你履歷的印象很深刻，因此我想跟你約面試。在面試當日請你攜帶有照片的身份證件。

面試者被要求要帶什麼？
（A）有照片的身份證件
（B）文件影本

解說 在「電話錄音」類的錄音裡，詢問要求事項的考題其答案線索在錄音的後段部分。該錄音裡出現要求／建議的暗示please並接著出現bring，所以在此之後就有答案線索。將picture ID做變化來表達的（A）為答案。　　　答案（A）

詞彙 **impressed** 印象深刻的　**resume** 履歷表　**bring** 帶來　**picture ID** 有照片的證件　**photo identification** 有照片的身份證件　**copy** 影本　**document** 文件

Q3 美 W

You have reached Alabama Power Company. Residents in the downtown area are currently experiencing a power outage. If you want to talk to a customer service representative, please stay on the line.

您所聯絡的是阿拉巴馬電力公司。市中心目前正停電中。若您想和客服專員說話，請等待別掛斷。

這位打電話者想要聯絡什麼人？
（A）電力公司
（B）網路服務供應商

解說 考題裡的trying to reach告訴你該錄音為「電話錄音」類型，且看到選項就可以知道是「機構的自動語音系統錄音」。這是詢問說話者的考題，答案線索在you have reached附近。Power company是指電力公司，所以使用相似詞的（A）為答案。 答案 (A)

詞彙 power company 電力公司 resident 居民 downtown area 市中心區 currently 目前 power outage 停電 representative 專員 stay on the line 在線上等待 electric company 電力公司 provider 供應商

Q4 澳 W

If you want to make a reservation, **press '1' now**. If you want to leave a message, please wait for the beep and then begin speaking.

若您想預約，請按「1」。若您想留言，等到聽見嗶聲再開始說話。

為什麼打電話者會按「1」？
（A）為了預約
（B）為了留言

解說 看考題就可以知道該錄音為「機構的自動語音系統錄音」。Press 1為核心詞彙，所以press 1 now附近就有答案線索。出現了與錄音裡相同說法make a resevation的（A）為答案。 答案 (A)

詞彙 make a reservation 預約 press 按 leave a message 留言 wait for 等… beep 嗶聲

STEP 01 若沒答對會後悔的考題

1 (A)	2 (A)	3 (B)	4 (B)
5 (A)	6 (A)	7 (B)	8 (A)
9 (C)	10 (C)	11 (A)	12 (B)
13 (B)	14 (B)		

1. 英 M

1 找出核心詞彙	purpose of the message
2 類型與答案的位置	主題／前面、中間部分
3 看選項	重新安排時間或參加運動俱樂部

Hello, Annie. This is Brian from Bodies Athletic Club. **I'm calling to** inform you that we have to reschedule this weekend's soccer game for next Saturday.

安妮您好。我是身體運動俱樂部的布萊恩。我打電話是要通知您，我們需要把這週末的足球比賽重新安排到下週六了。

這通留言的目的是什麼？
（A）為了重新安排一場比賽
（B）為了參加運動俱樂部

解說 透過考題裡的message與選項，就可以知道該錄音為「個人電話留言」類型。這是詢問主題的考題，答案線索出現於錄音的前段／中間部分。將核心詞彙I'm calling to後面出現的「要通知您，我們需要把這週末的足球比賽重新安排」做變化來表達的（A）為答案。 答案 (A)

詞彙 inform 通知 reschedule 重新安排（時間） this weekend 這個週末 join 加入

2. 美 W

1 找出核心詞彙	caller reached
2 類型與答案的位置	主題／前面、中間部分
3 看選項	重新安排時間或參加運動俱樂部

You've reached the Tokyo branch of International Bank. We are not open today. Our business hours are 9 a.m. to 4 p.m., except on weekends and national holidays.

您所聯絡的是國際銀行東京分部。我們今天沒有營業。除了週末和國慶假日以外，我們的營業時間為上午九點至下午四點。

這位打電話者聯絡到了什麼型態的公司？
（A）銀行
（B）大使館

解說 透過考題裡的caller reached與選項，就可以知道該錄音為「機構的自動語音系統錄音」類型。答案就出現於錄音的前段部分，透過在核心語彙you've reached後面出現的the Tokyo branch of International Bank，可以知道為「銀行」。 答案 (A)

詞彙 business hours 營業時間 except 除…之外 national holiday 國慶假日 embassy 大使館

3. 美 M

1 找出核心詞彙	speaker work
2 類型與答案的位置	說話者／前面部分
3 看選項	會計部門或行銷部門

Hi, Mary, **this is Jason** <u>from the marketing department</u>. I would like to know if you want to join us for our accounting director, Mr. Johnson's retirement party tonight.

瑪莉你好。我是行銷部門的傑森。我想知道你要不要跟我們一起參加我們會計部門經理強生先生的退休晚會。

說話者工作於什麼部門？
（A）會計部門
（B）行銷部門

解說 詢問說話者為誰的考題，答案線索都是在錄音的前段部分。from是出現公司或部門名稱時的線索。
答案 (B)

詞彙 marketing department 行銷部門 accounting director 會計部門經理 retirement party 退休派對

4. 澳 W

1 找出核心詞彙	intended for
2 類型與答案的位置	聽話者／前面部分
3 看選項	旅館員工或旅館顧客

Thank you for calling <u>the Oceanview Hotel.</u> **If you are calling to** <u>make a reservation, please press '1'.</u> For further assistance, please press 'zero' to be connected to an operator.

感謝您致電海洋風景飯店。若您打電話要預約，請按「1」。若需要別的服務，請按「0」來聯絡總機人員。

這通留言是給誰的？
（A）旅館的員工們
（B）旅館的顧客們

解說 透過考題裡的message與選項，就可以知道該錄音為「機構的自動語音系統錄音」類型。透過intended for，可以知道這是詢問聽眾為誰的考題，答案在錄音的前段部分。連接到的地方是旅館，訂房的人就是「旅館的顧客」。
答案 (B)

詞彙 make a reservation 預約 press 按 assistance 幫助；服務 operator 總機人員 employee 職員 customer 顧客

5. 英 M

1 找出核心詞彙	problem
2 類型與答案的位置	論及問題／中間部分
3 看選項	庫存不足或支付完成

Hi, Ms. Kim, this is Mark from Central Bookstore. I am calling regarding the book you ordered. **Unfortunately,** <u>it's sold out.</u> I can place a special order if you don't mind waiting a few days for delivery.

金小姐您好，我是中央書店的馬克。我打電話過來是有關於您所訂購的書。很不幸地，它都售完了。若您不介意再等幾天配送，我可以下特別訂單。

這個問題是什麼？
（A）有個東西不能提供了。
（B）帳單已經付了。

解說 詢問電話錄音裡是什麼問題狀況的考題，答案線索出現於錄音的中間部分。表示問題狀況的核心詞彙為unfortunately，其後面的「都售完了」就是這裡的問題狀況。available是有庫存的狀況，但這裡有not，所以是沒有庫存的意思。
答案 (A)

詞彙 regarding 有關於… order 訂購 unfortunately 很不幸地 sold out 售完 place an order 下訂單 don't mind -ing 不介意 wait 等待 delivery 配送 available 可用的 payment 支付

6. 美 M

1 找出核心詞彙	why closed
2 類型與答案的位置	具體內容／前面部分
3 看選項	整修或國定假日

Hello. This is an automated message from Verto's Law Firm. We're sorry, but we are closed all through this week **because** <u>our office is being remodeled.</u> Please call back next week.

你好。這是維多法律事務所的自動留言。很抱歉我們這周之內都不上班，因為我們的辦公室正在整修當中。請下周再次來電。

為什麼最近辦公室不上班？
（A）由於整修
（B）由於國定假日

解說 透過考題裡的「為什麼不上班」，就可以知道該錄音為「機構的自動語音系統錄音」類型。將核心詞彙because後面出現的「辦公室整修」做變化來表達的（A）為答案。
答案 (A)

詞彙 automated message 自動留言 law firm 法律事務所 all through this week 這整周 remodel 整修 call back 再次來電 due to 由於… renovation 整修

7. 英M

1 找出核心詞彙	suggest
2 類型與答案的位置	要求事項／後面部分
3 看選項	回撥電話或訪問門市

Hello, Ms. William, this is Brian from Anna Home Design. I wanted to tell you that the living room chairs you ordered aren't available in brown, but the gray fabric is available. I think you will like them in the gray fabric, too, but **need you to** stop by the store to confirm. Thank you.

威廉小姐您好。我是安娜住宅設計的布萊恩。我想跟您說，您訂購的客廳椅子沒有咖啡色的，但是有灰色布料。我覺得您也會喜歡那些灰色的布料，不過需要您順路到門市確認。謝謝。

打電話者建議接聽電話的人做什麼？
（A）回撥電話
（B）到門市來

解說 透過考題裡的caller，可以知道是「電話錄音」類型，由suggest得知這是詢問要求／建議事項的考題。答案出現於後段部分，將核心詞彙need you to後面出現的「順路到」做變化來表達的（B）為答案。 答案 (B)

詞彙 order 訂購 be available in 有…顏色的 fabric 布料 stop by 順路拜訪 confirm 確認 return the phone call 回撥電話

8. 美W

1 找出核心詞彙	ask
2 類型與答案的位置	要求事項／後面部分
3 看選項	在線上等候或按1

Thank you for calling Anywhere Tour Agency. All our lines are busy due to high volume of calls. **Please** hold the line, and our next available agent will answer your call shortly.

謝謝您撥電話到環遊旅行社。由於大量的來電，我們所有的專線都被佔用當中。請等待別掛斷，我們下一個有空的人員會立即接聽您的電話。

說話者要求打電話者做什麼？
（A）在線上等候
（B）按「1」

解說 對撥電話的人提出要求的錄音是「機構的自動

語音系統錄音」。答案在錄音的後段部分，核心詞彙please後面出現的「等待別掛斷」，用相同意思來表達的（A）為答案。 答案 (A)

詞彙 lines are busy 專線忙線中 volume of calls 通話量 hold the line 在線上等候 available 有空的 answer the call 接電話 shortly 立即 stay on the line 在線上等候

問題9～10，請參考以下訊息。 澳W

1 找出核心詞彙	business / closed
2 類型與答案的位置	說話者／前面部分
	具體內容／中間部分
3 看選項	餐廳，電影院，辦公用品店
	星期一，星期五，星期日
4 預測對話內容	聯絡到了辦公用品店，但周末休息

9Thank you for calling Fine Office Supplies, your place for the lowest prices on office supplies. Sorry, but we are currently closed. **10**Our hours of operation are from 10 a.m. to 6 p.m. on weekdays. If you would like to browse our stock and shop online, please visit our website. Thank you.

謝謝您致電精品辦公用品店，最低價辦公用品的總匯。很抱歉我們現在沒有營業。我們營業時間為平日上午十點至下午六點。若您想瀏覽我們的貨品以及線上購物，請至我們的網站。謝謝。

詞彙 the lowest price 最低價 office supply 辦公用品 closed 沒有營業的 hour of operation 營業時間 on weekdays 在平日 browse 瀏覽 shop online 線上購物 visit 訪問

9.
這是什麼型態的公司？
（A）餐廳
（B）電影院
（C）辦公用品店

解說 透過考題裡的business（營業場所）與「沒有營業」，就可以知道這是「機構的自動語音系統錄音」，因此考題是在詢問說話者為何，答案會在錄音的前段部分。核心詞彙Thank you for calling後面出現的名稱與「最低價辦公用品的總匯」都是答案的線索。 答案 (C)

詞彙 movie theater 電影院

10.
這家店什麼時候不營業？
（A）星期一
（B）星期五
（C）星期日

解說 在「機構的自動語音系統錄音」裡，營業時間公告是在中間部分出現。聽到「營業時間為平日」，所以可以猜測到週末是打烊的。 答案 (C)

詞彙 store 商店

問題11～12，請參考以下訊息。 英 M

1 找出核心詞彙	man calling / ask
2 類型與答案的位置	主題／前面、中間部
	要求事項／後面部分
3 看選項	傳遞訊息，重新安排會議
	得到同事的電話號碼
	到行銷部門，打電話，搭上早班飛機
4 預測對話內容	為了通知而撥電話，並要求回電

Good morning, Ms. Baker. This is Dan Henry calling from the marketing department. ¹¹Mr. Shawn asked me to let you know that he will be a little late for the 1:30 meeting with you. He's going to be back a little later from New York. ¹²Please call directly on his cell phone at 217-555-4738. Thank you very much.

貝克爾小姐早安。我是行銷部門的丹·亨利。尚恩先生要我通知您，和您約在一點半的會議他會晚一點到。他稍晚會從紐約回來。請直接撥電話到他的行動電話217-555-4738。謝謝。

詞彙 marketing department 行銷部門 meeting 會議 a little later 稍晚 directly 直接 cell phone 行動電話

11.
為什麼這個男人打電話來？
（A）為了傳遞一項訊息
（B）為了重新安排會議
（C）為了得到同事的電話號碼

解說 這是「個人電話留言」類錄音，且該考題為詢問主題的，所以答案在前段／中間部分。答案線索是接在自我介紹後面就出現。「通知」也可以說成是「傳遞一項訊息」。（B）是陷阱，因為這是Mr. Shawn的來電目的，並非錄音裡撥電話者的目的。 答案 (A)

詞彙 deliver 配送 reschedule 重新安排時間 co-worker 同事 phone number 電話號碼

12.
這個男人要求接聽電話的人做什麼？
（A）來到行銷部門
（B）打電話
（C）搭上很早的班機

解說 這是詢問「個人電話留言」裡的要求事項的考題，答案線索在錄音的後段部分。將核心詞彙please後面出現的「直接撥電話到他的行動電話」做簡化來表達的（B）為答案。 答案 (B)

詞彙 make a phone call 撥電話 catch 搭乘 early flight 早班飛機

問題13～14，請參考以下訊息。 美 W

1 找出核心詞彙	complaint / ask
2 類型與答案的位置	論及問題／中間部分
	要求事項／後面部分
3 看選項	貨物受損，貨物還沒送到，送錯東西
	退還總金額，打電話，立刻配送貨物
4 預測對話內容	訂購的商品尚未到達，而要求回電

Hello there. ¹³I'm calling about a problem with my order. My name is Gina Rotelli, and my order number is SBB-934. ¹³I was promised delivery within two weeks of the date I placed the order, but it still hasn't come in. ¹⁴Please check on this and give me a call today. My number is 555-0703. Thank you.

你好。我打電話過來是有關於我的訂單問題。我的名字是吉娜·羅泰里，我的訂單編號是SBB-934。我得到的保證是我下訂單之後兩周內配送，但它還沒有來。請確認這點，並在今天給我電話。我的號碼是555-0703。謝謝。

詞彙 problem 問題 order 訂單 delivery 配送 place an order 下訂單 come in 進來 check 確認

13.
這個打電話的人在抱怨什麼？
（A）送來的貨物受損了。
（B）貨物還沒送到。
（C）送錯東西了。

解說 透過考題裡的caller可以知道這是「個人電話留言」類錄音。complaint是「論及問題」類的核心詞彙，相關答案線索在錄音中間部分出現。將「還沒有來」做變化來表達的（B）為答案。 答案 (B)

詞彙 complaint 抱怨 arrive 到達 damaged 受損的 wrong item 不對的商品 deliver 配送

14.
打電話的人要求這家公司做什麼？
（A）退還總金額
（B）打電話
（C）立刻配送貨物

解說 這是詢問要求事項的考題。將核心詞彙please後面出現的「請確認、給我電話」做簡化來表達的（B）為答案。　　　　　　　　　　　　　　　　答案 (B)

詞彙　refund 退款　amount 金額　right away 立刻

1. (C)　2. (A)　3. (A)　4. (C)　5. (C)　6. (A)
7. (B)　8. (B)　9. (D)　10. (D)　11. (C)　12. (A)

問題1～3，請參考以下訊息。 美 M

Hi, Erica. **¹This is Madison Morton calling from Westwood Furniture store, and I'm the sales manager.** I'm calling about the dress hanger you ordered from us last week. **²Unfortunately, the second type model you selected is not in stock.** We can place a special order for it, but I don't think we can get it in less than two months. However, we have the third type model available now. So **³I'd like to know whether you want to order the third type model or would rather wait for the second type model.** I will leave for the day around six, so please call me back as soon as you get this message. Thank you.

您好，艾瑞卡。這是西木傢俱店麥迪森・摩頓的留言，我是銷售經理。我打來是有關上週您和我們訂購的衣架。很不巧地，您選的第二款沒有庫存。我們可以下特別訂單，但我不認為我們能在兩個月之內拿到。然而，我們目前有第三款可提供。所以我想知道您是否要訂購第三款，或寧願等第二款。我今天六點左右會離開，所以當您聽到這個留言，請儘快回電給我。謝謝。

詞彙　furniture 傢俱　sales manager 銷售部門負責人
dress hanger 衣架　unfortunately 不幸地　type 類型
select 挑選　in stock 有庫存的　place an order 下訂單
get 得到　available 可用的　wait for 等待
leave for the day 下班　as soon as …之後立刻
get the message 收到留言

1.
打電話是什麼人？
（A）一位會計
（B）一位服裝製造商
（C）一位銷售經理
（D）一位時尚設計師

解說　透過考題裡的caller與problem，可以知道這是「個人電話留言」類錄音。該考題是詢問說話者為誰的，所以其答案線索在錄音的前段部分。在前段的自我介紹的話語裡可以直接聽到「銷售經理」。　答案 (C)

詞彙　accountant 會計師　clothing maker 衣服製造業者

2.
這個問題是什麼？
（A）有個東西沒有了。
（B）有些文件遺失了。
（C）有些產品被損壞了。
（D）配送延誤了。

解說　問題狀況通常出現於電話錄音的中間部分。透過核心詞彙unfortunately，可以知道將「沒有庫存」做變化來表達的（A）為答案。　　　　答案 (A)

詞彙　item 商品　document 文件　missing 遺失的
product 產品　damaged 受損的　delivery 配送　late 晚；延誤

3.
這個打電話者想由艾瑞卡這兒知道什麼？
（A）她想要的款式。
（B）她回到辦公室的時間。
（C）特別訂購項目的費用。
（D）預計收貨的時間。

解說　在電話錄音裡，要求事項出現於後段部分。將核心詞彙I'd like to know後面出現的「是否要訂購第三款，或寧願等第二款」以概括性的敘述做變化來表達的（A）為答案。　　　　答案 (A)

詞彙　return 回來　cost 費用　specially 特別　expected 預估的　arrival time 到達時間

問題4～6請參考以下訊息和圖表。 美 W

Payment method	Rate charged
Annual payment	$179,671
Semi-annual payment	$93,429
⁵Quarterly payment	$47,074
Monthly payment	$15,811

Dear Mr. Anderson, this is May Lynn, **⁴customer service representative of AMEC Insurance Agency.** We are replying to your call regarding the change in payment method of your saving insurance. **⁵You stated earlier that you would like to change from annual payment to quarterly payment this year.** It is alright except we will need **⁶you to sign an application form. We will send the form by mail** with a prepaid return envelope. Please fill out the form and mail it back to us at your earliest convenience. Once we've received the form, your case will be processed right away. If you have any questions, please feel free to call back again at 0800-888-666. And thank you again for choosing AMEC Insurance Agency.

付款方式	繳交費率
年繳	$179,671
半年繳	$93,429
季繳	$47,074
月繳	$15,811

親愛的安德森先生，我叫瑪莉‧琳恩，AMEC保險公司的客服代表。我們回覆您的電話是有關於您的儲蓄險要變更付款方式的事宜。您稍早提到您今年想要將年繳的方式改為季繳。這是沒問題的，只是我們需要您簽一份申請表。我們會用郵寄方式，附上回郵信封，將表格寄送給您。請填寫表格並在您最快的方便時刻寄回給我們。一旦我們收到您的表格之後，我們會立即處理您的案子。若您有任何問題，請隨時撥打0800-888-666與我們聯絡。並再次感謝您選擇AMEC保險公司。

詞彙 customer service 客服 representative 代表 insurance agency 保險公司 reply 回覆 regarding 關於 change 改變 payment method 付款方式 saving insurance 儲蓄險 state 陳述 except 除⋯⋯之外 sign 簽署 application form 申請表 send by mail 以郵寄方式寄送 prepaid return envelope 回郵信封 fill out 填寫 convenience 方便 receive 接獲 appropriate 適當的 question 問題 choose 選擇

4.

講者在哪裡工作？
（A）旅行社
（B）租車公司
（C）保險公司
（D）藥房

解說 這是詢問「工作地點」的「簡短選項類考題」。一開始，講者便說「我叫瑪莉‧琳恩，AMEC保險公司的客服代表」，表明自己是保險公司的人。所以正確答案應該要選（C）。　　　　　答案 (C)

詞彙 travel agency 旅行社 car rental company 租車公司 insurance company 保險公司 pharmacy 藥房

5.

請看此圖，講者在申請案後，每次將付費多少錢？
（A）$179,671
（B）$93,429
（C）$47,074
（D）$15,811

解說 這是詢問繳費金額為何的「簡短選項類考題」。文中提到「您今年想要將年繳的方式改為季繳。」既然是想改變成「季繳」方式，而圖表中對應季繳金額為選項（C）47,074。　　　答案 (C)

詞彙 each time 每一次 application 申請

6.

聽者為了改變，被要求做什麼？
（A）他需要提出申請表

（B）他需要上線要求
（C）他需要寫道歉信
（D）他需要和業務代表談

解說 這是詢問要做繳款方式變更，所需要做的步驟。講者提到：「我們需要您簽一份申請表。我們會用郵寄方式，附上回郵信封，將表格寄送給您。」所以選項（A）是正解。　　　　　答案 (A)

詞彙 require 需要；要求 submit 提出 online request 線上請求 letter of apology 道歉信 sales rep (representative) 業務代表

問題7～9，請參考以下訊息。 英 M

Hello, this message is for Mr. Jefferson. My name is John Franklin. [7]I'm calling regarding the electronic engineering position posted in today's newspaper. I'm sure that I am an excellent candidate for the position. [8]I have over 5 years of experience working for an electronics company. I designed circuit layouts for a variety of electronic products. Also, I was the leader of my team for the last 2 years. I will be visiting near your downtown office next week, so I was wondering if I could show you my previous work at that time. [9]I will send you a copy of my resume this afternoon. I hope to hear from you soon. Thanks and have a good day.

您好，這是給傑佛森先生的留言。我的名字是約翰‧富蘭克林。我打電話是因注意到今天報紙上刊登的電子工程師職位。我肯定我會是這個職位出色的候選人。我在一家電子公司工作已經超過五年的經驗。我為多種電子產品設計電路佈局。而在過去兩年我也是團隊的領導者。下週我會在你們市中心辦公室的附近，所以我在想，那時是否能給你們看我以前的設計。今天下午我會寄出我的簡歷給您。希望能很快得到您的回覆。謝謝，祝您有美好的一天。

詞彙 regarding 有關於⋯ electronic engineering position 電子工程師職位 posted 公佈的 newspaper 報紙 candidate 申請者 design 設計 circuit layout 電路佈局 a variety of 多種的 wonder 想知道 at that time 那時候 copy 影印本 resume 履歷表

7.

這通留言的目的是什麼？
（A）為了訂一項電子產品
（B）為了申請一個職缺
（C）為了追蹤一項申請進度
（D）為了得到一家公司的資訊

解說 透過考題裡的message，可以知道是「個人電話留言」。該考題是詢問主題的，答案線索在錄音的前段／中間部分。透過在核心詞彙I'm calling regarding後面出現的「因注意到今天報紙上刊登的電子工程師職位」，可以猜測到（B）為答案。（C）是有關已提交申請書

之後的狀況，所以不是答案。　　　答案（B）

詞彙　electronic product 電子產品　apply for 申請
job opening 職缺　follow up on 追蹤　application 申請；
申請書　get information 得到資訊

8.
這位打電話者有關於他自己說了什麼？
（A）他在報社工作。
（B）他有相關的經驗。
（C）他聽說了很多關於這家公司的事。
（D）他最近搬到這個地區。

解說　個人電話留言的中間部分，通常出現與主題相關
具體內容，所以該考題的答案就在這兒。將「有超過五
年的經驗」做變化來表達「有相關的經驗」的（B）為
答案。　　　答案（B）

詞彙　relevant 相關的　recently 最近　move to 搬到…
area 地區

9.
這個男人說他將要做什麼？
（A）順道拜訪這間辦公室
（B）給對方看合約
（C）下周回電
（D）提交履歷

解說　這是詢問下一個行程的考題。該類考題的答案線
索通常在錄音後段部分，並且有核心詞彙I will出現。
將「寄出我的簡歷」做變化來表達的（D）為答案。
　　　答案（D）

詞彙　stop by 順道拜訪　contract 合約　call back
回撥電話　submit 提交

問題10～12，請參考以下訊息。 澳 W

10You've reached Countway Computers. We value
your call. All of our lines are busy now. If you want
to inquire about our computer products, hang up
and dial 222-3456. If you would like to speak to
a customer service representative, please stay
on the line, and your call will be answered in turn.
11Right now there is a wait of approximately five
minutes. Otherwise, please leave a brief voice
message with your name and telephone number
by pressing 2. **12**Your call will be returned by our
next available customer service representative.
Thank you.

您已連接至康威電腦。我們重視您的來電。目前所有線路均忙線中。
如果你想詢問我們的電腦產品，請掛斷電話並撥打222-3456。如果您
希望與服務人員通話，請在線上等待，您的電話將被依序接答。目前
大約要五分鐘等候。或是您可以按二，留下您的姓名和電話號碼的語
音訊息。我們下一位服務人員將回撥給您。謝謝您。

詞彙　reach 聯絡到　value 重視　line 電話專線
busy 忙線中　hang up 掛斷電話　dial 撥打電話
representative 專員　stay on the line 在線上等候
answer 回應　in turn 輪流　voice mail message
語音信箱留言　press 按

10.
這個打電話者聯繫的可能是什麼型態的公司？
（A）網路服務供應商
（B）電影院
（C）汽車修理廠
（D）電腦公司

解說　透過考題裡的caller reached，可以知道該錄音是
「機構的自動語音系統錄音」類。這是詢問說話者為誰
的考題，答案線索在錄音的前段部分。透過其公司名
稱，可以猜測到是「電腦公司」。「我們的電腦產品」
也是答案的線索。　　　答案（D）

詞彙　provider 供應商　movie theater 電影院　auto
repair shop 汽車修理廠

11.
這個打電話者需要等多久？
（A）一分鐘
（B）兩分鐘
（C）五分鐘
（D）十分鐘

解說　這是詢問具體事項的考題，答案出現於錄音的中
間部分。追蹤數字也是找答案的好方法。出現「五分鐘
等候」，所以（C）為答案。　　　答案（C）

詞彙　wait 等候

12.
為什麼接聽電話的人會按「2」？
（A）為了要有電話回覆
（B）為了訂票
（C）為了詢問產品
（D）為了了解付費的方式

解說　這是詢問各個號碼所提供的資訊是什麼的考題。
Press 2附近會出現答案。按2號的話，可以留姓名與電
話號碼，同時下一位能夠接電話的服務員會回覆，所以
（A）為答案。　　　答案（A）

詞彙　reserve 預約　payment option 支付方法

Quiz I

1. (A)　　2. (A)　　3. (A)　　4. (A)

Q1 美 W

Thank you for coming to today's meeting. I have a quick announcement before we start our meeting. The repainting of the underground parking garage will begin tomorrow, and it's going to last three days. So, please park in the outdoor parking area.

謝謝你們來到今天的會議。在我們會議開始之前，我有個簡短的公告。地下停車場重新粉刷的工程將於明天開始，而且會持續三天。因此，請在戶外停車區停車。

這則談話主要的目的是什麼？
（A）公告維修工作
（B）招募工作志願者

解說 這是詢問公告主題的考題。「地下停車場重新塗裝工程」是屬於維修工程。　　　答案 (A)

詞彙 announcement 公告 repaint 重新粉刷 underground 底下的 parking area 停車區 maintenance 維修

Q2 英 M

I've asked you all here for a short meeting to discuss our quarterly sales report. Sales went down by 10 percent. **I'd like** all of you to think of the reasons for the decline and come up with new strategies for increasing sales.

我召集你們開簡短的會議，是為了討論我們的季度銷售量報告。銷售掉了百分之十。我希望你們全部都思考其減少的原因，並且想出新的策略來增加銷售量。

說話者要求聽眾做什麼？
（A）對於改善計劃做腦力激盪
（B）策劃季度銷售資料

解說 會議上的公告裡，要求事項會出現於錄音後段部分。將核心說法I'd like後面出現的「思考其減少的原因，而且為了增加銷售量想出新的策略」做變化來表達的「對於改善計劃做腦力激盪」為答案。　答案 (A)

詞彙 quarterly sales report 季度銷售量報告 go down 掉下 reason 原因 decline 減少 come up with 想起（新的想法） strategy 策略 brainstorm 腦力激盪 improvement 改善 draw up 策劃

Q3 美 W

Ladies and gentleman, I'm sorry to announce that tonight's baseball game will be pushed back by one hour due to heavy rain conditions.

各位女士，各位先生。很抱歉要公告今晚的棒球比賽，由於豪雨的狀況將延後一個小時。

這則公告很有可能是在哪裡發出的？
（A）在戶外運動場
（B）在商店裡

解說 會聽到廣播延期棒球比賽的地方，應該就是棒球場吧。　　　答案 (A)

詞彙 announce 公告 baseball game 棒球比賽 push back 延後 heavy rain 豪雨 condition 狀況 stadium 戶外（露天）運動場

Q4 澳 W

Attention, shoppers. The store will be closing in ten minutes. **Please** proceed to the checkout counter immediately to complete your purchase. Thank you for your cooperation.

各位顧客請注意。本店即將在十分鐘之內打烊。請立刻到收銀台來完成您的採購。謝謝您的合作。

說話者建議顧客做什麼？
（A）到結帳處
（B）和經理做確認

解說 考題裡有suggest，就是在詢問要求事項的。將核心詞彙please後面出現的「到收銀台來」當中的proceed改成go來表達的（A）為答案。　答案 (A)

詞彙 shopper 顧客 proceed 到 checkout counter 收銀台 immediately 立刻 complete 完成 cooperation 合作 customer 客人 check with 和…確認

STEP 01 若沒答對會後悔的考題

1 (A)	2 (B)	3 (A)	4 (B)
5 (B)	6 (A)	7 (A)	8 (B)
9 (B)	10 (C)	11 (A)	12 (C)
13 (B)	14 (C)		

1. 英M

1	找出核心詞彙	speaker work for
2	了解類型	說話者／前面部分
3	看選項	連鎖咖啡店或人力中介公司

First on our staff meeting agenda today, I'd like to tell you about the results of our customer survey. As you may know, <u>we conducted a nationwide survey among our customers at all of our 100 coffee shop locations.</u>

今天員工會議的第一個議題，我想告訴你們我們的顧客調查結果。如同你們可能知道的，我們在我們全部一百個咖啡店地點，對我們的客人執行了全國性的調查。

說話者在什麼型態的公司工作？
（A）連鎖咖啡店
（B）人力仲介公司

解說 這是詢問說話者為誰的考題。在公告裡，說話者與聽話者相關的答案線索會在前段部分出現。之後再聽到「我們全部一百個咖啡店地點」，可以知道說話者是在連鎖咖啡店工作。 答案 (A)

詞彙 **agenda** 議題 **result** 結果 **survey** 調查 **conduct** 執行 **nationwide** 全國性的 **location** 地點

2. 美W

1	找出核心詞彙	purpose of the talk
2	了解類型	主題／前面部分
3	看選項	討論增加資金的計畫，或介紹新同事成員

Good afternoon. I'm glad you could all make it to this meeting. **I'm very pleased to** <u>introduce our new accountant at the GW Theater, James Donovan.</u> Mr. Donovan brings a great deal of money management experience to the job.

午安。我很高興你們全部都能來到這場會議。我非常高興介紹我們在GW戲院的新的會計師詹姆士‧唐納文。唐納文先生把相當多的資金管理經驗帶到這份工作上。

這則談話主要的目的是什麼？
（A）為了討論增加資金的計畫
（B）為了介紹新同事成員

解說 若錄音的前段部分出現introduce，很有可能是屬於「會議上公告」的「人物介紹」類型。將「新的會計師」做變化來表達成「新同事成員」的（B）為答案。 答案 (B)

詞彙 **make it** 能夠前來 **introduce** 介紹 **accountant** 會計師 **theater** 戲院 **bring** 帶來 **a great deal of** 相當多的 **management** 管理 **raise** 籌（款）

3. 美M

1	找出核心詞彙	ask
2	了解類型	要求事項／後面部分
3	看選項	送出某項要求給人事部門，或立即報告問題狀況

Before we start today's meeting, I'd like to tell you about the new company policy. From now on, **you must** <u>submit your vacation requests not to your immediate supervisor but to the personnel department.</u> Thank you for your cooperation.

在我們開始今天會議之前，我想告訴你們新的公司政策。從今以後，你們的休假申請單不是給你們的直屬上司，而是要交給人事部門。謝謝你們的合作。

說話者要求聽眾做什麼？
（A）送出某項要求給人事部門
（B）立即報告問題狀況

解說 將詢問要求事項的考題的核心說法you must後面的「提交休假申請單」做變化來表達的（A）為答案。 答案 (A)

詞彙 **policy** 政策 **from now on** 從此以後 **submit** 提交 **vacation request** 休假申請單 **immediate supervisor** 直屬上司 **personnel department** 人事部門 **cooperation** 合作 **report** 合作 **problem** 問題 **immediately** 立即

4. 澳W

1	找出核心詞彙	asked to check for
2	了解類型	要求事項／後面部分
3	看選項	工作時間表或每日的公告

I just want to give a quick reminder to all workers on the assembly line. As soon as you get here in the morning, **check** <u>the display board next to the factory manager's office for daily notices.</u>

我想給在裝配線上所有的員工一項簡短的提醒。早上你們一到這裡，就要確認工廠經理辦公室旁邊公佈欄上的當日公告。

聽眾被要求要確認什麼？
（A）工作時間表
（B）每日的公告

詞彙 quick 簡短的 reminder 提醒 assembly line 裝配線 as soon as 一…就 get 到達 display board 公佈欄 factory 工廠 daily 當日的

5. 英M

1 找出核心詞彙	topic of the meeting
2 了解類型	主題／前面部分
3 看選項	搭乘計程車或辦公室花費

Thank you for taking time to come to this meeting. Let me get straight to the point. As you all know, <u>many of you have been making unauthorized charges to the office expense account for things such as lunches and taxi rides that are not related to your jobs.</u>

謝謝你們撥冗來到這場會議。讓我直接切入重點。如同你們都知道的，你們當中許多人將未經許可的費用記在辦公室消費帳戶上，例如和你們的工作無關的午餐和計程車費用等。

會議的主題是什麼？
（A）搭乘計程車
（B）辦公室花費

解說 透過考題可以知道該錄音為「會議上的公告」。這是「未經許可的費用不可以記在辦公室消費帳戶上」的內容，所以（B）為答案。 答案(B)

詞彙 take time 撥冗 unauthorized 未經許可的 charge 費用 expense 消費 account 帳目 taxi ride 計程車 related 有關聯的 job 工作

6. 美M

1 找出核心詞彙	Where
2 了解類型	公告地點／前面部分
3 看選項	飛機或火車

Attention, passengers. <u>This is your captain speaking. I hope you're enjoying the flight.</u> It's a beautiful day out there. However, the radar indicates that we will be experiencing some turbulence soon, so please fasten your seat belt and stay in your seats.

各位乘客請注意。我是機長。我希望您正享受飛行。外面的天氣很好。但雷達顯示我們將經歷一些亂流，所以請繫安全帶，而且留在您的座位上。

這則公告是在哪裡發出的？
（A）在飛機上
（B）在火車上

解說 能聽到「我是機長」的地方，就是在飛機上了。 答案(A)

詞彙 captain 機長 radar 雷達 turbulence 氣流；亂流 fasten 繫緊 stay 留

7. 英M

1 找出核心詞彙	event taking place
2 了解類型	主題／前面部分
3 看選項	表演或歡迎會

Hello, everyone! **Welcome to** <u>Palmer Theater</u>. I know you're all looking forward to an exciting evening. <u>Before this evening's performance begins</u>, I have a couple of reminders.

大家好！歡迎來到帕瑪戲院。我知道你們都很期待一個很令人興奮的晚上。在今晚的表演開始之前，我有兩個提醒事項。

什麼活動將被舉辦？
（A）一場表演
（B）一場歡迎會

解說 透過「歡迎來到戲院」與「表演開始」，可以知道即將要發生的事情就是「表演」。 答案(A)

詞彙 theater 戲院 performance 表演 a couple of 幾個的 reminder 提醒事項 take place 發生 play 表演 reception 歡迎會

8. 美W

1 找出核心詞彙	asked
2 了解類型	要求事項／後面部分
3 看選項	測試警鈴或做日常的工作

Attention, employees. The fire alarm system is being tested this morning. You may hear the alarm go off several times through the morning. When you hear the alarm, **please** <u>remain calm and continue with your usual routine.</u> Thank you for your patience.

各位同仁請注意。今天早上火災警報系統正被測試。在整個早上您會聽到警報多次響起。在您聽到警報時，請保持平靜並持續做您日常的工作。感謝您的耐心。

員工被要求去做什麼？
（A）測試警鈴

（B）做他們日常的工作

解說 please為詢問要求事項考題的核心詞彙，透過在其後面出現的「保持平靜並持續做您日常的工作」，可以知道（B）為答案。　　　　　　　　　　　答案（B）

詞彙 alarm 警報　go off 響起　through 在整個…　remain calm 保持平靜　continue 持續　routine 日常工作　patience 耐心

問題9～10，請參考以下訊息。 澳W

1 找出核心詞彙	report say, happen next
2 類型與答案的位置	具體事項／中間部分
	下一個行程／前面部分
3 看選項	廣告成功，顧客滿意，銷售下降
	舉辦發表會，發出回應卡，討論調查結果。
4 預測對話內容	意見調查表示顧客滿意，所以另外討論。

Good afternoon. I'm glad so many of you could make it to this meeting. I'd like to share the results of our recent customer survey. As you know, we conducted a survey to find ways to boost our sales. Overall, ⁹customers show satisfaction with our product designs and our competitive prices. In front of you, you'll find the complete results of the survey. ¹⁰Let's discuss them now point by point.

午安。我很高興你們這麼多人能來到這場會議。我想分享我們最近的顧客意見調查結果。如您所知，我們為了大幅增加銷售量執行了調查。大致上，顧客對我們產品的設計和具有競爭力的價格表達了滿意。在你們面前，你們會看到完整的調查結果。現在我們針對每一項討論吧。

詞彙 make it 達到　share 分享　result 結果　survey 意見調查　conduct 執行　boost 大幅增加　customer 顧客　satisfaction 滿意　competitive 具有競爭力的　complete 完整的　discuss 討論　point by point 針對每一項

9.

這份調查報告說了什麼？
（A）廣告成功了。
（B）顧客很滿意。
（C）銷售下降了。

解說 透過「執行了調查、顧客對我們產品表達了滿意」，可以知道「顧客很滿意」。　　　　　　　　答案（B）

詞彙 report 報告書　advertisement 廣告　successful 成功的　satisfied 滿意的　decline 下降

10.

根據這則談話，接下來將會發生什麼？
（A）這個團體將舉辦發表會。
（B）將發出回應卡。
（C）這個調查結果將被討論。

解說 let's為詢問「下一個行程」的考題的核心說法，其後面出現的「針對每一項討論吧」，即是指對於意見調查結果進行討論。　　　　　　答案（C）

詞彙 happen 發生　make a presentation 發表　give out 分發　survey result 調查結果

問題11～12，請參考以下訊息。 英M

1 找出核心詞彙	announcement for, asked
2 類型與答案的位置	說話者／前面部分
	要求事項／後面部分
3 看選項	員工們，購物者，觀光客
	填表格，和保全經理談話，
	確認有沒有遺失的東西
4 預測對話內容	向員工公告：請確認是否遺失什麼東西

¹¹Attention, all staff. This is Alex Kim, the security manager at Walters Corporation. A set of house keys was found in the cafeteria this morning at approximately 10:30 a.m. ¹²Please check your wallets, pockets, and purses to make sure you haven't misplaced your keys. If you think the keys are yours, please come to the main office and ask for Mr. Chang to identify them. Thank you.

各位同仁請注意。我是沃特企業的保全經理艾力克斯·金。今天早上大概十點半的時候，在自助餐廳發現了一套房子的鑰匙。請看看你們的皮夾、口袋和手提包來確認你們是將鑰匙放錯地方。如果你覺得這些鑰匙是你的，請來到總辦公室並找張先生來認領。謝謝。

詞彙 cafeteria 自助餐廳　approximately 大概　wallet 皮夾　pocket 手提包　purse 放　misplace 放錯地方

11.

這則公告是要給誰的？
（A）員工們
（B）購物者
（C）觀光客

解說 這是詢問公告的對象，就是詢問聽眾為誰的考題，答案在錄音的前段部分，而且通常在attention後面出現。此題又出現了將staff改成employees來表達的方式。　　　　　　　　　　　答案（A）

詞彙 employee 員工　shopper 顧客　visitor 訪客

12.

聽眾被要求做什麼？

（A）填表格

（B）和保全經理談話

（C）確認有沒有遺失的東西

解說 please為詢問要求事項的考題的核心詞彙，其後面出現的「請確認你們是否將鑰匙放錯地方」，指的就是「確認有沒有遺失的東西」的意思。 答案(C)

詞彙 fill out 填寫 form 表格 security manager 保全經理 missing 遺失的 item 東西

問題13～14，請參考以下訊息。 [美 M]

1 找出核心詞彙	Where, park until the garage is completed
2 類型與答案的位置	地點／前面部分
	要求事項／後面部分
3 看選項	停車場，辦公室，購物中心
	在街上，沿著轉角
4 預測對話內容	在購物中心停車場
	在辦公室停車相關的公告

[13]This is the facility manager with an important announcement for all company employees. Since our company is building a new parking garage that will replace the old parking lot we've been using, [14]all employees should park their cars across the street during construction. We've made special arrangements with the shopping center to use one of their lots. We apologize for the inconvenience, but it'll be worth it.

我是設備部經理。我有項很重要的公告要給全公司員工。由於我們公司正在建設新的停車塔以取代我們一直以來用的舊停車場，在施工當中所有的員工們得將車子停在對面。我們和那邊的購物中心做了特約來使用他們的停車場。造成不便很抱歉，但這將會是值得的。

詞彙 facility 設備 important 重要的 announcement 公告事項 build 建設 parking garage 停車塔 replace 代替 parking lot 停車場 park 停車 construction 施工 arrangement 約定 apologize 道歉 inconvenience 不便 worth 值得

13.

這則公告很有可能是在哪裡發出的？

（A）在停車場

（B）在辦公室

（C）在購物中心

解說 「由於正在建設新的停車塔，所以將車子停在別的地方」這不能視為在停車場廣播的公告，應該是在辦公室對職員做的公告。 答案(B)

詞彙 office 辦公室 shopping mall 購物中心

14.

聽眾直到車庫完工前，應該在哪兒停車？

（A）在街上

（B）沿著轉角

（C）在購物中心停車場

解說 先說「員工們得將車子停在對面」，接著說「和那邊的購物中心做了特約來使用他們的停車場」，所以就是「在購物中心的停車場停車」的意思。在此必須注意，是在對面停車而不是在街上停車的。 答案(C)

詞彙 completed 完成的 corner 角落

STEP 02 考題實戰練習

1. (B)	2. (B)	3. (D)	4. (A)	5. (C)	6. (B)
7. (C)	8. (B)	9. (D)	10. (B)	11. (A)	12. (B)

問題1～3，請參考以下訊息。 [美 W]

Good afternoon, passengers for Star Train 157 to Budu station. [1]We are sorry to inform you of the change in our departure time. Unfortunately, a disabled train was ahead of us, and it caused a serious delay. Several maintenance crews are working on it now, and it should be moved off the tracks in 10 minutes. [2]The train is now scheduled to depart at 5:45 p.m. The boarding process will begin shortly. [3]Please stay adjacent to the gate.

午安，搭乘一五七星際列車到巴度站的乘客們。我們抱歉通知您出發時間變更，一台故障的列車停在前方，因而造成嚴重的延誤。維修團隊現在正處理中，列車應該在十分鐘內會離開軌道。火車目前定於下午五時四十五分離開。不久將開始登車。請待在閘口附近。

詞彙 passenger 乘客 inform 通知 change 變更 departure time 出發時間 unfortunately 很不幸地 disabled 拋錨的 cause 造成 serious 嚴重的 delay 延誤 maintenance crew 維修團隊 track 鐵路 be scheduled to 預定… depart 出發 boarding process 登記程序 shortly 不久；立刻 stay 留 adjacent to 接近…的 gate 出入口

1.

為什麼出發時間要重新安排？

（A）設備的一小部份壞了。

（B）有一台故障的火車。

（C）有些鐵軌還有沒被修理。
（D）鐵道封閉了。

解說 透過考題與選項就知道該錄音為火車站裡的公告。聽到「一台故障的列車停在前方」，所以（B）為答案。　　　　　　　　　　　　　　　答案（B）

詞彙 departure 出發　reschedule 重新安排時間　equipment 裝備　broken 故障的　malfunctioning 不正常運作的　repair 修理　railway 鐵道　closed 關閉的

2.
火車離開的時間是什麼時候？
（A）在下午四點三十分
（B）在下午五點四十五分
（C）在下午六點十五分
（D）在下午八點三十分

解說 在錄音裡就可以聽到「火車目前定於下午五時四十五分離開」。　　　　　　答案（B）

3.
乘客們被要求做什麼事？
（A）依團體編號上車
（B）看指南手冊
（C）確認他們的座位分配
（D）待在出發閘門附近

解說 please為詢問要求事項的考題的核心詞彙，在其後面出現的「待在閘口附近」以同義詞來表達的（D）就是答案。　　　　　　　　　　　　　　答案（D）

詞彙 board 搭乘　according to 依…　look at 看…　guidebook 旅行指南　assignment 安排　departure gate 出發閘口

問題4～6，請參考以下訊息。 英M

As you all know, our network equipment sales have gone up. We expect that sales will continue to increase, so we're planning to start a new branch in Busan in early August. ⁵I've been appointed to head the sales department in Busan, ⁴so I will be leaving my position as sales manager in July. Several new employees will be hired to deal with the increased business. ⁶ All of you are invited to consider the possibility of transferring to Busan. Please give us some feedback within the next few weeks if you're interested in making this move.

如同大家所知道的，我們的網絡設備銷售量上升了。我們期待銷售量將繼續增加，所以我們計劃在八月初開始在釜山有新的分公司。我被安排帶領釜山銷售部門，所以我在七月將離開銷售經理的職位。將有幾位新員工被雇用來處理增加的業務，你們也獲邀考慮調職到釜山的可能。若您有興趣此一變動，請在未來幾週之內給我們回應。

詞彙 equipment 裝備　go up 增加　branch 分部　appoint 任命　head 領導　sales department 銷售部門　leave 離開…　position 職位　hire 僱用　deal with 處理　invite 邀請　consider 考慮　possibility 可能性　feedback 回饋　interested 有興趣的　move 移動

4.
說話者是什麼人？
（A）一位銷售經理
（B）一位維修工人
（C）一位軟體設計師
（D）一位維修技師

解說 聽到「離開銷售經理的職位」就知道說話者為銷售經理。　　　　　　　　　答案（A）

詞彙 maintenance work 維修工人　designer 設計師　repair technician 維修技師

5.
在七月將會發生什麼事？
（A）一家公司將結束運作。
（B）一棟新大樓的整修將會開始。
（C）說話者將調動到新城市。
（D）一場發表將在會議中被舉辦。

解說 特定時間點是很重要的核心詞彙，所以錄音裡July附近就有答案。將「被安排帶領釜山銷售部門，所以我在七月離開銷售經理的職位」以概括性的敘述做變化來表達的（C）為答案。　　　　　　答案（C）

詞彙 operation 營運　renovation 整修　transfer 調動　make a presentation 做發表

6.
說話者要求聽眾考慮什麼事？
（A）遵守計畫的最後期限
（B）調到不同的辦公室
（C）招募更多員工
（D）變更一棟大樓的設計

解說 「be invited to 動詞原型」是「獲邀去做…」的意思，屬於詢問要求事項的考題的核心說法。在另一個核心詞彙consider後面出現了「轉換到釜山的可能」，將此做變化來表達的（B）就是答案。　　　　答案（B）

詞彙 meet 處理；面對　deadline 截止期限　recruit 招募　modify 變更；修正

問題7~9請參考以下對話和圖表。 [美 M]

Schedule	
Morning	
09:00~10:30 Bill Shun	Shadowing and speaking
11:00~12:30 Jessie Chen	8Improve listening through TED talk
Lunch break	
Afternoon	
02:00~03:30 Marie Lin	Read between the lines
04:00~05:30 Debbie Chang	How to build up your writing skills?

Dear teachers, 7welcome to the Seminar on Adult English Learning. I am your host Kim Garry Smith. Allow me to announce our program for the day. We have four speakers today–two in the morning and two in the afternoon. On the schedule, 8Dr. Bill Shun was planned to be our first speaker, but he just called in that due to the traffic jam, he can not make it on time. Therefore, we will have the second speaker Dr. Jessie Chen to speak for us first, and Dr. Bill Shun's speech will be postponed until later today. After lunch break, the afternoon sessions will resume at 2 o'clock sharp. 9In order not to affect the proceeding of the seminar, please return to your seats on time. Also, please keep your cell phones on silent mode at all times. Any forms of audio or video recording are forbidden. Thanks for your cooperation.

課程表	
上午	
09:00~10:30 比爾熊	跟讀法和說話術
11:00~12:30 潔西陳	透過TED talk增進聽力
午餐	
下午	
02:00~03:30 瑪莉林	弦外之音，言外之意
04:00~05:30 黛比張	如何增強寫作技巧？

各位親愛的老師，歡迎到成人英語學習研討會。我是您的主持人金蓋瑞密斯。容我公布今天的課程。我們今天有四位講者一兩位在上午，兩位在下午。在課程表上，比爾熊博士被安排做我們第一位講者。但是他剛剛來電，由於交通壅塞的因素，他將無法準時到。所以，我們將由第二位講者潔西陳博士先為我們開講，比爾熊博士的演說將延遲到今日稍晚的時段。午餐休息過後，下午的活動將於兩點整恢復。為了不影響研討會的進行，請準時回到您的座位上。另外，請隨時將您的手機保持靜音狀態。禁止任何形式的錄音及錄影。謝謝您的合作。

詞彙 welcome 歡迎 seminar 研討會 adult 成人 host 主持人 allow 允許 announce 宣布 program 節目 speaker 講者 schedule 日程安排；時刻表 due to 由於 traffic jam 交通壅塞 postpone 延遲 lunch break 午休 session 活動；節目 resume 恢復 affect 影響 proceeding 進行 return

返回 on time 準時 keep 保持 silent mode 靜音模式 at all time 隨時、一直 form 形式 audio 聲音的 video 錄像的 recording 錄製的音像 forbid 禁止 cooperation 合作

7.

聽者今天參加研討會的主要目標是什麼？
（A）學習政府的政策
（B）兒童照護與育兒經
（C）成人英語學習法
（D）如何在一年內賺到一百萬

解說 這是詢問「研討會目標」為何的「簡短選項類考題」。此題的提示在一開始講者提到的「歡迎到成人英語學習研討會」，所以研討會是關於「成人英語學習法」的內容，故正確答案選（C）。　　　答案 (C)

詞彙 objective 目標 attend 參加 government 政府 policy 政策 childcare 兒童照護 parenting 育兒 earn 賺 million 百萬

8.

請看此圖，哪一個演講會先講？
（A）跟讀法和說話術
（B）透過TED talk增進聽力
（C）弦外之音，言外之意
（D）如何增強寫作技巧？

解說 此題是有一點變化的題目。由於原訂的第一位演講者將因事遲到，所以由第二位演講者先演說。在圖表中第二位演講者的講題是「透過TED talk增進聽力」，所以（B）是正確答案。　　　答案 (B)

詞彙 speech 演講 shadowing 跟話 speaking 說話 improve 改進 through 透過 read between the lines 言外之意 build up 建立

9.

以下哪一項沒有被主持人提及？
（A）準時回到座位
（B）手機關靜音
（C）禁止錄音錄影
（D）不可喝水

解說 這是詢問哪一個選項「沒有」被提到的考題。文末提到「為了不影響研討會的進行，請準時回到您的座位上。還有，請隨時將您的手機保持靜音狀態。禁止任何形式的錄音及錄影。」4個選項中，只有（D）沒出現，故正確答案選擇（D）。　　　答案 (D)

詞彙 mention 提及 mute 啞巴、使……無聲 permission 允許 drink 喝

問題10~12，請參考以下訊息。 [美 M]

10Attention, shoppers. Our store will be closing in twenty minutes. Please make your final selections and proceed to the checkout lane. Don't forget to stop by the produce department for today's specials. There are fresh vegetables and a variety of fruit on sale, but only for a few more minutes. The customer service counter is now closed. [11]Please direct all questions to the manager on duty. [12]Shoppers purchasing fifteen or fewer items can use express checkout lanes. Just follow the red signs to the express lanes at the front of the store. Thank you for shopping with us, and we look forward to seeing you again.

顧客們請注意。我們的商店將在二十分鐘內打烊。請完成您的選購並前往結帳通道。別忘了於農產品部看看今天的特價品。有新鮮的蔬菜和多種水果在拍賣，但只限最後這幾分鐘。目前客戶服務櫃檯已關閉。所有的問題請直接向值班經理洽詢。購買十五個或更少物品可以使用快速結帳通道。只需依照店前方的紅色標誌前往快速結帳通道。感謝您來店購物，我們期待再次見到您。

詞彙 **shopper** 顧客　**final selection** 最後的選擇　**proceed to** 往…移動　**checkout lane** 結帳通道　**stop by** 順便訪問　**produce department** 農產品專區　**special** 特價品　**a variety of** 多種的　**on sale** 有折扣的　**customer service counter** 客服櫃檯　**closed** 關閉的　**direct questions to** 向…詢問　**manager** 負責人　**on duty** 執行任務當中的　**fewer** 少於…　**item** 商品　**look forward to V-ing** 期待…

10.
這則公告主要的目的是什麼？
（A）為了通知新的安全程序
（B）為了公告商店要打烊
（C）為了介紹付費的方式
（D）為了廣告肉品的價格

解說 詢問公告主題的考題，答案線索會在錄音的前段部分出現。聽到「將在二十分鐘內打烊」，所以（B）為答案。　　　　　　　　　答案 (B)

詞彙 **announcement** 公告　**inform** 通知　**safety procedure** 程序　**closing** 關閉　**introduce** 介紹　**payment** 支付　**advertise** 廣告　**price** 價格

11.
有疑問的顧客被指示到哪裡？
（A）找經理
（B）到結帳處
（C）到詢問處
（D）到客戶服務台

解說 這是詢問具體事項的考題。在錄音的中間部分會聽到「請直接向值班經理洽詢」，所以答案為（A）。
答案 (A)

詞彙 **question** 疑問　**be directed to** 被指向於…　**information center** 詢問處

12.
誰可以使用快速結帳處？
（A）買蔬菜的人
（B）買少於十五樣東西的人
（C）等候超過二十分鐘的人
（D）簽署意見調查表的人

解說 特定的名詞也能成為核心詞彙。在Express checkout lane附近會聽到「購買十五個或更少物品的購物者」，這就是答案。　　　　　答案 (B)

詞彙 **buy** 買　**wait** 等待　**sign** 簽名　**survey form** 意見調查表

Quiz I

1. (A)　　2. (A)　　3. (A)　　4. (A)

Q1 美W

Welcome everyone, and congratulations on starting a new career here at Mary Kacy Cosmetics. My name is Rebeca Mori, and I'm the sales manager. Let me start off by saying how happy we are to have you as part of the Mary Kacy Cosmetics sales team.

歡迎大家。恭喜你們在瑪莉凱西化妝品公司開始新的職業生涯。我的名字叫瑞貝卡·莫莉。我是銷售部門的經理。請讓我表達對於你們加入瑪莉凱西化妝品公司的銷售團隊讓我們有多高興做為開始。

聽眾很有可能是在哪裡？
（A）在員工迎新會
（B）在頒獎宴會

解說 透過考題與選項可以知道該錄音為活動相關公告。錄音內容裡，在welcome後面通常出現活動名稱。這是恭喜聽眾開始新的職業生涯，所以是在員工歡迎會上的話語。　　　　　　　　　　　答案 (A)

詞彙 career 職業生涯　start off 開始　be happy to 很高興…　as part of …的一部分　employee orientation 員工歡迎會　award banquet 頒獎宴會

Q2 英M

Make sure to make an appointment to get your I.D. photo taken before noon. We will have a short lunch break at 12:30, and then **in the afternoon**, each of you will meet the managers you'll be working with.

請你們確實記得預約，並於中午前拍你們證件的照片。我們在十二點半將會有簡短的午餐休息時間，然後在下午的時候你們每個人將要和你們一起工作的經理見面。

聽眾將會在下午做什麼？
（A）與經理見面
（B）為了身份證拍照

解說 時間點為很好的核心詞彙。錄音的後段部分出現in the afternoon，接著聽得到「和經理見面」。　答案 (A)

詞彙 make an appointment 預約　I.D. photo 證件照片　lunch break 午餐休息時間　work with 和…一起工作

Q3 英M

Good morning, class. My name is Tran, and I will be your biology professor this semester. I've been teaching at York College for over 15 years, and before that I was a student here, just like the rest of you. I'm going to begin today by talking about the scientific method.

全班同學，早安。我的名字叫泉恩。我將成為你們這個學期的生物課教授。我在約克大學教書教了十五年以上。之前，我和你們其他人一樣也是這裡的學生。今天晚上我想就討論科學的方法來開始。

這個演講的聽眾很有可能是什麼人？
（A）學生們
（B）教師們

解說 class也有「上課的學生們」的意思，且說話者說自己是教授，所以其聽眾應該是學生。　答案 (A)

詞彙 class 全班同學　biology professor 生物教授　semester 學期　rest 其餘的　by -ing 以…　scientific method 科學的方法

Q4 美M

Hello. **My name is Steven Reynolds**, and I'm very happy to speak today on Money Talk. I'd like to thank GW Radio for inviting me today. I've been a financial consultant for over twenty years, and I'm here to share several money management tips with today's listeners.

你好。我的名字叫史提芬·雷諾。我非常高興今天在「金錢開講」中演講。我想感謝GW廣播電台今天邀請我來。在過去二十多年我一直當財經顧問。我在這兒要和今天的聽眾一起分享一些金錢管理上的資訊。

史提芬雷諾是什麼人？
（A）一位財經顧問
（B）一位廣播主持人

解說 錄音裡，人名的附近有答案。這是在節目上說的話語，可以知道他是來賓。在錄音的中間部分論及自己為財經顧問。　　　　　　　　　答案 (A)

詞彙 invite 邀請　financial consultant 財經顧問　tip 資訊

STEP 01　若沒答對會後悔的考題

1 (A)	2 (B)	3 (B)	4 (A)
5 (B)	6 (B)	7 (A)	8 (A)
9 (A)	10 (B)	11 (C)	12 (A)
13 (A)	14 (B)		

1. 英 M

1 找出核心詞彙	asked
2 類型與答案的位置	要求事項／後面部分
3 看選項	看行程表或在會議廳做登記

Welcome, everyone. I hope you're enjoying the refreshments that we provided free of charge. I'm Jonathan Lee, the organizer for this year's Professional Cooking conference. First, **let's** take a look at the conference schedule.

歡迎大家。我希望你們正享受著我們免費提供的茶點。我是今年度專業烹飪會議的籌辦人強納生‧李。首先，我們來看會議行程吧。

聽眾被要求做什麼？
（A）看行程表
（B）在會議廳做登記

解說 這是詢問要求事項的考題。將核心說法let's後面出現的「看會議行程吧」以同義詞做變化來表達的（A）為答案。　　　　答案（A）

詞彙 refreshment 茶點　free of charge 免費的　organizer 籌辦人　take a look at 看　schedule 行程　conference hall 會議廳

2. 美 W

1 找出核心詞彙	changed
2 類型與答案的位置	具體事項／中間部分
3 看選項	演講者或研習會的時程

Attention, everyone. **I'd like to announce a slight change** to today's conference schedule. Because of a problem with the presenter's flight arrangement, the 11 a.m. workshop on management techniques will be postponed to 4 p.m., but will be held in the same conference room.

請大家注意。我想公佈今天會議行程上小小的變更事項。因為演講者的飛行時間的問題，上午十一點的管理技巧研習會將延後到下午四點，但是會在同樣的會議室舉辦。

什麼被改變了？
（A）演講者
（B）研習會的時程

解說 「活動前公告」裡常出現的就是活動行程上的變動。錄音裡change後面出現「會議行程」，接著可以聽到「講習會將延後」，所以（B）為答案。　答案（B）

詞彙 slight 小小的　change 變更事項　presenter 演講者　management technique 管理技巧　postpone 延後　hold 舉辦　conference room 會議室

3. 美 M

1 找出核心詞彙	in the afternoon
2 類型與答案的位置	下一個行程／後面部分
3 看選項	與部門經理們會面或熟悉顧客的問題

You will start today's session by greeting all the department managers from sales, advertising, accounting, and so on. **In the afternoon**, you will familiarize yourselves with customer service issues and learn about inventory management.

你們將和銷售、廣告、會計等所有部門的經理打招呼來開始今天的議程。在下午的時候，你們將認識客服議題，然後學習庫存管理。

聽眾在下午將會做什麼？
（A）與部門經理們會面
（B）熟悉顧客的議題

解說 時間點為很好的核心詞彙。將錄音裡出現的In the afternoon後面的「認識客服議題」做變化來表達的（B）為答案。　　　　答案（B）

詞彙 greet 和…打招呼　department 部門　and so on 等等　familiarize oneself with 熟悉…　issue 議題　inventory management 庫存管理

4. 英 M

1 找出核心詞彙	speaker
2 類型與答案的位置	說話者／前面部分
3 看選項	公司總裁或軟體工程師

Good evening, ladies and gentlemen. I'm Michael Chang. Welcome to our annual banquet. **As CEO and founder of this company, I'm pleased to present this year's award for best product developer to Jong Min Kim.**

各位先生、女士們晚安。我是麥可‧張。歡迎來到我們的年度宴會。以這家公司的總裁與創辦人的身份，我很高興將今年的最佳產品開發者獎頒給金鐘民。

說話者是什麼人？
（A）一位公司總裁
（B）一位軟體工程師

解說 詢問說話者為誰的考題，其答案線索在錄音裡以as來出現。As是身份的介系詞，所以將CEO做變化來表

達的（A）為答案。 答案(A)

詞彙 CEO 總裁 founder 創辦人 award 獎賞
developer 開發者

5. 澳W

1 找出核心詞彙	after the lecture
2 類型與答案的位置	要求事項／後續行程／後面部分
3 看選項	報名將來的演講或參加招待會

Our guest speaker today is Dr. Emma Lubiano,
who will be speaking to us about new advances
in the IT industry and how they affect software
companies like ours. **Following the lecture**, there
will be a reception. Please join us in the reception
where Dr. Lubiano will be answering questions.

我們今天的客座演講者為愛瑪‧露比安諾博士。她將告訴我們電子產
業裡的新進展，以及它們如何影響像我們一樣的軟體公司。演講之後
會有歡迎會。請你們參加歡迎會，在此露比安諾博士會答覆問題。

說話者邀請聽眾在演講後做什麼？
（A）報名將來的演講
（B）參加招待會

解說 after the lecture的近似說法following the lecture為
錄音裡的核心詞彙，所以將其後面出現的「請你們參加
歡迎會」做簡化來表達的（B）為答案。 答案(B)

詞彙 guest speaker 客座演講者 advance 進展
industry 產業 affect 影響 following …之後 lecture 演講
reception 歡迎會 join 參加 answer questions 答覆問題

6. 美M

1 找出核心詞彙	want to be when he was young
2 類型與答案的位置	具體事項／中間部分
3 看選項	教師或科學家

I'd like to start off by answering your questions
about how I started my career as a scientist. I
dreamed of being a scientist **from the time I was
very young**. It felt so interesting to read books
about science and many famous scientists, so I
hardly ever spent time with my friends.

我想以有關我如何開始我的科學家職業生涯，來開始回答你們的問
題。自從我很小的時候我夢想成為科學家。對於看有關科學和很多著
名科學家相關的書感到很有趣，所以我幾乎沒有花時間在我朋友們身
上。

演講者在年輕的時候想成為什麼？
（A）一位教師

（B）一位科學家

解說 考題裡的he就是「演說／演講」類錄音裡的
speaker，也就是錄音內容的I。將「自從我很小的時候
我夢想成為科學家」改成「想成為科學家」來表達的
（B）為答案。 答案(B)

詞彙 start off 開始 dream 夢想 hardly 幾乎不…
spend time 花時間

7. 英M

1 找出核心詞彙	purpose of the speech
2 類型與答案的位置	主題／前面部分
3 看選項	對頒獎表示感謝或解釋公司的規定

I'm very pleased to be honored for my research
into the use of the audio video materials to
improve language education. **I'd like to** thank all
of my fellow workers for this award. Without their
commitment, I couldn't have received this award.

我很高興我對視聽材料使用於語言教育的發展上的研究得到了榮譽。
為了這個獎賞我想感謝我所有的同仁們。若沒有他們的投入，我不可
能得到這個獎賞。

這個演講的目地是什麼？
（A）對頒獎表示感謝
（B）解釋公司的規定

解說 這是詢問演講目的的考題，所以在錄音前段部分
的內容有答案。將thank改成appreciation來表達的（A）
為答案。 答案(A)

詞彙 honor 榮譽 research 研究 material 材料
language 語言 education 教育 fellow 同仁
award 獎賞 commitment 投入 receive 得到

8. 美M

1 找出核心詞彙	giving out
2 類型與答案的位置	具體事項／中間、後面部分
3 看選項	發表記錄或軟體

Good morning, I'm Berry Moor, a senior manager
from the head office in Seoul. I'm really happy
to get a chance to visit the Bangkok office and
demonstrate the new database management
program. Before I tell you more about this new
program, I'd like to **hand out** these presentation
notes.

早安，我是首爾總部的首席經理貝瑞・摩爾。我很高興有機會訪問曼谷辦公室，並示範新的資料庫管理軟體。在我告訴你們更多有關這個新的軟體之前，我想分發這些報告資料。

說話者發給參加的人什麼東西？
（A）報告資料
（B）軟體

解說 錄音裡出現give out的同義詞hand out，在其附近會有答案。「報告資料」為記載發表內容的文件。
答案（A）

詞彙 senior 首席的　head office 總部　chance to 動詞原型 做…的機會　demonstrate 示範　hand out 分發　give out 分給

問題9～10，請參考以下訊息。 澳 W

1 找出核心詞彙	Where, Sofia Russo do
2 類型與答案的位置	地點／前面部分
	具體事項／中間部分
3 看選項	宴會廳，在會議室，在書店
	在醫院工作，出版書籍，開發醫療藥物
4 預測對話內容	在宴會介紹演講者的經歷

⁹Good evening, and welcome to the Connor Company's Annual Employee Appreciation Dinner. I would like to extend special thanks to the Grace Hotel for providing us with this wonderful banquet hall. And now it's time to introduce our guest speaker for this evening. ¹⁰Please welcome Dr. Sofia Russo, author of the best-selling book *The Future of Medicine*, who will tell us about her experiences writing this book.

晚安。歡迎來到康納公司的年度員工感恩晚餐。我想表達特別感謝葛莉思飯店提供給我們這麼棒的宴會廳。那麼現在是介紹今晚的客座演講者的時間。請歡迎暢銷書《醫學的未來》的作者蘇菲亞・羅素博士來告訴我們她寫這本書時的經驗。

詞彙 extend 表達（歡迎、同情等）　provide A with B 提供B給A　banquet hall 宴會廳　guest speaker 客座講師　author 作者　experience 經驗

9.
說話者在哪兒？
（A）在宴會廳
（B）在會議室
（C）在書店

解說 在錄音的前段部分出現「晚餐」，所以（A）或（B）為可能的答案。透過「感謝提供給我們這麼棒的宴會廳」，可以知道演講的地點為宴會廳。　答案（A）

詞彙 conference room 會議室　bookstore 書店

10.
蘇菲亞羅素做過什麼？
（A）她曾在醫院工作。
（B）她曾出版書籍。
（C）她曾開發醫療藥物。

解說 錄音內容裡出現的人名附近會有答案。受邀而來的講師很多時候是作者。將「作者」改成「出版書籍」來表達的（B）為答案。　答案（B）

詞彙 hospital 醫院　publish 出版　develop 開發　medical 醫學的

問題11～12，請參考以下訊息。 英 M

1 找出核心詞彙	speaker work, his previous work experience
2 類型與答案的位置	說話者／前面部分
	具體事項／中間部分
3 看選項	電腦程式編寫，會計，新聞業
	有助於學習如何執行多種工作，
	沒有包含新的工作，到國外出差
4 預測對話內容	說話者在面試當中說明自己足夠的經歷

First of all, I'm very happy for the opportunity to tell you more about my qualifications for this position. ¹¹I have been a reporter with the Korea Times for the last 5 years. ¹²During those 5 years, I've learned patience, the ability to multi-task and the importance of hard work. Now I can manage a variety of tasks and these have become my professional strengths. I think these are probably the most valuable skills for any journalist.

首先，我很高興有機會告訴你們我對於這個職位我的資格條件。在過去五年當中，我在韓國時報當記者。在這五年的時間裡，我學會了耐心、同時處理多項工作的能力、以及勤勞的重要性。現在我能處理多種的任務，而且這些成為我的專業上的優勢。我認為對任何一位新聞工作者而言，這些可能是最具有價值的技術。

詞彙 opportunity 機會　qualification 資格條件　position 職位　patience 耐心　ability 能力　multi-task 多項工作　importance 重要性　hard work 勤勞　manage 管理　a variety of 多種　task 任務　professional 專業上的　strength 優勢　probably 可能是　valuable 具有價值的　journalist 新聞工作者

11.

說話者在什麼領域工作？
（A）電腦程式編寫
（B）會計
（C）新聞業

解說 「在過去五年當中當了記者」是「在新聞業工作的」的意思。 答案 (C)

詞彙 programming 編寫電腦程式 accounting 會計 journalism 新聞業

12.

關於他之前的工作經驗，說話者說了什麼？
（A）有助於他學習如何執行多種工作。
（B）它沒有包含新的工作。
（C）他常到國外出差。

解說 「在五年當中學會的東西」就是指「工作經驗」，而且也說了「現在我能處理多種的任務」，所以可以了解成「工作經驗有助於執行多種工作」。

答案 (A)

詞彙 previous 以前的 various 多種 cover 包含

問題13～14，請參考以下訊息。 美 M

1 找出核心詞彙	purpose of the talk, happen after the speech
2 類型與答案的位置	主題／前面部分
	後續行程／後面部分
3 看選項	介紹客座演講者，公告旅館的開幕，
	說明旅遊的行程，簡短的中場休息，
	問答時間，播放短片
4 預測對話內容	介紹演講者之後有提問時間

[13]Welcome to the Business Management lecture series. Our speaker this evening is Mr. John Thompson, an accountant with over twenty years' experience, and he also coordinates the annual Small Business Conference at City College. The title of his talk tonight is "What Every Small Business Administrator Needs to Know About Taxes." [14]After his speech, Mr. Thompson will answer questions in the Great Hall, and coffee and snacks will be served.

歡迎來到企業管理系列講座。我們今晚的演講者為約翰·湯普生先生。他是具有超過二十年以上經驗的會計師，而且也籌辦城市大學的小型企業年度研討會。今晚他的演講題目為「每一個小型企業管理者都需知的稅務」。演講之後，湯普生先生將會在「宏偉廳」回答問題，而且也提供咖啡和茶點。

詞彙 lecture 講座 accountant 會計師 experience 經驗 coordinate 籌辦 speech 演講 answer questions 回答問題

13.

這段談話的目的是什麼？
（A）為了介紹客座演講者
（B）為了公告一間旅館的開幕
（C）為了說明旅遊的行程

解說 「演講者為某某」即為介紹演講者的狀況。

答案 (A)

詞彙 guest speaker 客座演講者 explain 說明 travel itinerary 旅遊行程

14.

在演講之後很有可能將會發生什麼事？
（A）將有一個簡短的中場休息。
（B）將會接著進行問答時間。
（C）將播放短片。

解說 考題裡的after the speech為核心詞彙。將錄音裡的「將會回答問題」改成了「將會接著進行問答時間」。

答案 (B)

詞彙 intermission 休息時間 a question and answer session 問答時間 follow 接續著 video footage 短片

STEP 02 考題實戰練習

1. (A)	2. (C)	3. (C)	4. (C)	5. (B)	6. (B)
7. (A)	8. (D)	9. (C)	10. (A)	11. (B)	12. (A)

問題1～3，請參考以下訊息。 美 W

[1]Welcome everyone to this year's Global Conference on Community Health. We're pleased to have more than 200 professionals who work in various fields of community health programs throughout the world to give presentations. Our presenters will be sharing their experiences, survey results, and ideas for providing medical treatment to citizens of the world. Before I present our keynote speaker, [2]I have an important announcement about the small group sessions on the program. Because of limited space, you need to register for the sessions in advance. Your tickets should be in your welcome kit for each session you sign up for. If not, [3]check our website to confirm that you are really registered.

歡迎大家來到今年的社區衛生服務全球會議。我們很高興能有超過兩百名工作在世界各地社區衛生計畫多樣領域的專業人員來演講。我們的發表者將分享他們為世界公民提供醫療的經驗、調查結果和想法。在介紹今天的主講人之前，有關於活動當中的小團體會議，我有一項重要的公告。因空間有限，這個會議您需要預先登記。每一場您登記的會議門票應該在您邀請卡上。如果沒有，請於我們的網站確認您是否已真正註冊。

詞彙 be pleased to 很高興… professional 專家 various 多種的 field 領域 throughout 遍布於… presentation 發表 presenter 發表者 keynote speaker 主要演講者 important 重要的 announcement 公告事項 limited 有限的 register for 登錄 in advance 提前 sign up for 報名

1.

這場會議的主題是什麼？
（A）社區衛生
（B）報告方式
（C）軟體設計
（D）醫療工具

解說 透過這三個考題與選項可以知道該錄音為「活動前公告」類型。錄音前段部分出現介系詞on，接著聽得到「社區衛生」，所以很容易找到答案。　　答案(A)

詞彙 method 方法 tool 工具

2.

有關於小團體會議，說話者說了什麼？
（A）它們將在不同的地點被舉辦。
（B）它們不包含在活動中。
（C）它們需要預先登記。
（D）它們是產品演示的一部份。

解說 這是詢問具體事項的考題，所以答案會在錄音內容的中間部分。將「需要預先登記」以相似說法表達的（C）為答案。　　答案(C)

詞彙 location 地點 include 包含 prior registration 事前登錄 a part of …的一部分

3.

根據說話者所言，聽眾能在會議網站上找到什麼？
（A）調查報告
（B）一項評估
（C）登記確認
（D）活動單

解說 錄音內容裡的website附近有答案。若是與website資訊相關內容，大部分在後段部分出現答案線索。尤其第三個考題的答案線索通常是在錄音的後段部分。將「確認是否已真正註冊」做變化來表達的（C）為答案。　　答案(C)

詞彙 report 報告 estimate 評估資料 registration 註冊 confirmation 確認資料 list 目錄

問題4～6，請參考以下訊息。英 M

Welcome to our annual conference. Before we get started with this morning's program, [4]I'd like to make an important announcement regarding the schedule. Our first group speaker will begin her presentation thirty minutes later than originally scheduled. She will now speak at nine-fifteen, instead of at eight forty-five, in our main meeting room. At twelve o'clock, [5]lunch will be served in the Red River Room instead of the Blue Mountain Room, which will be used for dinner. [6]This evening, as listed in your pre-printed schedules, don't forget to attend our keynote speaker's presentation. Thank you.

歡迎來到我們的年度會議。在我們開始今天上午的活動前，有關時間表我想做個重要的公告。我們第一組的演講者將比原本預定的時間晚三十分鐘開始她的演講。現在她將於九點十五分在大會議室演講，而不是八點四十五分。在十二點鐘，將在紅河室用午餐，而不是用於晚餐的藍山室。今晚，如同印好的時間表所列，別忘了參加我們主講人的演講。感謝您。

詞彙 start with 以…開始 important 重要的 announcement 公告事項 schedule 行程 presentation 發表 originally scheduled 原來預定的 instead of 而不是… meeting room 會議室 serve 提供 pre-printed 已印好的 attend 參加 keynote speaker 主要演講者

4.

為什麼發出這則公告？
（A）為了表揚一位員工
（B）為了介紹一些新菜色
（C）為了公告時間表變更
（D）為了慶祝公司的成功

解說 透過下一題題目的「提供午餐」，可以猜測到該錄音為「活動前公告」類。這是詢問主題的考題，所以答案在錄音的前段部分。將「有關時間表我想做個重要的公告」以相似說法來表達的（C）為答案。　　答案(C)

詞彙 honor 表揚 introduce 介紹 dish 菜 celebrate 祝賀 success 成功

5.

將會在哪裡提供午餐？
（A）在主會議室
（B）在紅河室
（C）在藍山室
（D）在自助餐廳

解說 錄音裡的lunch附近會出現答案。（C）是陷阱，因為（C）是晚餐場地。　　答案(B)

詞彙 cafeteria 自助餐廳

6

說話者建議聽眾在晚上做什麼？

（A）與好友吃晚餐

（B）參加一場報告

（C）領取問卷

（D）拿到已簽名的書

解說 時間點為很重要的核心詞彙。錄音裡的this evening附近會出現答案。將錄音後段聽到的「參加我們主講人的演講」做簡化來表達的（B）為答案。 答案（B）

詞彙 close friend 要好的朋友 pick up 領取 questionnaire 問卷

問題7～9請參考以下對話和圖表。 英 W

New Dawn to Alzheimer's Disease
May 25 – Grand Conference Hall

The history of the disease	9:00~10:20
The early symptoms of the disease	10:30~11:50
Lunch break	
[8]Gene screening	14:00~15:20
Q & A	15:30~16:50

Dear audience, welcome back to the conference hall. [7,8]We are sorry to announce that due to some short circuit during lunch hour just now, the electric systems of this building have temporarily broken down. Fortunately, [8]the sponsor of our activity has made an emergency arrangement for our guest speaker to resume the rest of the speech at another meeting place nearby. And a shuttle bus has been booked to take all of us together over there directly. Please leave through the exits of the room, take the stairs and gather at the lobby area of the conference hall. [9]For your safety, do not take the elevators. Our speaker, Ms. Helena Jo, has already left early to the new meeting place for preparation. So, let's go now carefully.

阿茲海默症新曙光
5月25日——圓山會議廳

疾病的歷史	9:00~10:20
疾病的早期症狀	10:30~11:50
午休	
基因篩檢	14:00~15:20
Q & A	15:30~16:50

親愛的觀眾，歡迎回到會議廳。我們很抱歉要宣布，剛剛中午時刻因為電線短路的因素，造成本建物的電力系統暫時中斷。所幸的是，活

動的主辦單位緊急安排，讓我們的受邀的演講者在附近的另一個會議廳，繼續完成剩下的演講。而且已經訂了一台接駁公車接送我們所有人一起過去。請經由會議廳的安全門離開，走樓梯到會議廳大廳集合。為了您的安全起見，請勿搭乘電梯。我們的演講者，海倫娜·喬小姐，已經先行離開到新會場準備。好！讓我們現在小心走。

詞彙 audience 聽眾 conference hall 會議廳 announce 宣布 short circuit 短路 electric system 電力系統 building 建築物 temporarily 暫時地 break down 故障 fortunately 幸運地 sponsor 贊助者 activity 活動 emergency 緊急情況 arrangement 安排 resume 恢復 nearby 附近 shuttle bus 接駁車 exit 出口、安全門 take the stairs 走樓梯 gather 聚集 lobby area 大廳 safety 安全 take the elevator 搭乘電梯 preparation 準備 carefully 小心地 dawn 曙光、黎明 Alzheimer's Disease 阿茲海默症

7

根據講者的話，是發生了什麼問題？

（A）電力中斷

（B）記憶消失

（C）交通阻塞

（D）地震來襲

解說 這是詢問發生什麼意外狀況的「簡短選項類考題」。講者說「剛剛中午時刻因為電線短路的因素，造成本建物的電力系統暫時中斷」所以，選項（A）是符合的答案。 答案（A）

詞彙 shutdown 關閉 memory lost 記憶消失 traffic jam 交通壅塞 earthquake 地震

8

請看此圖。哪一個時段的節目會在別處舉行？

（A）疾病的歷史

（B）疾病的早期症狀

（C）午休

（D）基因篩檢

解說 這是詢問「節目安排更動」的「簡短選項類考題」。由文中得知，電力中斷是發生在中午時分，而隨後的節目則被安排在他處舉行。所以答案是（D）基因篩檢。 答案（D）

詞彙 take place 舉行 history 歷史 symptom 症狀 gene 基因 screening 篩檢

9

聽眾被警告不要做什麼？

（A）碰觸電源

（B）爬行樓梯

（C）搭乘電梯

（D）搭接駁車

解說 這是詢問「何選項為非」的「簡短選項類考題」。核心語是「警告不要做什麼」。因為電力中斷，聽眾被警告「為了您的安全起見，請勿搭乘電梯」，所

以要選（C）。 答案 (C)

詞彙 touch 碰觸 power switch 電源開關 climb 爬升 stairs 樓梯 elevator 電梯 shuttle bus 接駁車

問題10～12，請參考以下訊息。 美 M

Good afternoon, everyone. Thanks for taking time to attend this training session out of your busy schedule. I'm Mario Rossi, software engineer from the head office in New York. As you all know, **11**our team recently developed a new software system to keep track of our warehouse inventory. The new system will enable us to keep our warehouse well-stocked and organized. **10**As inventory manager, you have to become familiar with using this software, so I'd like to make sure all of you know how the new system works. **12**First, I'd like to play a short video footage that shows you the general features of this new system. Please direct your attention to the screen.

各位午安，感謝大家在百忙之中抽空參加本次培訓會議。我是紐約總部的軟件工程師馬力歐羅西。如你們所知，我們小組最近開發出掌握我們倉庫庫存的新軟體系統。新系統將能使我們的倉庫能充份儲存和系統化。身為庫存經理，您必須會熟悉使用這個軟體，所以我想確認你們全體都知道這個新系統如何運作。首先，我想先放一段錄影短片讓大家看這個新系統的一般功能。請將您的注意力朝向螢幕。

詞彙 take time 撥冗 attend 出席 training session 訓練課 head office 總公司 recently 最近 develop 開發 enable 使得可能 inventory 庫存 manager 經理 familiar with 熟悉…的 work 運作 general 一般的 feature 功能

10
聽眾很有可能是什麼人？
（A）公司的經理們
（B）農民協會的會員們
（C）在電腦店的顧客們
（D）在餐廳的員工們

解說 若是詢問聽眾為誰的考題，大部分在錄音的前段部分出現答案，但這是比較難的錄音，必需要聽到中間部分才能找的到答案。身份的介系詞as後面出現「作為庫存經理」，以此做簡化來表達的（A）為答案。
答案 (A)

詞彙 audience 聽眾 association 協會 customer 顧客 store 商店

11
最近開發出了什麼？
（A）潛在的客戶們
（B）一套軟體系統
（C）辦公室用品

（D）一項醫療設備

解說 在錄音中間出現developed。將「新軟體系統」以簡化來表達的（B）為答案。 答案 (B)

詞彙 potential customer 潛在的顧客 office supply 辦公用品 device 裝置

12
說話者接下來將會做什麼？
（A）做視聽發表
（B）引導參觀設備
（C）介紹公司的總監
（D）採購一套軟體系統

解說 這是詢問下一個行程的考題。將「放一段錄影短片」改成「做視聽發表」來表達的（A）為答案。
答案 (A)

詞彙 show 顯示 audiovisual 視聽的 tour 參觀 facility 設備 director 主管 purchase 購買

Quiz

1. (A)   2. (A)   3. (A)   4. (B)

Q1 [美W]

This is Angela Booth with your 30-second afternoon weather report. Though it's been a relatively dry week for this time of year, we can expect showers tonight. There's an 80 percent chance of precipitation tomorrow morning.

我是三十秒氣象報導的安琪拉‧布斯。儘管相較於每年的這個時間，目前算是較乾燥的一週，但我們預測今晚有陣雨。明天早上則有百分之八十的降雨機率。

說話者很有可能是什麼人？
（A）一位廣播播報員
（B）一位旅館經理

解說 在錄音內容的前段部分就可以決定是廣播節目種類的「天氣預報」類型，說話者就是廣播播報員。

答案 (A)

詞彙 weather report 氣象報導 relatively 相對地
dry 乾燥的 shower 陣雨 precipitation 降雨

Q2 [英M]

If you are coming into the city from the east side now, try to avoid Clover Street. **We recommend you take highway 15 where traffic is running smoothly.** Stay tuned. I'll be back in 10 minutes with another traffic update.

如果您現在要從東側進入本市，請盡量避開幸運草街。我們建議您行駛目前交通順暢的十五號高速公路。請繼續收聽。我將在十分鐘之後回來報導另一項路況更新。

說話者建議聽眾做什麼？
（A）行駛備用道路
（B）開慢一點

解說 若為「路況報導／天氣預報」，在錄音後段部分會提供有用的資訊。在此篇錄音裡，用suggest的同義詞recommend來提供了答案線索。「不要走Clover Street，而改走十五號高速公路」是「行駛備用道路」的意思。

答案 (A)

詞彙 east side 東邊 try to 試著；盡量 avoid 避開
recommend 建議 highway 高速公路 smoothly
流暢地 stay tuned 繼續收聽 traffic update 路況報導

Q3 [美W]

Good evening. **This is Sandra Johnson** and with your Business World Now. Hana Computer Group's chairman, Michael Rogers, announced today that the company's new laptop 'the Sensation' will go on sale next Friday.

晚安。這是商業世界新聞，我是珊卓拉‧強生。漢納電腦集團的董事長麥可羅傑斯今天公佈，該公司的新筆記型電腦「轟動」在下週五將開始銷售。

珊卓拉強生很有可能是什麼人？
（A）一位新聞播報員
（B）一位企業總裁

解說 在錄音裡提到的名字附近有答案。出現了新聞節目的名稱，所以說話者為主持新聞節目的人。 答案 (A)

詞彙 chairman 董事長 announce 公佈 laptop
筆記型電腦 go on sale 開始銷售

Q4 [英M]

The construction of the new highway will begin on May 1st and is estimated to cost two million dollars. **The project will take** approximately four months. However, citizens are skeptical that the current traffic congestion will be alleviated.

新高速公路的建設將在五月一日開始，且預計花費兩百萬元。該計劃大約將需要四個月。然而，市民對於現在的交通堵塞將變緩和感到懷疑。

這個計畫將會進行多久？
（A）兩個月
（B）四個月

解說 這是詢問具體內容的考題。只要有聽到錄音內容裡出現的project... take後面的數字「四」就可以了。

答案 (B)

詞彙 construction 建設 estimate 預計
approximately 大概 citizen 市民 skeptical 懷疑的
current 現在的 traffic congestion 交通堵塞
alleviate 緩和

STEP 01 若沒答對會後悔的考題

1 (A)	2 (B)	3 (B)	4 (A)
5 (B)	6 (A)	7 (A)	8 (B)
9 (B)	10 (B)	11 (C)	12 (B)
13 (C)	14 (C)		

1. 美 M

	找出核心詞彙	reason of the delay
1	找出核心詞彙	reason of the delay
2	類型與答案的位置	具體內容／中間部分
3	看選項	車禍或馬路維修

Thanks for listening to 102.7, your local station for news, traffic and weather. I'm Chris Lee with a traffic report. **We have heavy traffic** this morning because of a car accident on Route One near the airport. Avoid Route One if possible.

感謝您收聽102.7新聞，您的新聞、交通資訊和氣象的在地電台。我是路況報導的克里斯‧李。由於一號路線上機場附近的車禍，今天早上交通堵塞。如果可以的話請避開一號路線。

延遲的原因是什麼？
（A）一起車禍
（B）馬路維修

解說 透過考題與選項可以預測該錄音內容為「路況報導」。這是詢問問題狀況原因的考題，所以在錄音裡because of後面出現的「車禍」為答案。　　答案 (A)

詞彙 traffic report 路況報導　because of 因為　accident 事故　if possible 如果可以的話　delay 延誤　repair 維修

2. 美 W

	找出核心詞彙	asked
1	找出核心詞彙	asked
2	類型與答案的位置	要求事項／後面部分
3	看選項	調高收音機的聲量或繼續收聽廣播

This is a special weather report. Please be aware that the entire region is under a flood watch. We are currently experiencing heavy rains, which we expect to continue for the next twenty-four hours. **Everyone** living within a mile of the Han River **should** stay tuned for evacuation orders.

這是特別氣象報導。請注意，全區域正發布洪水特報。目前正在下豪雨，而且預計它會持續二十四小時。居住於漢江一英哩以內的所有的人，請務必不要轉台並注意疏散令。

聽眾被要求做什麼？
（A）調高收音機的聲量
（B）繼續收聽廣播

解說 stay tuned是「將電台維持固定」，也就是「不要轉台持續收聽」的意思，所以（B）為答案。　答案 (B)

詞彙 weather report 氣象報導　be aware that 注意到…　entire region 全區域　flood watch 洪水特報　heavy rain 豪雨　stay tuned 不要換台　evacuation order 疏散令

3. 英 M

	找出核心詞彙	report mainly concern
1	找出核心詞彙	report mainly concern
2	類型與答案的位置	主題／前面部分
3	看選項	天氣或交通

You will be happy to know this is the last day for the renovation of Clover Street, and it will be open to the public again tomorrow morning. So from tomorrow, it will be wise to take Clover Street instead of Main Street, where traffic is always heavy. I'll be back for another traffic update in 15 minutes.

你們將很樂於知道今天是幸運草街維修工程的最後一天，而且它將於明天早上重新對大眾開放。因此從明天起，行駛幸運草街來代替總是堵塞的幹線道路將是明智的選擇。我在十五分鐘之後，將帶著另一項路況更新回來。

這則報導主要在關切什麼？
（A）天氣
（B）交通

解說 是否為「廣播節目」的類型，大部分能在錄音的前段部分決定。但此篇錄音在前段部分先提供路況，用以暗示出類別，在後段部分再說出「將帶著另一項路況更新」來確定其節目類型。　　答案 (B)

詞彙 renovation 維修　public 大眾　again 重新　instead of 而不是…　traffic update 路況報導

4. 澳 W

	找出核心詞彙	needed in the morning
1	找出核心詞彙	needed in the morning
2	類型與答案的位置	具體內容／後面部分
3	看選項	厚外套或雨傘

Cold weather will continue, but that is usual for this time of the year. You may want to take a heavy coat when you go out **in the morning**. That's the morning weather report on SY Radio. Now back to our regular classical music program.

冷天氣將會持續，但這是每年此時很正常的事。早上外出時，您可能要帶著很厚的外套。這是SY廣播電台的晨間氣象報導。現在回到我們固定的古典音樂節目。

根據說話者所言，在早上將會需要什麼？
（A）一件厚外套
（B）一把雨傘

解說 時間點為很好的答案線索。透過該考題與選項可以預測該錄音為「天氣預報」。在該錄音裡的時間說法in the morning附近可以聽到heavy coat。　　答案 (A)

詞彙 usual 平常的　heavy coat 厚外套　go out 外出
weather report 氣象報導　regular 固定的

5. 美 M

1 找出核心詞彙	recommend
2 類型與答案的位置	要求事項／後面部分
3 看選項	小心開車或帶雨傘

Good morning, it's time for the GW Radio morning weather report. We'll have heavy rain throughout the morning. After the rain stops, temperature will drop sharply in the afternoon. So **we recommend** taking an umbrella and keeping yourself warm when you go out.

早安。現在是GW廣播電台的晨間氣象報導時間。我們在上午將持續有豪雨。雨停了之後，下午氣溫將會劇降。因此我們建議您外出時要帶著雨傘並且保暖。

說話者建議聽眾在今天下午做什麼？
（A）小心開車
（B）帶雨傘

解說 這是與「天氣預報」有關，詢問有用資訊的考題。在錄音裡recommend後面就出現答案。　　答案 (B)

詞彙 heavy rain 豪雨　throughout 整個
temperature 氣溫　drop 下降　sharply 劇烈地
recommend 建議　warm 溫暖　go out 外出

6. 澳 W

1 找出核心詞彙	Mr. Chen
2 類型與答案的位置	具體人物／前面或中間部分
3 看選項	公司總裁或廣播業者

Good morning and welcome to the Morning 4 on national radio. I am your host, Maria Rega. We're happy to have **Mr. James Chen**, the president of James Enterprises, in our studio as our special guest today. Mr. Chen will talk about how his childhood experiences helped him develop his career.

早安。歡迎收聽公共電台的晨間四節目。我是主持人瑪莉亞・瑞佳。我們很高興邀請詹姆士企業的董事長詹姆士・陳先生，來到我們的播音室作為特別來賓。陳先生將談談他兒童時代的經驗如何幫助他發展出他的事業。

陳先生是什麼人？
（A）一位公司總裁
（B）一位廣播業者

解說 這是「受訪節目」類的錄音內容，會在人名附近出現答案，很有可能是詢問有關來賓或主持人的內容。該錄音的前段部分，人名附近出現了「詹姆士企業的董事長」，而這就是答案。　　答案 (A)

詞彙 host 主持人　president 董事長　guest 來賓
childhood experience 童年時代的經驗　career 職業
broadcaster 廣播員

7. 美 W

1 找出核心詞彙	report mainly about
2 類型與答案的位置	主題／前面部分
3 看選項	商業收購或建設計劃

And now for this evening's business news. Nanjing Industries formally announced that their acquisition of GW Package will proceed as planned. The profits of Nanjing Industries this quarter increased sharply nearly 12 percent over the second quarter, which convinced the company to proceed with the acquisition.

現在是今晚的商務新聞。南京工業正式公佈他們對GW包裝公司的收購案將依照計劃進行。南京工業這一季的利潤比起第二季劇增了將近百分之十二，這使該公司有信心將收購案進行下去。

這則報導主要是有關於什麼？
（A）一項商業收購
（B）一個建設計畫

解說 這是詢問廣播節目類型的考題，看選項就可以知道為「一般報導」類。在錄音前段部分的announced後面出現答案。　　答案 (A)

詞彙 formally 正式地　acquisition 收購　profit 利潤
quarter 季　sharply 急劇地　nearly 幾乎　over 比起…
convince 使相信　proceed with 進行…

8. 美 M

1 找出核心詞彙	at noon
2 類型與答案的位置	後續行程／後面部分
3 看選項	廣告或聽眾來電

Good morning Vancouver. This morning, we invited a famous critic, Arthur George to our studio. He will be discussing changes in the film industry over the last century. Then **at noon**, Mr. George has agreed to take calls from our audience.

早安，溫哥華。今天早上我們邀請了著名評論家亞瑟‧喬治到我們的播音室。他將要討論上一個世紀裡電影產業的變化。接下來在中午的時候，喬治先生同意接聽我們聽眾的電話。

在下午將會發生什麼？
（A）插播商業廣告。
（B）聽眾們將會打電話到廣播電台。

解說 時間點為很好的答案線索。將錄音後段部分的「同意接聽聽眾的電話」改成了「聽眾們將會打電話到廣播電台」來表達。　　　　　　答案 (B)

詞彙 invite 邀請　critic 評論家　discuss 討論
take a call 接電話　audience 聽眾

問題9～10，請參考以下訊息。 澳W

1 找出核心詞彙	Who, tomorrow
2 類型與答案的位置	說話者／前面部分
	具體內容／中間部分
3 看選項	飛機駕駛，氣象播報員，旅行社職員
	雨天，晴天，陰天
4 預測對話內容	氣象預報員說明天是晴天

⁹Welcome to the five o'clock weather report. I know you're all tired of this long day of rain, but the good news is that the skies will finally clear up tonight. ¹⁰By tomorrow morning there shouldn't be a cloud in the sky, and it'll be warm and sunny all day. For all you people who've been waiting to make a trip to the beach, tomorrow should be the perfect day for it.

歡迎收聽五點整氣象報導。我知道你們對這次漫長的下雨天都感到厭倦，但有個好消息是今晚天空將會變晴朗。到明天早上天空應該不會有雲彩，而且一整天都會溫暖又有陽光。對於一直等待到海邊旅行的所有的人來說，明天應該是最完美的一天。

詞彙 finally 終於　clear up 變晴朗　warm 溫暖　sunny 有陽光的　all day 一整天　make a trip 旅行　beach 海邊

9.
正在說話的人很有可能是誰？
（A）一位飛機駕駛
（B）一位氣象播報員
（C）一位旅行社職員

解說 錄音前段部分以出現「氣象報導」，可以判斷出類型，所以該位說話者為氣象播報員。　　答案 (B)

詞彙 pilot 飛機駕駛　weather forecaster 氣象播報員
travel agent 旅行社職員

10.
明天將可能是什麼樣的天氣？
（A）下雨
（B）晴朗
（C）多雲

解說 在錄音裡出現tomorrow相關的具體說法tomorrow morning，又說了「不會有雲彩、有陽光」，所以以sunny為答案。　　　　　　答案 (B)

詞彙 rainy 下雨的　cloudy 陰天的

問題11～12，請參考以下訊息。 英M

1 找出核心詞彙	subject of the report, new product arrive
2 類型與答案的位置	主題／前面部分
	具體內容／後面部分
3 看選項	商業合併，行銷活動，新電腦的上市今天，兩週之內，三週之內
4 預測對話內容	新電腦將在兩週之內上市的新聞

Computer Magazine reported today that the ¹¹California Computer Company has announced that it will launch a new computer. The spokesman of the company said the new computer will be smaller and faster than other computers currently on the market. ¹²The new computer will be available in stores within the next two weeks. To learn more about these innovative systems, visit Computer Magazine's website.

電腦月刊今天報導，加州電腦公司公佈將推出新款電腦。該公司的發言人說該新款電腦和現今市場上其他電腦相比更小又更快。該款新電腦在接下來的兩個星期之內在商店可以購買。若想知道更多有關這些創新的系統，請至電腦月刊網站。

詞彙 report 報導　launch 開賣　currently 目前　on the market 在市場上　available 可購買的　within 在…之內
innovative 創新的

11.
這則報導的主題是什麼？
（A）一項商業合併
（B）一項行銷活動
（C）新電腦的上市

解說 這是「一般報導」類型的錄音內容，在錄音前段部分的announced附近有答案。將「推出新款電腦」以相似說法來表達的（C）為答案。　　答案 (C)

詞彙 subject 主題　merger 合併　release 上市

12.

新產品將於什麼時候到達商店？
（A）今天
（B）在兩週之內
（C）在三週之內

解說 「新產品」是指「新的電腦」，所以如果注意聽「在商店可以購買」後面出現的時間點，就可以知道「兩週之內」為答案。　　　　　　答案 (B)

問題13～14，請參考以下訊息。 美 M

1 找出核心詞彙	recommend, next traffic report
2 類型與答案的位置	要求事項／後面部分
	後續行程／後面部分
3 看選項	搭乘大眾運輸，慢速開車，行駛替代道路
	五分鐘，十分鐘，十五分鐘
4 預測對話內容	請走別的道路、下一次路況報導在十五分鐘之後

This is Ken Harrison from Radio 5's traffic desk. A traffic accident downtown is causing major delays on several main roads. Drivers are asked to avoid North State Street. ¹³So, if you must drive downtown, we recommend using Constitution Avenue instead. Even on Constitution Avenue, however, you may experience some delays. ¹⁴Our next traffic report will be in 15 minutes, so keep listening.

我是廣播五交通部門的肯·哈里遜。市中心的一場車禍正造成一些幹線道路上嚴重的延誤。請駕駛人避開北州街。若是您得開到市中心，我們建議改行駛憲法路。但即使在憲法路上，您可能也會遇到一些延誤狀況。我們下一次的交通播報將於十五分鐘之後，所以請繼續收聽。

詞彙 accident 事故　downtown 市中心的 cause 起因 delay 延遲　road 道路　avoid 避開 recommend 建議 instead 代替　traffic report 路況報導　keep V-ing 繼續⋯

13.

說話者建議了什麼？
（A）搭乘大眾運輸系統
（B）開車比平常開慢一點
（C）行駛替代道路

解說 透過考題與選項可以知道該錄音為「路況報導」類型。這是詢問「路況報導」的有用資訊的考題。核心詞彙recommend後面出現了「改行駛憲法路」，而將此改以「行駛替代道路」來表達的（C）為答案。
　　　　　　答案 (C)

詞彙 recommend 建議　public transportation 公共交通　than usual 比起平時　alternate route 替代道路

14.

下一次的交通報導是在什麼時候？
（A）在五分鐘之後
（B）在十分鐘之後
（C）在十五分鐘之後

解說 這是「廣播節目」類型，在錄音後段部分就能找到答案的簡單考題。在此直接就可以聽到數字十五。
　　　　　　答案 (C)

STEP 02　考題實戰練習

1. (A)	2. (C)	3. (D)	4. (D)	5. (A)	6. (B)
7. (A)	8. (A)	9. (D)	10. (B)	11. (D)	12. (C)

問題1～3，請參考以下訊息。 英 M

¹,³This is Jeffrey Jones in the GWC Traffic Helicopter. It's now quarter to five. Traffic is running smoothly on most streets into and out of the city. ²However, Route 4's northbound lane is blocked because of a major accident. Cars are backed up for more than three kilometers. It will take a few hours to clear the road, so we recommend taking the South Central by-pass into the city. Other than that, there are no major incidents to report, and it looks like most of you will have a smooth commute home. I'll be back for another traffic update in 15 minutes. ¹,³This is Jeffrey Jones in the GWC Traffic Helicopter wishing you safe travel!

這是在GWC交通直升機上的傑弗瑞瓊斯。現在是四點四十五分。進城和出城大部分的街道交通運行流暢。不過，四號路線的北向車道因為一個重大事故而被封閉。車輛受阻超過三公里。這要花幾小時來疏通道路，因此我們建議由市區南邊繞路進城。除此之外，沒有重大的事件報告，看來你大部分都能順暢下班回家。我會在十五分鐘後回來做路況更新。這是在GWC交通直升機上的傑弗瑞瓊斯，祝您行車安全。

詞彙 smoothly 流暢地　block 封鎖　accident 事故 clear 疏通　recommend 建議　by-pass 旁道　traffic update 路況報導

1.

這則公告是給誰的？
（A）駕駛人
（B）飛機駕駛
（C）新聞報導者
（D）警官

128

解說 透過考題與選項可以預測該錄音為「路況報導」類型。在錄音前段與後段出現答案線索traffic，同時整體內容是在說明交通狀況，因此是給駕駛人聽的廣播節目。　　　　　　　　　　答案 (A)

詞彙 driver 駕駛人 pilot 飛機駕駛 police officer 警官

2.

四號路線有了什麼問題？
(A) 有施工。
(B) 有直升機墜毀。
(C) 有意外事故。
(D) 有太多的旅行者。

解說 具體的地名為很好的答案線索。「四號路線」附近出現「事故」，所以 (C) 為答案。　　答案 (C)

詞彙 problem 問題 construction 施工；建築工程 crash 墜毀

3.

說話者在什麼地點？
(A) 在新聞播音室
(B) 在車上
(C) 在地面上
(D) 在直升機上

解說 在錄音前段與後段出現了兩次「在直升機上」，所以 (D) 為答案。(A) 是陷阱。　　答案 (D)

詞彙 studio 播音室 on the ground 在地上

問題4～6，請參考以下訊息。澳W

The following is a public service announcement, brought to you by Radio ABC. <u>4Because of the drought, government officials are asking all city residents to conserve water.</u> <u>5Residents are asked not to fill their swimming pools or water their gardens until further notice.</u> Right now, the government is asking residents to do this on a voluntary basis, although if the situation becomes severe, it is possible that fines will be imposed. For more information, <u>6find energy conservation tips at our website at www.energytips.or.uk.</u>

以下由ABC電台為您帶來一則公共服務公告。由於乾旱，政府官員要求各城市的居民節省用水。直到進一步通知前，居民被要求不在游泳池注水或花園澆水。此刻，政府要求居民基於自願來做這些，但如果情況變嚴重，有可能會加以罰款。想知道更多訊息，請在我們網站www.energytips.or.uk搜尋節能小建議。

詞彙 public service announcement 大眾服務公告 because of 由於… drought 旱災 government official 政府官員 resident 居民 conserve 節省 fill 灌注；加滿 swimming pool 游泳池 water 澆水 until further notice 到後續通知之前 right now 現在 on a voluntary basis

自願地 situation 狀況 severe 嚴重的 possible 有可能的 fine 罰款 impose 徵收；課取

4.

這則談話是要指示什麼人？
(A) 廣播電台員工
(B) 公務員
(C) 政府官員
(D) 居民

解說 透過考題與選項可以預測該錄音為「一般報導」類型。錄音裡重複出現「要求居民」這類的話，所以可以知道居民為聽眾。　　　　　答案 (D)

詞彙 radio station 廣播電台 public servant 公務員

5.

聽眾被要求避免些什麼？
(A) 給植物澆水
(B) 在游泳池游泳
(C) 散步
(D) 丟垃圾

解說 「要求不要在花園澆水」也可以說是「避免給植物澆水」，所以 (A) 為答案。　　　答案 (A)

詞彙 avoid 避免 plant 植物 throw 扔 garbage 垃圾

6.

在說話者提到的網站上可以發現什麼？
(A) 目前氣象資訊的地圖
(B) 節約能源的方式的列表
(C) 政府官員的地址
(D) 園藝工具的價格表

解說 網站名稱附近出現「節能小建議」，將此內容做變化來表達的 (B) 為答案。　　答案 (B)

詞彙 mention 論及 (a) list of …的列表 way to …的方法 address 地址 tool 工具

問題7～9，請參考以下訊息。美W

And now for this afternoon's lead news story. Residents of Melton City are still without power. <u>7The heavy rains and strong winds swept through the county last night and tore down power lines.</u> As a result, 150,000 residents are without electricity until this afternoon. Work crews have been working hard to restore power, <u>8but the winds, which remain strong, are making their work difficult.</u> The Power Company expects that the western part of the city will be able to turn on their lights this evening, but <u>9the rest of the city will be lucky to have electricity by tomorrow morning.</u>

現在是今天下午頭條新聞。梅爾頓市的居民依然沒有電力。昨晚大雨和強風席捲該郡同時摧毀了電力線。導致十五萬居民到今天下午仍無電使用。施工團隊盡全力恢復供電，但因風勢仍強，而使他們的工作困難。電力公司預計今天傍晚該城西部將能夠開燈，但城市其餘地區若到明天早上供電就算是幸運的。

詞彙 resident 居民　heavy rain 豪雨　sweep through 橫掃；席捲　tear down 拆毀　power line 電線　as a result 其結果　restore 復原　be able to 能…　turn on the light 開燈

7.

為什麼該城市的居民失去了電力？
（A）有大風暴。
（B）有太多居民住在該城市。
（C）機組工作人員正在安裝新系統。
（D）電力公司員工罷工。

解說 這是詢問具體內容的考題。透過考題與選項可以知道該錄音為「一般報導」類型。錄音裡，在without electricity的前面有問題狀況的原因。將「大雨和強風」改以「風暴」來表達的（A）為答案。　　　答案 (A)

詞彙 lose 失去　electric power 電力　big storm 大規模暴風雨　install 安裝　on strike 罷工當中

8.

是什麼使得工作人員的工作變困難？
（A）強風
（B）低溫
（C）有霧的狀況
（D）豪雨

解說 difficult為核心詞彙，在錄音裡的difficult附近會出現答案。　　　答案 (A)

詞彙 low 低　temperature 氣溫　foggy 有霧氣的　condition 狀態

9.

什麼時候整座城市將會有電力？
（A）今天下午
（B）今天傍晚
（C）今晚
（D）明天早上

解說 「今天傍晚該城西部將能夠開燈、城市其餘地區在明天早上供電」，就是指整座城市在「明天早上」才有電的意思。　　　答案 (D)

詞彙 entire 全部的

問題10～12請參考以下對話和圖表。 [美 M]

	The name of the dish
1	Appetizer
2	Fruit Salad
3	Steamed fish
4	[11]Stewed beef

Hello everyone! I'm your good friend, Gavin Hunter. Winter is approaching. In the cold winter, one of my favorite pastimes is to stay home and stew myself some hot soup, then to enjoy it with my family. [11]Do you like cooking, too? Wanna learn some nice winter dishes to warm up the stomachs of your loved ones? [10]Our special guest today, Teacher Jennie Chen, is a famous cooking expert who is often invited on TV cooking shows. She is also the author of several bestselling cook books, including the most recently published [11,12] 'Don't Nuke, Let's Stew'. During our program today, we will also give out three of this book as free gifts to listeners who call in and share your [11]favorite pot dish recipes. This is Gavin Hunter. We'll be right back after the music. Stay tuned.

	菜名
1	開胃菜
2	水果沙拉
3	蒸魚
4	燉牛肉

哈囉！大家好！我是你們的好朋友，蓋文·杭特。冬天的腳步近了。在寒冷的冬天裡，我最喜歡的消遣就是待在家中，為自己燉一些熱湯，然後和家人分享。 您也喜歡料理嗎？要不要學幾樣好棒的冬季菜餚，來暖暖心愛的人的腸胃呢？我們今天的特別來賓，是珍妮·陳老師，陳老師是一位知名的料理專家，時常受邀參加電視的烹飪秀。她同時也是許多暢銷食譜的作者，包括近期出版的《別用微波爐了，來燉鍋熱湯吧！》在我們今天的節目當中，如果聽眾能來電分享您最愛的煲湯食譜，我們也會送出3本食譜，作為免費禮物。我是蓋文·杭特，音樂過後我們馬上回來，不要換電台喔！

詞彙 approaching 將近　favorite 最喜愛的　pastime 消遣　stew 燉燉　families 家人　dish 菜餚　stomach 胃　expert 專家　invite 邀請　author 作者　several 幾個　bestseller 暢銷書　book 暢銷書　including 包括　recently 不久前　publish 出版　nuke 用微波爐烹飪　during 在……期間　listener 聽眾　share 分享　recipe 食譜　stay tuned 保持收聽；不要轉台

10.

誰是今天的特別來賓？
（A）格雷西·杭特
（B）珍妮·陳

（C）克萊兒‧詹森
（D）艾瑪‧牛頓

解說 這是詢問「對象是誰」的「簡短選項類考題」。文中提到「我們今天的特別來賓，是珍妮‧陳老師」，所以要選（B）。 答案（B）

詞彙 special 特別的 guest 來賓

11.

請看此圖，節目上最可能介紹什麼菜色？
（A）開胃菜
（B）水果沙拉
（C）蒸魚
（D）燉牛肉

解說 此題可由多處尋得線索。首先，我們知道會是一道「冬季」的菜餚；再者文中提到的食譜名稱《別用微波爐了，來燉鍋熱湯吧！》也和熱湯有關；最後，節目也是要聽眾call-in分享自己的「煲湯食譜」。可推測此節目將介紹（D）燉牛肉。 答案（D）

詞彙 introduce 介紹 appetizer 開胃菜 fruit 水果 salad 沙拉 steam 蒸 fish 魚 stew 煨燉 beef 牛肉 soup 湯

12.

會被送出當禮物的書名是什麼？
（A）如何烤出美味的蛋糕
（B）小朋友最愛的便當
（C）別用微波爐了，來燉鍋熱湯吧！
（D）烤牛排與海鹽

解說 這題是詢問書名為何的「簡短選項類考題」。正確答案是（C）「別用微波爐了，來燉鍋熱湯吧！」。 答案（C）

詞彙 gift 禮品 bake 烘焙 delicious 美味的 cake 蛋糕 lunch box 便當 children 孩子 nuke 用微波爐烹飪 roast 烤 sea 海洋 salt 鹽巴

Chapter 22 購買、參觀、觀光

Quiz

1. (A)   2. (A)   3. (A)   4. (A)

Q1 英 M

Is your company looking for skilled computer technicians? Do you want to hire technicians who have been trained with state-of-the-art equipment? Look no further. You can find highly trained and skilled graduates at the Computer Technology Institute.

貴公司正在尋找熟練的電腦技師嗎？您想雇用以最先進的設備來訓練的技師嗎？不用再殷殷盼了。在電腦技術學院您能找到有完善訓練與技術一流的畢業生。

什麼型態的公司正在被廣告？
（A）一家訓練機構
（B）一家電腦店

解說 這是詢問在廣告哪項產品的考題。錄音裡的疑問句後面有答案線索。培養「有完善訓練與技術一流的畢業生」的地方就是教育訓練機構。 答案（A）

詞彙 look for 尋找 skilled 熟練的 technician 技師 hire 僱用 train 訓練 state-of-the-art 最先進的 equipment 設備 highly 相當高地 graduate 畢業生 institute 學院

Q2 澳 W

Are you satisfied with your health insurance? Does it cover all your needs? Don't spend your life worrying as your insurance rates get higher and higher. Our insurance plan covers all your medical expenses at reasonable prices. **Call 555-1942** to obtain a free consultation.

您對您的健康保險滿意嗎？它涵蓋了您所有的需求嗎？別將您的人生浪費在擔心變得越來越貴的保險費率上。我們合理的價格的保險商品涵蓋了您所有的醫療費用。請撥555-1942來得到免費諮詢。

根據這則廣告，為什麼聽眾會撥這個電話號碼？
（A）為了得到諮詢
（B）為了看醫生

解說 這是「廣告」類型的錄音。將「得到免費諮詢」簡化成「得到諮詢」來表達的（A）為答案。 答案（A）

詞彙 satisfy 滿足 health insurance 健康保險 cover 提供保障 need 需求 rate 費率 insurance plan 保險商品 expense 費用 at reasonable prices 以合理的價錢

obtain 得到　free consultation 免費諮詢

Q3 英M

Welcome to the Garnet Company. My name is Ditman. I am a sales manager in charge of this factory tour. I'll be leading you around the production plant today and help you understand how we make our product durable and reliable.

歡迎到佳網公司。我的名字叫迪特門。我是負責這間工廠導覽的銷售經理。我將帶領你們到生產工廠，並幫助你們了解我們如何製造耐用又可靠的產品。

這則公告是在哪裡發出的？
（A）在一間工廠
（B）在一場銷售會議上

解說 詢問地點的考題，答案線索大部分在錄音的前段部分。尤其是「參觀／觀光」類的錄音，在welcome後面會出現線索。說話者「負責這間工廠導覽」，所以該錄音是在「工廠」做的公告。　　　　　　答案 (A)

詞彙 sales manager 銷售經理　in charge of 負責…的
factory 工廠　tour 參觀　lead 帶領　plant 工廠　durable
耐用的　reliable 可靠的

Q4 美M

Please remember that eating and drinking are not allowed in the exhibit areas. Instead, you can go to a very good restaurant on the second floor of the museum. **Now let's** look at the large piece of pottery standing in the center of the room.

請記得在展示區不可以飲食。但是你們可以去博物館二樓的一間很棒的餐廳。現在我們來來立在這間房間中央的大型陶器。

接下來很有可能會發生什麼事？
（A）一場導覽將開始。
（B）一部電影將播放。

解說 這是詢問「參觀／觀光」後續行程的考題。先出現禁止事項的公告，之後聽到「開始」的核心詞彙Now let's look at，所以可以知道接下來就是開始參觀。
　　　　　　答案 (A)

詞彙 remember 記住　allow 允許　exhibit 展示會
instead 代替；反而　museum 博物館　pottery 陶器

STEP 01　若沒答對會後悔的考題

1 (A)	2 (B)	3 (A)	4 (A)
5 (B)	6 (A)	7 (A)	8 (B)
9 (C)	10 (A)	11 (B)	12 (B)
13 (A)	14 (C)		

---

1. 美M

1 找出核心詞彙	advertised
2 類型與答案的位置	主題／前面部分
3 看選項	雜誌或電視節目

Do you get your sports news from television? Are you getting tired of all the commercial interruptions on TV? You don't have to be annoyed by commercials anymore. Our magazine gives you all the latest sports news commercial-free.

你從電視上得知運動新聞嗎？你對於被電視廣告打斷感到厭倦嗎？你再也不用被廣告煩擾了。我們的雜誌給你所有最新的運動新聞，而且沒有廣告。

什麼東西正在被廣告？
（A）一本雜誌
（B）一個電視節目

解說 這是詢問在廣告哪項產品的考題。在錄音裡疑問句後面出現「我們的雜誌給你新聞，而且沒有廣告」，所以（A）為答案。　　　答案 (A)

詞彙 tired 感到厭倦的　commercial interruption
因廣告而來的中斷　annoyed 被煩擾　anymore 不再
magazine 雜誌　latest 最新的　commercial-free 沒有廣告

2. 美W

1 找出核心詞彙	true about the restaurant
2 類型與答案的位置	特點／中間部分
3 看選項	提供免費點心或專門做海鮮料理

Want to try the traditional Japanese food with a modern style? Then stop by Fuji House, which is full of wonderful aromas and tastes. We specialize in seafood, and our sushi is the best you can't find anywhere else. All the dishes are moderately priced. Visit us today!

想嘗試具有新風味的傳統日本料理嗎？那麼請來一趟充滿美妙香氣和味道的富士之家吧。我們專門做海鮮，而且我們的壽司是你在任何地方都找不到的頂級品。所有的餐點都有合理的價錢。今天就來到我們這裡吧！

有關於這個餐廳，何者為真？
（A）它提供免費點心。
（B）海鮮料理是它的專業。

解說 該錄音為餐廳的廣告。這個考題是在詢問特色為何。出現「我們專門做海鮮」，所以（B）為答案。
　　　　　　答案 (B)

詞彙 traditional 傳統的 stop by 順便來 full of …充滿的 aroma 香氣 taste 味道 specialize in 專門做… seafood 海鮮 anywhere else 別的地方 dish 餐 moderately 合理地 priced 有定價的 visit 訪問

3. 澳 W

1 找出核心詞彙	speaker
2 類型與答案的位置	說話者／前面部分
3 看選項	導遊或保全人員

Good morning, and welcome to the ruins of Machu Picchu. <u>My name is Lisa, and I'll be your guide this morning.</u> We'll start our walk at the main gate of the city, where you'll see the Temple of the Sun, and finish at the main plaza, which you can see behind me.

早安。歡迎到馬丘比丘遺址。我的名字叫莉莎,是你們今天早上的導遊。我們將由該城市的大門開始,在此你會看到太陽神殿,然後在你所看到我身後的大廣場結束。

說話者是誰?
(A) 一位導遊
(B) 一位保全人員

解說 錄音裡聽到「Welcome to + 地點名稱」就能知道為「參觀／觀光」類型。該錄音裡接著出現「我是你們今天早上的導遊」,所以 (A) 為答案。 答案 (A)

詞彙 ruin 遺址 main gate 大門 temple 神殿 finish 結束 main plaza 大廣場

4. 英 M

1 找出核心詞彙	stay at the Wilson House
2 類型與答案的位置	具體內容(參觀行程)／前面或中間部分
3 看選項	半小時或一小時

Good afternoon. I hope you're all feeling well-rested and energetic after that delicious lunch. For our next stop, <u>we'll visit</u> **the Bob Wilson House**. Mr. Wilson was our city's first mayor. <u>We'll spend 30 minutes</u> **there**.

午安。我希望你們在好吃的午餐之後都感到休息且有活力。我們的下一站將參觀鮑伯威爾森之家。威爾森先生是我們城市的第一任市長。我們在那兒會花三十分鐘的時間。

他們將會在威爾森之家停留多久?
(A) 半小時
(B) 一小時

解說 這是詢問參觀行程的考題。在錄音中專有名詞用 there 來替代,並且在其後接著說出「三十分鐘」。 答案 (A)

詞彙 well-rested 休息得好的 energetic 有活力的 delicious 好吃的 stop 停靠站 mayor 市長 spend 花(時間)

5. 美 M

1 找出核心詞彙	offering discounts
2 類型與答案的位置	主題／前面部分
3 看選項	為了慶祝它的週年或為了結束營業

<u>Corner Bookstore is going out of business.</u> Come in today for the most amazing bargains you've ever seen. <u>All books are 80 percent off the ticketed price.</u> So hurry on down to Corner Bookstore before we are gone forever.

轉角書店即將歇業。請今天就來來得到你所見過的最令人驚喜的優惠。所有的書以標價打二折。所以在我們永遠消失之前,請趕快到轉角書店吧。

為什麼這家店提供折扣?
(A) 為了慶祝它的週年。
(B) 為了結束營業。

解說 「廣告」類型錄音當中,打折活動經常出現。活動的背景、理由出現在錄音前段部分。將「歇業」以相似說法來表達的 (B) 為答案。 答案 (B)

詞彙 go out of business 歇業 amazing 令人驚訝的 bargain 特價品 ticketed price 定價 gone 消失的 celebrate 慶祝 anniversary 紀念日 close 關門

6. 澳 W

1 找出核心詞彙	use the service
2 類型與答案的位置	具體內容(購買方法)／後面部分
3 看選項	打電話或看網站

Do you want to make your house look like a new house? If so, GW's Painting and Decorating is the answer. We specialize in both interior and exterior painting. We've been painting homes in this city for 13 years. Don't wait. <u>Call us today.</u>

你想讓你的家看起來像新家一樣嗎?若是如此,GW油漆與裝飾公司就是答案。我們專門做室內和室外油漆。我們在此城市塗裝住宅十三年了。請別等待,今天就打電話給我們。

人們如何能使用這項服務?
(A) 藉由打電話過去
(B) 藉由拜訪網站

解說 這是「廣告」類錄音，購買方法的線索出現在後段的部分。最常出現以撥打電話為方法的內容，而此處果然也在最後句子裡出現了。使用call的同義詞give a call的（A）為答案。 答案 (A)

詞彙 look like 看起來像… answer 答案 specialize in 專門做… wait 等待 call 撥打電話

7. 美 W

1 找出核心詞彙	receive if they call now
2 類型與答案的位置	具體內容（優惠）／後面部分
3 看選項	免費配送或免費安裝

And if you order today, you'll also **receive** free shipping. But remember! This offer is good only until the end of this week. Don't wait any longer! Call 216-555-3411 now to place your order.

若於本日訂購，您將會得到免費配送的服務。但請記住！這項優惠只在這週有效。別再等待了！現在撥打216-555-3411來下訂單吧。

若顧客現在就打電話，他們將會得到什麼？
（A）免費的配送
（B）免費的安裝

解說 這是詢問「廣告」的優惠內容為何的考題。「現在打電話」在錄音裡是以「本日訂購」與「現在撥打」來表達。在錄音前段就可以聽到「免費配送」。
答案 (A)

詞彙 order 訂購 receive 得到 free shipping 免費配送 remember 記住 offer 優惠 good 有效的 place an order 下訂單

8. 美 M

1 找出核心詞彙	asked
2 類型與答案的位置	要求事項／後面部分
3 看選項	安靜或帶走垃圾

We value our environment, so please don't throw your garbage on the trail. Since there are no garbage cans while climbing up the mountain, **you need to** carry your garbage with you until we return. Now, let's begin our hike.

我們非常重視我們的環境，所以請不要在小徑上丟垃圾。由於在登山途中沒有垃圾桶，您需要帶著您的垃圾直到我們返回。現在，讓我們開始健行吧。

觀光客被要求做什麼？
（A）安靜地待著
（B）帶走他們的垃圾

解說 這是「參觀」類錄音當中，談論「注意事項」的。考題裡的asked，在錄音裡是以you need to表達，因此接在後面聽到的「帶著您的垃圾」就是答案。
答案 (B)

詞彙 value 重視 throw 丟 garbage 垃圾 trail 小道 climb up 登 carry 帶 return 回來 begin 開始 hike 健行

問題9～10，請參考以下訊息。 澳 W

1 找出核心詞彙	being offered, the sale start
2 類型與答案的位置	具體內容（優惠）／中間或後面部分
	具體內容（期間）／後面部分
3 看選項	免費禮物包裝，免費配送，免費安裝
	星期一，星期五，星期天
4 預測對話內容	免費安裝的優惠在星期一開始

Looking for a new appliance with affordable prices? As of tomorrow, Sweet Home Appliances is having our annual sale with fantastic bargains for every appliance. We have a variety of products, such as stoves, dishwashers, drying machines and more. And during this time only, [9]we are offering free installation services for all appliances. [10]The sales start at 8 a.m., Monday and continue until 7 p.m. Sunday night. Don't miss this fantastic deal.

正在找經濟實惠的新家電嗎？從明天起，甜蜜家庭家電行舉辦年度行銷活動，每一件家電都有令人驚豔的特價。我們有多種產品，例如爐子、洗碗機、烘乾機等等。而且只有在此期間，我們將對所有的家電提供免費安裝服務。銷售活動在星期一上午八點開始持續到星期天晚上七點。別錯過這個超級好的交易。

詞彙 look for 尋找 appliance 家電 affordable price 負擔得起的價錢 as of 自從… annual 年度的 fantastic 令人驚豔的 bargain 特價品 a variety of 多種的 product 產品 stove 爐子 dishwasher 洗碗機 drying machine 烘乾機 offer 提供 installation 安裝 start 開始 miss 錯過 deal 交易

9.

什麼服務將被提供給顧客們？
（A）免費的禮物包裝
（B）免費的配送
（C）不收費的安裝

解說 若選項裡出現free，其錄音內容很有可能是「廣告」類。考題裡的being offered，在錄音裡是變成are offering，在其後面聽到的內容就是答案。錄音裡的free，在選項裡變成以without charge來表達。 答案 (C)

詞彙 customer 顧客 complimentary 贈送的 gift wrapping 禮物包裝 delivery 配送 installation 安裝 without charge 免費

10.
銷售活動什麼時候開始？
（A）在星期一
（B）在星期五
（C）在星期日

解說 這是詢問優惠期間的考題。大部分在錄音內容後段部分出現答案線索。透過「星期一八點開始」可以知道（A）為答案。　　　　　　　　　答案（A）

問題11～12，請參考以下訊息。 英 M

1 找出核心詞彙	come to see, asked to return
2 類型與答案的位置	地點／前面部分
	要求事項／後面部分
3 看選項	美術館，歷史遺址，汽車工廠
	機場，巴士，禮品店
4 預測聽話內容	參觀古蹟的民眾在公車上集合。

Hello everybody, **11**I'd like to welcome you to the most historic and beautiful site in Namwon City. The building before us was first built nearly 500 years ago, and it was once destroyed, but recently restored to its original 16th century condition. Since the ground here is very slippery from the rain, please watch your step while walking around the site. We'll spend one hour here, so **12**be sure to return to the bus on time since we'll be leaving promptly at 2 o'clock.

大家好。歡迎你們到南園市裡最具有歷史價值又最美麗的地點。我們前面的這棟建築物是將近五百年前初次建造的，並且曾有過一次的破壞，但最近修復為原本十六世紀的狀態。由於下雨，這裡的地面相當滑溜，因此走動的時候請注意您的腳步。我們將在這兒待一個小時，所以請你們記得準時回到巴士上，因為我們將在兩點立刻出發。

詞彙 historic 具有歷史價值的 building 建築物 build 建造 nearly 幾乎 destroy 破壞 recently 最近 restore 修復 original 原來的 condition 狀態 ground 地面 slippery 滑溜的 watch one's step 注意腳步 site 地點 return 回來 on time 準時 leave 出發 promptly 立刻

11.
觀眾要看看什麼？
（A）一間美術館
（B）一個歷史遺址
（C）一間汽車工廠

解說 透過考題與選項可以預測到該錄音為「參觀／觀光」類型。該考題是詢問訪問地點為何的，答案線索在錄音裡welcome後面出現。將「具有歷史價值又最美麗的地點」簡化成「具有歷史價值的地點」即「歷史遺址」的（B）為答案。　　　　答案（B）

詞彙 art museum 美術館 historic site 歷史遺址 automobile factory 汽車工廠

12.
人們被要求返回到哪裡？
（A）到機場
（B）到巴士
（C）到禮品店

解說 透過考題裡的asked可以知道這是詢問要求事項的。錄音裡，在be sure to後面就是答案線索。其要求為回到公車上。　　　　　　　　　　答案（B）

詞彙 airport 機場 gift shop 禮品店

問題13～14，請參考以下訊息。 美 W

1 找出核心詞彙	convenient, find the product
2 類型與答案的位置	具體內容（優點）／中間部分
	具體內容（購買方法）／後面部分
3 看選項	容易攜帶，能被折疊，非常輕
	百貨公司，美髮店，超市
4 預測聽話內容	商品很容易搬運、在超市有貨

Do you like healthy beverages? Not only healthy but also tasty? Well, Lion Beverage has something for you. Try "Naturalia", which is full of only natural ingredients without any type of preservatives. In addition, **13**it's packaged in a small, convenient box, so you can conveniently carry it to work or to school. If you are health conscious, "Naturalia" is the best choice for you. **14**Find it now at your local supermarket.

你喜歡健康的飲料嗎？不僅要健康而且也要美味嗎？那麼，獅子飲料公司為你有了某樣東西。嚐嚐「自然飲」，它只有充足的天然成分，不含任何防腐劑。此外，它是小巧又方便的盒裝，所以能便於攜帶到職場或學校。如果你在意健康，「自然飲」對你來說就是最好的選擇。現在就在你們當地的超市尋找它吧。

詞彙 healthy 健康的 beverage 飲料 full of …充滿的 ingredient 成分 preservative 防腐劑 in addition 另外 package 包裝 convenient 方便的 carry 攜帶 conscious 在意的 supermarket 超市

13.

關於這個產品，有什麼是很便利的？

（A）它很容易攜帶。
（B）它能被折疊。
（C）它非常的輕。

解說 透過考題與選項可以知道該錄音為「廣告」類型。該考題是詢問優點的。在錄音的中間部分出現convenient，可以聽到用被動語態表達的「容易攜帶」。　　　　　　　　　　　　答案（A）

詞彙 easily 容易地　fold 折疊　lightweight 輕的

14.

聽眾可以在哪裡找到這個產品？

（A）在百貨公司
（B）在美髮店
（C）在超市

解說 這是詢問「廣告」敘述的購買方法為何的考題。該錄音最後的句子出現了find，在此後面就能聽到答案。　　　　　　　　　　　　　　　　答案（C）

詞彙 department store 百貨公司　hair salon 美髮店

STEP 02　考題實戰練習

1. (A)	2. (D)	3. (A)	4. (B)	5. (D)	6. (A)
7. (A)	8. (B)	9. (A)	10. (A)	11. (C)	12. (C)

問題1～3，請參考以下訊息。 澳W

Have you ever been late for an important meeting due to bad weather or heavy traffic? Looking for a comfortable way to get to your destination on time? [1]Then check out Korean Railways. Korean Railways has trains to every major business destination throughout the country, and to better meet customers' business needs, [2]we've just started providing wireless Internet service on board, so you can get on the Internet while moving to your destination. In addition, [3]we are offering special discounts for new customers. This offer will be good until the end of the month. For more information, visit our website at www. koreanrailway.com. We look forward to seeing you soon at Koreana Railways.

你曾因惡劣的天氣或繁忙的交通而在重要會議中遲到嗎？在尋找一種舒適的方式讓您準時到達目的地嗎？那麼看看韓國鐵路吧。韓國鐵路有到全國各地每一個主要商業區的列車，同時為了更適合於客戶的需求，我們開始於車上提供無線上網服務，因此您能在移動到目的地的時候上網。此外，我們也提供特別折扣給新客戶。這項優惠將持續到

本月底。有關更多訊息，請至我們的網站www.koreanrailway.com。我們期待很快與您在韓國鐵路相見。

詞彙 late 晚到　important 重要的　bad weather 壞天氣　heavy traffic 交通堵塞　comfortable 舒服的　way to …的方法　destination 目的地　on time 準時　throughout the country 整個國內　meet needs 滿足需求　provide 提供　wireless Internet 無線網路　in addition 另外　offer 提供　discount 折扣　good 有效的　look forward to V-ing 期待…

1.

什麼型態的公司正在被廣告？

（A）火車
（B）網路服務
（C）搬家公司
（D）飯店

解說 這是詢問廣告商品為何的考題，錄音前段部分的疑問句之後會出現答案。藉由錄音裡聽到的公司名稱能得到線索，而透過「有列車」也可以知道有關火車的廣告。　　　　　　　　　　　　　　答案（A）

詞彙 advertise 打廣告　moving company 搬家公司

2.

這家公司最近做了什麼改變？

（A）它僱用了更多人員。
（B）它擴大進入了新市場。
（C）它更新了網站。
（D）它增加了服務。

解說 錄音中間出現的we've just started是指「最近做了某事」的意思。將其後出現的「開始於車上提供無線上網服務」做簡化來表達的（D）為答案。　　　　答案（D）

詞彙 change 變更　recently 最近　hire 招募　add 增加

3.

根據說話者所言，這個月誰將會得到折扣？

（A）第一次來的顧客
（B）老顧客
（C）本地居民
（D）競賽優勝者

解說 discount為核心詞彙。錄音裡，在discount附近出現了new，將此改成first來表達的（A）為答案。

答案（A）

詞彙 receive 得到　first-time 第一次的　patron 老顧客　contest 競賽　winner 優勝者

問題4～6請參考以下對話和圖表。 美 W

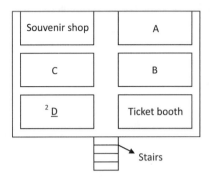

Dear guests, welcome to the Municipal Art Gallery. ⁴I'm your guide Marie-Clare Cooper. Before we start the tour today, allow me to introduce the layout of the gallery for you. After we go to the second floor, we will see the ticket booth at our right hand side. ⁵Please check your coats at the coatroom across from the booth while I purchase tickets. Today, ⁶there are three different themes of exhibition being shown: "Promise of Something New" - A photography display, "True Love of Yesterday" - A show on sculptures, and "Garden of Spring" - A pot culture exhibition. We will spend roughly 15 minutes at each show room. Now let's first scan the QR-code by the stairs, so later we can get discounts on certain souvenir items at the shop. All right, are you ready? Let's go.

親愛的來賓，歡迎來到市立美術館。我是您的導覽員瑪莉・克萊兒・庫柏。在我們開始今天的參觀之前，請容我為您介紹美術館的配置。上二樓之後，我們將看到右手邊有售票處。在我購買門票的時候，請在售票處對面的衣帽間寄放您的外套。今天有三場不同主題的展覽展出，分別為「新之允諾」一相片展、「昨日真愛」-雕刻作品展、「春之園」一盆栽展出。我們將在每一個展場停留約15分鐘。現在，讓我們先掃描樓梯旁的QR-code，這樣之後我們在店裡，能有特定紀念商品的折扣。好了，準備好了嗎？我們出發！

詞彙 municipal 市立的 gallery 美術館 guide 導遊 allow 允許 introduce 介紹 layout 配置，排版 ticket booth 售

票亭 check 寄放，檢查 coatroom 衣帽間 across from 在……對面 purchase 購買 promise 允諾 photography 攝影 display 展出 sculpture 雕刻 pot culture 盆栽 roughly 約略，大致 scan 掃描 discount 折扣 souvenir 紀念品

4.
誰是瑪莉・克萊兒・庫柏？
（A）老師
（B）導覽員
（C）雕刻家
（D）園丁

解說 這是詢問「職業別」的「簡短選項類考題」。說話者一開始就自我介紹「我是您的導覽員瑪莉・克萊兒・庫柏。」所以答案要選（B）。　　　答案 (B)

詞彙 teacher 老師 tour guide 導遊 sculptor 雕刻家 gardener 園丁

5.
請看此圖。衣帽間在哪裡？
（A）A
（B）B
（C）C
（D）D

解說 這是詢問「地點」的「簡短選項類考題」。導遊請遊客們「請在售票處對面的衣帽間寄放您的外套。」圖表中，售票處對面的房間是（D）。　　答案 (D)

詞彙 coatroom 衣帽間

6.
哪一種藝術品沒有被展出？
（A）繪畫
（B）雕刻
（C）盆栽
（D）相片

解說 這是詢問「何者為非」的「簡短選項類考題」。文中導遊說明「今天有三場不同主題的展覽展出「新之允諾」一相片展、「昨日真愛」一雕刻作品展、「春之園」一盆栽展出，所以只有選項（A）繪畫不在此列。
答案 (A)

詞彙 artwork 藝術品 painting 繪畫 sculpture 雕刻 potted plant 盆栽 photograph 相片

問題7～9，請參考以下訊息。 英 M

Hello everyone, welcome to Big Mountain National Park. My name is George, and I'll be your guide for the day. I have a few reminders before we begin our tour. This morning, ⁷we will have a 90-minute drive to the Big Waterfalls. On the way, we'll see a lot of animals. ⁷, ⁸We will stop a few times along the way so that you can take photos if you want. However, please don't attempt to feed the animals. Also, it's so warm today, ⁹it is recommended to drink water frequently. After spending an hour at the Big Waterfalls, we will have lunch for one hour at the Jinsan Restaurant ⁷where our bus will be standing by for us to move onto the next stop.

您好，大家好，歡迎來到巨山國家公園。我的名字是喬治，我將是你今天的導遊。在我們開始行程之前我有幾項提醒。今天上午，我們將開90分鐘車程去大瀑布。在路上，我們會看到很多動物。沿路上我們會停車幾次，因此如果您想要的話您可以拍照。不過，請不要企圖餵食動物。另外，今天如此溫暖，我們建議您經常補充水份。在大瀑布待一小時之後，我們將在津森餐廳用餐一小時，我們的巴士將在那兒等候我們前往到下一站。

詞彙 reminder 提醒事項 on the way 在路上 stop 停留 take photos 拍照 attempt 嘗試；試圖 feed 餵 warm 溫暖的 recommend 建議 frequently 頻繁地 stand by 等候；待命

7.
這則公告很有可能會在哪裡被聽到？
（A）在巴士上
（B）在船上
（C）在火車上
（D）在飛機上

解說 「參觀／觀光」類錄音裡，地點相關線索總是在前段部分出現。但此考題的選項為交通工具，所以答案線索可能不在錄音前段部分。該錄音內容裡有「九十分鐘車程」、「停車」、「巴士等候」等說法，所以（A）為答案。　　　　　　　　　　答案 (A)

詞彙 announcement 公告事項

8.
他們今天早上為什麼會有數次的停車？
（A）為了購買一些食物
（B）為了照相
（C）為了休息
（D）為了搭載其他團體

解說 錄音中間部分能聽到「如果您願意您可以拍照」，此為停車的理由。在這一句裡的pictures與photos是同義詞。　　　　　　　　　　　答案 (B)

詞彙 purchase 購買 take pictures 拍照 take a rest 休息 pick up 搭載

9.
說話者鼓勵人們做什麼事？
（A）喝水
（B）餵食動物
（C）輕聲說話
（D）帶走他們的垃圾

解說 「參觀／觀光」類型的後面部分會出現注意／勸導／許可事項。該考題裡的核心詞彙encourage，在錄音裡以recommended來表達，其後面就有答案線索。
　　　　　　　　　　　答案 (A)

詞彙 encourage 鼓勵 quietly 安靜地 carry 帶

問題10~12，請參考以下訊息。 美M

¹⁰Hi, I'm Richard Steves, director of the award-winning film, *The Exodus*. To celebrate Busan's International Film Festival, we're offering free admission or discounts to previews scheduled during the next two weeks. ¹¹We've been sponsored by Busan City Council to offer a special package to audience members. For the low price of two dollars, you can take a guided city tour and enjoy refreshments before or after the film. The festival venue is conveniently located near public transportation stops. ¹²Sign up for the special package online at www.busanfestival.com. Availability is limited, so don't wait!

您好，我是獲獎影片《出埃及記》的導演李察‧史提夫。為了慶祝釜山國際電影節，我們在未來兩週已安排好的試映提供免費入場或折扣。我們被釜山市議會贊助，提供觀眾一個特別配套方案。用兩塊錢的低價，能得到一趟市區導覽和在看片之前或之後享受茶點。電影節舉辦的地點接近大眾運輸站。請上網到www.busanfestival.com登記這個特別的配套方案。名額有限，所以請不要等待！

詞彙 director 導演 award-winning 得獎的 celebrate 慶祝 offer 提供 free admission 免費入場 discount 折扣 preview 試映會 sponsor 贊助 guided tour 導覽 refreshment 茶點 venue 活動場地 conveniently located 位置方便的 public transportation 大眾交通運輸工具 sign up for 登錄… online 線上 availability 可得性 limited 有限

10.
說話者很有可能是誰？
（A）一位電影導演
（B）一位導遊
（C）一位餐廳經理
（D）一位市長

解說 在錄音前段部分出現I'm與說話者的身份。於此題中直接說「導演」。　　　　　　答案 (A)

詞彙 tour guide 導遊 manager 經理 mayor 市長

11.
這個特別配套方案中包含了什麼？
（A）博物館的票
（B）在紀念品店的折扣
（C）市區觀光
（D）導覽手冊

解說 在錄音當中直接能聽到有關special package的說明，也就是「用兩塊錢能享受旅遊與茶點」。 答案 (C)

詞彙 include 包含 museum 博物館 gift shop 紀念品店 guidebook 手冊

12.
為什麼聽眾應該到網站看？
（A）為了得到停車指示
（B）為了看目前表演的清單
（C）為了登錄一項配套活動
（D）為了更多了解城市的景點

解說 錄音內容裡，在網址的附近可以聽到register for的同義詞sign up for。在其後面出現的special package改成了event package來表達。因此（C）為答案。 答案 (C)

詞彙 visit 訪問 parking 停車 tip 資訊 a list of... ...的目錄 register for 登錄 attraction 旅遊景點

STEP 01 若沒答對會後悔的考題

1 (C)

1. 美W

1 找出核心詞彙	order
2 了解類型	詢問產品訂購資訊
3 看圖表	產品報價單
4 看選項	產品資訊
5 聽錄音來確認答案	

Furniture	
Royal Series	$12,500
Renaissance Series	$11,200
Minimalism Series	$9,700
Country Series	$9,500

Hello, Mr. Black. It's Sherri from Palace Furniture. I'm calling regarding your order. You have ordered the Country Series yesterday, [1]but I have just learned the series has sold out. According to your budget that is about 10,000 dollars, I recommend the third series to you. Please kindly check and call me back. Thanks.

家具	
皇家系列	12,500元
文藝復興系列	11,200元
極簡風系列	9,700元
鄉村系列	9,500元

嗨，布萊克先生。我是皇宮家居的雪莉，就您的訂單致電給您。您昨天訂購了鄉村系列家具，但我剛剛得知這個系列已銷售一空。根據您約一萬元的預算，我推薦第三個系列給您。請您確認並回電給我，謝謝。

請看圖表。布萊克先生將訂購哪個系列的家具？
（A）皇家系列
（B）文藝復興系列
（C）極簡風系列
（D）鄉村系列

解說 這是與產品訂購資訊有關的問題。為家具行員工

打電話給顧客的獨白。電話中提到顧客訂購的產品已經銷售一空（sold out），所以顧客須重新選擇訂購商品。再根據獨白中提到顧客的預算為一萬元，再搭配圖表的產品報價單，符合顧客預算且有貨的產品為（C）Minimalism Series。

答案(C)

1 (A)	2 (C)	3 (C)	4 (B)
5 (D)	6 (C)	7 (A)	8 (C)
9 (D)	10 (C)	11 (B)	12 (A)

問題1～3請參考以下獨白與圖表。 英W

Program	
Speaker	Time
Ms. Green	1:00-1:45
Mr. Crews	1:50-2:35
BREAK	2:35-3:00
³Mr. Tropper	3:00-3:45
³Ms. Davies	3:50-4:35

Hello, everyone. I hope you've all enjoyed the first half of our program this morning. ¹I'd like to remind you that there will be another training session given in the afternoon. We invite four professional reporters to share their precious interview experience. ³Please note there will be a change for the last two speakers. Ms. Davies will leave early. ²Let's take a break for one hour. Thank you.

議程表	
講者	時間
葛林女士	1:00-1:45
古魯斯先生	1:50-2:35
休息時間	2:35-3:00
崔布爾先生	3:00-3:45
戴維斯女士	3:50-4:35

大家好。我希望大家都喜歡今天上午我們前半段的課程。我想提醒大家下午有另一場培訓課程。我們邀請四位專業的記者來分享他們寶貴的採訪經驗。請注意最後兩名講者的順序將調整，戴維斯女士將提早離開。我們休息一個小時。謝謝。

詞彙 program 計畫，節目 training 訓練 session 會議；集會；授課 professional 專業的 reporter 記者；報導者 precious 珍貴的 interview 採訪 leave 離開 take a break 休息

1.

聽者被提醒關於什麼？
（A）關於下午的課程
（B）關於如何填表格
（C）關於餐桌禮儀
（D）關於胸章在哪裡

解說 這在詢問獨白中的細節，如果獨白是作為研討會的開場白，通常這類的訊息會在獨白的中後段出現。但這則獨白是研討會上半場結束的公告內容，若此時有需要提醒聽者注意的事項，通常會在獨白的前半段作說明，後半段會做感謝詞或是接續活動的宣布。 答案(A)

詞彙 remind 提醒 table manner 餐桌禮儀 badge 胸章

2.

接下來將發生什麼事情？
（A）培訓課程將被取消。
（B）演講將於十分鐘後開始。
（C）參加者將休息。
（D）講者將離開。

解說 在錄音音檔開始播放前，要記得先瀏覽題目，這個題目在詢問接下來會發生的事情，此時要特別留意獨白的中後段。 答案(C)

詞彙 speech 演講 participator 參加者

3.

看圖表，最後一名講者是誰？
（A）葛林女士
（B）古魯斯先生
（C）崔布爾先生
（D）戴維斯女士

解說 看到圖表是議程的時間表，便可知道這四名講者的順序將會有所變動，聽到獨白中說there will be a change for the last two speakers，便可將（A）和（B）選項先刪除，將重點放在後面兩名講者上。可能會發生的情況有兩種：演講取消或是順序對調，接下來聽到Ms. Davies will leave early.可知戴維斯女士因為要提早離開所以順序對調，故可知答案為（C）崔布爾先生。 答案(C)

問題4～6請參考以下獨白與圖表。 美M

	Weekday	Weekend
Morning	Web Design	⁵Computer Skills
Afternoon	Computer Programming	⁵Computer skills
Evening	Software Design	X

Do you want to upgrade your occupational skills and earn more money? ⁴Hi-Q computer training school will help you attain your goal. We offer courses that are up to date and market oriented. All our teachers are academically trained and well certified. <u>⁶We guarantee that you will learn what you need to know in a time of three months.</u> <u>⁵Our courses are offered on the weekend.</u> What are you waiting for? Call now and register!

	平日	周末
早上	網站設計	電腦技能
下午	程式設計	電腦技能
晚上	軟體設計	X

您想要提升您的職業技能並且賺更多的金錢嗎？Hi-Q電腦訓練學校將幫助您實現您的目標。我們提供最新而且市場導向的課程。所有我們的老師都有學術訓練並有合格證書。我們保證您將在三個月的期間內學習您所需要知道的技能。我們的課程是在周末。您還在等什麼？現在就來電註冊吧！

詞彙 upgrade 提升 occupational 執業的 attain 達到 goal 目標 oriented 以…為目的 academically 學術上 certificated 持有合格證書的 guarantee 保證 register 註冊 web 網頁 programing 程式設計 software 軟體

4.
學校提供哪種訓練？
（A）外國語文
（B）電腦技能
（C）公眾演說
（D）工業設計

解說 這則是在推銷產品的廣告留言，在之前學到的攻略法可知，若是廣告類型的獨白，其產品資訊會出現在最前面。從最前面透露的訊息可知這是一間電腦公司的課程廣告，提供的是電腦技能的訓練課程。 答案 (B)

詞彙 training 訓練 foreign 外國的 skill 技能 public 公眾的 industrial 工業的

5.
看圖表，哪個課程正在被廣告？
（A）網站設計
（B）程式設計
（C）工業設計
（D）電腦技能

解說 獨白中提到他們提供的課程是在「周末」，再觀看課程表，可知目前廣告推銷的課程為（D）電腦技能。 答案 (D)

詞彙 advertise 做廣告

6.
訓練將是多長？
（A）一個月
（B）兩個月
（C）三個月
（D）四個月

解說 這在詢問獨白的細節，因此要特別留意獨白中與時間有關的訊息。這則獨白是推銷課程的廣告，而這種與產品資訊相關的細節會出現在獨白的中間，專心聆聽獨白內容，只要抓到關鍵字「three months」就可以得到答案。 答案 (C)

問題7～9請參考以下獨白與圖表。 美W

<u>⁷Welcome to the Modern Art Museum.</u> My name is Kristin, and I'll be your guide. The museum has many different art collections. We are in front of the information center now. You can see <u>⁹there is a gift shop next to the information center.</u> And beside the coffee shop is Venus Hall which displays sculptures. Opposite the Venus Hall, you can see the famous sculpture *The Thinker*. <u>⁸We'll begin our tour at Zeus Hall, the biggest room at the end of the aisle.</u> All right. Everyone ready? Follow me!

歡迎來到現代藝術博物館，我是克莉絲汀，你們的導遊。這座博物館有許多不同的藝術品。我們現在在諮詢中心前面，你可以在諮詢中心旁邊看到禮品部。而在咖啡廳旁，是展示許多雕像的維納斯廳。在維納斯廳對面，你可以看到那座知名的雕像《沉思者》。我們將從走廊底端最大房間——宙斯廳開始導覽。好的，大家準備好了嗎？跟著我走！

詞彙 collection 收藏品 beside 在旁邊 display 展示 sculpture 雕像 opposite 在對面 aisle 走廊

7.
在哪裡可以聽到這則公告？
（A）在博物館
（B）在工廠
（C）在車站
（D）在會議

解說 這個問題在詢問公告的發生地點，通常在獨白的最前面就可以找到答案。這則獨白是導遊在開始導覽之

前說的話，一開始會先致歡迎詞，歡迎大家到博物館參觀，並告知自己的名字。故可知答案為（A）。

答案 (A)

詞彙 announcement 公告 station 車站

8.

接下來可能發生什麼事情？
（A）電影將播放。
（B）商店將開幕。
（C）導覽將開始。
（D）博物館將閉館。

解說 詢問接下來的會發生的事情，答案會在獨白的中後段，通常在導覽前的歡迎詞之後，接下來就會開始導覽。但記得，雖有預設的答案，還是要確認錄音內容之後再進行作答，會比較保險。 答案 (C)

詞彙 happen 發生 open 開始 tour 導覽 close 關閉

9.

看圖片。禮品中心在哪裡？
（A）A室
（B）B室
（C）C室
（D）D室

解說 此題需要搭配圖表解題。圖片中有四間房間，說話者有逐步介紹了四間房間，但這題是在詢問gift shop的位置，所以不要被過多的資訊所迷惑，只要專心聽核心詞彙「gift shop」。說話者說gift shop在information center的旁邊，在觀看圖片，information center旁邊只有一間房間，故可知答案為（D）Room D。 答案 (D)

問題10～12請參考以下獨白與圖表。 英W

¹²Leader Program	Copper Program	Dulcet Program
- on the First Floor - with French windows - 7-day lease period	- on the First Floor - without French windows - 14-day lease period	- on the Second Floor - 30-day lease period

Dear Mr. Jones, ¹⁰this is Lynn Jefferson calling from Trend Gallery. About your inquring about the site rental, ¹¹I sent you an email with a quote few minutes ago. Our gallery has three different programs. ¹²First one is on the first floor which has a limited lease term of seven days. It's more expensive, but the benefit is this showroom has French windows and pedestrians walking by can see your exhibition from outside the building. The second one is also one on the first floor, has a 14-day lease period, without French windows. The third one is on the second floor. It's cheaper

and has a longer lease period. If you have any questions, please give me a call back again. Thanks.

領導者方案	紅銅方案	宜人方案
- 在一樓 - 有落地窗 - 租期七天	- 在一樓 - 沒有落地窗 - 租期十四天	- 在二樓 - 租期三十天

親愛的瓊斯先生，我是趨勢畫廊的琳恩·傑佛森。關於您來電詢問場地租借的事宜，我幾分鐘前寄了一封報價單給你。我們畫廊有三種租借方案。第一種方案是在一樓，有七天的限制租期，比較貴，但好處是這個展覽室有落地窗，路過的行人能從建物外面看見您的展品。第二種方案也是在一樓，十四天的租期限制，但沒有落地窗。第三種方案在二樓，比較便宜且租期較長。如果您有任何問題，請再回電，謝謝。

詞彙 gallery 畫廊，美術館 rental 租借 inquire 詢問 quote 報價 program 方案 limited 受限的 lease term 租借期限 benefit 優點 French window 落地窗 pedestrian 行人 exhibition 展覽

10.

講者在哪裡工作？
（A）旅行社
（B）汽車經銷商
（C）畫廊
（D）電影院

解說 無論獨白的主題是什麼，碰到詢問講者的身分、工作地點…等題目，答案的資訊都會出現在獨白的最前面。碰到這類題目，不要懷疑，作答順序要排在第一個。以此題組為例，為電話留言告知產品資訊的獨白內容，一開始便先告知自己的身分——畫廊的工作人員，故答案要選（C）。 答案 (C)

詞彙 agency 經銷處，代辦處 dealer 商人 theater 戲院

11.

什麼訊息被透過電子郵件給聽者？
（A）一件藝品的照片。
（B）一個場地租借的報價單。
（C）一封道歉函。
（D）一份銷售報告。

解說 根據獨白內容提到I send you an email with a quote few minutes ago，因此講者傳了報價單給對方，故此題要選（B）。 答案 (B)

詞彙 picture 照片 artwork 作品，藝術品 apologetic 道歉的 sales report 銷售報告

12.

看圖表，哪個方案最貴？

（A）領導者方案

（B）紅銅方案

（C）宜人方案

（D）它們的費用一樣。

解說 這題需要聽完所有的獨白內容後，搭配圖表作答。獨白中介紹了三個方案，並講述方案的細項與特色，也對於費用做了基本介紹，只要抓到關鍵字「expensive」，再對照獨白中介紹的方案細項：在一樓、有落地窗、租期七天，便可推敲出答案應為（A）。雖然獨白中沒有明確講述方案所需花費的金額，但有出現核心字彙expensive和cheaper，可推知三個方案的價錢不一樣，所以選項（D）不是正確答案。

答案 (A)

模擬試題答案與解析

001 (D)	002 (C)	003 (C)	004 (C)	005 (A)	006 (C)	007 (B)	008 (C)	009 (A)	010 (C)
011 (A)	012 (B)	013 (B)	014 (B)	015 (A)	016 (C)	017 (A)	018 (B)	019 (A)	020 (B)
021 (B)	022 (C)	023 (A)	024 (B)	025 (B)	026 (B)	027 (C)	028 (B)	029 (B)	030 (B)
031 (A)	032 (C)	033 (D)	034 (B)	035 (B)	036 (C)	037 (B)	038 (B)	039 (D)	040 (A)
041 (B)	042 (A)	043 (B)	044 (D)	045 (D)	046 (A)	047 (D)	048 (A)	049 (D)	050 (A)
051 (B)	052 (B)	053 (D)	054 (B)	055 (D)	056 (C)	057 (C)	058 (C)	059 (D)	060 (B)
061 (B)	062 (C)	063 (D)	064 (C)	065 (B)	066 (A)	067 (C)	068 (B)	069 (C)	070 (D)
071 (C)	072 (B)	073 (B)	074 (D)	075 (B)	076 (D)	077 (B)	078 (A)	079 (B)	080 (B)
081 (D)	082 (B)	083 (A)	084 (C)	085 (D)	086 (B)	087 (C)	088 (C)	089 (C)	090 (D)
091 (A)	092 (B)	093 (C)	094 (B)	095 (C)	096 (D)	097 (D)	098 (B)	099 (B)	100 (C)

1. 美W

(A) She is planting a tree.
(B) She is arranging some flowers.
(C) She is taking a picture.
(D) She is sitting at a table.

(A) 她在種樹。
(B) 她在插花。
(C) 她在照相。
(D) 她坐在桌旁。

解說 這張照片是考「人與物」的關係，照片內出現的物件（如：花、樹、照片），在答案的選項中皆有出現，但卻搭配了錯誤的動作，只有答案(D)才是符合邏輯的答案。正確答案為(D)。 答案 (D)

詞彙 plant trees 種樹 arrange flowers 插花 take photos 照相 sit at a table 坐在桌旁

2. 英W

(A) The toys are packed in a box.
(B) The curtains are wide open.
(C) The toys are scattered around the room.
(D) The light is on the ceiling.

(A) 玩具裝在箱子中。
(B) 窗簾是敞開著。
(C) 玩具散放整個房間。
(D) 燈在天花板上。

解說 這題是考「景物」的題目。(A)玩具並未裝箱中，(B)窗簾並未敞開，而(D)並無法從相片中看到天花板有無燈飾，所以只有(C)玩具散放一地才是正確答案。 答案 (C)

詞彙 be packed 收好 curtain 窗簾 scattered around 散落在⋯⋯ light 燈 ceiling 天花板

3. 英M

(A) A man is assembling a bookcase.
(B) A man is bending to pick up the newspaper.
(C) The women are sitting next to each other.
(D) Some benches have been disassembled.

(A) 一個男人正在組裝書櫃。
(B) 一個男人正在彎腰拿起報紙。
(C) 女人們正並排坐著。
(D) 一些長椅被拆解了。

解說 有兩位女性並排坐著，所以(C)為答案。(A)是用與book相近的發音bookcase來誤導的選項。(B)論及了照片裡沒有的名詞newspaper，所以不是答案。(D)是故

意用周遭背景的單字benches來誤導的選項。 答案 (C)

詞彙 assemble 組裝 bookcase 書櫃 bend 彎腰 pick up 拾取 newspaper 報紙 each other 互相 disassemble 拆解

4. 美M

(A) The school bus driver is parking the bus.
(B) The teacher is guiding the children by the car.
(C) The students are riding in the school bus.
(D) The boys are facing each other in the car.

(A) 校車司機正在停車。
(B) 老師在車旁邊引導孩子。
(C) 學生們正在登上校車。
(D) 男孩們在車上面對面。

解說 此篇是考「人與物」的關係。(A)車已靜止，而非司機正在停車，(B)並未看到有老師，(D)圖中兩位學生正一前一後地在上車，也看不到是否車上學生是面對面，故選(C)才是正確答案。 答案 (C)

詞彙 school bus driver 校車司機 parking 停車 guide 引導 ride in 搭乘 face each other 面對面

5. 美W

(A) They are having a meeting.
(B) They are turning off the laptop.
(C) They are going to lunch.
(D) They are having a day off.

(A) 他們正在開會。
(B) 他們正關閉筆電。
(C) 他們正要去午餐。
(D) 他們正放一天假。

解說 這題是在考「人的關係」。(B)圖中並無顯示正在關電腦的動作，(C)從圖片並無法判斷他們是否即將去用餐，(D)他們正在開會，並沒有放假一天。所以正確答案為(A)。 答案 (A)

詞彙 have a meeting 開會 turn off 關閉 laptop 筆電 go to lunch 去午餐 have a day off 放一天假

6. 美W

(A) Some trees line both sides of the street.
(B) Some people are riding on a boat.
(C) Some cars are crossing a bridge.
(D) Some pedestrians are crossing a bridge.

(A) 一些樹木排列在街道的兩側。
(B) 一些人正在搭船。
(C) 一些車輛正在通過橋樑。
(D) 一些行人正在通過橋樑。

解說 有一些車子正在過橋，所以(C)為答案。(A)不是

答案，因為樹木是在道路的單側。選項(B)和(D)不是答案，因為在照片中沒有人出現。 答案 (C)

詞彙 line 排成一列 both sides of the street 街道的兩側 ride 搭乘 cross a bridge 通過橋樑 pedestrian 行人

Part 2

7. 美W 英W

Who will you go to the concert with?
(A) She's a famous pianist.
(B) I don't know yet. Do you want to go?
(C) Yes, I enjoyed it a lot.

你會跟誰去演奏會？
(A) 她是很有名的鋼琴家。
(B) 我還不知道，你要去嗎？
(C) 是的。我很喜歡。

解說 以Who開頭問的句子是問「對象是誰」。此題的核心語是go with，是問要跟誰去演奏會。(A)沒有針對題目作答，(C)用yes回答也不合文法，而(B)雖沒有確實回答誰，但是有反問並邀請提問者一同前往，所以正確答案為(B)。 答案 (B)

詞彙 concert 演奏會 famous 有名的 pianist 鋼琴家 don't know yet 還不曉得 enjoy it a lot 很喜歡

8. 美W 美M

What are you reading?
(A) She's reading a newspaper.
(B) Yes, I like reading.
(C) Just an old novel.

你在讀什麼？
(A) 她在讀報紙。
(B) 是啊，我喜歡閱讀。
(C) 只是一本舊小說。

解說 以What開頭問的句子是問「什麼」。此題的核心語是you reading？用you問要用I回答，因此(A)用she回答用錯主詞，此外(B)用yes回答不合文法，而(C)是I'm just reading an old novel.的簡略答句（I'm省去），合乎題意，故正確答案為(C)。 答案 (C)

詞彙 read newspaper 讀報 read 閱讀 novel 小說

9. 英W 美M

When does the guest check in today?
(A) 4 in the afternoon.
(B) It is a bounced check.
(C) Yes, they'll check out tomorrow.

今天客人會何時入住呢？
(A) 下午四點。

(B) 這是空頭支票。
(C) 是的，他們明天退房。

解說 以When開頭問的句子是問「時間點」。題目check in入住是飯店住房用語，(A)下午四點是正確答案，其餘的(B) bounced check的check在此指的是支票，為誘答選項，(C)用yes回答不合文法。 答案 (A)

詞彙 guest 客人 check in 入住（飯店） in the afternoon 在下午 a bounced check 空頭支票 check out 退房

10. 美M 美W

Where's the weekly report?
(A) No, you don't need to do that.
(B) The sales are low these years.
(C) The manager has it.

週報告在哪裡？
(A) 不，你不必這麼做。
(B) 這幾年銷售很低迷。
(C) 在經理那兒。

解說 以Where開頭問的句子是問「地點」。(A)用no回答不合文法，(B)答非所問，(C)才是有回應到問題的答案。 答案 (C)

詞彙 weekly report 週報告 sales are low 銷售低迷 manager 經理

11. 美M 英M

Have you read the new software manual?
(A) Not yet. Where is it?
(B) He's in charge of the annual banquet.
(C) Here's your newspaper.

你看過新的軟體手冊嗎？
(A) 還沒有，它在哪裡？
(B) 他負責年度晚宴。
(C) 這是您的報紙。

解說 這是一般疑問句的考題。對於詢問是否「看過」，以否定與補充說明方式來回答的(A)為答案。(B)是故意用manual的類似發音annual來誤導的選項。(C)是故意用new的類似發音newspaper來誤導的選項。 答案 (A)

詞彙 manual 手冊；說明書 in charge of 負責…的 banquet 宴會 newspaper 報紙

12. 美W 澳W

How do you commute to work every day?
(A) No later than 7:00.
(B) I walk there.
(C) Yes, in the afternoon.

你每天如何上下班？
(A) 不晚於七點。
(B) 我走路到那裡。
(C) 是的，在下午。

解說 這是詢問通勤方式的how。(B)「用走路去」指的就是通勤的方式，就是答案。(A)是對於when的回答方式，所以不是答案。(C)是對於疑問詞疑問句用Yes／No來回答，所以不是答案。 答案 (B)

詞彙 commute to work 通勤 no later than 不晚於… walk 走路

13. 英M 美W

Can you tell me your camera's serial number?
(A) Contact me at 555-6556.
(B) Where is it?
(C) Yes, very serious.

你能告訴我你相機的序號嗎？
(A) 撥555-6556與我聯絡。
(B) 它在哪裡？
(C) 是的，非常嚴重。

解說 這是建議疑問句的考題。(B)是反問形式的回答方式，總是能成為答案。(A)是故意用電話號碼來與number產生聯想做誤導的選項。(C)故意用了serial的類似發音serious來誤導的選項。 答案 (B)

詞彙 serial number 序號 contact 聯絡 serious 嚴重的

14. 美M 英W

Why don't we meet at the lobby?
(A) It has been a long time.
(B) That sounds like a good idea.
(C) Because it is too late.

我們何不在大廳見面呢？
(A) 已經好久了。
(B) 那聽起來不錯。
(C) 因為太晚了。

解說 以Why not開頭的句子是「建議」的意思，不可以回答Because，所以(C)自動刪除，(A)答非所問，而(B)才是回應題目的合理答案。 答案 (B)

詞彙 meet 會面 lobby 大廳 a long time 一段長時間 a good idea 好主意 too late 太晚了

15. 英W 美W

How do you usually go to work?
(A) My husband drives me there.
(B) We don't need to work today.
(C) Yes, I love my job.

你平常如何去上班？
(A) 我先生會送我去。
(B) 我們今天不需要工作。
(C) 是的，我愛我的工作。

解說 此題以How開頭問的句子是問「方法」，go to work問如何去上班，(A)選項是合理的答案，(B)答非所問，只是同樣出現work這個單字來誘答，而(C)的答案不適用於此，若選項(C)反推的題目會是Do you like your job? 答案 (A)

詞彙 usually 通常 go to work 上班 husband 丈夫 drive 開車 love 喜愛

16. 英W 美M

Have you seen any movies lately?
(A) No, I haven't seen him.
(B) I think he's a good director.
(C) Oh, I've been too busy.

你最近有沒有看什麼電影？
(A) 沒有，我沒有看到他。
(B) 我覺得他是個好導演。
(C) 喔，我最近太忙了。

解說 這是一題Yes/No問句，詢問「經驗」，核心語have you seen... ? (A)用No回答原本是可以的，但是問句是問movies，答句不可以用him回覆。(B)用了同樣是影劇字彙的director導演，但並非合邏輯的選項。而(C)才是正解，因為(C)雖然沒有明顯地用yes或no回答，但說自己太忙是間接地說喔，最近太忙了，沒時間看電影。 答案 (C)

詞彙 see a movie 看電影 lately 最近 director 導演 too busy 太忙了

17. 美W 美M

Would you like to meet on Monday or Tuesday?
(A) Either is fine with me.
(B) I don't like him to stay.
(C) It is terrific.

你要星期一還是星期二見面？
(A) 我都可以。
(B) 我不要他留下來。
(C) 太棒了。

解說 這是選擇A或B的題目。本來答案應該是擇一回答，但這裡(A)是都可以，也算是合理的回應。(B)和(C)都是答非所問。 答案 (A)

詞彙 Monday 星期一 Tuesday 星期二 either 兩者中的任何一個 stay 留下來 terrific 很棒的

18. 美M 美W

What are you doing this afternoon?
(A) Yes, I have to.
(B) I'm going shopping.
(C) Fine, thanks.

今天下午你將要做什麼？
(A) 是的，我得做。
(B) 我將去購物。
(C) 很好，謝謝您。

解說 這是詢問行為的what疑問句。回答中包含了行為的(B)為答案。(A)不是答案，因為對疑問詞疑問句不能用Yes／No來回答。(C)是對於How的回答方式。

答案 (B)

詞彙 have to 得… **go shopping** 去購物 **fine** 很好

19. 美W 美M

Didn't you think the speech was interesting?
(A) No, it was long and boring.
(B) No, there's no interest fee.
(C) Sure, let's have some coffee.

你不覺得演講很有趣嗎？
(A) 不，它漫長又無聊。
(B) 不，它沒有利息。
(C) 當然，我們來一點咖啡吧。

解說 該考題是否定疑問句。對「有趣」以No來回答，之後再附加說明的(A)為答案。(B)是故意用interesting的相似發音interest來誤導的選項。(C)是對建議的說法回答的方法。

答案 (A)

詞彙 speech 演講 **interesting** 有趣的 **boring** 無聊 **interest fee** 利息

20. 英M 美W

Where did you leave the new catalog?
(A) Sorry, we're going to produce them next year.
(B) In the top drawer of this cabinet.
(C) Of course not.

你把新的型錄放在哪了？
(A) 對不起，我們明年才要生產它們。
(B) 在這個櫃子最上面的抽屜裡。
(C) 當然不是。

解說 對where疑問句用地點說法來回答的(B)為答案。(A)沒有包含地點說法，所以不是答案。(C)是對Do you mind...?疑問句的回答方式。

答案 (B)

詞彙 leave 留置 **catalog** 型錄 **produce** 生產 **drawer** 抽屜

21. 美W 英W

Do you know where Martha lives?
(A) No, she'll leave tomorrow morning.
(B) She lives on Cambie Street.
(C) Yes, she's already left.

你知道瑪莎住在哪裡嗎？
(A) 不，她明天早上離開。
(B) 她住在坎比街。
(C) 是，她已經離開了。

解說 這是一題以Do you know提問的間接問句，但注意答案不見得是用Yes或No回答。主要疑問詞Where是問「地點」，其實這一句相當就是在問Where does Martha live？選項(A)及(C)都出現了和題目的lives諧音的leave及left，但是皆為誘答選項。所以正確答案是(B)。

答案 (B)

詞彙 Do you know...? 你知道…？ **live** 居住 **leave** 離開 **tomorrow morning** 明晨 **on...street** 在……街上 **already** 已經

22. 澳W 英M

Who's going to lock up the office tonight?
(A) I bought it at the office supply store.
(B) For three night only.
(C) I'm working late, so I will.

今晚誰要鎖辦公室？
(A) 我在辦公用品店買到它的。
(B) 只有三個晚上。
(C) 我將工作到很晚，所以我會。

解說 對who疑問句的回答方式中，包含有「我」的(C)為答案。(A)是故意用同音詞office來產生混淆的選項。(B)是對how long疑問句的回答方式。

答案 (C)

詞彙 lock up 將……鎖上 **office supply store** 辦公用品店 **work late** 工作到很晚

23. 美M 美W

Let's go for a walk, shall we?
(A) Why not? I'd love to.
(B) I can't talk when I walk.
(C) Yes, you'd better run.

我們去散步，好嗎？
(A) 何不？我很樂意。
(B) 我走路時無法交談。
(C) 是，你最好用跑的。

解說 此題Let's..., shall we? 這種句型是「詢問對方意向」的問句。(A)回答是接受了邀約，為正確答案。(B)同樣出現了walk這個字在選項，但沒有針對問題做答。

(C)的前半部回答Yes似乎合理，但後半部you'd better run答非所問。 答案 (A)

詞彙 **go for a walk** 散步 **shall we?** 好嗎？ **Why not** 何不 **I'd love to** 我很樂意 **talk** 談話 **you'd better** 你最好…… **run** 跑、快走

24. 美M 英M

Can I expect your reply today or tomorrow?
(A) By regular mail.
(B) This afternoon, if possible.
(C) Yes, I can.

我今天可以得到你的回覆，還是明天？
(A) 通過普通郵件。
(B) 如果可能的話，是今天下午。
(C) 是的，我可以。

解說 該考題是選擇疑問句。(B)的this afternoon是today的變化說法。(A)是對how的回答方式。而選項(C)其主詞不對。 答案 (B)

詞彙 **reply** 回覆 **regular mail** 普通郵件 **if possible** 如果可能的話

25. 美W 美M

Which is the key to the supply closet?
(A) We don't need supplies.
(B) The one with the yellow tag.
(C) No, it isn't very close.

哪一隻是供應品倉庫的鑰匙？
(A) 我們不需用品。
(B) 有一個黃色標籤的那個。
(C) 不，它不會很近。

解說 which疑問句也是一種選擇疑問句。用代名詞one來回答的(B)為答案。(A)是故意用supply的相近發音supplies來誤導的選項。(C)是故意用closet的相近發音close來誤導的選項。 答案 (B)

詞彙 **supply closet** 供應品倉庫 **tag** 標籤 **close** 近

26. 美W 英W

Can somebody answer the phone?
(A) That's a good answer to the question.
(B) I'll get it right away.
(C) The phone is broken.

誰接一下電話好嗎？
(A) 這是解題的好答案。
(B) 我馬上去接。
(C) 電話壞了。

解說 這原本是一句「祈求協助」的Yes / No問句。正確答案是(B)，但在此，Yes已省略。選項(A)也有answer這

個字，但在這裡的用法是當名詞，沒有針對題目作答，選項(C)有出現題目中的phone這個字，但答非所問。 答案 (B)

詞彙 **answer the phone** 接電話 **good answer** 好答案 **question** 問題 **I'll get it** 讓我來 **right away** 立刻 **broken** 壞了

27. 英W 美W

How soon can you be ready?
(A) Yes, I've already been there.
(B) About 3 kilometers an hour.
(C) In about 5 minutes.

你多快能準備好？
(A) 是，我有去過那裏。
(B) 大約時速3公里。
(C) 大約再5分鐘。

解說 用How soon問是詢問「多快？多久之後？」的意思。(A)答非所問，(B)是回答How fast「多快速度」的答案，非針對題目作答。而(C)才是正確答案。 答案 (C)

詞彙 **how soon** 多快 **be ready** 準備好 **already** 已經 **about** 大約 **kilometer** 公里 **an hour** 一小時 **in 5 minutes** 再5分鐘

28. 美M 澳W

How do you turn off the copy machine?
(A) I'll return it soon.
(B) Press the red button.
(C) The copier is over there.

怎麼關影印機？
(A) 我將很快就歸還它。
(B) 按紅色的鈕。
(C) 影印機就在那兒。

解說 該考題是方法的how疑問句，因此有表達方法的(B)為答案。(A)是故意用turn的相近發音return來產生混淆的選項。(C)是對where的回答方式。 答案 (B)

詞彙 **turn off** 關掉 **copy machine** 影印機 **return** 返回 **press** 按 **copier** 影印機 **over there** 在那兒

29. 美M 美W

Could you please turn the radio up?
(A) It's Sandy's turn to go.
(B) No problem. I'll turn it up.
(C) Down the hall and to the right.

你可否將收音機聲量開大一點？
(A) 現在輪到珊蒂去了。
(B) 沒問題，我會開大一點。
(C) 到大廳底之後右轉。

解說 該考題是建議的疑問句。因此以肯定／允許回答

之後再附加說明的(B)為答案。(A)是故意用同音詞turn來產生混淆的選項。在選項(C)中，若將考題裡的turn解釋為「轉彎」，是可以列入考慮的選項，但不是答案。

答案 (B)

詞彙 **turn up** 提高聲量

30. 美W 美M

Don't we need to order more office supplies?
(A) It's hard to open.
(B) No, let's do it later.
(C) Yes, I was surprised.

我們不需要訂購更多的辦公用品嗎？
(A) 它很難打開。
(B) 不，晚一點做吧。
(C) 是的，我很驚訝。

解說 該考題是間接建議的疑問句。以否定／拒絕回答之後，再附加說明的(B)為答案。(A)是完全無關的選項。(C)是故意用supplies的類似發音surprised來產生混淆的選項。 答案 (B)

詞彙 **order** 訂購 **office supply** 辦公用品 **hard** 困難 **open** 打開 **later** 稍晚一點 **surprised** 驚訝

31. 美W 英M

The printer's run out of ink.
(A) You can get some in the top drawer of this cabinet.
(B) Yes, I'm having trouble running this program.
(C) No, I think she headed out for lunch.

印表機的墨水用完了。
(A) 你可以在這個櫃子最上面的抽屜裡拿到一些。
(B) 是的，我在運用這個程式時遇到困難。
(C) 不，我想她出去吃午餐了。

解說 該考題是論及問題狀況的陳述句。因此提供解決方法的(A)為答案。(B)是論及另一個問題來產生混淆的選項。(C)是故意用同音詞out來產生混淆的選項，而且也不知道she指的是誰。 答案 (A)

詞彙 **out of ink** 沒有墨水的 **drawer** 抽屜 **have trouble V-ing** 於…遇到困難 **head out** 出去

Part 3

問題32～34請參考以下對話。 美W 美M

W : Sir, let's see... To fly to Toronto from Taipei, you can change flights at Los Angeles.

M : [32]Isn't there a direct flight from Taipei to Toronto?

W : No, I'm sorry, Sir. There is no direct flight between these two cities. [33]Or, maybe you can change planes in Vancouver. It will save you almost an hour's time. And this way, you don't need a visa for the US.

M : [33]That's better. Can you [32]book me a round-trip ticket to and from Toronto, please? I plan to leave latest by tomorrow afternoon.

W : [34]There is an 11:00 o'clock flight tomorrow morning. Is it all right?

M : [34]Good. I'll take it.

女：先生！我幫您看看……從台北飛多倫多，您可以在洛杉磯轉機。
男：從台北飛多倫多沒有直航班機嗎？
女：沒有耶，對不起，先生。這兩個城市間沒有直航班機。或者，或許您可以在溫哥華轉機，您將節省快一個小時的時間。而且這樣的話，您也不需要飛美國的簽證。
男：這樣比較好。可以幫我訂一張到多倫多的來回機票嗎？我計劃最晚明天下午就要出發。
女：明天早上11點有一個班次。可以嗎？
男：好！我訂下來。

詞彙 **fly** 飛 **Toronto** 多倫多 **change flight** 轉機 **Los Angeles** 洛杉磯 **direct flight** 直達機，直飛 **Vancouver** 溫哥華 **almost** 幾乎 **visa** 簽證 **book** 訂（票）**round trip ticket** 來回票 **to and from** 往返於 **latest** 最晚

32.

男士計畫去哪裡？
(A) 溫哥華
(B) 洛杉磯
(C) 多倫多
(D) 舊金山

解說 這是詢問「地點」的「簡短選項類考題」。男士想要購買到多倫多的來回機票，所以目的地是(C)選項的多倫多。 答案 (C)

詞彙 **plan** 計畫 **Vancouver** 溫哥華 **Los Angeles** 洛杉磯 **Toronto** 多倫多 **San Francisco** 舊金山

33.

他將怎麼飛？
(A) 直飛多倫多
(B) 在台北轉機
(C) 在洛杉磯轉機
(D) 在溫哥華轉機

解說 這是詢問「手段、方法」的「簡短選項類考題」。女士建議「您可以在溫哥華轉機，您將節省快一個小時的時間」，而男士也覺得這樣比較好，所以選項(D)是正解。 答案 (D)

詞彙 **direct flight** 直飛 **change flight** 轉機

34.

他將何時離開？

(A) 今晚11點

(B) 明晨11點

(C) 明晚10點

(D) 明晨10點

解說 這是詢問「時間點」的「簡短選項類考題」。男士要搭的班機是「明天早上11點」出發的班次，所以選(B)。　　　　　　　　　　答案 (B)

詞彙 leave 離開　tonight 今晚　tomorrow morning 明晨　tomorrow night 明晚

問題35～37請參考以下對話。 英W 美M

W : Hey, Joe, what a coincidence to see you here! Where are you going?

M : Hello, Lynn, [37]I'm having a dentist's appointment in 20 minutes, and you?

W : I took some time off from work early this afternoon [36]to visit a colleague. It's Cindy. Remember her? She just gave birth to a baby in the hospital.

M : [36]Congratulations! I was invited to her wedding as well two years ago. It was the last colleague's wedding I went to before I quit that job.

W : [35]Here is my stop. I'll get off first now. Bye! Joe.

M : Lynn, you take care. And give my regards to the new mom.

女：嘿！喬！真巧在這裡遇到你！你要去哪裡？

男：哈囉！琳恩！我20分鐘以後要看牙醫，你呢？

女：我今天下午提早下班，要去拜訪一位同事，是辛蒂！記得她嗎？她剛在醫院生了一個寶寶！

男：恭喜啊！她兩年前也有邀請我去她的婚禮。這是我離職以前參加的最後一場同事的婚禮了！

女：我的站到了！我要先下車了！再見！喬。

男：琳恩！你保重了！幫我跟新手媽媽問候一下！

詞彙 coincidence 巧合　dentist 牙醫　appointment 約會　take time off 空出時間　colleague 同事　hospital 醫院　congratulations 恭喜　be invited to 受邀　wedding 婚禮　quit 辭職　stop 車站　get off 下車　take care 保重　regards 問候

35.

此對話在哪裡發生？

(A) 在汽車經銷商

(B) 在公車上

(C) 在醫院

(D) 在超市

解說 這是詢問「地點」的「簡短選項類考題」。女士在對話最後提到「我的站到了。我要先下車了！」所以可推斷他們是在車上，選項(B)最符合。　　答案 (B)

詞彙 conversation 對話　take place 發生　dealer 經銷商　hospital 醫院　supermarket 超市

36.

說話者最有可能是什麼關係？

(A) 鄰居

(B) 師生

(C) 老同事

(D) 親戚

解說 這是詢問「關係」的「簡短選項類考題」。核心語是speakers' relationship。對話中的兩個人在談論一位在醫院生產的女同事，男士也說離職前有受邀參加同事婚禮，所以最可能的答案是(C)。　　答案 (C)

詞彙 relationship 關係　neighbor 鄰居　teacher 老師　student 學生　colleague 同事　relative 親戚

37.

男士接下來最可能做什麼？

(A) 和女士去醫院

(B) 去看他的牙醫

(C) 去買糖果

(D) 回家

解說 這是詢問「下一個行程」的考題。核心語是do next。男士在對話中提到「我20分鐘以後要看牙醫」，所以巧遇舊同事後，應該會繼續去辦正事。選項(B)最符合。　　答案 (B)

詞彙 next 下一個、緊隨其後　hospital 醫院　dentist 牙醫　buy 購買　candy 糖果

問題38～40請參考以下對話。 美M 美W

M : Hi, Ms. Anderson, this is Henry Gou calling from Jamison computer. [38,39]I called you two days ago, inquiring about a conference room rental case at your hotel.

W : Yes, Mr. Gou, I remember. I had my assistant send you the material with a quote. Did you receive it?

M : I did. I've looked closely over the different room types and their prices. They all seem very nice. But before we make a decision, [39]I think I'd better come take a look in person. Will it be all right if I make an appointment with you tomorrow?

W：Oh, ⁴⁰unfortunately, I won't be available tomorrow because I need to be away on a business trip. But my assistant Sherry will be able to help you and show you around.

男：嗨！安德森女士，我是傑米森電腦公司的郭亨利。我兩天前有打電話給你，問關於你們飯店的會議室租借事宜。

女：有的，郭先生。我記得。我有讓我的助理寄發相關資料及報價給您，您有收到嗎？

男：有！我有仔細看了一下不同房型及價位。都很不錯。但是在我們做決定之前，我想我最好來親自參觀一下。我可以和你約明天見面嗎？

女：喔！很不巧，我明天不行。我必須出差。但是我的助理雪莉可以協助您，帶您到處看看。

詞彙 computer 電腦 inquire 詢問 conference room 會議室 hotel 飯店 remember 記得 assistant 助理 material 資料 quote 報價 receive 接獲 look over 瀏覽 closely 仔細地 room type 房型 price 價格 make a decision 做決定 take a look 看一看 in person 親自 make an appointment 約見面 unfortunately 不幸地，不巧地 available 有空的 on a business trip 出差

38.
女士的職業最可能是什麼？
(A) 醫生
(B) 經理
(C) 教師
(D) 傳道士

解說 這是詢問「職業」的「簡短選項類考題」。核心語是occupation。男士說「我兩天前有打電話給你詢問關於你們飯店的會議室租借事宜。」而女士也回應有請助理寄資料給男士，所以最有可能的選項是(B)經理。

答案 (B)

詞彙 occupation 職業 doctor 醫生 manager 經理 teacher 教師 preacher 傳道士

39.
男士來電主要的目的是什麼？
(A) 他想詢問房間的報價。
(B) 他想商談價格的事宜。
(C) 他想要有折扣。
(D) 他想來看看飯店。

解說 這是詢問「目的」的「句子選項類考題」。核心語是main purpose of call。男士想租借場地，而且說「做決定之前，我想我最好來親自參觀一下。」所以選項(D)是正確答案。

答案 (D)

詞彙 purpose 目的 inquire 詢問 cost 花費，成本 negotiate 談判，商量 discount 折扣 pay a visit 拜訪

40.
女士明天會做什麼？
(A) 她將會出差。
(B) 她將會見男士。
(C) 她將送一份報價給男士。
(D) 她將請事假。

解說 這是詢問「明天的行程」的「句子選項類考題」。女士提到「我明天不行。我必須出差。」所以正解是(A)。

答案 (A)

詞彙 on a business trip 出差 meet 會見 quote 報價 ask for leave 請事假

問題41～43，請參考以下對話。 美M 英M

M1：Well, ⁴¹I've almost finished all of the work for the roof except I have to drive nails into these last pieces of woods. After that we can start painting. Have you prepared all of the supplies we need for the painting?

M2：Yes, ⁴²except the brushes. I couldn't find them in the truck. I must have left them at the store this morning. I'll call the store to see if the brushes are still there.

M1：Sounds like a good plan. ⁴³I think we can still have the roof completed by this afternoon. I mean, it won't take longer than two hours for us to finish the painting.

男1：嗯，除了在最後這塊木頭上得把釘子敲進去，我幾乎完成屋頂所有的工作了。之後我們就可以開始塗油漆了。你有把我們塗油漆時需要的所有用品準備好了嗎？

男2：是的，除了刷子。我在卡車上找不到它們。我一定是今天早上把他們留在店裡了。我會打電話給店裡看看刷子是否還在那兒。

男1：聽起來是個好計劃。我想我們仍然可以在今天下午完成屋頂工作。我的意思是，我們完成塗油漆不會需要兩小時以上。

詞彙 finish 完成 work 工作 roof 屋頂 except 除了 drive 敲 wood 木頭 prepare 準備 brush 刷子 leave 留置 still 仍然 completed 被完成的

41.
說話者正在做什麼？
(A) 正在訂辦公室用品
(B) 正在屋頂工作
(C) 正在儲存建材
(D) 正在修理卡車

解說 該考題是詢問主題的，因此答案大部分在錄音的前段部分。出現「我幾乎完成屋頂所有的工作了」與大致的作業行程，所以可以了解成「正在屋頂工作」。

答案 (B)

詞彙 order 下訂單 office supply 辦公室用品 store 儲存 building material 建材 fix 修理

42.

說話者遺忘了什麼？

(A) 刷子

(B) 汽車零件

(C) 一些畫作

(D) 工作時間表

解說 考題中的lost，在錄音裡是變化為「找不到」來表達，並作為線索。在其前面出現的brushes為答案。

答案 (A)

詞彙 automobile part 汽車零件 painting 圖畫

43.

這個工作很有可能在什麼時候被完成？

(A) 今天上午

(B) 今天下午

(C) 明天上午

(D) 明天傍晚

解說 這是若有錄音的後段部分聽到時間點，就能回答的考題。在錄音裡，以finished的同義字completed來出現答案線索，其後面的「今天下午」為答案。 答案 (B)

問題44～46，請參考以下對話。美W 美M

W: Good afternoon. ⁴⁴I'd like to make a reservation for dinner tonight at 7. I'd like a table that accommodates a large group.

M: Let me check. ⁴⁵I'm afraid we don't have any large tables at 7. However, 6 o'clock should be okay. Will that time work for you?

W: As a matter of fact, that works too because we will go there directly from work. ⁴⁶My name is Susan, and do you need anything else to reserve our table?

M: That's enough. So I'll put you down for a large table at 6 o'clock tonight.

女：午安。我想預約今天晚上七點的晚餐。我想要可以容納大團體的桌子。

男：讓我確認一下。在七點時我們恐怕沒有任何大的桌子。但是六點的時候應該可以。那個時間對您方便嗎？

女：事實上那也可以，因為我們會直接從公司去那裡。我的名字是蘇珊，你還需要其他任何資訊來預訂我們的桌位嗎？

男：那就夠了。那麼我將安排你們在今晚六點的大桌子。

詞彙 make a reservation 做預約 accommodate

能容納 as a matter of fact 事實上 directly from 直接從… reserve 預約 enough 足夠的

44.

這則談話的主題是什麼？

(A) 一個工作職缺

(B) 一項產品的價錢

(C) 一個團體發表會

(D) 一項餐廳的預約

解說 這是詢問主題的考題。在錄音前段部分出現「預約晚餐」，所以以「餐廳預約」為主題。 答案 (D)

詞彙 main 主要的 topic 主題 conversation 談話 job opening 工作職缺 product 工作職缺 presentation 發表會 reservation 預約

45.

這個男人建議什麼？

(A) 稍晚回電給他

(B) 和經理談話

(C) 寄一些推薦函

(D) 在不同的時間過來

解說 出現「七點不行，但六點可以」，所以將此以概括說法來做表達的(D)為答案。 答案 (D)

詞彙 recommend 建議 later 晚一點 send 寄 reference 推薦函 different 不同的

46.

這個女人提供了什麼訊息？

(A) 她的名字

(B) 她的訂單號碼

(C) 她的住宅地址

(D) 她的電話號碼

解說 在該女生的最後一句話裡出現她的名字，所以(A)為答案。 答案 (A)

詞彙 provide 提供 order number 訂單編號 home address 住宅地址

問題47～49請參考以下對話。英W 美M

W: Sorry I'm late today. ⁴⁷My bus was delayed due to the heavy rain. The traffic was just terrible.

M: I think you should try taking the MRT next time. The Metro is much faster, and it won't be affected by bad weather.

W: It might be a good idea, and I do take the MRT from time to time. ⁴⁸But you see, I prefer taking the bus since it's more cost effective. The city government grants senior citizens 60 complimentary rides each month. I get to ride for free!

M：How nice! [49]Can't wait to turn 65 soon!

女：抱歉，我今天遲到了！我的公車因為大雨耽擱了。交通狀況糟透了！

男：我想你下次應該搭捷運。捷運快多了，而且不會受到壞天氣的影響。

女：這點子或許不錯，我有時候也會搭捷運。但是你知道嗎？我比較喜歡搭公車，因為比較划算。市政府准許銀髮族每月60次優惠搭乘。我可以免費搭公車喔！

男：真好！真等不及要趕快65歲！

詞彙 delay 延誤 heavy rain 傾盆大雨 traffic 交通 take the MRT 搭捷運 Metro 地鐵 affect 影響 weather 天氣 good idea 好主意 from time to time 偶爾 prefer 較喜歡 effective 有效的，有力的 grant 准予，發放 senior citizen 銀髮族 complimentary 贈送的，免費的 ride 乘坐，搭乘 for free 免費 turn 達到，超越

47.
為何今天女士遲到？
(A) 她睡過頭了。
(B) 她發生意外。
(C) 她上錯公車。
(D) 她受困於交通。

解說 這是詢問「原因」的「句子選項類考題」。女士遲到的原因是「我的公車因為大雨耽擱了。交通狀況糟透了！」選項(D)是同義表達。　　　　答案 (D)

詞彙 sleep in 睡過頭 accident 意外 get caught 受困，被抓

48.
為何女士喜歡搭公車多於捷運？
(A) 搭公車不花她一毛錢。
(B) 公車比較方便。
(C) 捷運站不透氣。
(D) 她不喜歡爬樓梯。

解說 這是詢問「理由」的「句子選項類考題」。女士表示較喜歡搭公車是因為「市政府准許銀髮族每月60次優惠搭乘。我可以免費搭公車」。所以選(A)。
　　　　答案 (A)

詞彙 prefer... over... 喜歡……勝於 cost 花費 penny 一分錢 convenient 方便的 station 車站 stuffy 不透氣的 climb 攀登，爬上 stairs 樓梯

49.
女士最有可能是幾歲？
(A) 52
(B) 59
(C) 63
(D) 68

解說 這是詢問「年齡」的「簡短選項類考題」。從第二題我們可得知女士是銀髮族，而男士也說自己恨不得也快點65歲。只有選項(D)符合銀髮族的年齡。
　　　　答案 (D)

詞彙 how old 多大年紀

問題50～52，請參考以下對話。 英 M 美 W

M：Hi, [50]I saw some car photos posted on your website. Are they all available for sale?

W：Most of them are for sale except some of them have already been sold. If you could tell what type of cars you are interested in, I can check the inventory for you.

M：[51]I'd like a car that is fuel-efficient and reliable since I drive to a lot of places. I don't need a luxury car.

W：That narrows it down a little bit. [52]I'll check the computer for cars that have what you're looking for.

男：您好，我看到您的網站上張貼了一些汽車的照片。它們全部都是可供出售的嗎？

女：他們大部分都可供出售，除了其中一些已經售出的。如果你能告訴我你對什麼類型的車感興趣，我可以幫你查查庫存。

男：由於我要開車去很多地方，我想要省油又可靠的車。我不需要豪華的車子。

女：這樣範圍縮小了一點。我會在電腦上確認有沒有你要找的汽車。

詞彙 post 刊登；張貼 available 可供的 except 除了 fuel-efficient 省油的 reliable 可靠的 drive to 開去（某處）a lot of 很多 place 地點 luxury car 豪華的汽車

50.
這個男人想要做什麼？
(A) 買一輛汽車
(B) 換不同的工作
(C) 租公寓
(D) 為一台車拍照

解說 該考題是詢問主題的，答案線索在錄音前段部分的疑問句裡出現。該男生說「看到了一些汽車的照片、都是可供出售的嗎」，所以可以知道他想「買汽車」。
　　　　答案 (A)

詞彙 buy 買 automobile 汽車 different 不同的 rent 租 apartment 公寓 photograph 拍照

51.
這個男人說了什麼有關於他的偏好？
(A) 他想要一台昂貴的車子。
(B) 可靠性很重要。

(C) 他喜歡一家薪水更高的公司。

(D) 他通常使用大眾交通工具。

解說 「我要開車去很多地方，我想要省油又可靠的車」，可以簡單了解為「可靠性很重要」。　答案 (B)

詞彙 expensive 貴的　usually 通常　public transportation 大眾交通工具

52.

這個女人接下來可能會做什麼？

(A) 簽一份合約

(B) 在電腦上做確認

(C) 給折扣

(D) 安裝一些設備

解說 這是詢問下一個行程的考題。在錄音的後段部分該女生的話語裡，出現核心詞彙I'll，接著可以聽到「在電腦上確認」。　　　　　答案 (B)

詞彙 sign 簽名　contract 合約　check 確認　discount 折扣 install 安裝　equipment 設備

問題53～55，請參考以下對話。 美W 美M

W：Hi, Peter. This is Jenny. The printer in our marketing department isn't working. This is the third time it broke down. ⁵³I thought you placed an order for a new one. Is that right?

M：Yes. I ordered the new printer last week and the company said ⁵⁴it will be delivered tomorrow afternoon.

W：If that's the case, it doesn't pay to try to get the old printer up and running. ⁵⁵I'm going to use the printer in the accounting department until tomorrow. Thanks.

女：你好彼得，我是珍妮。我們行銷部門的印表機不能運作了。這是它第三次故障了。我想你已訂了一台新的了，對嗎？

男：是的，我上週訂了新的印表機，該公司說明天下午將會送到。

女：若是那樣，就不用讓舊印表機運作。到明天之前，我會用會計部門的印表機。謝謝你。

詞彙 marketing department 行銷部門　work 運作 break down 故障　place an order 下訂單　order 訂購　deliver 配送　if that is the case 若是那樣 up and running 正常運轉的　accounting department 會計部門

53.

為什麼這個女人打電話來？

(A) 為了取消會議

(B) 為了安排約會

(C) 為了要求服務

(D) 為了詢問有關一份訂單

解說 這是詢問主題的考題。在錄音前段部分的疑問句裡會出現答案線索。「印表機不能運作了、已訂了一台新的了，對嗎？」，所以(D)為答案。　　答案 (D)

詞彙 cancel 取消　meeting 會議　appointment 約定 inquire about 詢問有關於…

54.

在明天下午將會發生什麼？

(A) 一位新會計師將被雇用。

(B) 一項產品將被配送。

(C) 一份合約將被簽署。

(D) 一個預約將被取消。

解說 時間點為很好的答案線索。錄音裡的tomorrow afternoon附近出現「送達」。(B)的product是指printer。　　　　　　　　　　　　　　答案 (B)

詞彙 accountant 會計師　hire 雇用　contract 合約　sign 簽名　reservation 預約

55.

根據珍妮所言，員工們能在會計部門做什麼？

(A) 取得薪水資訊

(B) 使用新影印機

(C) 領取辦公室用品

(D) 列印一些文件資料

解說 accounting department為核心詞彙。將「用印表機」改成「列印文件」來表達的(D)為答案。　答案 (D)

詞彙 access 取得　copier 影印機　pick up 領取　office supply 辦公室用品　document 文件資料

問題56～58請參考以下對話。 美M 英W

M：Excuse me. We are visitors to this town and are ⁵⁶looking for a place to have lunch. Is there any restaurant nearby?

W：Yes, there's a nice restaurant about 5 to 10 minutes walk away. Just go straight to the corner and turn left. Then go one more block. It is right next to an ice cream shop.

M：Turn left at the corner? Do you mean by the post office?

W：No, the other corner, the one across the street by the bank. But you'd better hurry. ⁵⁷They take their last order at two o'clock, and ⁵⁸it's almost one forty now.

男：不好意思。我們是遊客，正在找用午餐的地方。這附近有餐廳嗎？

女：有的。大約步行5到10分鐘的距離有一家不錯的餐廳。直走到街角然後左轉，再走一條街，餐廳就在一家冰淇淋店的旁邊。

男：在街角左轉。你是說郵局旁邊？

女：不是，另一個角，對街銀行旁邊的那個角。不過你們最好趕快，他們兩點鐘接受最後點餐，現在已經快一點四十分了。

詞彙 visitor 遊客 town 城鎮 look for 尋找 have lunch 吃午餐 restaurant 餐廳 nearby 在附近 go straight 直走 block 街區 ice cream 冰淇淋 shop 商店 post office 郵局 across 在……對面 bank 銀行 had better 最好… hurry 趕快 order 點菜 almost 幾乎，快要

56.
男士要做什麼？
(A) 寄信
(B) 領錢
(C) 吃午餐
(D) 買冰淇淋

解說 這是詢問「想要做什麼」的「簡短選項類考題」。男士問女士「正在找用午餐的地方。這附近有餐廳嗎」，所以是想用餐了，選(C)。　　答案 (C)

詞彙 mail 郵寄 withdraw 提取，撤回

57.
為什麼女士叫男士要趕快？
(A) 餐廳很遠
(B) 銀行快打烊了
(C) 主廚很快要休息了
(D) 時鐘快停了

解說 這是詢問「原因，理由」的「句子選項類考題」。女士提醒男士「你們最好趕快，他們兩點鐘接受最後點餐」，也可推斷說選項(C)「主廚很快要休息了」。　　答案 (C)

詞彙 far away 遙遠的 closed 打烊的 chef 主廚 take a break 休息 clock 時鐘

58.
現在幾點？
(A) 08:37
(B) 11:55
(C) 13:36
(D) 14:40

解說 這是詢問「時間點」的「簡短選項類考題」。女士說「現在已經快一點四十分了」，四個選項中，最接近一點四十分（13:40）是(C) 13:36。　　答案 (C)

詞彙 what time 什麼時間

問題59～61，請參考以下對話。 美M 美W

M : Hi, ⁵⁹I'm here to talk to someone about hosting a company dinner in your restaurant. My boss said that the food and the service are excellent here.

W : I'm just a restaurant server, and ⁶⁰the manager in charge of hosting events isn't here at the moment. You'll need to contact her. Here is her business card.

M : Thanks. I'll get in touch with her as soon as I can. By the way, when is she available?

W : ⁶¹She'll be in tomorrow. How about calling her in the morning? I'm sure you can set up a meeting with her within a few days.

男：你好，我來這兒是要和你們的人洽談在你們餐廳主辦一場公司的晚宴。我的老闆說這裡的食品和服務都很優質。
女：我只是個餐廳的服務生，負責舉辦活動的經理此刻不在。你將會需要與她聯繫。這是她的名片。
男：謝謝。我會儘快與她聯繫。順便問一下，她什麼時間可以呢？
女：她明天會在。早上打電話給她怎麼樣呢？我相信在幾天之內你可以安排與她會面。

詞彙 host 舉辦 in charge of 負責…的 at the moment 此刻；現在 contact 聯絡 business card 名片 get in touch with 與…連繫 as soon as 儘快 by the way 順便提一下 available 有空的 set up a meeting 約定見面

59.
這個男人為什麼去餐廳的？
(A) 為了要應徵一個職位
(B) 為了要和同事一起晚餐
(C) 為了配送一件貨物
(D) 為了安排一場活動

解說 這是詢問理由的考題。將錄音前面部分出現的「來洽談主辦一場公司的晚宴」做簡化來表達的(D)為答案。　　答案 (D)

詞彙 apply for 應徵… position 位置 colleague 同事 deliver 配送 order 訂單；貨物

60.
有什麼樣的問題？
(A) 所有的房間都被預訂了。
(B) 經理不在。
(C) 餐廳因假日而不營業。
(D) 一位客人抱怨服務。

解說 詢問問題狀況為何的考題，答案大部分會包含否定詞或論及問題的說法。將錄音裡出現的「經理此刻不在」以相近意思的not available表達的(B)為答案。
　　答案 (B)

詞彙 problem 問題 fully 完全地 book 預約 closed 不營業的 due to 由於… holiday 假日 complain 抱怨

61.

這個女人建議了什麼？

(A) 去不同的餐廳

(B) 隔天打電話來

(C) 參考網站資訊

(D) 和朋友一起回來

解說 這是詢問建議事項為何的考題。錄音裡，接在 how about 後面的「早上打電話」改成「隔天打電話」來表達的(B)為答案。 答案 (B)

詞彙 recommend 建議 consult 參考 come back 回來

問題62～64請參考以下對話。 美M 美W

Dishes	Price / per person
Entrée: [64]fish / chicken	$ 100
[64]Rice	$ 50
Soup: [64]corn / tomato	$ 50
Coffee and cake	$ 50
Combo	$ 200

M : Hi, Ma'am. Are you [62]ready to order?

W : What are the [63]lunch specials today?

M : I recommend you try our fish or chicken set lunch. It will be served with a bowl of rice, soup, a cup of coffee and dessert.

W : May I order individual items instead of a combo? I don't usually drink coffee, and I don't need desserts, either.

M : Sure, but individual items may cost a little more.

W : That's all right. What kind of soup do you have for today?

M : We offer corn soup or tomato soup.

W : All right, I think I'll have an order of [63,64]fish with just rice and corn soup, please.

M : Sure. No problem.

餐點	每人價格
主菜：魚 / 雞	$ 100
米飯	$ 50
湯：玉米 / 番茄	$ 50
咖啡及蛋糕	$ 50
套餐價	$ 200

男：嗨！小姐好！您準備好要點餐了嗎？

女：今天中午特餐是什麼？

男：我推薦您試試我們的鮮魚定食或雞肉定食。會附一碗飯、湯、一杯咖啡和甜點。

女：我可不可以單點，不要套餐？我不常喝咖啡，而且我也不需要點心。

男：當然可以。但是單點可能比較貴喔！

女：沒關係。你們今天有什麼湯？

男：我們提供玉米湯或番茄湯。

女：好！我想要點：魚、飯、還有玉米湯。

男：沒問題！

詞彙 ready to 準備好做某事 order 點餐 lunch 午餐 special 特餐 recommend 推薦 try 嘗試 set lunch 定食 a bowl of 一碗 a cup of 一杯 dessert 點心 individual 單獨的，個別的 item 項目 instead of 而不是 combo 套餐 don't usually 通常不 either 也（不） what kind of 哪一種

62.

這段對話在哪裡發生？

(A) 在戲院

(B) 在超市

(C) 在餐廳

(D) 在洗衣店

解說 這是詢問「對話場景」的「簡短選項類考題」，核心語是Where... take place? 對話內容不離「點餐」、「食物」等餐廳用語，所以答案是(C)餐廳。 答案 (C)

詞彙 conversation 對話 take place 發生 theater 劇院 supermarket 超市 restaurant 餐廳 laundry 洗衣店

63.

女士想要點什麼主菜？

(A) 雞肉

(B) 豬肉

(C) 牛肉

(D) 魚肉

解說 這是詢問「點餐選項」的「簡短選項類考題」。核心語是want to order?在對話中女士提到要點「魚、飯、還有玉米湯」，所以其中的主菜是(D)魚肉。 答案 (D)

詞彙 entrée 主菜 chicken 雞肉 pork 豬肉 beef 牛肉 fish 魚

64.

請看此圖。女士需要付多少錢買午餐？

(A) $ 100

(B) $ 150

(C) $ 200

(D) $ 250

解說 這是詢問「總共需要付費多少」的「簡短選項類考題」。接續上一題，女士要點「魚、飯、還有玉米湯」，從圖表中對應，此3項價格共是$100 + $50 + $50 = $200。所以選(C)。 答案 (C)

詞彙 how much (money) 多少錢 pay for 支付

問題65～67請參考以下對話。 英W 美M

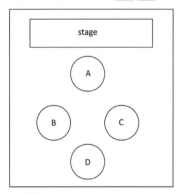

W : ⁶⁵Have you got everything ready for the welcoming dinner banquet for Dr. Hamilton?

M : Almost! The food and beverages have been ordered, and the hotel staff will help to set the table.

W : ⁶⁷How about the entertainment? Did you hire any performing artists?

M : Yes, ⁶⁷I hired a live band and a singer. Don't worry! The event is going to be great.

W : Is this the seating chart for the evening? ⁶⁶Make sure that Dr. Hamilton will sit as close to the stage as possible, so he can have a clear view of the performance.

M : I'll do that.

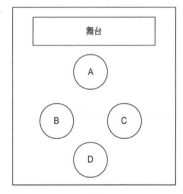

女：你都安排好漢彌爾頓博士的歡迎晚宴的各項事宜了嗎？
男：差不多了。吃的喝的都訂好了，飯店的人員會幫忙擺設桌子。
女：餘興節目呢？你有沒有請藝人表演？
男：有。我請了一個樂隊和歌手。別擔心，節目會很棒的。
女：這是那天的座位表嗎？確認漢彌爾頓博士坐在盡可能靠近舞台的地方，這樣他才能清楚看到節目。
男：知道了。

詞彙 ready 準備好的 welcoming 歡迎的 dinner banquet 晚宴 almost 幾乎 food and beverage 食物和飲料 hotel staff 飯店員工 entertainment 娛樂 performing artist 會表演的藝人 hire 雇用 live band 現場樂隊 singer 歌手 don't worry 別擔心 event 場面、事件 make sure 確認 as... as possible 盡可能的 clear view 清晰的視野 performance 表演 stage 舞台

65.
對話是關於什麼？
(A) 關於一場會議
(B) 關於歡迎晚宴
(C) 關於到洛杉磯一遊
(D) 關於才藝表演

解說 這是詢問「對話內容」的「簡短選項類考題」。核心語是「關於什麼」。女士一開始便問男士「你都安排好漢彌爾頓博士的歡迎晚宴的各項事宜了嗎？」，所以應選(B)。 答案 (B)

詞彙 conference meeting 研討會議 welcoming banquet 歡迎晚宴 trip 旅遊 talent show 才藝秀

66.
請看此圖。漢彌爾頓博士會坐在哪裡？
(A) A桌
(B) B桌
(C) C桌
(D) D桌

解說 這題的關鍵在女士說的「確認漢彌爾頓博士會坐在盡可能靠近舞台的地方，這樣他才能清楚看到節目」，在對照圖表，最接近舞台的是A桌。 答案 (A)

詞彙 where 哪裡 sit 坐

67.
晚宴將安排哪一種餘興節目？
(A) 芭蕾舞表演
(B) 魔術表演
(C) 歌唱與樂隊
(D) 街舞表演

解說 這題是詢問「內容」的「簡短選項類考題」。男士提到他安排的餘興節目是「請了一個樂隊和歌手」。所以(C)為正解。 答案 (C)

詞彙 entertainment 娛樂 arrange 安排 ballet 芭蕾舞 magic 魔術 singing 歌唱 band 樂隊 street dance 街舞

問題68～70請參考以下對話。 美W 美M

```
Sears Department Store
Coupon
$50

⁶⁸Valid through March 31
Purchase number 331
```

W：⁶⁸,⁷⁰Sir, it'll come up to $265 dollars in total, cash or charge, please?

M：Oh, ³I'll pay by cash, and I have a $ 50-dollar coupon. Please deduct it from total. Here you go!

W：Let me see. I'm sorry, Sir, ⁶⁹,⁷⁰This is a coupon we printed for the promotion last month. It is no longer valid.

M：That's too bad! I missed the expiry date? What a waste of the $50 dollars!!

W：Well, Sir, ⁷⁰what I can do is to give you a 10-percent-off voucher with no expiry date which you can use on your future purchase.

M：Great! May I use it right away today?

W：No, Sir. ⁷⁰It doesn't apply to your current purchase.

```
席爾斯百貨公司
優惠券
$50

有效至3月31日
採購號碼 331
```

女：先生，總共265元。您要付現還是刷卡？
男：喔！我付現，另外，我有一張五十元的優惠券，請從總金額去扣。給你！
女：讓我看看。先生抱歉。這是我們上個月印來做活動的優惠券。已經失效了。
男：真糟糕！我錯過最後限期了？真是浪費了50元！
女：先生！我可以給您一張9折的優惠券，無效期限定。您可以之後消費時使用。
男：太棒了！我可以今天立刻用嗎？
女：不行耶！先生，這不適用於您目前的採購。

詞彙 **come up with** 達到、總計 **in total** 全部地 **cash or charge** 付現還是刷卡 **coupon** 優惠券 **deduct** 扣除 **promotion** 促銷 **no longer** 不再 **valid** 有效 **miss** 錯過 **expiry date** 有效日期 **what a waste** 真浪費 **10 percent off** 打九折 **voucher** 禮券 **purchase** 購買 **right away** 立即、馬上 **apply to** 適用於 **current** 目前的

68.
女士的工作可能是什麼？
(A) 店經理
(B) 業務代表
(C) 收銀員
(D) 董事長

解說 這是詢問「工作職業」的「簡短選項類考題」。文中雖然沒有明確出現工作職稱，但由女士的第一句對白「總共是$265元，您要付現還是刷卡？」可推斷，她的工作應是(C)收銀員。　　　　答案 (C)

詞彙 **store manager** 店經理 **sales rep** 業務代表 **cashier** 收銀員 **chairman** 董事長

69.
請看此圖。講者說話的月份是何時？
(A) 二月
(B) 三月
(C) 四月
(D) 五月

解說 這是詢問「說話時間」的「簡短選項類考題」。女士說「這是我們上個月來做活動的優惠券。已經失效了」而在圖表中，顯示優待券有效期限是3/31，若上個月是3月，則講話的月份應該是4月。答案(C)為正確答案。　　　　答案 (C)

詞彙 **month** 月份 **February** 二月 **March** 三月 **April** 四月 **May** 五月

70.
此對話沒有引申何事？
(A) 男士今天需要付265元。
(B) 他的50元優惠券過期了。
(C) 男士將付現，不用信用卡。
(D) 他今天的購物能打九折。

解說 這是詢問「何者為非」的「句子選項類考題」。(A)、(B)、(C) 3個選項都在文中有出現，唯有(D)是不能適用於今日男士的採購。故要選(D)。　　　　答案 (D)

詞彙 **imply** 暗示，引申 **conversation** 對話 **need to** 需要 **expired** 期滿的，到期的

Part 4

問題71～73請參考以下電話留言。 美M

Hello, Mr. J. P. Sward, ⁷¹this is Jeffrey Ford, customer service representative calling from the Makoto Bank. We got your inquiry about getting a loan for starting a small business. Since you are one of our credit card holders and I can see on the record that your credit has been pretty good, getting a loan should not be a problem. [72]However, we still need you to provide a financial statement for evaluation as a formal procedure. Starting a business can be difficult in the beginning since you need to pay overheads such as rent, employee wages, and so on. And we have different services for customers like yourself who wants to start a new business. For more information, [73]please contact our small loan office and set up an appointment with the officer. We will be very happy to assist you. Thank you.

哈囉！J. P.斯沃德先生，我是誠信銀行的客服代表傑佛瑞‧福特。我們收到您關於微型創業小額借貸的詢問。因為您是我們的卡友，而且從記錄上看來，您的信用一直都很好，所以貸款應該不成問題。不過我們仍需要您提供財力證明，作為正式的程序。創業在一開始可能較辛苦，因為您需要支付像房租、員工薪資等等的經常性開銷。我們有提供不同的服務給像您這樣想創業的客戶。想進一步了解，請聯絡我們的小額貸款營業處，和我們的主管約見面。我們將很樂意協助您。謝謝！

詞彙 customer service 客服 representative 代表 inquire 詢問 loan 借款 credit card 信用卡 holder 持有者 record 紀錄 provide 提供 financial statement 財力證明 evaluation 評估 formal 正式的 procedure 程序 difficult 困難的 overhead 經常性支出 rent 房租 employee 員工 wage 工資 contact 聯絡 set up 安排 appointment 約會 officer 長官 assist 協助

71.
講者在哪裡工作？
(A) 自助餐廳
(B) 診所
(C) 銀行
(D) 雜貨店

解說 這是詢問「工作地點」的「簡短選項類考題」。說話者在一開始便自我介紹「我是誠信銀行的客服代表傑佛瑞‧福特」所以答案是(C)。 答案 (C)

詞彙 cafeteria 自助餐廳 clinic 診所 bank 銀行 grocery store 雜貨店

72.
申請小額借貸需要什麼？
(A) 畢業證書
(B) 財力證明
(C) 病歷
(D) 結婚證書

解說 這是詢問「所需文件為何」的「簡短選項類考題」。說話者提到「我們仍需要您提供財力證明，作為

正式的程序」所以答案(B)是正確答案。 答案 (B)

詞彙 apply 申請 diploma 畢業證書 financial statement 財力證明 medical record 病歷 marriage certificate 結婚證書

73.
講者建議聽者做什麼？
(A) 隨時來見他
(B) 去電小額貸款營業處約見面
(C) 申辦新的信用卡
(D) 上網查看更多資料

解說 透過recommend the speaker to do，可以知道是「詢問建議事項的考題」。核心語please contact後面出現的「請聯絡我們的小額貸款營業處，和我們的主管約見面」是關鍵，所以本題要選(B)。 答案 (B)

詞彙 anytime 任何時間 check online 上網查

問題74～76，請參考以下訊息。 英 M

Good morning! [74]I called this meeting to announce that next week new security software will be set up on all employees' computers. This software will help boost computer speed, increase stability, and protect confidential information from unauthorized users much more efficiently. Now, to prepare you for this change, [75]our head technician will demonstrate how to use this software in the training session next Friday. [76]Please register for this session on our company website by the end of this week. Do you have any questions?

早安！我召集這次會議是要宣布，下週將在所有員工的電腦安裝新的安全軟體。這個軟體將有助於提高電腦的速度、增加穩定性，並且更有效地保護機密信息免於被未經授權用戶取得。現在為了讓你們對這樣的改變做好準備，在下星期五的訓練研習會，我們的首席技師將會示範如何使用這個軟體。請在這週結束前，上我們公司的網站報名這場研習會。有沒有任何疑問呢？

詞彙 call a meeting 召集會議 announce 公告 security 安全 set up 安裝 boost 提高 increase 增加 stability 穩定性 protect 保護 confidential 機密的 unauthorized 未經授權的 efficiently 有效地 prepare 準備 head technician 首席技師 demonstrate 示範 training session 訓練研習 register for 報名…

74.
什麼事情被公告了？
(A) 一項新的聘用程序
(B) 一項員工滿意度調查
(C) 一場會議日期
(D) 一套軟體的安裝

解說 透過這裡的三個考題，可以猜測該錄音為「公司內公告」或「會議上公告」類型。該考題是詢問主題的，在錄音的前段部分會出現答案線索。將「安裝新的安全軟體」以簡略表達的(D)為答案。　　答案 (D)

詞彙 hiring procedure 聘用程序　survey 調查　satisfaction 滿意　installation 安裝

75.

下星期五將會發生什麼？
(A) 一件預算將被審閱。
(B) 調查結果將被公布。
(C) 電腦將被更換。
(D) 員工將被訓練。

解說 錄音裡提到的時間點附近會有答案線索。「首席技師將會示範」是「員工將被訓練」的意思。　答案 (D)

詞彙 budget 預算　review 審閱　survey 調查　replace 替換　train 訓練

76.

聽者們被要求在週末之前做什麼？
(A) 送出開銷報告
(B) 打電話給人事部門
(C) 與他們的經理見面
(D) 報名訓練研習會

解說 這是詢問「要求事項」為何的考題，且有兩個答案線索。在Please和未來時間點之間出現的「報名研習會」為答案。　　答案 (D)

詞彙 submit 送出　expense 花費　personnel department 人事部門

問題77～79，請參考以下交通廣播。 美 M

Good morning. It's 9 o'clock, and this is the latest Radio XKY traffic update. I'm Michael Walker. Well, it's not common that a traffic report can bring you good news, but I'm pleased to announce that all highways are comparatively clear. ⁷⁷The expanded train service that was recently launched into operation has resulted in reduced traffic volume, so most drivers on the expressway will not be tied up in traffic. ⁷⁸There is about a 20-minute delay on Highway 100 toward the Oak Street bridge, though. A tractor-trailer is turned over on the left lane there. ⁷⁹I'll be back in 10 minutes with another traffic update, so keep listening.

早安。現在是九點鐘，這是XKY電台最新的交通更新。我是邁克·沃克。很少有路況報導給您帶來好消息，但我很高興公布所有的高速公路都相對地通暢。最近開始運作的擴增的火車班次使得交通量減少，所以在快速道

路上大部分的駕駛人不會被困在車陣中。不過，在一百號高速公路上往橡樹街橋方向有大約二十分鐘的延誤，一台拖車翻覆在左車道上了。我會在十分鐘之後回來做另一則路況報導，請繼續收聽。

詞彙 common 平常的　bring 帶來　be pleased to 很樂於…　highway 高速公路　comparatively 相對地　clear （道路）通暢　expanded 擴大的　launch 開始　operation 運作　result in 導致　reduced 降低的　expressway 快速道路　delay 延遲　though 雖然　turn over 翻覆　keep V-ing 持續

77.

為什麼高速公路交通量降低？
(A) 近期的道路施工完成了。
(B) 天氣狀況不適宜。
(C) 市民在放假中。
(D) 火車服務改善了。

解說 該錄音裡沒有能直接聽到的核心詞彙。「高速公路交通量降低」在錄音裡是以reduced traffic volume與expressway來表達的。目前情況的原因是expanded train service，將此做變化來表達的(D)為答案。　　答案 (D)

詞彙 decrease 降低　complete 完成　weather condition 天氣狀況　unfavorable 不適宜　citizen 市民　on holiday 在假期中

78.

什麼事情造成了一百號高速公路上的延誤？
(A) 一台翻覆的卡車
(B) 一個故障的交通號誌
(C) 滑溜的道路狀況
(D) 道路維修

解說 數字為核心詞彙，且也很容易記憶。將Highway 100附近的「一台拖車翻覆」改成「一台翻覆的卡車」來表達的(A)為答案。　　答案 (A)

詞彙 overturned 翻覆的　broken 故障的　traffic sign 交通號誌　slippery 滑的　condition 狀況　repair 修理

79.

下一次的報導將會在什麼時候？
(A) 在五分鐘後
(B) 在十分鐘後
(C) 在十五分鐘後
(D) 在三十分鐘後

解說 這是詢問「廣播節目」的下一個時程的考題。在錄音最後出現的「十分鐘之後回來」就是提到下一次播放時間的線索。　　答案 (B)

詞彙 occur 發生

問題80～82請參考以下公告內容。 英 W

Hello, Miss Woody. This is Tina Rexford calling

from MPJ Technology Company. I'd like to congratulate you that you have passed the screening of our interviews, and are hired as sales assistant. Please come to the company and report for duty by 8:50 next Monday. Also [81]we need you to bring a copy of each of the following materials including: ID, passbook cover, highest academic proof, TOEIC certificate and a photo. After checking in, Tracy Bowe will have a work transfer with you. [80]Tracy has been the sales assistant of MPJ for the past 5 years and is recently promoted to be our new sales representative. [82]There will be a celebration for her at the cafeteria after work on Monday. It'll be fun. You are welcome to attend. If you have any questions, you can call me back at 776-8547. Thanks.

哈囉！伍迪小姐。我是MPJ科技公司的緹娜，雷克斯福德。我要恭喜您，您已通過我們的面試篩選，並被雇用為業務助理。請在下週一的八點五十分以前，到公司來報到。還有，我們需要您各帶一份以下資料的影本，包括：身分證、存款簿封面、最高學歷證件、多益證書以及一張照片。報到完成之後，崔西．博韋會和您做工作交接。崔西已經在MPJ擔任過去5年的業務助理，而且最近被晉升為我們的新科業務代表。週一下班後在員工餐廳將會為她舉辦一場慶祝會，會很好玩喔，歡迎您參加。如果您有任何問題，可以回電給我，電話是776-8547。謝謝！

詞彙 technology 科技 congratulate 恭喜 screen 篩選 interview 面試 hire 雇用 sales assistant 業務助理 report for duty 報到 bring 攜帶 material 資料 include 包括 passbook 存款簿 academic 學業的 proof 證明 certificate 證書 photo 照片 work transfer 工作交接 recently 最近 promote 晉升 sales rep 業務代表 celebration 慶祝 cafeteria員工餐廳 welcome 歡迎

80.
誰是崔西．博韋？
(A) 新任經理
(B) 新任業務代表
(C) 新任會計師
(D) 新任助理

解說 這是詢問「工作職務」為何的「簡短選項類考題」。核心語是is recently promoted...。講者提到「崔西已經在MPJ擔任過去5年的業務助理，而且最近被晉升為我們的新科業務代表。」所以答案是(B)。
答案 (B)

詞彙 manager 經理 sales rep 業務代表 accountant 會計師 assistant 助理

81.
星期一聽者不需要帶什麼？

(A) 多益證書影本
(B) 身分證影本
(C) 畢業證書影本
(D) 成績單影本

解說 這是詢問「何者為非」的「簡短選項類考題」。文中提到需要攜帶的資料有「我們需要您各帶一份以下資料的影本，包括：身分證、存款簿封面、最高學歷證件、多益證書以及一張照片」只有(D)成績單影本不包含在其中。
答案 (D)

詞彙 copy 影本 TOEIC certificate 多益證書 ID 身分證 diploma 畢業文憑 transcript 成績單

82.
星期一將有什麼活動？
(A) 周年紀念
(B) 慶祝派對
(C) 休閒活動
(D) 年終尾牙

解說 這是詢問「活動為何」的「簡短選項類考題」。因為有同仁升官，所以「周一下班後在員工餐廳將會為她舉辦一場慶祝會」正確答案是(B)。
答案 (B)

詞彙 anniversary 周年紀念 celebration party 慶祝派對 leisure activity 休閒活動 year-end banquet 年終尾牙

問題83～85，請參考以下電話留言。 美 W

Hi, I'm calling from Anderson Realtor. [83]You called our office a few days ago and asked about an apartment. I remember you were interested in a two-bedroom apartment. Unfortunately, only one-bedroom apartments are available now. However, [84]if you're willing to wait, a two-bedroom apartment will be available next month; it is being renovated at the moment. If you'd like to see in advance what the renovated apartment would look like, [85]please call me to visit an occupied apartment with a similar floor plan.

您好，這是由安德森不動產經紀公司打來的。您前幾天致電到我們辦公室詢問有關一棟公寓。我記得你對兩房的公寓感興趣。很可惜，現在只有一房臥室的公寓可以提供。然而，如果你願意等候，一間有兩房的公寓將於下個月可提供，它目前正在裝修。若你想要提前看看這間裝修的公寓看起來如何，請打電話給我，來參觀一間已被租用、但有類似平面佈置的公寓。

詞彙 unfortunately 可惜；不幸地 available 可用的 be willing to 願意做… renovate 裝修 at the moment 此時；現在 in advance 提前 visit 參觀 occupied 被佔用的 floor plan 樓層平面圖

83.
說話者打電話來要說什麼？

(A) 一個近期的詢問
(B) 一個新的規定
(C) 一個取消的預約
(D) 下降的租金

解說 這是詢問「電話錄音」的主題的考題。在錄音前段部分出現「前幾天致電、詢問有關一棟公寓」，所以可以了解說話者要談「一個近期的詢問」。 答案 (A)

詞彙 inquiry 詢問 regulation 規定 canceled 被取消的 reservation 預約 reduced 減少的

84.
說話者說了什麼關於兩房公寓的事？
(A) 它已經被租用。
(B) 它非常昂貴。
(C) 它正在裝修當中。
(D) 它在老人當中很受歡迎。

解說 這是詢問意見為何的考題。透過在錄音裡 two-bedroom apartment 後面出現的「正在裝修」可以知道 (C) 為答案。 答案 (C)

詞彙 expensive 貴的 undergo 經歷 senior citizen 老人

85.
說話者建議聽者做什麼？
(A) 比較兩間公寓的價錢
(B) 確認樓層平面圖
(C) 保留租賃合約
(D) 打電話聯繫看屋

解說 這是詢問建議事項為何的考題。錄音裡與 suggest 相關的說法，是在 please 後面出現的「打電話給我來參觀」，因此將這句做變化來表達的 (D) 為答案。
答案 (D)

詞彙 compare 比較 price 價格 retain 保留 contract 合約 tour 參觀

問題86～88請參考以下演講內容。 美 M

Thank you. Please be seated. Welcome to the Laurie Springfield Center. I'm your host Danny Luke. When people face the barriers in life, some would surrender and give up on themselves, yet others would persist and seek for break through. [86]Our guest tonight, Dr. Jamie Blake, is a perfect example of someone who makes a comeback after a cruel crisis in life. [87]Dr. Blake was a successful physician before an accident that took his eye sight. But he did not give away his hope and became an inspirational public speaker since then. His story has motivated millions of people who are in despair. Dr. Blake will be entering our conference hall with his seeing-eye dog, Jenny. [88]Please pay attention that the dog is working. Do not touch or feed or play with the dog at all times. Let's welcome Dr. Blake onto the stage patiently and quietly. Thank you.

謝謝！請就座！歡迎來到洛里‧斯普林菲爾德中心。我是您的主持人丹尼‧路克。當面對人生的難關時，有些人會屈服並自暴自棄；然而有些人會堅持不懈並尋求突破。我們今晚的來賓傑米‧布萊克博士，就是一位克服人生殘酷的危難，又東山再起的一個活生生的例子。布萊克博士曾經是一位成功的醫師，在一起意外中他失去了視力。但是他不放棄希望，並且之後成為了一位勵志公眾演說家。他的故事激勵了數百萬絕望的人們。布萊克博士即將和他的導盲犬珍妮一同進入會場。請注意，他的狗在工作。任何時候請不要碰觸、或餵食、或和狗玩耍。讓我們安靜地、耐心地歡迎布萊克博士上台。謝謝大家。

詞彙 be seated 就座 face 面對 barrier 難關 surrender 屈服 give up 放棄 persist 堅持不懈 seek 尋求 break through 突破 perfect 完美的 example 例子 comeback 東山再起 cruel 殘酷的 crisis 危難 successful 成功的 physician 醫師 accident 意外 eye sight 視力 give away 放棄 hope 希望 inspirational 勵志的 public speaker 公眾演說家 motivate 激勵 million 百萬 in despair 絕望中的 enter 進入 conference hall 會場 seeing-eye dog 導盲犬 pay attention 注意 stage 舞台 patiently 耐心地 quietly 安靜地

86.
誰是今晚受邀的講者？
(A) 丹尼‧路克
(B) 傑米‧布萊克
(C) 洛里‧斯普林菲爾德
(D) 珍妮‧布萊克

解說 這是詢問「受邀講者是誰」的「簡短選項類考題」。文中提到「我們今晚的來賓傑米‧布萊克博士……一個活生生的例子」可見答案是 (B)。 答案 (B)

詞彙 guest speaker 受邀的講者

87.
受邀的講者以前的職業是什麼？
(A) 律師
(B) 歌手
(C) 醫生
(D) 老師

解說 這是詢問「來賓之前職業為何」的「簡短選項類考題」。司儀提到「布萊克博士曾經是一位成功的醫師，在一起意外中他失去了視力」可知答案為 (C)。
答案 (C)

詞彙 occupation 職業 lawyer 律師 singer 歌手 doctor 醫師 teacher 老師

88.

聽眾能對導盲犬做什麼？

(A) 拍打
(B) 餵食
(C) 觀看
(D) 與之玩耍

解說 這是詢問對導盲犬「能做什麼」的「簡短選項類考題」。文中聽眾被告誡「請注意，他的狗在工作。任何時候請不要碰觸、或餵食、或和狗玩耍。」所以只有 (C) 觀看不在此限。 答案 (C)

詞彙 guide dog 導盲犬 pat 拍打 feed 餵食 watch 觀看 play with 與……玩耍

問題89～91請參考以下公告內容。 美W

[89]Dear fellow workers, your attention, please! On behalf of the board, I would like to thank all for your efforts in the past years. Because of your diligent hard work and selfless devotion, [90]our company has flourished quickly in the market, and not only did we a establish good reputation, but also accumulated lucrative profits. Therefore, the board has decided to provide all of us [91]some new fringe benefits in addition to the wages. First of all, we will organize an annual company outing which will be discussed in detail by the welfare committee. Secondly, we will arrange an employee health check at a designated hospital every year since your well-being is an asset to the company. Finally, there will also be stock bonuses distributed to every employee. It's the company's wish to run the business as if running a big family.

親愛的同事們，大家請注意！僅代表董事會，我想要感謝在過去這些年來大家的努力。因為有您努力不懈的辛勤工作，以及無私的投入，我們公司才能快速地在市場上成長。而且我們不僅建立了良好的名聲，也累積了豐厚的利潤。因此，董事會決定提供我們大家一些除了工資以外的附加福利。首先，我們會安排年度員工旅遊，福利委員會將討論細節。其次，我們會在一家指定的醫院安排每年的員工健康檢查，因為大家的健康就是公司的資產。最後，還會有股票分紅分配給每一位員工。公司希望將企業經營成一個大家庭。

詞彙 fellow 同事 attention 注意 on behalf of 代表 board 董事會 efforts 努力 diligent 堅持不懈的 selfless 無私的 devotion 投入 flourish 興旺 establish 建立 reputation 名聲 accumulate 累積 lucrative 有利的 profit 利潤，益處 decide to 決心做 provide 提供 fringe benefit 附加福利 in addition to 除……之外 annual 年度 outing 短途旅遊 discuss 討論 in detail 詳細地 welfare committee 福利委員會 arrange 安排 employee 員工 health check 健康檢查 designated 指定的 well-being 福

祉 asset 資產 stock bonus 股票分紅 distribute 分配 run 跑，運轉，經營

89.

聽眾最有可能是誰？

(A) 學生
(B) 遊客
(C) 員工
(D) 客戶

解說 這是詢問「聽者的身分」的「簡短選項類考題」。由於在一開始，說話者便提到「親愛的同事們，大家請注意！」可見聽者的身分是(C)員工。 答案 (C)

詞彙 student 學生 tourist 遊客 employee 員工 client 客戶

90.

講者暗示了什麼？

(A) 部分員工將被資遣。
(B) 今年是艱困的一年。
(C) 人們很自私。
(D) 這家公司有潛力。

解說 這是詢問「引申暗示訊息」的「句子選項類考題」。講者先感謝聽者的努力，然後告訴他「我們公司…在市場上成長。而且……建立了良好的名聲，也累積了豐厚的利潤。」可推測這家公司很有潛力。 答案 (D)

詞彙 imply 暗示 lay off 資遣 rough 艱難的 selfish 自私的 potential 有潛力的

91.

談話中沒有提及哪一項福利？

(A) 商務旅行
(B) 員工旅遊
(C) 健康檢查
(D) 股票分紅

解說 這題是詢問「何者為非」的「簡短選項類考題」。這也來到本篇的重頭戲，講者提到有「我們會安排年度員工旅遊...。其次，我們會在一家指定的醫院安排員工年度健康檢查……。最後，還會有股票分紅分配給每一位員工。」所以是(A)商務旅行沒被提到。另外，同學不要把business trip（出差）和company trip員工旅遊弄混淆喔！ 答案 (A)

詞彙 measure 措施 business trip 商務旅行 company trip 員工旅遊 health checkup 健康檢查 stock bonus 股票分紅

問題92～94，請參考以下談話內容。 美W

Good afternoon, everyone. Thanks for coming to

this meeting on a short notice. The first agenda of this meeting: [92]I'd like to discuss a minor change in our technical support protocol. Previously, [93]if a problem cannot be resolved for a customer, we requested that the customer call us again later. From now on, [94]you'll need to give customers a reference number if they must call back. Also, you'll need to type in the computer what information you know about the situation so that when the customer calls back, the problem can be solved more easily.

各位午安，感謝您前來在短時間內通知的本次會議。這次會議的第一個議題，我想討論在我們的技術支援服務規定上的一個小小的改變。以前，如果無法為客戶解決問題，我們要求客戶稍後再次打電話給我們。從現在開始，如果他們必須回撥，你將必須給客戶一個參考編號。而且，你也需要把有關這個狀況你所知的訊息輸入電腦，所以當顧客回電話來時，這個問題可以更容易的被解決。

詞彙 agenda 議題 discuss 討論 minor 微小的 protocol 規定；程序 resolve 解決 customer 顧客 request 要求 from now on 從現在起 reference number 參考編號 situation 狀況 solve 解決 easily 容易地

92.
這段談話的目地是什麼？
(A) 為了討論顧客的抱怨
(B) 為了公布政策改變
(C) 為了介紹新員工
(D) 為了腦力激盪而出新的廣告策略

解說 透過考題與選項可以猜測該錄音為「會議上的公告」。這是詢問主題的考題，所以答案線索在錄音的前段部分。將「想討論在技術支援服務規定上的一個小小的改變」以概括的說法來表達的(B)為答案。 答案 (B)

詞彙 purpose 目的 complaint 抱怨 policy 政策 brainstorm 腦力激盪 advertising 廣告 strategy 策略

93.
說話者很有可能是對什麼人談話？
(A) 會計人員
(B) 倉庫監督人員
(C) 客服專員
(D) 旅行社職員

解說 「會議上的公告」，這類型的說話者大部分為公司職員。「無法為客戶解決問題、要求客戶再次打電話」的人可以被視為「客服專員」。 答案 (C)

詞彙 accountant 會計人員 warehouse 倉庫 supervisor 倉庫 travel agent 旅行社職員

94.
說話者要求聽者做什麼？
(A) 經常打電話
(B) 提供參考編號
(C) 提出想法
(D) 紀錄來電

解說 這是詢問要求事項為何的考題。透過該錄音裡的 you'll need to 可以知道答案線索。將「給客戶一個參考編號」做變化來表達的(B)為答案。 答案 (B)

詞彙 ask 要求 frequently 經常地 provide 提供 come up with 提出

問題95～97請參考以下對話。 英 W

Agenda of the semiannual meeting
Market trend
New recruit training
Oversea expansion
[97]Budgetary reduction

Good. I think everyone is here now except Lucy. [95]Lucy will be joining us in about 10 minute's time. She is on an international phone call with our CEO, Mr. Block, and will let us know what Mr. Block has to tell us. She wants us to just go ahead without her. So, [96]welcome to our semiannual meeting. First of all, please take a look at the agenda. I'd like to make a small change on the order of what we will discuss today. [97]Let's start with the final item first about how to cut down on our budgets since it is crucial for the cost. By the end of the discussion, everyone should be clear about the spending limits of your department each month. All right, let's start with the first slide I projected on the screen.

半年會會議議程表
市場趨勢
新進人員訓練
海外拓展
預算刪減

好！我想除了露西之外，大家現在都到了。露西大概10分鐘以後會進來開會。她在和總裁布拉克先生通國際電話，會讓我們知道布拉克先生要交代我們什麼事情。她要我們不用等她，先開始。那麼！歡迎參加我們的半年會的會議。首先，請看看我們的議程表。我想在我們今天要討論事項的順序，做一個小變動。讓我們先從最後一項關於如何削減預算開始，因為這對我們的成本很重要。討論結束以後，大家應該會清楚每一個月你們部門的花費限制。好的，讓我們從我投影在屏幕上的頭一張投影片開始吧！

詞彙 except 除……之外　join 加入　international phone call 國際電話　CEO 首席執行長　go ahead 開始進行　semiannual 一年兩次的　agenda 議程表　order 順序　discuss 討論　item 項目　cut down 削減　budget 預算　crucial 重要　cost 成本　spending limit 花費限制　department 部門　slide 投影片　project 投射　screen 屏幕, 螢幕

95.

為何露西不能準時來開會？

(A) 她在製作投影片

(B) 她在影印資料

(C) 她在講電話

(D) 她沒來上班

解說 這是詢問「原因」為何的「句子選項類考題」。核心語是「不能準時來開會」。講者提到「Lucy大概10分鐘以後會進來開會。她在和總裁Mr. Block通國際電話」，所以正確答案為 (C)。　　　答案 (C)

詞彙 copy material 影印資料　talk on the phone 講電話　absent from work 上班缺席

96.

員工多久開一次這種會議？

(A) 每月一次

(B) 每年一次

(C) 每月兩次

(D) 每年兩次

解說 這是詢問「頻率」的「簡短選項類考題」。核心語是how often，講者提到「歡迎參加我們的半年會的會議」（semiannual），半年開一次會，所以每年會有兩次，選(D)。　　　答案 (D)

詞彙 how often 多常（問頻率）　staff 員工　type 類型　once 一次　twice 兩次

97.

請看此圖，哪一個主題會先討論？

(A) 市場趨勢

(B) 新進人員訓練

(C) 海外拓展

(D) 預算刪減

解說 這是詢問「會議議程變動」相關的「簡短選項類考題」。文中提到「讓我們先從最後一項關於如何削減預算開始，因為這對我們的成本很重要。」所以會從選項(D)預算刪減開始討論。　　　答案 (D)

詞彙 topic 主題　market 市場　trend 趨勢　recruit 新成員　oversea 海外　expansion 拓展　budgetary 預算　reduction 刪減

問題98～100請參考以下對話。　美 Ｗ

Dr. Anderson's appointment chart					
	Mon	Tue	Wed	Thu	Fri
5:30		A		C	
99 6:30			B		
7:30					
8:30					D

Hi! Mr. Gibson, good afternoon. **98**This is Big Smile Dental Clinic calling. I'm returning your call regarding your request on changing the date of your appointment. We are sorry that Dr. Anderson is fully booked for the week, but **98,99**we do have a cancelation at 6:30 Wednesday evening with Dr. Anderson. And I'm afraid this is the only available time we have before your original appointment at 8:30 on Friday. If you don't mind seeing a different doctor at this time, **100**we'd appreciate it if you can call back at least 24 hours ahead of time to secure your appointment. Thank you.

安德森醫生門診約診表					
	一	二	三	四	五
5:30		A		C	
6:30			B		
7:30					
8:30					D

嗨！吉布森先生，午安。這裡是微笑牙科診所。我回電給您是關於您想更改門診日期的事情。很抱歉，安德森醫生這個星期已經全部滿診，但是我們在星期三傍晚六點半，安德森醫生的診有人取消。而且恐怕這是您原來在星期五八點半的診之前，唯一有可能的開放時間。如果您不介意這個時間，看別的醫師的診的話，麻煩請您至少在事前24小時來電，以確保您的門診時間。謝謝！

詞彙 smile 微笑　dental 齒科的　clinic 診所　return 回應, 回覆　regarding 關於　request 要求　change 改變　date 日期　appointment 約會　fully booked 訂滿　cancelation 取消　afraid 恐怕　available 有空的　original 原來的　mind 介意　appreciate 感謝　at least 最少　ahead of time 提前時間　secure 確保

98.

誰是安德森醫生？

(A) 律師

(B) 牙醫

(C) 外科醫師

(D) 教授

解說 這是詢問「職業別」的「簡短選項類考題」。講者一開始便提到「這裡是微笑牙科診所」，而安德森醫

生是診所的一名醫師，所以正確答案是(B)。　　答案 (B)

詞彙 lawyer 律師　dentist 牙醫　surgeon 外科醫師
professor 教授

99.

請看此圖，講者提供哪一個門診時間？

(A) A

(B) B

(C) C

(D) D

解說 這是詢問「門診時間」是什麼的「簡短選項類考題」。文中提到「我們在星期三傍晚6:30，安德森醫生的診有人取消」，再對應到圖表，選項(B)是答案。
　　　　　　　　　　　　　　　　　　答案 (B)

詞彙 which 哪一個　appointment time 門診時間

100.

聽者被建議做什麼？

(A) 解釋問題

(B) 提供報告

(C) 回覆來電

(D) 遞出履歷

解說 透過suggested to do可知道是詢問「建議事項的考題」。核心語是「麻煩請您至少在事前24小時來電，以確保您的門診時間」，講者是建議聽者回撥電話。
　　　　　　　　　　　　　　　　　　答案 (C)

詞彙 listener 聽者　suggest 建議　explain 解釋，說明
problem 問題　provide 提供　report 報告　return 回覆
call 電話　submit 提交　resume 履歷表

怪物講師的
Part 3、Part 4
特訓班

Part 3 怪物講師的特訓班

1. Where most likely are they?

(A) At a movie theater　　(B) At a shopping mall

(C) At a museum　　(D) At a school

2. What can the women carry with them?

(A) Coats　　(B) Hats

(C) Cell phone　　(D) Juice

3. What is offered at the exhibition?

(A) On-the-site tour guides　　(B) Audio tour service machines

(C) Free speeches　　(D) Free drinks

美M 英W 美W

M: Welcome to the exhibition. May I have your tickets, please?

W1: There you go. There are the two of us.

M: Sure. Please enter through the front door. There is a locker room at the very end of the first floor. Please check your coats, hats, and bags.

W2: Can we carry our cell phones?

M: Cell phones are allowed but no food or drinks, please.

W1: You'd better finish drinking your juice now.

W2: All right. Give me a minute. Is there a tour guide for the exhibition?

M: Unfortunately not. But we do offer the audio tour service machines that include a multilingual system.

男:歡迎來展覽。請問我可以有您的門票嗎?
女1:在這裡。有我們兩個人。
男:當然。請由前門進入。一樓的最裡面有個置物間。請寄放您的外套、帽子、還有包包。
女2:我們可以帶手機嗎?
男:手機可以,但是食物和飲料不行。
女1:妳最好現在就把果汁喝完。
女2:好吧!給我一分鐘。展覽有沒有導覽員?
男:很抱歉沒有。不過我們有提供多語系統的語音導覽服務器。

1. 他們最可能是在哪裡? 答案 (C)

(A) 在電影院　　(B) 在購物中心

(C) 在博物館　　(D) 在學校

2. 女士能隨身攜帶什麼? 答案 (C)

(A) 外套　　(B) 帽子

(C) 手機　　(D) 果汁

3. 展覽有提供什麼? 答案 (B)

(A) 現場導覽　　(B) 語音導覽器

(C) 免費演講　　(D) 免費飲料

Part 3　怪物講師的特訓班

1. Who is the man?

(A) A supervisor　　　　　　(B) A coworker

(C) A client　　　　　　　　(D) A superintendent

2. What is likely to be Lucy's age?

(A) 15　　　　　　　　　　　(B) 18

(C) 22　　　　　　　　　　　(D) 25

3. What does Mary suggest doing?

(A) Prepare a meeting　　　　(B) Preparing for lunch

(C) Conduct a speech　　　　(D) Conduct an orientation

美M　美W　英W

M: Good morning, Mary. You are early today.

W1: Yes, have you met Lucy? Lucy, this is John, our product engineer. John, this is Lucy, the new assistant in the sales department.

M: Nice to meet you, Lucy.

W2: Nice to meet you, John.

M: Hi, you look fairly young, Lucy. Are you still a student?

W2: Yes, I just graduated from High School last month. And will be admitted to night school of local university from September.

W1: All right, Lucy, why don't we start the orientation now? I'll show you around and let's meet more colleagues from the company.

W2: Sure. Talk to you later, John.

男：瑪莉，早安。你今天來早了！
女1：是啊。你有見過露西了嗎？露西，這是約翰，我們的產品工程師。約翰，這是露西，新進業務助理。
男：很高興認識妳，露西。
女2：很高興認識你，約翰。
男：嗨！妳看起來真年輕。露西。你還是學生嗎？
女2：是的。我上個月剛從高中畢業。從九月起，會入學當地大學念夜間部。
女1：好吧！露西。我們開始員工培訓吧。我帶妳四處看看，再讓我們再去見見其它的公司同事！
女2：好的！約翰，我們回頭再聊。

1. 男子是誰？　答案 (B)

(A) 主管人員　　　　　　　　(B) 同事

(C) 客戶　　　　　　　　　　(D) 管理員

2. 露西可能幾歲？　答案 (B)

(A) 15　　　　　　　　　　　(B) 18

(C) 22　　　　　　　　　　　(D) 25

3. 瑪莉建議要做什麼？　答案 (D)

(A) 準備會議　　　　　　　　(B) 準備午餐

(C) 進行演說　　　　　　　　(D) 進行培訓

Part 3 怪物講師的特訓班

1. What is this conversation about?

(A) Inquiring information (B) Expressing gratitude
(C) Filing complaint (D) Lost and found

2. What is the course that the women are hoping to have?

(A) Chinese (B) Japanese
(C) English (D) Korean

3. What will the women do after the conversation?

(A) Register an online course (B) Take an English course.
(C) Look for a course they need elsewhere. (D) Become a teacher

---

英 W 美 M 美 W

W1: Excuse me, we'd like to know if you offer any training course for tour guides.

M: Let me see. Yes, we have a course for people who are interested in becoming professional tour guides or tour managers.

W1: Is it for Japanese division?

M: I'm sorry. We used to offer courses for the Japanese division, but now we only have English division left.

W2: Why is that? I thought the Japanese market ought to be quite big in our country.

M: Well, don't know why. But if not enough people register for the course, we will stop recruiting new students. Then gradually the class will be discontinued.

W2: Lorena, if we can't find a course we need here, maybe we have to check with other schools.

W1: That's the only thing to do now.

女1：不好意思！我們想知道你們是否有開任何導遊的訓練課程。
男：我看看。有的！我們有一門課專為有興趣從事專業導遊或領隊的人所開設。
女1：是給日文組別的嗎？
男：抱歉！我們曾經提供課程給日文組，但是我們現在只剩下英文組了。
女2：為什麼呢？我以為日文市場在我們國家應該蠻大的。
男：嗯！不知道為什麼。但是若沒有足夠的人註冊課程，我們會停止招新生。那漸漸地，課程就會終止了。
女2：洛蕾娜，若我們無法在此找到我們需要的課程，或許我們必須查查其他學校。
女1：現在只好這樣了！

1. 此對話是關於什麼？ 答案 (A)

(A) 詢問資訊 (B) 表達感謝
(C) 表達抱怨 (D) 失物招領

2. 女士希望修什麼課？ 答案 (B)

(A) 中文 (B) 日文
(C) 英文 (D) 韓文

3. 女士在對話過後會做什麼？ 答案 (C)

(A) 註冊線上課程 (B) 修英文課
(C) 到別處尋找他們需要的課 (D) 當老師

Part 3 怪物講師的特訓班　　　　　請聽音檔，練習下面題目

1. Why can't the man go to the movie with the woman?

(A) He doesn't want to see movies. (B) He has other plans.

(C) He has seen the movie already. (D) He will have a day off on Friday.

2. When does the movie begin?

(A) 6:45 (B) 7:15

(C) 7:30 (D) 7:45

3. What will Clare do for the woman in return?

(A) Take her out for movie next week. (B) Treat her a burger for dinner.

(C) Give her a free ride home. (D) Buy her a beer.

美W 美M 英W

W1: Thank God it's Friday. I've been looking forward to today for 5 days.

M: Why? Do you have any plans?

W1: Yes, I'm going to see the movie 'The Day After'. Do you want to go with me? I have 2 free tickets.

M: I'd love to, but sorry, I can't. I already have another pre-engagement. Maybe you can ask Clare.

W1: Are you free tonight, Clare? Do you want to go with me to the movie? It's an Oscar winning film.

W2: It seems fun. A free movie, why not?

W1: Great! The movie is playing at the Sakura Theater starting 7:15. We can leave right after work.

W2: Sure. Since you are treating me a free movie, why don't I buy you a burger for dinner in return? We'll have a great time this evening.

女1：太棒了！終於是星期五了！我等這天已經等了5天了！
男：為什麼？妳有什麼計畫嗎？
女1：是的。我要去看電影「明天過後」。妳要不要跟我去？我有兩張免費票。
男：我很想，但是抱歉我不行耶。我已經有其他的約了。或許你可以問問克萊兒。
女1：克萊兒，你今晚有空嗎？你要不要和我去看電影？是一部奧斯卡得獎電影喔！
女2：好像蠻有趣的。免費電影，好啊。
女1：太棒了！電影7:15在櫻花戲院播放。我們可以下班後直接去。
女2：當然！你請我看免費電影，那何不我買個漢堡回請你當晚餐？我們會有個很棒的夜晚。

1. 為何男子不能和女子去看電影？　答案 (B)

(A) 他不想看電影 (B) 他有其它計畫

(C) 他已經看過這部電影了 (D) 他星期五休假

2. 電影何時開始？　答案 (B)

(A) 6:45 (B) 7:15

(C) 7:30 (D) 7:45

3. 克萊兒會回報女子什麼？　答案 (B)

(A) 下週帶她去看電影 (B) 請她晚餐吃漢堡

(C) 讓她搭便車回家 (D) 買啤酒請她

Part 4 怪物講師的特訓班　　　　　　　　　　請聽音檔，練習下面題目

1. What kind of organization does the speaker record for?

    (A) A school   (B) A police office

    (C) A bank   (D) A gallery

2. Which is NOT one of the good ways to reach a representative?

    (A) Hang up and dial again   (B) Stay on the line

    (C) Dial an extension number   (D) Dial for operator

3. What is the alternative to reach the bank other than making a call?

    (A) To use the web page   (B) To send an email

    (C) To mail a letter   (D) To send a fax

美 W　電話錄音

Thanks for calling THBC bank. Our lines are all busy at the moment. Please do not hang up and stay on the line. The next representative available will answer your call as soon as possible. If it is an emergency, please dial 0, our operator will take your call right away. Or if you know the extension number of the bank clerk you are looking for, please dial the extension number now. We can also be reached at our web page www.thbc.com Our office hours are 9 AM to 5 PM, Mondays to Fridays, and we are closed on Saturdays and Sundays. Thank you again for calling THBC bank. Your satisfaction is very important to us.

感謝您來電THBC銀行。我們的電話線現在都在忙線中。請不要掛斷並留在電話線上，下一位有空的代表將會儘速接聽您的電話。若這是緊急情況，請撥0，我們的總機將立即回覆您。或者若是您知道您要找的銀行員分機號碼，請現在就撥打分機。也可以透過網頁www.thbc.com與我們聯絡。我們的辦公時間是星期一到星期五，上午九點到下午五點，星期六及星期日公休。再次感謝您來電THBC銀行。您的滿意度對我們非常重要。

1. 講者是為哪一種組織錄音？　答案 (C)

    (A) 學校   (B) 警局

    (C) 銀行   (D) 藝廊

2. 哪一個不是聯繫代表的一個好方法？　答案 (A)

    (A) 掛斷再撥一次   (B) 保留在線上

    (C) 撥打分機號碼   (D) 撥打總機

3. 除了打電話之外，什麼是聯繫銀行的可替代的選擇？　答案 (A)

    (A) 使用網頁   (B) 發送電郵

    (C) 郵寄信件   (D) 發送傳真

Part 4　怪物講師的特訓班

1. What kind of training does the school offer?

(A) Foreign languages　　　　　(B) Computer skills
(C) Public speaking　　　　　　(D) Industrial design

2. How long will the training be?

(A) 1 month　　　　　　　　　(B) 2 months
(C) 3 months　　　　　　　　　(D) 4 months

3. What special service is provided to the trainees?

(A) Free consultation　　　　　(B) Course discount
(C) Free courses　　　　　　　(D) Job hunting

美 M　廣告台詞

Do you want to upgrade your occupational skills and earn more money? Hi-Q computer training school will help you attain your goal. We offer courses that are up to date and market oriented. All our teachers are academically trained and well certified. We guarantee that you will learn what you need to know in a time of three months. Job hunting service is also provided for all trainees. Our courses are offered in the evenings and on weekends for someone who still holds a day job just like you. What are you waiting for? Call now and register!

您想要提升您的職業技能並且賺更多的金錢嗎？Hi-Q電腦訓練學校將幫助您實現您的目標。我們提供最新而且市場導向的課程。所有我們的老師都有學術訓練並有合格證書。我們保證您將在三個月的期間內學習您所需要知道的技能。也有提供求職服務給所有的學員。我們的課程是在傍晚和周末，為了像您一樣仍有白天工作的人。您還在等什麼？現在就來電註冊吧！

1. 學校提供哪種訓練？　答案 (B)
(A) 外國語文　　　　　　　　　(B) 電腦技能
(C) 公眾演說　　　　　　　　　(D) 工業設計

2. 訓練將是多長？　答案 (C)
(A) 一個月　　　　　　　　　　(B) 兩個月
(C) 三個月　　　　　　　　　　(D) 四個月

3. 有什麼特別服務被提供給學員？　答案 (D)
(A) 免費諮詢　　　　　　　　　(B) 課程折扣
(C) 免費課程　　　　　　　　　(D) 求職服務

Part 4　怪物講師的特訓班　

1. Where does the speaker work?

(A) A travel agency

(B) A car dealer

(C) A gallery

(D) A movie theater

2. What's the benefit of the showroom on the first floor?

(A) It is more spacious.

(B) It costs less.

(C) It attracts attention.

(D) It has a longer lease term.

3. What information was given to the listener by email?

(A) A picture of artwork.

(B) A quote on rooms.

(C) An apologetic letter.

(D) A sales report.

英 W ｜ 電話留言

Dear Ms. Jefferson, this is Melody Jones calling from Caves Art Gallery. My colleague left me a note saying that you called to inquire about the site rental matters. Our gallery has three different spaces available to the public. Two of them are on the upper floors of the building. They are cheaper and has a longer lease period. There is also one on the first floor which has a limited lease term of seven days. But the benefit is this showroom has French windows and pedestrians walking by can see your exhibition works from outside the building. The rental fee for this room is higher, but the ad performance is rather satisfactory. I will send you an email with a quote on these room types. If you have any questions, please give me a call back again. Thanks.

親愛的傑佛遜女士，我是敦煌藝術美術館的美樂蒂‧瓊恩斯。我的同事留紙條給我說您來電詢問場地租借的事宜。我們的美術館有三個不同的空間供大眾租借。其中兩個是在建物較高的樓層。它們比較便宜而且租期較長。還有一個在一樓，有七天的限制租期。但是好處是這個展覽室有落地窗，路過的行人能從建物外面看見您的展品。這間展覽室的租金較高但是廣告效益頗令人滿意。我將給您一封有房型報價的電郵。如果您有任何問題，請再來電給我，謝謝！

1. 講者在哪裡工作？　答案 (C)

(A) 旅行社

(B) 汽車經銷商

(C) 美術館

(D) 電影院

2. 一樓的展覽間有何優點？　答案 (C)

(A) 較寬敞

(B) 較便宜

(C) 吸引注意

(D) 租期較長

3. 聽者透過電子郵件得到什麼訊息？　答案 (B)

(A) 一件藝品的照片

(B) 一個房型的報價

(C) 一封道歉函

(D) 一個銷售報告

Part 4 怪物講師的特訓班　　　　　　　　　　　　　請聽音檔，練習下面題目

1. Which department does the listener belong to?

   (A) Logistic department　　　　　　　(B) Sales department
   (C) Human resource department　　　(D) Marketing department

2. What can be inferred about conference room B?

   (A) It will be vacant tomorrow afternoon.　(B) It has all necessary equipment.
   (C) It can hold up to 15 people.　　　　　(D) It is doubled booked.

3. How is the listener asked to reply to the speaker?

   (A) By email　　　　　　　　　　　(B) By phone
   (C) By fax　　　　　　　　　　　　(D) In person

美 W　電話留言

Hi, Jessie, this is Mary calling from the logistics department. The logistics officers are holding an on-the-job training at 3 o'clock tomorrow afternoon and we need a conference room accommodating 15 people. The only room big enough is conference room A, yet as I know that the sales department will have the routine monthly meeting in room A at the same time. Therefore I am calling to see if it is possible for your meeting to be moved to conference room B which is also fully equipped and can hold as many as 10 people. Would you please give me a call back as soon as possible to see if there can be a change in arrangement? Thanks.

嗨！潔西，我是物流部門的瑪莉。物流人員將在明天下午三點召開一場在職訓練，我們需要一個能容納15人的會議室。唯一夠大的房間是A會議室，但就我所知，業務部門將於同時段在A會議室召開例行性的月會。所以我來電想看看是否你們的會議可以挪到B會議室，它一樣也是配備齊全，而且能容納多達10人。麻煩請盡快回電給我看看是否能做安排上的改變。謝謝！

1. 聽者屬於哪一個部門？　答案 (B)
   (A) 物流部門　　　　　　　(B) 業務部門
   (C) 人事部門　　　　　　　(D) 行銷部門

2. 關於會議室B，這裡提到了什麼？　答案 (B)
   (A) 明天下午將空出　　　　(B) 包括所有需要的設備
   (C) 能容納高達15人　　　　(D) 被重複預約

3. 講者要求聽者如何回覆她？　答案 (B)
   (A) 用電郵　　　　　　　　(B) 用電話
   (C) 用傳真　　　　　　　　(D) 親自造訪

Part 4 怪物講師的特訓班　　　　　　　　　請聽音檔，練習下面題目

1. Who most likely is the speaker?

(A) Auditor
(B) Assistant
(C) Executive officer
(D) Accountant

2. Who is Tina Gomez?

(A) Supplier
(B) Customer
(C) Section Chief
(D) New employee

3. What will Jessie Shun do next Monday?

(A) Train a coworker
(B) Report in a meeting
(C) Repair computers
(D) Check some documents

美 M 發布公告

Good morning, everyone. I have an announcement to make. Our IT department will have a newcomer next Monday. Tina Gomez will work as our new system analyst. She has been in the industry for 12 years and is very skillful in dealing with different programming languages. She is also one of the participants in designing the famous Janova case. We are very happy to have her join our team. On Monday, Jessie Shun will give her an orientation showing her around the different departments of the company, the staff cafeteria, and most importantly our computer systems and our processes for handling technical components.

大家早。我有一個通告要發布。下週一我們的資訊部將有一位新成員。緹娜‧戈麥斯將擔任我們的新系統分析師。她在業界已經12年而且對於處理不同的程式語言技術很好。她也是設計著名的Janova案的其中一位參與者。我們很高興有她加入團隊。在星期一，潔西‧珊將幫她做職前訓練，帶她看看公司的不同部門、員工餐廳、最重要的是我們的電腦系統還有處裡技術零件的程序。

1. 講者可能是誰？ 答案 (C)

(A) 審計員
(B) 助理
(C) 主管人員
(D) 會計師

2. 誰是緹娜‧戈麥斯？ 答案 (D)

(A) 供應商
(B) 客戶
(C) 科長
(D) 新員工

3. 下周一潔西‧珊將做什麼？ 答案 (A)

(A) 訓練一位同事
(B) 在會議報告
(C) 修理電腦
(D) 檢查一些文件

Part 4 怪物講師的特訓班　　　　　　　請聽音檔，練習下面題目

1. What are the listeners being reminded of?

   (A) About programs in the afternoon　　(B) About how to fill out a form

   (C) About table manners　　(D) About where their badges are

2. What will be changed?

   (A) The time for lunch　　(B) The place of the session

   (C) The topic of the speech　　(D) The speaker of the talk

3. What will be given to the listeners?

   (A) Yellow vests　　(B) Name tags

   (C) Lunch boxes　　(D) Meeting minute

美 W　司儀公告

Thank you. I hope you've all enjoyed the first half of our program this morning. I'd like to remind you that there will be another training session given in the afternoon. Our guest speaker Dr. Harvey from The Harvard Consultation Center is going to give a lecture right after the lunch break. There will be more trainees coming for the afternoon session, so the event will be held in the bigger auditorium next door. We are going to give out lunch boxes to trainees who signed up for the whole day session. Please get them from the staff members in yellow vests. Let's take a break for one hour, and please show your badge for re-entry. Thank you.

謝謝！我希望大家都喜歡今天上午我們前半段的課程。我想提醒大家下午有另外一場培訓課程。特邀講師——哈佛諮詢中心的哈維博士將在午休過後為我們上課。因為下午有較多的學員來參加這堂課，所以課程將於隔壁的大禮堂舉行。我們將給登記上全天課的學員便當。請向穿著黃背心的工作人員領取。我們休息一個小時，請出示名牌重新進場。謝謝！

1. 聽者被提醒了什麼？　答案 (A)
   (A) 關於下午的課程　　(B) 關於如何填表格
   (C) 關於餐桌禮儀　　(D) 關於胸章在哪裡

2. 什麼將被改變？　答案 (B)
   (A) 午餐的時間　　(B) 課程的地點
   (C) 演講的主題　　(D) 演講的講者

3. 聽眾將被給予什麼東西？　答案 (C)
   (A) 黃背心　　(B) 名牌
   (C) 便當　　(D) 會議記錄

Part 4 怪物講師的特訓班

1. Where will the train pause?

(A) Karate station
(B) Boxing station
(C) Judo station
(D) Tai Chi Station

2. What caused the damage to the track?

(A) A flood
(B) A lightening
(C) A car accident
(D) An earthquake

3. What should commuters do?

(A) Take another train back.
(B) Transfer onto shuttle bus
(C) Get off the train and walk
(D) Take a taxi home

英 W ｜ 廣播公告

Dear passengers, may I have your attention, please. This is your train conductor speaking. We are approaching Karate Station and will be making a pause there due to damages to the track after a car accident. Passengers are required to get off the train there and transfer by shuttle buses to your destination. The train is being repaired now and hopefully will resume working state tomorrow morning. For passengers who need to transfer to the shuttle bus, please get a free transfer ticket from the desk. Sorry about the inconvenience.

親愛的乘客，請注意。這是火車列車長報告。我們即將要接近空手道站，並會在該站暫停，因為一場車禍後鐵軌有毀損。乘客必須在該站下車並轉搭接駁車到您的目的地。火車正在搶修當中並希望明天早上就能恢復通車。需轉搭接駁車的乘客，請在服務台領取免費轉乘車票。造成不便請諒。

1. 火車將於哪裡暫停？ 答案 (A)

(A) 空手道站
(B) 拳擊站
(C) 柔道站
(D) 太極站

2. 是什麼造成了鐵道的毀壞？ 答案 (C)

(A) 洪水
(B) 閃電
(C) 車禍
(D) 地震

3. 通勤者應該做什麼？ 答案 (B)

(A) 搭另一台火車回去
(B) 轉搭乘接駁車
(C) 下車用走的
(D) 搭計程車回家

國家圖書館出版品預行編目（CIP）資料

全新制50次多益滿分的怪物講師TOEIC多益聽力攻略+模擬試題+解析 / 鄭相虎、金映權 著. -- 初版. --
臺北市：不求人文化, 2018.1
　面；　公分
ISBN 978-986-95195-3-3（平裝附光碟）
1.多益測驗
　805.1895　　　　　　　　　　　106018312

書名 / 全新制 50 次多益滿分的怪物講師 TOEIC 多益聽力攻略 + 模擬試題 + 解析
作者 / 鄭相虎、金映權
審訂者 / 怪物講師教學團隊（台灣）
譯者 / 高俊江、賈惠如
發行人 / 蔣敬祖
出版事業群副總經理 / 廖晏婕
副總編輯 / 劉俐伶
校對 / 林佳樺、紀珊、劉兆婷
視覺指導 / 姜孟傑、鍾維恩
排版 / 張靜怡
法律顧問 / 北辰著作權事務所蕭雄淋律師
印製 / 金濱印刷事業有限公司
初版 / 2018 年 1 月
初版六刷 / 2019 年 4 月
出版 / 我識出版教育集團──不求人文化
電話 / (02) 2345-7222
傳真 / (02) 2345-5758
地址 / 台北市忠孝東路五段 372 巷 27 弄 78 之 1 號 1 樓
郵政劃撥 / 19793190
戶名 / 我識出版社
網址 / www.17buy.com.tw
E-mail / iam.group@17buy.com.tw
facebook 網址 / www.facebook.com/ImPublishing
定價 / 新台幣 699 元 / 港幣 233 元
시나공 토익 Listening（전면 개정판）
Copyright©2011 by Jeong Sangho & Kim Youngkwon
Original Korea edition published by Gilbut Eztok, Seoul, Korea
Taiwan translation rights arranged with Gilbut EZtok
Through M.J Agency, in Taipei
Taiwan translation rights©2018 by I'm Publishing.Co., Ltd

總經銷 / 我識出版社有限公司業務部
地址 / 新北市汐止區新台五路一段 114 號 12 樓
電話 / (02) 2696-1357 傳真 / (02) 2696-1359

地區經銷 / 易可數位行銷股份有限公司
地址 / 新北市新店區寶橋路 235 巷 6 弄 3 號 5 樓

港澳總經銷 / 和平圖書有限公司
地址 / 香港柴灣嘉業街 12 號百樂門大廈 17 樓
電話 / (852) 2804-6687 傳真 / (852) 2804-6409

2011 不求人文化

2009 懶鬼子英日語

I'm 我識出版集團
I'm Publishing Group
www.17buy.com.tw

2005 意識文化

2005 易富文化

2003 我識地球村

2001 我識出版社

2011 不求人文化

2009 懶鬼子英日語

www.17buy.com.tw

2005 意識文化

2005 易富文化

2003 我識地球村

2001 我識出版社